PRAISE FOR
MORE THAN A STRANGER

"This sweet treat of a romance will entrance you with its delicious humor, dollop of suspense, and delectable characters. It'll make your mouth water!"
　　—*New York Times* bestselling author Sabrina Jeffries

"*More Than a Stranger* is more than a romance—it's a witty and engaging love story that had me turning pages well into the night, just so I could find out what would happen next. It's a truly captivating tale of two headstrong friends who become much more to each other than they could have imagined."　　　　　　—Lydia Dare

ERIN KNIGHTLEY

More Than a Stranger

A SEALED WITH A KISS NOVEL

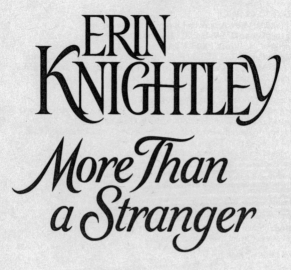

A SIGNET ECLIPSE BOOK

SIGNET ECLIPSE
Published by New American Library, a division of
Penguin Group (USA) Inc., 375 Hudson Street,
New York, New York 10014, USA
Penguin Group (Canada), 90 Eglinton Avenue East, Suite 700, Toronto,
Ontario M4P 2Y3, Canada (a division of Pearson Penguin Canada Inc.)
Penguin Books Ltd., 80 Strand, London WC2R 0RL, England
Penguin Ireland, 25 St. Stephen's Green, Dublin 2,
Ireland (a division of Penguin Books Ltd.)
Penguin Group (Australia), 250 Camberwell Road, Camberwell, Victoria 3124,
Australia (a division of Pearson Australia Group Pty. Ltd.)
Penguin Books India Pvt. Ltd., 11 Community Centre, Panchsheel Park,
New Delhi - 110 017, India
Penguin Group (NZ), 67 Apollo Drive, Rosedale, Auckland 0632,
New Zealand (a division of Pearson New Zealand Ltd.)
Penguin Books (South Africa) (Pty.) Ltd., 24 Sturdee Avenue,
Rosebank, Johannesburg 2196, South Africa

Penguin Books Ltd., Registered Offices:
80 Strand, London WC2R 0RL, England

First published by Signet Eclipse, an imprint of New American Library,
a division of Penguin Group (USA) Inc.

First Printing, June 2012
10   9   8   7   6   5   4   3   2   1

PUBLISHER'S NOTE
This is a work of fiction. Names, characters, places, and incidents either are the
product of the author's imagination or are used fictitiously, and any resemblance
to actual persons, living or dead, business establishments, events, or locales is
entirely coincidental.
  The publisher does not have any control over and does not assume any
responsibility for author or third-party Web sites or their content.

For Kirk, my very own perfect hero. Because of you, I know what it is to be well and truly loved.

Acknowledgments

What an incredible journey it has been getting this, my first book, to publication—one that would have never been possible without the help of a veritable army of people! A big thanks to Lydia Dare, Sabrina Jeffries, Heather Snow, and each and every member of my critique group. Your support, advice, wisdom, and humor not only kept me going, but helped me to thrive.

I am forever grateful to my phenomenal agent, Deidre Knight. I can't imagine where I'd be without your council, cheerleading, and superagent talents. Also to my wonderful editor, Kerry Donovan, whose expert eye and skilled guidance helped to make this book something I will always be incredibly proud of.

Last but never least, I'm so thankful for my outrageously supportive family. A special thanks to my talented brother, Andy McLeroy, who composed an original piano piece to share with readers on my Web site that somehow took my words and transformed them into music notes. Thanks as well to my sister Kara, whose experience as a writer helped to keep me sane, and finally to my parents, whose constant support has buoyed me in all aspects of my life. The world is truly limitless for the person whose loved ones believe in them.

Prologue

Lady Evelyn Moore paused to look behind her one last time before slipping into the little-used music room in the east wing. Closing the door, she grinned. Thank goodness no one had seen her. Given the number of rooms in her family's sprawling country home, she should have plenty of time to read the newly arrived letter from her brother before anyone found her. Her governess would *not* be pleased, but really, Mrs. White should have known Evie would never be able to delay such a treat until after her lessons.

Skipping across the room to the sun-drenched settee by the window, she plopped down in a heap on the warm velvet cushions. She could hardly wait to read all about Richard's latest adventures. Even though he had been gone to Eton only two months, it felt more like two years. Without her coconspirator, life at Hertford Hall was considerably duller these days. Not that there was anyplace else on earth she would rather be. It was just that, with her three sisters being entirely too young to be of any use to her—no respectable eleven-year-old would play with children of four and three—and the local villagers always acting so reserved around the daughter of a marquis, excitement came in short bursts, coinciding with either the arrival of the post or her daily riding lessons.

Today, the arrival of the post trumped all. Ripping open the seal, Evie unfolded the letter, the paper still cool from the crisp autumn wind outside, and smoothed a palm over the creases. She tucked her feet beneath her and pored over Richard's words.

Within moments, however, her excitement began to fade, trickling away like water from a cracked cup, until at last she wrinkled her nose in disgust and flicked the letter away. Honestly, if she had to read one more glowing word about that new friend of his, she was going to scream. She glared at the offending piece of paper beside her, its familiar, messy scrawl repeatedly spelling out the name she had already come to despise.

Hastings.

The boy had shown up in Richard's very first letter from school—something about his supposed riding skills. Since then, her brother mentioned him more and more, until this new letter was naught but *Hastings this* and *Hastings that*.

As if *she* cared how wonderful Hastings was.

He surely couldn't be a better friend to Richard than she. With only two years between them, Richard had been her best friend since . . . since—well, until he left for school, Evie couldn't remember a single day when they were not at each other's sides. Surely since the day she was born.

Who did this Hastings think he was, anyway?

Jumping to her feet, she slipped out of the music room, down the corridor, and up to her own bedchamber. Relieved not to have been discovered by Mrs. White—or worse, Mama—Evie hurried to her writing desk, pulled out a fresh piece of paper, and dipped her quill in the heretofore unused pot of red ink. With slow and deliberate lettering, she labored to spell out exactly the right words in her best possible handwriting.

> *Dear Mr. Hastings,*
>
> *I am sorry to tell you that my brother already has a best friend. I don't care that you can shoot and ride well. Besides, I promise that you cannot ride better than me. Kindly leave Richard alone.*

She reread the missive and, finding it satisfactory, carefully signed her name. She painstakingly folded the letter onto itself and sealed it with a gummed wafer. Dipping her quill once more, this time in the more elegant black ink, she simply wrote *Hastings* across the top. Having already written a letter to her brother the previous evening, she added a postscript requesting Richard give the letter to his friend.

Well, that ought to take care of that.

Two weeks later, a letter, addressed in an unfamiliar hand to Lady Evelyn, arrived at the Hall. With her lessons complete and anticipation coursing through her, Evie thundered up the stairs to her room, slammed the door, and flopped down on her window seat before opening the letter.

> *Dear Lady Evelyn,*
>
> *I would first like say that, as a dear family friend to your brother, I give you leave to address me simply as Hastings. I hope you will likewise allow me to address you as Evie, since that is how I think of you, thanks to your brother's many stories.*
>
> *Second, I would like to point out that Richard is free to befriend whomever he chooses. As it is, we*

*get along rather well, so I don't expect I shall aban-
don our acquaintance, particularly over his little
sister's complaint. We are, as I have stated, great
friends by now.*

*Third, as Richard is here at Eton, and you are
off in the country, I don't think it is very well done
of you to begrudge him a friend. As his friend, I,
for one, would want him to have as many acquaintances as would make him happy.*

*And finally, I am sure you do ride very well—
for a girl.*

*I am, my lady, your most humble servant,
The Honorable Benedict Hastings*

Evie's mouth hung wide at the impertinent response.
Why, the little weasel! Insinuating that she, who loved
her brother most of all, would begrudge him a friend.
And to further goad her by claiming to be such *dear
friends* already—it just made her sick.

Dear Hastings,

*You have it all wrong. Richard may have as many
friends as he likes. You just need to know he
already has a best friend. And just so you know, I
am eleven years old, and I can tell when someone
is taunting me.*

*Regards,
Lady Evelyn Moore. NOT Evie.*

Dear Evie,

*Yes, I see now how I must have misinterpreted
your meaning when you wrote (and I quote),
"Kindly leave Richard alone." You see, I seem to*

have a wild imagination and thought you wished for me to leave Richard alone. I do apologize.

I would like to propose a compromise. I shall be his friend (best or otherwise, it is up to him), as long as he is on Eton's grounds. At all other times, I leave him to you. Does this sound fair enough to you?

Awaiting your response with a hopeful heart, I am, as always, your most humble servant,

Hastings

Dear Hastings,

Fine. Just be sure not to visit Richard here during breaks. Speaking of Richard, what a pity it was to hear from him that you almost failed your English literature exam. I suggest you spend less time playing your silly sports and more time studying.

And stop calling me Evie.

Lady Evelyn

Dear Evie,

Thank you for your concern about my academics. Have no fear; I have passed my exams and will be back next term to keep Richard, my best friend, company. How is your pony, Buttercup? Have you taken her for a nice, slow, ladylike walk recently?

Hastings

Much to her surprise, it wasn't long before Evie began to actually look forward to Hastings's letters. Over the years, his biting wit made her laugh out loud, and she spent hours crafting tongue-in-cheek replies. Hastings never failed to promptly respond, and she considered him to be one of her most reliable correspondents.

And then, the letters stopped coming.

After nearly five years of constant communication, a veritable river of correspondence flowing between them uninterrupted, suddenly the waters had dried up. There had not been a single word, not even one small note from Hastings in almost two months. It was positively rude—not to mention uncharacteristic.

Leaning forward as far as she could manage from her place on the sofa in the Rose Salon, Evie squinted at the wavy image of the butler through the front window. The bright sunshine glinted off Finnington's bald pate as he waited for the dark-clothed rider to hand over the post.

Why was it when one was anxious for something, things seemed to move at an extraordinarily slow pace? She tapped her fingers on her knees, willing the men to move faster.

Honestly, for all her anticipation, there had *better* be a letter in there from Hastings. If not . . . well, she didn't know what she was going to do, but she would certainly do something. The bothersome, inconsiderate boy. Make that man—*she* at least had sent him a very nice letter upon his eighteenth birthday not five weeks earlier, which was more than she could say for him and what he had done for *her* birthday.

Which just happened to be today.

Evie blew out a frustrated breath and slumped back onto the cushions. Surely Hastings would send her something to commemorate her sixteenth year on this earth. For him to do otherwise was simply unthinkable.

At last, the front door creaked open, and Finnington shuffled inside. Evie hastily straightened and grabbed up her book, pretending to read as she listened to the approaching footsteps. When he paused at the doorway and cleared his throat, she looked up, a serene, questioning smile on her lips. "Yes?"

"A letter for you, my lady. From Lord Raleigh," he rushed to clarify, his wrinkled brow betraying a hint of sympathy for the space of a second before his expression cleared to its normal impassiveness.

Blast.

Blast, blast, blast. She was going to kill Hastings—death by tongue-lashing. Pressing her lips into something she hoped resembled a smile, she accepted Richard's letter and waited while Finnington retreated from the room. Thank goodness for the man's loyal discretion—it was embarrassing enough simply knowing he knew she was desperate to hear from Hastings. She couldn't bear it if anyone else suspected.

The second the door closed, she ripped into the letter, nearly tearing the thick paper in the process. Her eyes skimmed over Richard's words, hunting for mention of Hastings. Nothing. Not a single mention. Really, *what* was going on?

Pushing to her feet, she headed for the small writing table in the corner situated below the imposing portrait of Papa's father. His stern, accusing stare bored straight into her as she plotted what she would write. "Oh, don't look at me like that," she muttered, riffling through the drawers for paper and quill. "As far as I'm concerned, he has it coming."

Dear despicable, reprehensible, no-good, sorry excuse for a nonfriend,

We are in our fourth fortnight since last you put quill to paper for my benefit—and now you have officially missed my birthday. Yes, I am certain you think yourself very busy and important now that your graduation from Eton is at hand, but I believe "rude" must be added to the list if we are to properly describe your current state.

You must agree I am owed some sort of explanation. If I don't hear from you before we come for the ceremonies, you will sorely regret it. Really, do you want our first meeting to be one of animosity? I should think not. Now, you'd best get to work composing your response. I shall watch the post with bated breath to read what is sure to be a riveting explanation for your delinquency.

Yours in annoyance,
Evie

P.S. — It occurred to me that you might be nervous about losing in the race we were to have. Rest easy, for Mama has utterly forbidden me from bringing Epona along. You may continue (erroneously, of course) to believe you are the superior horseman, though someday I shall prove you wrong.

***

Eton College, Windsor, England, 1809

He should have known.

Benedict Hastings tossed the letter onto his desk, causing the single flame of his candle to waiver in the small gust of air. He should have realized delaying writing to Evie would only make matters that much worse.

His wooden chair creaked in protest as he leaned back and scrubbed a hand over his eyes in frustration. This was madness. Here he was, only a week away from turning his entire life upside down, and still he hadn't found a way—or the proper resolve—to cut this one last tie to his old life. He should have done it weeks ago, but really, how could he ever find the right words to sever the truest, deepest relationship he had ever known?

All his attempts had ended up either crumpled or burned, each filled with completely inadequate words to the girl who had somehow become his closest confidant over the years. Evie knew everything about him.

Almost everything.

He sighed and looked around at the nearly empty room. She knew all but the one most important thing about his life. And he knew that if he kept up their correspondence, there was no way he could keep his secret from her. His only choice was to say nothing at all.

In a week's time, when Miss Dubois—Lisette, he must remember to call her—arrived to whisk him off on their supposed Grand Tour, he would have no problem looking his school friends in the eye and waggling his brow when they asked why he had decided to accompany the seductive older woman instead of pursuing university.

When he informed his parents that he was hopping over to the Continent to see the sights for the next few years, they wouldn't bat an eye. They'd probably rejoice at that prospect of seeing even less of their *worthless* second son.

But the moment he wrote a letter to Evie filled with the falsehoods of his practiced story, he had no doubt she would see right through it. And, even if it was for the greater good, he couldn't bear to feed lies to the one person to whom he'd practically bared his soul.

He smacked a fist on the desk, welcoming the burst of pain. Why now? Why did his orders have to be for Thursday, and not two days later, when he could finally meet Evie in person? For five years he had tried to picture her, first as an annoying little girl, then as an amusing young sprite of a female, and then . . . Well, he didn't know when it had happened, but lately visions of a blond-haired, blue-eyed beauty with a devilish smile haunted his dreams.

If he was honest with himself, there was another reason he had to set her aside. She would be a distraction he couldn't afford. His chosen path would be dangerous enough without complicating things further with a female. There was simply no way around it. His letter must be written in such a way as to assure she wouldn't try to contact him again.

Benedict squeezed his eyes shut. The mere thought of hurting and subsequently losing Evie stole his breath and seared his heart. Resolutely, he opened his eyes and reached for his quill. It was for the greater good, he reminded himself. Besides, no matter how much she had meant to him, he was surely just a small, faceless part of her childhood. She had plenty of other people who cared about her. In a few months she would forget all about him and move on to the next thing in her life.

As he set to work, his nib scratched over the paper with resolute strokes, severing the ties that bound them with each callous word. Though he knew she would never notice, he carefully composed the letter so that the unforgiving words offered up something else all together, if she but only read it the right way. When at last he signed his name, he carelessly dropped his quill and reread what he had written.

It was exactly right and terribly wrong all at once.

Chapter One

'Tis very easy to make pronouncements of equestrian greatness when you have forbidden me from visiting Hertford Hall. If I were to simply arrive unannounced one day prepared to race, I wonder—would you be so brave?

—*From Hastings to Evie*

Alyesbury, England, 1816

She had done it. She had actually done it, and it was all Evie could do not to burst with excitement before making a dignified exit. Shutting the door behind her, Evie did a silent little victory dance right there in the corridor outside her father's study.

She was one step closer to achieving her ultimate goal. Now all she had to do was come up with a way—

"Mama will never allow it."

Evie squeaked in surprise as her hand flew to cover her thudding heart. Blast it all, *where* had her sister come from? "Good heavens, are you trying to stop my heart? Really, Beatrice, you shouldn't sneak up on people."

"I didn't sneak up on you. You just didn't see me. And as I was saying—"

"I know what you said," Evie said, scowling. "I can't believe you are speaking on a matter you know nothing about. And even if you did, it doesn't concern you in the least."

In a household with three younger sisters running around, Evie should have known her private conversation with Papa wouldn't be private at all. At least it was only Beatrice lurking about and not the twins. Evie loved them all dearly, but she knew Jocelyn and Carolyn well enough to realize that if they had overheard Evie's conversation with Papa, the whole household would be privy to the details by nightfall.

Beatrice crossed her arms over her small chest and returned Evie's scowl. "You're my sister; of course it's of concern to me. And it matters not whether or not it is my business, Mama still will never agree to your proposal. It's utterly ridiculous."

Leave it to Bea to put her finger on the exact thing Evie was worried about. After nearly seven years of working by her father's side, she had been fairly sure she could garner his approval, and indeed she had. But only with the caveat that she win her mother over as well. That was a much more challenging proposition.

Evie cast a furtive glance at the study door, then hooked an arm none too gently around Beatrice's thin elbow and towed her down the corridor. Best not to chance Papa—or anyone else, really—overhearing them. Pulling her into the formal Rose Salon, Evie shut the door with a soft click and turned to face the little spy.

"First of all, my proposal was not ridiculous, and it is unkind of you to say so. Second of all, Papa was perfectly amenable to the idea, and third of all, sixteen is a little old to be listening at keyholes, don't you think?"

Faint pink blotches appeared on her sister's cheeks, making her deep blue eyes even darker. "I was only passing by when Papa had his not-so-*amenable* outburst.

You must admit that is a strange enough occurrence to warrant pausing outside the door."

She had a point. Not that Evie could blame Papa. What other reaction would a father have when his daughter announced that, after five tedious Seasons, she wanted to withdraw from the marriage market altogether? After his initial cry of objection, inquiring as to her sanity, Evie had eventually won him over with her well-laid arguments. After all, one mustn't approach a battlefield unless one was prepared to do battle.

She sighed and made her way over to the busy floral sofa overlooking the decidedly soggy gardens. The dull gray skies cast little light into the room, even though all the drapes were wide open. "He was just a bit surprised, is all. He came to see the logic of my reasoning."

"Evie," Beatrice said, plopping down on the cushions beside her, "just because you haven't yet found the man you wish to marry doesn't mean you won't ever find him. You can't just give up." She fluffed her pale yellow skirts out demurely around her legs, one of a thousand little things she did lately to remind Evie that her little sisters were turning into proper young ladies. Well, somewhat proper young ladies who occasionally spied on others.

Evie pulled a gold-tasseled cushion into her lap and eyed her sister. She really did not want to have this conversation right now. After her partial victory with Papa, she had thought to head straight to Mama and begin her campaign. But without Beatrice's support—and more important, silence—Evie had little hope of winning Mama over.

Perhaps the best tactic was to simply be frank. "You must not have been listening too closely if that is what you think. If you had, you would have heard that I am not giving up—I'm finally getting what I really want. I'm very happy with things just the way they are. I absolutely love working with Papa in the stables, and, to be quite blunt, there hasn't seemed to be a man in the whole of the *ton* who is not conceited, or dull, or old, or status climbing, or simply *wrong* for me in one way or another. No offense to Richard or Papa, but I vastly prefer the company of a horse to that of a man."

Beatrice giggled, covering her mouth as she always did to hide her crooked front tooth. "I thought I heard something about horses' manners being superior to those of gentlemen."

Evie exchanged a grin with her sister. It might not say much for the male population of England, but it was true. In five Seasons, she had yet to meet even one man with whom she could imagine spending a month, let alone a lifetime. Of course, she had learned early on that even if one thought one knew a person, one could be completely wrong about that person's character. What if she found someone she thought she could love, only to have him turn out to be just another thoughtless, lying male, intent on toying with her? Evie's jaw clenched as she pushed back the memories floating to the surface for the second time that day.

Now was not the time to be thinking of Hastings the Betrayer.

She squared her shoulders a bit and met her sister's eyes. "I'm simply finding a way to take control of my own future, not leaving it in the hands of some man. It's all I've ever wanted, really."

"You say that, but you've never even given any of your suitors a fighting chance."

If only Beatrice knew how wrong she was. The memories pushed past the barrier Evie had erected in her mind, bringing an uncomfortable pang to her heart. She had given one man much more than a fighting chance, and she had paid the price. Never again.

At least her sisters would never know how foolish

she had been. Her father was the only person who knew about her rash actions some seven years ago. Not even Richard knew. She had a sneaking suspicion that Papa's knowledge of that day had a lot to do with his agreement to her proposal.

Sighing, Evie nudged Beatrice's shoulder, offering a small, teasing smile. "You should be happy, you know. When you come out next year, you won't have a nearly on-the-shelf older sister holding you back."

"No, I'll have a *firmly* on-the-shelf sister missing out on all the best things in life. Marriage, children . . . dancing."

"You know dancing has never been my forte. Now foxhunting, on the other hand . . ." She grinned when Beatrice rolled her eyes. "Bea, it's the right thing for me. Now, you must promise me that you will keep your mouth shut about my plans until I figure out the best way to present it to Mama."

"There *is* no best way to present it—because it's a *bad* idea."

"Oh, stop," Evie said, shaking her head. Would it be so hard for her sister to support her? "I just need to butter her up a bit. Papa is delaying the trip to London in order to have a little more time with the new Irish hunter. That leaves me with seven days to convince Mama to allow me to stay behind and live my dream. Now promise you'll keep mum."

Bea sighed. "Very well, I promise."

Evie released the breath she hadn't realized she'd been holding. If she were to have any hope at all with Mama, she couldn't have Beatrice ruining things at the wrong moment. "Thank you. I do hope I can trust you."

"Of course you can." She stood and shook out her skirts, still eyeing Evie skeptically. "I suppose I should wish you good luck."

"Why thank you, Bea. I appreciate the sentiment."

"Yes, well, you're most definitely going to need it."

Generally speaking, Mayfair was where one went to attend a much-anticipated ball, call upon a highly regarded peer, or stroll down the street in one's finery in order to see and be seen. It was not where one went when one's whole life came crashing down like a centuries-old tree, struck down by a single, searing bolt of lightning.

And yet, here he was.

Standing in the shadows across the street from the stately old building he had visited only a few times before, Benedict counted the windows a second time. *Oh, thank God.* He exhaled a long breath, the puff of warm air in the chilly London night a visible testament to his relief.

Richard was home.

Benedict waited for a break in the early night traffic before dashing across the street and up the stairs. Though Richard kept these rooms year round, he occupied them only when his family was in town for the Season. The lighted windows above meant two things: Benedict's oldest and most trustworthy friend was home, and Hertford Hall was unoccupied.

He had taken only a few steps toward Richard's door when the muffled sound of angry footsteps and the shrill voice of an aggravated female brought him up short. Seconds later, the door burst open and a dark-haired, flush-faced beauty stormed into the corridor. She clutched her half boots to her chest while her long, thoroughly tousled hair tumbled down her back. Oblivious to Benedict's presence, she shouted over her shoulder in Italian, a language Benedict knew well enough to raise his eyebrows at her choice of words.

A second later, Richard appeared in the doorway,

hastily buttoning his wrinkled breeches. "Isabella, wait! Don't be like this, angel."

She whirled around, pointing a long, thin finger at Richard's chest. "No, I no wait for you anymore. You can go to the devil, Raleigh." With that, she turned and hurried for the stairs, pushing past Benedict without a break in the colorful Italian curses flowing like water from her ruby red lips.

Frozen in place, Benedict looked back toward his old friend. "Still have that golden touch with the ladies, I see."

Richard's gaze snapped to his, confusion flashing for a half second before he broke out in a grin. "Bloody hell, Hastings, what cat dragged your sorry arse in?"

Simply seeing his old friend—someone who actually gave a damn about him—brought a trickle of light to relieve the darkness in Benedict's heart. He crossed his arms and hitched up a single eyebrow. "You know, I'm not sure I'm comfortable conversing with a half-naked man in public. Do you think you can make yourself decent before commenting on the state of my arse?"

Letting out a bark of laughter, Richard motioned for Benedict to join him. "Come on inside. I can't wait to hear what has brought you to my doorstep tonight after nearly two years away."

Richard led him into the small parlor and pointed to the crystal decanters on a sideboard. "Pour us some drinks, will you? I'll go fetch the rest of my clothing. And sorry about calling you Hastings—I forget sometimes that you prefer Benedict now."

"You can call me anything you want, so long as you put a shirt on." He was glad Richard remembered, though. Going by the family name just seemed to give them more power over him, as strange as it might sound to others. Why would he go by the name of his father when the man hadn't even cared that he'd existed? The point was moot, as his father had been gone for years, but now more than ever Benedict wanted—*needed*—to distance himself from his family.

As his friend padded barefoot down the hall, Benedict headed to the sideboard and sniffed at the various containers. The spicy, earthy scent of aged scotch caught his attention, and he poured a few fingers for each of them. At last the knot of tension in his shoulders began to unravel a little. He had no doubt Richard would grant him the use of Hertford, the haven Benedict so badly needed as he sorted out what the hell he was going to do next.

He sat in the chair in front of the small writing desk close to the crackling fire and took a long sip of the scotch. It burned a hot trail to his gut, though it still couldn't warm the part of him that had gone cold the moment he heard the words that had changed everything. He doubted anything could. He rubbed a weary hand over his eyes, which were still gritty after his pounding ride from Folkestone only hours earlier. He'd never ridden so hard in his life. If he planned to leave tonight, he'd have to rent a horse—poor Samson deserved a rest.

He took another drink and leaned against the hard wooden back of his chair. He knew what it would look like if anyone discovered what had happened: escape, cowardice, guilt. But it wasn't any of those things. Nearly a decade in the service of the Crown had taught him when retreat was most prudent, and that time was now. Until he could look on the disastrous events of the past twenty-four hours with any amount of objectivity, he needed to step away. He would regroup, reevaluate, and then come up with a plan.

He needed a place to disappear, and Hertford Hall was that place.

He'd never been, but in his mind there was no better place to go. Throughout his years at Eton, he had patched together a picture of what the Hall must be like from Evie's glowing descriptions of her pastoral home. Ironically enough, Richard had lamented the same things she loved about it: the solitude, the peacefulness, the distance from London. In his battered state, Benedict knew it was exactly the sanctuary he needed. He was glad now for all the times Richard had suggested he visit.

Now all he had to do was figure out what to say to the man. He could tell him the truth, but Benedict knew his friend well enough to realize he would want to help—insist on it, in fact. But this was his fight. He didn't want anyone else to be sullied by the inevitable repercussions.

Soft footsteps on carpet heralded Richard's return. Benedict straightened and relaxed his features just as Richard reappeared, rolling up the sleeves to a plain white shirt. Pushing the whole mess from his brain, Benedict held out the second glass. "Here—I imagine you need this after displeasing the fiery Isabella."

Richard chuckled, shaking his head. "Fiery indeed. She and I have enjoyed each other's company for a few months now, and she told me tonight she had a very enticing offer from Lord Hamilton that she would accept if I didn't counter."

"I'm guessing you didn't counter?"

Richard lifted his glass and grinned. "I told her I hoped they would be happy together."

"And you waited until you were half dressed to bring this up?"

Settling onto a leather chair, Richard shrugged. "Her timing, not mine." He took a long drink before continuing. "What can I say? I much prefer a more casual arrangement. Mistresses can be such a bother. She's been angling for a more permanent arrangement for weeks, and I do believe I just called her bluff." He waved his drink dismissively. "Enough about that. What I want to know is when did you get into town and what the hell were you doing on my doorstep?"

"Glad to see you, too." Benedict ducked to avoid the small book Richard lobbed at him. "Actually, I came to ask a favor."

"Now there's something new. What is it that I can do for you, my friend?"

"I've only just returned to England—come straight from the coast as a matter of fact—and I can't bear the thought of being thrown into all the chaos of the Season. You know I'll not set foot on my brother's estate, especially not with Mother demanding that I do my duty and marry some wealthy chit or another."

"All these years of utter indifferences, and she thinks she can force you to do her bidding now?"

Benedict shrugged. "The estate needs money now." His jaw clenched. He didn't want to speak of his family more than absolutely necessary. Besides, any good spy knew the key to a good story was keeping it simple.

His chair squeaked as he leaned forward, rolling the tumbler between his palms. "It didn't take long to decide to make the most of my time in England and head to the country for a spell. In the past, you had mentioned I could—"

The rest of Benedict's sentence was cut off when the door banged open and the angry *signorina* stormed in once more. With her shoes and dress now properly in place and her hair pulled into a low knot on her head, she would have looked respectable if not for the sneer on her face. "I jus' wanted you to know that nobody disrespects Isabella and gets away with it. Enjoy your parties this week, *signor*."

With a sickly smile marring her lovely face, she backed

up, slamming the door with enough force to rattle the furnishings. Silence engulfed the room as the two men stared at the closed door.

"You know," Richard said, never taking his gaze from the front door, "the country suddenly sounds rather nice."

Benedict glanced toward Richard, an unexpected smile coming to his lips. "Oh?"

"Yes. And I know just the place."

Chapter Two

If you will recall, Hastings, it was you who suggested the compromise of abstaining from the Hall four years ago. I would happily trounce you at the location of your choice. The question is, would you be brave enough to try?

—From Evie to Hastings

Evie had never before noticed how utterly *regular* the ticking of a clock was. Clip, clop, clip, clop—like the steady pace of an elderly workhorse, all the joy and verve beaten out of it long ago.

"Is something wrong, sweetheart?"

Evie looked up from her uneven, pathetic stitches to see her mother watching her, her gray eyes oddly amused. "No, of course not."

Unless one counted being killed by boredom, because in that case, something was definitely wrong. After two days of pursuing nice, ladylike activities in an attempt to gain her mother's good grace, Evie was beginning to wonder how the whole of the female population of England didn't revolt against such mind-numbing boredom. Honestly, the rack would have been better.

It didn't help that it was the most gorgeous day ever, with bright sunshine filling every corner of Mama's cheery sitting room. Evie was dying to check on Ronan's progress. The new addition to their operation was high-spirited and handsome, a full nineteen hands of burnished red, Irish glory. He had been her choice, and it was torture leaving his care to others. Of course, that was exactly what she would be doing for the whole of the Season if she couldn't convince Mama to allow her to stay in the country.

Setting her own sampler down beside her on the cream cushions of the sofa, Mama folded her hands and smiled. "Evie, I never thought I would say this, but why don't you go join your father in the stable block?"

"No, no. I'm perfectly happy here with you." It was quite possibly the biggest lie Evie had ever told.

Mama's eyes softened, and she reached over to take the mangled sampler from Evie's hands. "Go, my dear. I so appreciate your desire to spend some time with me, but after two days of watching you fidget and fuss and make a perfect mess of those poor ivy leaves you have been attempting to stitch, I think it's time you exhaust some of your restlessness."

Oh, thank goodness. Evie did her best not to look too satisfied. Her plan to play the perfect daughter wasn't working in the way she had intended, but apparently it *was* working. Clearly Mama could see how ill-suited Evie was to such ladylike pursuits. Tonight might be the perfect time to present her proposal. But in the meantime . . . "Thank you, Mama, I believe I will join Papa."

In less than fifteen minutes, Evie had changed into her riding habit and was headed for the stables. The brisk spring air was absolute heaven compared to the stuffiness of the sitting room. It rather felt like freedom. With the afternoon sun already dipping toward the trees, she didn't want to waste a single minute she could spend on the back of her horse.

Lifting the hem of her skirt, she hurried along the gravel path, stepping carefully so as to avoid the puddles left over from yesterday's rain. She half ran the last few steps, grasping the edge of the door with her gloved hand to propel herself around the corner.

"Oof!"

The air was knocked right from her lungs as she collided at full speed with an unmoving brick wall that she knew for a fact should not be there. Evie stumbled, almost falling backward when a pair of large strong hands grasped her upper arms and steadied her.

"I beg your pardon. Are you quite all right?"

The brick wall spoke surprisingly good English for an inanimate object.

Evie's gaze traveled up the dark gray greatcoat, past the sharp, lightly stubbled jaw, and settled briefly on a very inviting set of masculine lips before reaching the man's dark, velvet brown eyes. Words failed her completely. *Where* had this gorgeous man come from? For endless seconds she stood stock-still, held not only in his grasp, but in his curious gaze as well. He had the loveliest eyes she had ever seen, like the burnished mahogany of her father's heirloom desk.

"Miss? Are you injured?"

Evie blinked. She should say something. She should *really* say something. "Um. . . quite."

His dark eyebrows scrunched together as he tilted his head slightly. "Quite . . . injured?"

"No! Quite all right. I'm fine, really. Um, thank you." Oh Lord, why must she lose her wits, now of all times? Here, now, with a gorgeous stranger very nearly holding her in his arms? She finally understood what it meant to be struck dumb by something, and at the worst possible time.

And now he was looking at her as if she was one horse short of a matched pair. "You're certain?"

Evie almost laughed. Was she certain? Not in the

slightest. She felt as though she had just been spun around in circles, but there was no way she would tell him as much. She took a quick step back, pulling away from his steadying hands. It was far enough to miss his warmth, but at least she could still detect the subtle, enticing hint of leather and sandalwood. She took a slow breath and offered him a smile. "Yes, I'm certain. Please accept my apologies for not watching where I was going, Mr. . . . ?"

"Evie!"

Evie jumped, whirling around at the unexpected voice from behind her. "Richard! What on earth are you doing here?"

She wouldn't have been more surprised if Prinny himself had been standing in her stables. Joy swooped through her, and she opened her arms to her brother. Grinning, he came forward and scooped her up in a bear hug, giving her a little spin so that her feet swung out as if she were a child. "Richard, put me down!" The admonishment didn't have much effect, couched by her laughter. Only her brother could make her feel like a ten-year-old girl again.

When at last he set her down, she giggled and stepped back. Evie looked him over, taking in his tousled blond hair and wind-reddened cheeks. She could hardly believe he was here at the Hall, now of all times. "What on earth are you doing here? It's such a lovely surprise!"

"Well, it's good to see you, too, Little Bit. Are you headed out for a ride?"

"Yes, I was before I ran into our visitor. A friend of yours, I presume?" She motioned toward the stranger but froze when their eyes met. He was watching her with such intensity, she instinctively took a tiny step back. The look was gone in an instant. Evie blinked in confusion. How completely odd. Could she have possibly

imagined the fierceness of his gaze? Surely she had—
she had only just met the man! He'd have no cause to
care one way or another about her. Nonetheless, a tiny
shiver raced down her spine.

A chuckle drew her attention back to Richard. He
flashed a broad, cheeky grin her way, shaking his head
slowly. "I can't believe I haven't introduced the two of
you yet."

Evie raised an eyebrow. He was up to something.

Without thinking, she backed up a step. The move
only made his smile grow. She cut her eyes toward the
other man. She did *not* want to embarrass herself in
front of him any more than she already had. Fortunately,
he paid her no mind at all. The whole of his attention
was focused sharply on Richard.

For some reason, her brother seemed to enjoy the
moment. With his usual flare for dramatics, he said, "My
dear Evie, it is my great pleasure to introduce you to my
friend, the venerated, the enigmatic, the long-aw—"

And at that moment the stranger stepped forward.

Chapter Three

And don't you dare lie to me, Hastings. Our conversations may be formed through ink and paper, but I promise you I will know if you are fibbing, and you will regret it. Did you, or did you not send the blasted book?
— From Evie to Hastings, upon the arrival of an anonymously sent copy of Mrs. Seeton's Book of Etiquette: Rules, Direction, and Proper Behavior for the Fair Sex

One second, Benedict's brain had been frozen from the shock of discovering that the incredibly beautiful blond goddess before him was, in fact, Evie. *His* Evie. The Evie who was *supposed* to be in London, far away from the house he sought refuge in.

The next thing he knew, he was jerking into action, opening his mouth without a clue about what he would say, only suddenly very sure that Evie could *not* know he was Hastings. "Mr. James Benedict, at your service, my lady."

The lie was like vinegar in his mouth, and he gritted his teeth with the effort to keep his expression neutral. God, what had he done? His gaze shot to Richard, who stood just to the right of his sister. At any other time, his face would have been comical. Not then. No, at that moment, Benedict could do nothing but pray his old friend wouldn't call him out right then and there.

Blessedly oblivious to the silent battle between the men, Evie grinned. "It's a pleasure to make your acquaintance, Mr. Benedict. And thank you for speaking up; my brother does tend to like to hear himself speak." She bumped Richard with her shoulder teasingly. Thank God she didn't look to his face. With his mouth frozen open and his eyes akin to those of a startled owl, she would have known in an instant something was not right.

Benedict met Richard's gaze straight on, willing him to go along with the ruse. The damned lie had just come out, as natural as taking a breath of air. Really, what the hell else could Benedict have done? Bits and pieces of that dreadful last letter came rushing back to him. If she knew who he was, she would probably eviscerate him — with words, if he were lucky, though he deserved worse.

Damn it all, he had too much to handle as it was; adding in an irate ghost from his past would make the situation unbearable.

Loosening the muscles of his jaw, he offered her his best impersonation of a lighthearted smile. "Yes, I was beginning to wonder if he'd simply forgotten who I was."

Richard's mouth snapped shut then, and he gave Benedict a considering look. "No," he said slowly, "*I* for one, have not forgotten who you are, *Mister* Benedict."

The emphasis was subtle, but unmistakable. Still, Benedict's galloping pulse slowed a little. Richard would go along with him — for now, at least. Even as he tried to concentrate on the farce in front of him, Benedict's mind raced to think of an explanation for when he and Richard were next alone. Whatever it was, it had to be damned good.

"Well, allow me to welcome you to Hertford Hall." Evie gave a small flick of her wrist, encompassing the whole of the house and grounds past the stable door. Obediently, Benedict wrenched his gaze from her attractive form and surveyed the scenery as any normal guest would. It truly was impressive—even more so than his own family's estate in Leicestershire. With the massive stone facade rising from the gently sloping hill, it had the effect of somehow presiding over the neatly manicured lawns and rolling forestland beyond. The stable block, which he knew to be the home of the family's horse-breeding operation, paid homage to the house itself, with great arching windows and stately stone walls. There was no mistaking the pride the family took in the place.

"Thank you, my lady. It is a pleasure to finally see the place for myself." He could have bitten his tongue. *Finally?*

Her hand went to her trim waist, which was nicely emphasized by the cut of her light blue riding habit. "I hadn't realized you'd been acquainted so very long. How is it that you and my brother know each other, Mr. Benedict?"

A very good question. Beside her, Richard crossed his arms and tilted his head to the side, the first hint of amusement coloring his expression. With both siblings waiting expectantly, Benedict decided to go with the most obvious answer. "Eton, actually. We met in the early days."

As a person who spent half his time living a lie, he knew it was best to stick as close to the truth as possible.

"When was it, exactly?" Richard asked, the very picture of innocence. "I can't seem to remember."

Oh yes. Clearly he was starting to enjoy himself.

Benedict opened his mouth to respond, but the distant thunder of an approaching horse gave him pause. Whoever it was, he had Benedict's undying gratitude. He turned in time to see a lone rider on a very handsome red mount rapidly approaching. Though the man sported gray hair to Richard's blond and a slightly stockier build, the resemblance was impossible to miss. "Richard, is that your father?"

"Indeed it is," he responded, waving hugely at the older man. The marquis returned the gesture, and the siblings hurried forward to greet him.

Benedict hung back, glad for a second to try to gather his wits. Granville had no idea how indebted Benedict was to him for his timely—and inadvertent—rescue. He took a long, slow pull of air, trying to calm his overworked nerves.

After all these years—after all those letters—it was nothing short of shocking to see Evie in the flesh. To hear her smooth, clear voice and fleetingly feel her lithe body pressed against his.

Even toward the end, when she had invaded both his thoughts and his dreams as an ethereal, indistinct beauty, he could have never imagined how lovely she would be in person. All those emotions he had pushed into the far recesses of his mind almost a decade earlier now roared through his body, heating his blood. Her luminous, nearly crystalline blue eyes, her open yet somehow enticing smile—even her slightly tanned skin added to her allure. It was as though the forbidden fruit had been placed before him, perfect in all its untouchable glory.

Benedict swallowed, cursing his wretched luck.

Why the hell was she even here? Why wasn't she in London, batting those long eyelashes at some dandy on the ballroom floor? He started forward, slowly approaching the chattering trio as Richard and his father embraced. Evie laughed beside them, the afternoon sun behind her turning her hair into a golden halo about her head.

A golden halo? Benedict raked a hand through his hair—he had to get a hold of himself.

Richard stepped back and beckoned. "Benedict, come meet my father."

The implications of the statement hit Benedict anew. Of course Evie's presence here would mean that the whole blasted family would be there. He forced a grin as he closed the distance between them. Great, now he would be lying to the lot of them. Though he had never met them, Benedict had always respected them. Richard and Evie had spoken of them often and with great fondness, and it was almost as if Benedict already knew them. They were exactly the sort of family he had dreamed of during the loneliest times of his childhood, when his own father had ignored him in favor of his hunting dogs and his mother had so thoroughly disliked him. And though his brother had once been a decent-enough companion when they were in leading strings, that all changed when he went away to school and was surrounded by those who pandered to the future earl.

After the introductions, the marquis beamed in welcome. "So good of you to join Richard for a visit, Mr. Benedict. I do hope you will feel at home."

Granville was every bit as jovial and welcoming as Benedict had always pictured him to be. He was a good, respectable man who did not deserve to be deceived in his own home.

"Thank you, my lord. It's so good of you to have me."

Though he smiled and conversed easily with others, complimenting the grounds and admiring the marquis's new mount, unease turned Benedict's stomach. He hated concealing the truth from them, but what could he do? He had to figure out a way to leave as soon as possible. He had no clue where else he could go, but it wouldn't be right to stay. As soon as he came up with a reasonable excuse to do so, he would leave.

Of their own volition, his eyes strayed to his beautiful former correspondent. He could fool the others, but not himself. Having finally laid eyes on her, the idea of turning around and leaving was nearly inconceivable.

Soon, he would be gone from their lives forever, but just not quite yet.

                      *   *   *

With the initial excitement of her brother's arrival
waning, Evie could not wait to get her brother alone
and learn what had really brought them to the Hall. In
answer to Papa's inquiry, Richard had claimed they had
grown bored of the city and wanted a change of scenery
before the Season began in earnest.

It had been all she could do not to snort. Richard grow
tired of the city? Not a chance. As they climbed the shallow limestone steps to the house, she waited impatiently
for the opportunity to question him alone. She stole a
quick glance at their guest and bit her bottom lip against
the fresh flutter of butterflies within her stomach. She
couldn't wait to hear more about who the devil this Mr.
Benedict was and why she had never heard of him before.

Honestly, it really wasn't fair that such a man existed
in England and she had not yet had the pleasure of laying eyes on him. She might not want to marry, but she
certainly wasn't dead.

The heavy oak door swung open on well-oiled hinges,
and Finnington appeared, dipping his head to Papa.
"Lord Raleigh's chamber and a guest suite are nearly
prepared, my lord."

Evie offered the butler a discreet wink. One should
never underestimate the efficiency of a well-trained
staff. They had probably gone to work the moment the
men reached the drive.

Papa rubbed his hands together. "Excellent. I imagine you gentlemen will want a moment to collect yourselves. Why don't we meet for some refreshments in a
half hour or so?" He turned to Richard and clasped him
on the shoulder. "You should go surprise your mother
before you head up to your bedchamber. She's probably
still in the drawing room. Finnington can show Mr.
Benedict to his room while I go freshen up."

Richard agreed, and Papa, Mr. Benedict, and Finnington headed up the curving staircase. Evie couldn't have planned it better herself. As Richard turned toward the Rose Salon, Evie pounced, snagging him by the arm. She waited until the sound of the others' footsteps receded before releasing him. "All right, out with it. What is going on?"

"Whatever do you mean?" The very picture of nonchalance, he grabbed a handful of nuts from a crystal bowl on the ornately carved side table and tossed a few in his mouth. "Nothing is 'going on.'"

"Yes, and I'm the lead in the next production of *Othello*."

"Really? Well, good for you, Bit. I always knew you had a flare for the dramatic." He grinned cheekily, and she smiled despite herself.

"Don't be an ass. You wouldn't leave London so close to the Season without a reason."

"As I told Father, I simply decided the country sounded like a bit of a reprieve from the city. It can get tiresome, you know."

"Yes, I know, but *you* know no such thing. My whole life you've done nothing but wax poetic about the offerings of the city." A reprieve from the city, indeed. He must think she was born yesterday. "Let me see. . . ."

She folded her arms and tilted her head to the side, narrowing her eyes. "Using the most scientific of approaches, I have derived that you are here"—she paused for dramatic effect—"because of a woman."

A sheepish grin lit her brother's face. "Yes, of course. It was never going to be a great mystery. Though I do hate being so damned predictable."

"If there is trouble with you, there is sure to be a woman at the heart of the matter," she said knowingly. Their close relationship meant that she knew far more about his vices than could be called proper.

"Truer words have never been spoken, though I never thought you would admit it."

She scowled at him, causing him to laugh.

"You didn't think I would pass that up, did you? It was practically handed over on a silver platter. Besides, I'm sure you'll be causing your fair amount of trouble next week when you head to town."

"For your information, I have some very big news."

"Oh?" he said, raising an eyebrow.

She reached out and grabbed his forearm, unable to hide her excitement. "I talked with Papa earlier this week and . . ." She trailed off, enjoying the anticipation on Richard's face.

"Yes?"

"He said that if I can gain Mama's blessing, I can sit this Season out. Isn't that wonderful?"

"Sit the Season out? Why ever would you want to do a thing like that?"

She smacked him soundly on the shoulder. "You cad. You know it is my greatest wish to forego the husband hunt and concentrate on my work here."

He chuckled and gave her a one-armed hug. "I'm only teasing you, Bit. It really is very exciting for you, though for the life of me I can't imagine why the country life enthralls you so." He shuddered. "Give me the city any day."

"Yes, I am counting on that. I fully intend to make Hertford my home even after you inherit, so you'd best get used to the idea. The stables are my domain, and I plan to keep it that way."

Richard adopted a perfectly snobbish expression. "And have a woman sully her hands with business on my watch? Never."

She giggled. He could have been impersonating just about anyone in the *ton*. It really was nice to have him here—provided he didn't cause any trouble before the family departed. That particular thought gave her pause. Whenever Richard was around, they tended to get into mischief together, despite their supposedly mature ages. She had best not leave anything to chance.

Placing her hands on her hips, she looked him in the eye meaningfully. "I have Papa's blessing, but only if I can garner Mama's as well. I have not yet spoken with her; I'm waiting for just the right moment. *Nothing* can go wrong between now and when they leave. I mean it," she said, raising an eyebrow for emphasis. "I won't have you and your friend upsetting the delicate balance of things while you are here. The last thing I need is Mama and Papa rethinking the mental capacity of their offspring."

Richard barked with laughter. "You do have a way with words, Bit. Are you sure you don't want to take another look at that lead in *Othello*?"

"Very funny. I'm quite serious, however. If you do *anything* to mess this up for me, you will live to regret it, I assure you."

This time Richard rolled his eyes. "Yes, Mother. Although I think if you wanted to be truly dramatic, you could say, 'You'll *rue* the day you messed with me.'" He shook his fist theatrically to punctuate "rue." "It has a certain flair, don't you think?"

She shook her head at his antics. "Yes, a good ruing always spices things up." She paused and fiddled with the cuff of her sleeve. As casually as she could manage, she said, "Speaking of spicing things up, who, exactly, is this Mr. Benedict?" Just saying his name made a tiny thrill dance through her.

"As he said, just an old friend."

"If he is such an old friend, why have I never heard of him before? I would have sworn that I knew all of your friends, old or otherwise."

"I'm sure I mentioned him at some point," he said, waving a dismissive hand in the air. "You must have just forgotten. And really, what does it matter? We'll be here only a few days, and then we will be on our way."

Evie furrowed her brow. He hadn't ever mentioned the man, she was sure of it. But perhaps he was right; it didn't really matter. "All right, then. You'd best go freshen up before our little gathering. You look and smell like somebody dragged you through the stables."

Richard exhaled, sounding as if he had been holding his breath. "Right. I am going to say hello to Mother before washing up, and you are going to go gather the girls. In"—he checked his watch fob—"approximately twenty-six minutes, I will see you in the drawing room. I fully expect you to revert to your earlier enthusiasm at the divine pleasure of my company by then. No more worries about Richard behaving badly, all right?"

She nodded, and he winked before taking his leave. Despite his nonchalance about the whole thing, she found herself thinking there was just something . . . *off* about Mr. Benedict. She gave a little shrug and started up the grand, curving staircase. It was probably nothing. And really, when one was as handsome as he, one could get away with a bit of peculiarity here and there.

When she reached the top of the stairs, the door to a nearby guest room clicked closed, catching her attention. Evidently, Mr. Benedict had been given the Blue Room.

Anticipation skittered through her at the thought of seeing him again, and she bit her lip against the delectable feeling. Why was it she had the sudden desire to go knock on the man's door? She shook her head at the scandalous thought.

Perhaps it wasn't Richard's behavior she should be concerned with.

Chapter Four

*Bravery aside, I am a man of my word, and I wouldn't
break an agreement with a lady. I also wouldn't break
one with you. Besides, it is much more fun to banter
with you by letter than to mind my manners in person.
Wouldn't you agree?*

— From Hastings to Evie

When the last servant shuffled from the room and
pulled the door closed behind him, Benedict
closed his eyes and blew out a long breath.

Thank God *that* was over.

Too bad he had mere minutes to come up with an
explanation for Richard that would not result in Benedict either being kicked out on his arse or meeting Richard on a grassy knoll at dawn, weapon in hand. Or
worse—being handed over to Evie as the liar he was.

Peeling off his jacket, Benedict tossed it across the
foot of the gigantic four-poster bed and inspected his
surroundings. Across from the bed, a small sitting area
was arranged around a fireplace where freshly lit logs
cracked and popped noisily. The meager warmth of the
fire worked to chase the faint chill from the enormous
room. Huge, nearly floor-to-ceiling windows lined the
back wall, and the afternoon sunlight poured through in
slanted columns, highlighting the stirred-up dust in the
freshly prepared room.

He dropped onto the upholstered bench at the foot of the bed and went to work removing his boots.

What could he possibly say to Richard to explain his reasoning? Perhaps he should say he was running from the law and had assumed a false identity to avoid capture. Or that a jilted lover was after him. Or that he had suffered an attack of the mind and had momentarily forgotten his own name.

He dropped his left boot on the floor with a thud. No, he should tell Richard the truth—or at least as much of it as possible. He was Benedict's closest friend, for God's sake. He couldn't look himself in the eye if he just started piling on the lies.

A sharp knock sounded on the door. "Enter," he called, yanking off the right boot.

Richard strode in, looking remarkably refreshed. "All settled? Yes? Good—now I am positively rapt to know what the devil possessed you to introduce yourself the way you did, *Mister* Benedict." The question was said without anger, but with genuine curiosity. He settled on one of the blue-and-white-striped chairs beside the fireplace and waited for Benedict's response.

Benedict ran a hand through his hair, blowing out a breath. *Here goes nothing.* "I know—not my most intelligent decision today. But you remember the correspondence your sister and I shared when we were children?" Richard nodded, and Benedict continued. "From what I have gathered over the years, she never actually shared with you how that particular relationship ended."

Richard's left eyebrow rose. "I had assumed it died naturally when you left school, but my astounding powers of deductive reasoning now lead me to believe that wasn't the case."

"Not exactly. I was young, and an idiot, and I didn't want my old life following me to my exciting new one.

Evie is a bit, well, persistent, shall we say, and when she wouldn't take the hint that I didn't wish to continue writing, I sent a rather strongly worded letter that ended the correspondence." Benedict tried not to cringe when the wording of that last letter flitted through his mind. God, all these years later and he still felt like the worst sort of cad. It was definitely for the best that Hastings remained in the past when it came to Evie.

Richard looked genuinely surprised. "How odd. She never said a word about it."

"Which should tell you something about how she felt about the letter. I know how close the two of you are. Has she ever kept anything from you before?"

"Not that I'm aware of, though I must admit now I'm not so sure." Richard sat forward, rubbing his palms over his knees. "Still, that was nearly a decade ago—do you really think it's necessary to lie about your name?"

"Not a lie so much as a rearranging, really. My middle name is James, after all. But really, would you want to be me when she realized that the blackguard who called her an 'annoying little pest of a girl with all the grace and decorum of a horsefly' is here in the flesh?"

Richard smothered a horrified laugh beneath his hand. "No, I most definitely would not. That was not well done of you at all, my friend. As a matter of fact," he said, rubbing a hand over his chin, "it might be worth it to tell her the truth just to see what she will do to you."

"You did go along with it when I introduced myself," Benedict reminded him. His tone was lighthearted despite the disquiet slipping through his belly. With so much turmoil in his life right now and all that was at stake with his future, he could ill afford to be distracted by further drama.

"True enough. Interestingly, despite bringing up the fact she has never heard mention of a James Benedict, Evie seemed to take our sudden appearance relatively in stride. Rather worrisome, really. She is bound to pin me down sooner or later."

"Perhaps she'll let it drop."

Richard snorted. "Certainly. And I can expect to sprout wings and take flight sometime in the next hour or so. Care to join me?"

An unexpected grin lifted the corner of Benedict's mouth. It was a gift really, that Richard could make him laugh, even now. "All right, I suppose we should get our story straight. I can be an old friend passing through on the way to take a new fellowship position in the north."

"An academic? That is rich."

"Well, if I were a peer, they would know my family name, and I'd rather not impersonate a parson or military man. Simple, respectable, and unremarkable."

"I suppose that could work," Richard said doubtfully.

"Just keep to the story, and I will strive to be as uninteresting as I can manage."

"Yes, but what are you going to do differently?"

Benedict ignored him completely. "And I will do everything I can to stay out of her way while I am here."

An odd sound filtered through the door, and the men exchanged glances. Dread dropped in Benedict's stomach like a lead weight. He'd been a spy too long not to know a suspicious sound when he heard one. Richard held a finger to his lips and rose from the chair. Benedict shook his head and pointed to his stocking feet. Quick as a wraith, he was out of his chair and across the room.

In one swift movement, he twisted the knob and yanked the door open. A blond-headed female stumbled into the room and right into his chest for the second time that day. Oh God, had Evie heard—

"Beatrice!" Richard exclaimed, his brow knitted in consternation. "What do you think you are doing, you little eavesdropper?"

Beatrice? Benedict breathed a long sigh as relief swept through him. Quickly, he set the interloper away from him and closed the door. It was obvious now that she was just a look-alike to her older sister. Both her hair and her eyes were darker, and she was of a much slighter build.

The girl's pale skin flared a dull red as she lifted her shoulders in a sort of half shrug. "Well, I'm sorry, but when you didn't come to see us, I slipped away from our lessons to come see you, but just as I came down the stairs, you disappeared into the guest room, and then I heard your voices, and, well"—she paused to suck in a breath—"I didn't want to interrupt if it was an important conversation, after all."

Richard's lips were pursed, and his hands rested on his hips; yet his expression was rather indulgent. "And what did you hear, you naughty girl?"

She grinned and turned to Benedict, dropping a quick curtsy. "Hello, Mr. Hastings. It is *so* thrilling to finally meet you in person."

Richard and Benedict groaned in unison. Bloody hell, this was *not* going to be his day—or his week. Perhaps not even his year.

"All right, Bea," Richard said, hooking an arm about his sister's shoulders and guiding her to the settee by the windows. "What is it going to take to keep you quiet?"

"Why doesn't anyone think I can keep a secret?" she grumbled, managing to look genuinely miffed.

"Well, my dear, everyone knows you can't trust a spy."

Benedict made a face. That little quip really stung. Giving himself a mental shake, he retraced his steps to the bed to retrieve his jacket. If he must have the disadvantage of being bootless in front of the girl, he could at least be properly outfitted from the knees up. "Lady

Beatrice, I apologize that you have been drawn into our little ruse. I know that you wouldn't want to mislead your sister—"

"Is that what we are calling lying through one's teeth these days?" She smiled innocently as she spoke.

Benedict ground his teeth against the retort that sprang to his lips. He needed the girl in his corner, whether he liked it or not. Grabbing one of the chairs by the fireplace, he carried it over to the settee and set it directly in front of her. Any good manipulator knew that being on eye level was important when trying to garner an opponent's favor. "I merely wish to spare your sister the hurt of dredging up old memories. Had I known she was in residence, I never would have come. As I will be here only a short time, surely you can see I simply wished to spare her feelings."

Beatrice snorted. "You merely wished to spare *yourself* the hurt of her thrashing you when she discovers who you really are."

"That is uncalled for, Bea," Richard warned, his features for once looking serious.

"Says the man who played along with the deception."

"Says the girl who relies on her only brother to send her oil paints."

Beatrice gasped, drawing back in horror. "What has that to do with anything?"

Richard leaned back against the cushions, smug now. "Only that if you choose to tattle to anyone—Evie, Mother or Father, or even your maid—you'll soon be reacquainted with the delights of painting only with watercolors. You know, just as a proper young lady should."

"But that isn't fair!"

"Such is life, my dear."

A cautious smile came to Benedict's lips. Beatrice looked truly appalled by the threat. He held his peace, however, waiting to see what she would say.

After several seconds, her thin shoulders drooped and she gave a tiny nod. "Very well. I won't tell her anything. But just so you know," she said, straightening a little, "it's not just because of the paints. She wants something very badly, and I think her reaction to Hastings's presence could jeopardize her plans."

"Duly noted," Richard said, smiling in triumph. "Now then, give your brother a hug and get back to your tutors before you get in trouble."

Benedict waited as Richard escorted his sister to the door. Despite the skirmish between them, there didn't appear to be any hard feelings whatsoever. If it had been his own brother locked in a battle of wills, Benedict had no doubt things would have ended much worse. He clenched his jaw at the thought, shoving Henry as far from his mind as possible. He didn't want to think about the bastard just yet, not with Richard in the room.

When the door shut, Benedict rose and ran a hand through his hair. "Well, that does make a bit of a muddle of things. Do you think she can keep her tongue behind her teeth?"

"I wouldn't worry too much. She is quite a bit older than she was when she tattled to our parents about that little midnight ride to the Rose and Thorn a few summers back."

"Great, now I feel much better."

Richard laughed and slapped him on the shoulder. "She wants those paints far too much to chance it. Now, let's speak no more on the matter. No amount of bribery could keep Jocelyn or Carolyn quiet if they discovered what was afoot."

Bloody hell. Things just kept getting better and better. "Perhaps I should take my leave. This is becoming far too complicated." Even as Benedict said it, a voice deep within him protested. He had only just laid eyes on

Evie—how could he possibly up and walk away so soon? In the midst of all the rotten things he was mired in, could he not have a day or two to soak in Evie's presence? Then store it up like wheat for the winter?

Richard waved a dismissive hand. "Oh, no. You are not leaving me now. Besides, this is the most fun I've had in ages. Now then, I'm anxious to get my hands on some of Cook's delectable food. Shall we?"

Was it possible to feel relief and dread at once? "Very well. Let me just get my boots."

As he tugged them back on, Benedict steeled himself against the unease winding through his veins like quicksilver. Though he fairly ached with the desire to see Evie again, God help him if he found himself the target of her wrath.

Once his boots were in place, he stood and nodded toward the door. "Lead the way."

"Is he handsome?"

Evie, who had been the first to arrive in the drawing room for tea, turned from the window and raised an eyebrow at her youngest sister, Carolyn, whose large blue eyes were wide with curiosity.

"I daresay you can see for yourself in a few minutes." Releasing the drape, Evie walked around the sofa, smoothing the voluminous skirts of her habit as she sat. She hadn't had enough time to change, but after scrutinizing the sky, she wondered if she might still have the opportunity to ride after all. Just a quick one, of course—she wouldn't be out past sunset.

Carolyn's hopeful expression fell, and she plopped on the sofa opposite Evie, the blond sausage curls framing her face bouncing on impact. Sitting beside her twin on the sofa, Jocelyn wrinkled her nose. "That must mean he is not."

"Jocelyn," Beatrice exclaimed, scowling as she tucked her feet beneath her, "Evie meant no such thing." She was only a year older, but she nevertheless seemed to think herself vastly more mature, which continually irked her younger sisters.

Today was no exception. Jocelyn scowled right back. "How would you know? He could be some sort of ogre for all we know."

Evie grinned, picturing the handsome stranger, with his chocolate eyes and deliciously broad shoulders. An ogre he was not. "I meant exactly what I said. He shall be down any minute, and I expect you to mind your manners."

"Yes, please." Mama breezed into the room, her burnished orange gown whispering briskly as she walked. "I would very much appreciate it if you would all be on your best behavior." She paused behind the twins to kiss their cheeks before moving on to inspect the tea tray.

"Of course, Mama. I only wish we had been given a bit of warning. I would have chosen my pink and white muslin instead of this old thing." Jocelyn plucked unhappily at her perfectly lovely gown, its only sin being that it boasted green trim instead of pink.

Satisfied that the tray was in order, Mama took a seat beside Evie. "I certainly would have appreciated a bit of advance notice myself, poppet, but such is the mind of a man. I'm merely happy he came now and not a week from now. We would have already been halfway to London by then, and I would have been sorely disappointed to miss him."

Evie blanched at her mother's mention of London. How on earth would she find the opportunity to speak to her mother privately with Richard and his guest causing so much excitement? Evie knew she couldn't wait much longer, or the opportunity would pass. In the meantime, she must behave absolutely above reproach. She discreetly straightened her shoulders and softened her smile.

"Ah, here they are; my dear family."

At Richard's greeting, the girls jumped up to greet him, giggling as he hugged all three of them at once. Mama and Evie rose as well, and a moment later Papa entered the room.

Evie stood back a little as the girls talked animatedly with Richard, their voices rising an octave or two to be heard over each other. Through the cacophony, Evie suddenly felt compelled to look to the doorway. Mr. Benedict stood just outside the drawing room, his eyes leveled directly at her. She sucked in a surprised breath, a tiny thrill racing across the back of her neck.

The moment their eyes met, he looked away, seeking out Richard instead. As he stepped into the room, the girls stopped talking at once, leaving a vacuum of silence that seemed to echo off the rose-colored wallpaper.

Jocelyn and Carolyn shared identical looks of wonder, with their eyes wide and lips slightly parted. Beatrice bit her lip and blushed before looking down to her hands. Struck anew by his chiseled features and wide shoulders, Evie knew all too well what her younger sisters must have been thinking. Mr. Benedict shifted under the sudden scrutiny, looking uncomfortable. Richard took it all in stride, extending a hand to his friend. "Mr. Benedict, come meet my family."

As her brother made the introductions, Evie stood to the side and observed their guest. He greeted each member of her family graciously, if a bit reservedly. Though his eyes never strayed to hers again, she wondered if he could possibly be as aware of her as she was of him.

Pasting a generic smile on her face, she didn't hear a word of the conversation; instead, she let her eyes follow the strong line of his shoulders down his broad chest all the way to his slim waist. She looked away before her eyes could dip lower and barely resisted the urge to fan her cheeks.

"Evie?"

Her head snapped up to see her mother looking at her strangely. "Yes?"

"I said would you like to pour the tea?"

Drat, how had she missed the question? She smiled brightly at Mama. "Of course." Cringing, Evie scurried to the tea tray. She really needed to get herself together. She picked up the dainty porcelain pot and poured the first cup, a ribbon of fragrant steam curling pleasantly before her nose and calming her nerves a bit. She looked askance at Mr. Benedict. "How do you take your tea, sir?"

He cocked his head slightly to the side as if she had asked him if he wanted snails with his tea. After the slightest hesitation, he said, "Just a splash of milk, please."

Her eyebrows drew together briefly before she smoothed her expression. Honestly, what had she said to earn that particular look? She was beginning to think the man was a little odd.

She nodded nonetheless and returned her attention to the tea while Richard regaled her family with an overly dramatic tale about the inn they had stayed in the previous night. Setting down the creamer, Evie straightened and stepped forward to offer Mr. Benedict the tea.

He accepted with another one of those almost nonexistent smiles. Clearly social niceties were not this man's forte. She started to turn back to the tea when the lightest touch of his fingers on her bare wrist stopped her cold. "Lady Evelyn?"

Though he immediately withdrew his hand, she felt as though hot wax had been dripped on her skin, fierce but strangely pleasurable all at once. "Yes?" Her voice sounded breathy to her own ears, and she drew a steadying breath. Thank heavens her family was preoccupied with the story.

"How do you take *your* tea?" He looked to her with genuine interest, and she belatedly realized she was probably giving him the same odd look he had given her moments ago.

"Um, one lump of sugar, no milk."

He nodded as if it were the most normal conversation in the world and moved forward to take a seat. What on earth? Evie gave her head a little shake and went back to her hostess duties. As she poured and distributed the tea, she couldn't seem to stop herself from sneaking glances in Mr. Benedict's direction, watching his expressions as he conversed with the others. Never once did he give them one of those odd looks or ask them strange questions.

As Evie passed the last cup of tea to Carolyn and sat back on the stuffy antique sofa, Mama turned to Mr. Benedict and smiled. "I certainly hope you don't mind the informal nature of our little gathering. We tend to be very relaxed when we are here at the Hall."

He glanced around the bright and spacious drawing room. "Not at all, my lady. And I must say, your home is lovely. I can see why you don't often find yourselves in the city with such a place as this available to you."

"Why, thank you, Mr. Benedict." Mama flushed with pleasure. She had extensively refurbished much of the house over the years, and Evie knew he could not have given her mother a better compliment. "Do tell us more about yourself. I know where you are headed, but from where do you hail?"

"Bath," Richard interjected around a mouthful of cucumber sandwich. "He hails from Bath."

Mr. Benedict froze, his teacup halfway to the table, for a fraction of a second. Setting the cup down, he nodded. "Yes—Bath, my lady." He pressed a napkin to his lips, his eyes flitting to Richard before continuing. "Since leaving for university, however, I very rarely find myself outside the school's grounds. Indeed, it seems I am to go directly from being educated to being the educator, as it were, and will again find myself sequestered within a new school's walls."

"Bath, you say?" Every eye turned in Evie's direction. Drat, had she just said that aloud?

She had been thinking Richard didn't have any good friends in Bath, which was why he hadn't sampled that particular city's offerings. She had to say something now, lest she look like a dimwit. She licked her lips and forced a smile. "How interesting. I myself have never been. As my mother has already pointed out, our family spends most of our time here at the Hall, but I hear the Roman Baths are quite the phenomenon. It is said the waters there are miraculously restorative. Tell me, do you take the waters when you do find yourself in the area, Mr. Benedict?"

Inwardly, she winced. Well, that didn't sound inane at all.

"Yes, they are quite the thing. However, as I have returned so infrequently, I have not indulged in that particular offering of the city."

Evie frowned. He just did it again—giving her a strange, unreadable look. He had been perfectly pleasant with her parents. When normally she might have let the topic drop, she tilted her head as if very interested in what he had to say. "Really? I would have expected a resident to have experienced so fine a local offering."

He reached out for the tea again, breaking eye contact. "Ancient history is not really my forte, I suppose."

"But the beauty of the baths lies in their being the past come to life, so to speak."

His eyes flickered up to meet hers. "Sometimes the past is better left behind, I think." The intensity was back, if only for a moment. She shivered, not sure what to make of him. Then he smiled, though it did not seem to reach his eyes. "Are you interested in ancient peoples, then, Lady Evelyn?"

It was hard to think straight with the full force of his gaze leveled at her. She hadn't realized his left cheek dimpled when he smiled. "Um, yes, I find them to be quite fascinating. Sadly, I often find them to be more interesting than people in the present."

Immediately realizing the possible interpretation of the statement, she rushed to clarify. "Not *present* present people, er, company, of course. I was speaking in general terms. Oh dear, I do apologize if I have just now managed to insult the entirety of the British Empire," she finished weakly. Had she really said that? Cringing, Evie bit into a chocolate biscuit to keep from making any further asinine comments.

Mr. Benedict raised an eyebrow but nodded nonetheless, as if she had actually made some amount of sense. She swallowed and smiled faintly back, then turned to her mother. "Shall I ring for more tea?"

Mama looked to her with interest, nodding slowly, and Evie valiantly suppressed a blush as she rose and made her way to the bellpull. After all her warnings to Richard, she was the one earning her mother's famous raised eyebrow.

Evie sighed. All she needed to do was act like a normal human being between now and when her family departed. Really, was that too much to ask of herself? Her gaze slid to Mr. Benedict, now engrossed in a conversation with her father. What was it about him that so intrigued her, anyhow? No one had ever captured her attention quite so thoroughly—at least not in person.

She pressed her lips together. As much as she was curious about the man, she refused to make a fool of herself. What she needed was a ride. Being cooped up in the house with Mama had clearly muddled her brain, and a jaunt across the grounds would be just the thing. Perhaps then her heart wouldn't race every time she made eye contact with the enigmatic stranger.

As if on cue, he looked up, his eyes immediately finding hers. She drew in a quick breath, light-headed from the sudden pounding of her heart.

Oh heavens, she was in trouble.

Chapter Five

If Grandmama ever receives a letter from you, the terms of our agreement shall become null and void. You'd best lock your doors, lest I find you alone and dole out a proper punishment for such meddling.
　　　　　　　　　　　— From Hastings to Evie

He really needed to get some air.

After the excruciatingly polite tea with Richard's family, Benedict needed to get away from everyone, outside where the crisp evening air could help to clear his mind. Perhaps when he was away from the house, he could think of something else besides the delectable Lady Evelyn. God, he felt like a damned degenerate for even thinking of Evie in those terms; seeing her and Richard together for the first time had truly driven home that she was his best friend's little sister. Still, there was simply no denying Benedict's attraction to her.

Being in the same room with Evie was an almost dreamlike experience. For all of the very personal things he knew about her—her aspirations, her interests, her occasionally sharp tongue—he had never considered how much he *didn't* know about her. He hadn't known she fidgeted when she sat, smoothing her hands over her gown or tapping her foot lightly beneath her skirts. He had never thought about which flavor of biscuit she preferred—chocolate—or how she took her tea—one lump of sugar, no milk. And he had certainly never pictured her babbling on about ancient peoples.

A smile lifted the corner of his mouth. God only knew what all that had been about. Was it possible that his presence here somehow flustered her? It was certainly flustering *him*.

The small smile vanished. He knew what he was doing. Without conscious thought, he was allowing himself to be diverted from the real issues in his life.

He paused by one of the windows, pushed aside the heavy damask drapes, and rested his forehead against the cool glass. His whole reason for coming here was to figure out what the hell he was going to do about the unthinkable decision he had to make, and in a matter of hours he had been distracted. The window began to fog where his skin touched the glass, and he stepped away.

The problem was, he wasn't ready. He needed just a little more time before he could look on the situation with any amount of objectivity. Not that one could ever look on betrayal with any amount of detachment. Ruthlessly, he shoved the whole ordeal to the back of his brain.

Later. He would deal with it all later.

He strode to the door, pausing only long enough to retrieve his hat and gloves, and headed for freedom.

The earlier sunshine had given way to clouds, obstructing the setting sun. He took a deep breath, filling his lungs with the satisfyingly clear country air—*English* country air, which was infinitely sweeter than, say, French country air. He had missed that indefinable quality of English air. After everything that had happened in the last week, he couldn't for the life of him recall why he had ever thought it thrilling to leave the country. After the last few years, he had treaded on far more foreign soil than was healthy.

"Oh, I beg your pardon!"

Benedict's breath caught. Without even turning around,

he already knew who it was. Already her voice was imprinted on his brain, along with many of the letters they had shared through the years. She was, after all, the one and only person who had ever written to him in all his years at Eton.

Smoothing his expression, he swiveled on his heel and dipped his head in greeting. "Lady Evelyn. Have I intruded upon your privacy?"

Of course, it would have to be her—the one person he should avoid. She looked completely adorable in her mud-speckled riding habit, her cheeks flushed with color and her hair slightly mussed where it was coiled below her hat. A small smudge of dirt decorated her chin, and he very nearly reached out to wipe it away. Instead, he clasped his hands tightly behind his back.

She smiled up at him, somehow looking sunny despite the weather. "Not at all. I was taking the long way back to the house after a lovely ride. I've been a bit cooped up this week. How are you enjoying the gardens?"

"I find them quite agreeable." He offered the briefest possible smile—more of a grimace, really—before looking past her into the distance. He was so damned curious about her, but no good could come from engaging her in conversation.

She hesitated for a moment, and he steadfastly avoided looking back at her. Finally, she said, "I'm glad to hear it. Are you a nature enthusiast?" Her voice carried hints of determined politeness, and he firmly suppressed a grin. How long would it take for her sharp tongue to emerge? Would she be able to hide it from her brother's guest?

Turning slightly away from her, he lifted one shoulder in a halfhearted shrug. "Not particularly."

She tilted her head, her golden eyebrow hitching up. "Really?" There was no hesitation this time. "I find the outdoors to be quite refreshing. Even when the weather is less than agreeable, the air is always fresh and clean—provided one avoids London." She gave a little shudder, as if London constituted the worst of fates. Of course, he was well aware of her aversion to the city—one that for the most part he agreed with, but he wasn't about to commiserate with her. Instead, he simply nodded in polite acknowledgment.

She eyed him for a moment, and he wished he could read what was going through her mind. She rubbed a gloved hand absently along her arm. "Am I to believe you share my brother's preference for the city life?" Her statement was punctuated by the muted whinny of a horse in the near distance.

"I harbor no preference one way or the other."

"Truly? I can hardly conceive of a man without an opinion . . . whether it is warranted or not." The last was said beneath her breath, but he was glad he had caught it. That tongue was catching up to her.

"Oh?"

She colored faintly, like the first hint of sunset on a warm summer evening. "It is just that most gentlemen of my acquaintance tend to express their positions on subjects rather freely, whether or not they have any actual knowledge to support their views."

"It is a good thing a woman would never do such a thing."

She raised her eyebrows in surprise. Blast, why did he let the quip slip out?

"Touché, Mr. Benedict. However, women rarely force their opinions on others. Men, on the other hand, seem to do so at every possible opportunity. Alas, since men are in a position of authority, women have no choice but to acquiesce."

He made a sound that sounded rather close to a snort. "If only that were true."

Her eyes abruptly narrowed into a scowl. Damn it, he shouldn't be provoking her. He offered her a conciliatory smile. "A joke, Lady Evelyn, although, apparently a poorly executed one."

Her face relaxed, and she crossed her arms, looking at him as if taking his measure. "I wouldn't have taken you for the joking type. Clearly I need to work on my powers of perception." A gust of wind tugged at the loosened strands of hair, which fell from beneath her hat. He had a sudden, clear image of tucking the pieces behind her ear.

"No, you were right the first time. I generally keep to myself. As a matter of fact, that is why I fit well in academia." His heart squeezed within his chest. Speaking falsehoods to the one person he had always been so honest with felt like a crime against the heavens. Wasn't that why he had ended their correspondence in the first place? He half expected her to narrow her eyes and brand him as the liar he was.

Instead, she merely nodded, turning to look out over the gardens. "Well, normally, you could not have chosen a better place for solitude. Other than when Beatrice comes outdoors to paint, I am generally the only one who spends much time out here. And really, I was just passing through on my way back to the house."

He surreptitiously glanced around. He wouldn't put it past Beatrice to hide among the bushes somewhere. She had behaved perfectly at their little gathering, but it galled him that she knew who he really was. Distractedly, he offered Evie a polite smile. "Don't let me keep you, then."

Despite his words, he could clearly picture himself reaching out to her, sliding his hands around her waist, and embracing her like the long-lost friend she was. He pushed the vision from his mind.

Oblivious as she was to his thoughts, her eyes reflected disappointment. "Well, I shall leave you be. I merely wished to see what you thought of one of my favorite places in the world. By day, the lovely plants showcase their beauty, but at night . . ." Glancing to the clouds above them, she trailed off, her expression softening. At night . . . what?

With her eyes averted, he drank in the sight of her profile. He still could not grow used to her beauty—masses of honey blond hair, shiny even in the dull light of the overcast day and elegant despite the effects of a brisk ride, and those expressive blue eyes that were so like Richard's but somehow so much *better*. Realizing he was holding his breath, he discreetly exhaled.

At last she lowered her gaze to his. Her eyes widened the smallest bit, but it was enough for him to wonder what his expression betrayed. Years of training in the art of deceit, and all it took was one blond, impish young woman to ruin it all. He had always known she would be his weakness.

Her lips slowly turned up in a pleased grin. "Do forgive me, Mr. Benedict, for interrupting your solitude. Enjoy the afternoon, sir, and I shall see you at dinner."

With that, she turned and headed toward the house, leaving him slack-jawed behind her. Damn it all to hell, *what* had she seen on his face?

Well, goodness.

Clearly, Mr. Benedict had some amount of interest in her. His words might be few, but his eyes spoke volumes.

Evie felt the hint of a giddy smile come to her lips. She didn't know what had possessed her to sneak up on him like that. It *might* have had something to do with her inability to quite put a finger on how he viewed her. He went from utterly disinterested one minute to rather startlingly intense glances the next. She supposed one liked to know where one stood with others. The truth was, he represented a challenge, and Evie *loved* a good challenge.

Particularly when the challenge looked like a modern

day, in-the-flesh Greek god. Not that it mattered in any way, shape, or form, but it was awfully delicious to realize that someone as handsome as he held some amount of regard for her. It occurred to her when she saw him strolling through the garden alone that he would be leaving in a few days. Surely it couldn't hurt to indulge in a little harmless flirting. Even if she wanted to lose her heart to him—which she didn't—she wouldn't have time to. And it was rather fun to meet a man outside of the *ton*, outside of her set altogether. She relished the freedom of being far away from the prying eyes and wagging tongues of the gossipmongers who filled every ballroom in London this time of year.

And the hint of mystery about him only served to make him more . . . alluring.

She smiled as she made her way into the house and headed up the stairs to change. As she reached the landing and turned toward the west wing where the family's quarters were, Mama emerged from her private sitting room, grinning.

"How was your ride, dear? Lovely, I hope."

Evie slowed, suspicious. It was not the question itself that was unusual, but rather the way in which it was delivered. Mama looked like the cat that had gotten the cream. Evie didn't know what her mother was up to, but she had a feeling she wasn't going to like it. "Yes, quite nice. Thank you for asking."

She pushed open her door and rang for her maid. The room seemed overly warm after the brisk air of the outdoors. She pulled off her gloves, tossed them on the bureau, and set to work unbuttoning the stiff wool jacket of her habit. Her mother followed in behind her and placed a casual hand on the back of one of the chairs facing the fireplace, brushing her fingers idly over the moss green velvet. "Anything of interest happen afterward?"

Ah. Clearly, she had been spotted with Mr. Benedict.

Evie shimmied out of the jacket and laid it on a nearby stool, careful not to drop any mud on the carpet. "Interesting? Not that I can think of. Why do you ask?"

Her mother grimaced at Evie's deliberate obtuseness but wasn't about to be deterred. "I happened to see you outside in the garden speaking with Mr. Benedict. I merely wondered what the two of you were talking about."

A little warning bell went off inside Evie's head. The last thing she needed was for her mother to think there was a chance Evie would fall for their guest. For heaven's sake, the man might be handsome, but he certainly wasn't worth abandoning her dreams for. The alarm quieted somewhat when she realized she had a ready out—thank goodness for Mr. Benedict's fellowship. Even she knew that in order to accept the position, one must be unmarried.

Perhaps a little reminder was in order. She busied herself removing her hat, offering a perfectly innocent smile to her mother. "His new position, of course. He is looking forward to beginning the fellowship. Apparently, the position opened up unexpectedly when the last fellow married, and he is quite pleased with the opportunity." At least, Evie hoped that was what had happened. With any luck, her mother would not bring that particular fib up to Mr. Benedict.

Mama's face fell, and Evie *almost* felt guilty. "I see."

A scratch at the door announced Morgan's arrival. Evie breathed a sigh of relief as the maid bustled in and stood to the side to await Evie's instructions. "Well, I believe I will get out of these clothes and perhaps take a bath before dinner."

Her mother smoothed a hand over her hair and nodded. "That sounds like a very good idea." She walked over to where Evie stood, licked the pad of her thumb, and brushed it over Evie's chin. "I don't believe mud is intended to be a cosmetic, after all."

Evie wrinkled her nose at the gesture. "And here I thought it was the newest thing."

Her mother chuckled, the skin around her soft gray eyes crinkling. "Well, I suppose that explains a great deal. Enjoy your bath, dear, and I will see you at eight." She patted Evie's cheek before heading for the door, then paused just before exiting. Her hand on the doorknob, she half turned and said over her shoulder, "Do be sure to wear something nice."

As her mother slipped from the room and closed the heavy oak door with a quiet click, Evie's smile fell. Drat. She had a sneaking suspicion her mother had not given up on Mr. Benedict, after all.

Chapter Six

Proper punishment, indeed! When it comes to you, I shall never respect my elder. And by the way, I just added that last letter to my list of letters to send to Grandmama Hastings. The poor dear—I hope her heart can handle her grandson's wickedness.

—From Evie to Hastings

"Good God, man—who tied your cravat—a wild animal?"

"And good evening to you, too," Benedict said, pulling back the door to admit Richard into his chambers. Outfitted in a deep blue velvet tailcoat with silver buttons, light blue trousers, and an elaborately tied white cravat, Richard could not have looked more the opposite of Benedict. "At least I don't look as though I've been assaulted by a French dressmaker."

Richard's mouth dropped open in mock affront. "I'll have you know, my *tailor*, Mr. Babcock, is as British as I am." He waved a dismissive hand in Benedict's direction and grinned. "You, on the other hand, don't look as though you even *have* a tailor. Where did you even find such a plain jacket? And those trousers—good God, is that a frayed hem on the bottom of the left leg?"

Benedict chuckled. "It sounds as though I look the part of an academic short on funds and fashion sense."

"You can say that again. You do realize it wouldn't kill

you to wear some color now and again. After all, I have it on the best authority that women love a stylishly dressed man."

"I'll leave the rainbow to you, my friend." Benedict had learned long ago that the simpler his wardrobe, the broader the range of situations into which he could blend. Besides, he preferred not to look like a damned peacock. He bent to search through his bag for the pair of evening gloves he had brought. Slipping them on, he took one last look in the mirror. Plain, but classic. His physique did look a little more toned than one would expect of an academic, but all in all, it would do.

Turning back to Richard, he said, "After you."

When they arrived in the drawing room, only Lord Granville was present, despite their being right on time.

"Good evening, gentlemen," the marquis said, rising from his position on the sofa to greet them. "Well, Richard, what did Benedict think about the hunt?"

The hunt? Benedict looked askance at his friend.

"Actually, it completely slipped my mind. Earlier, my father and I were discussing his new Irish hunter—the one he was riding when we arrived. We are most anxious to put the horse through its paces. Would you like to join us for an impromptu hunt on Friday? It will merely be an exercise, an informal affair. It is quite the end of the season, but we are sure to enjoy ourselves, nonetheless."

Enjoying himself was not exactly something Benedict could imagine doing at the present moment—or in the foreseeable future, for that matter. But of course, Richard had no way of knowing the circumstances that weighed like boulders hanging from Benedict's neck. And he was not yet ready to confide in his friend. Richard surely saw no reason why Benedict couldn't enjoy himself while they were there, especially since Richard knew what an accomplished horseman Benedict was.

Having no way to get around it, Benedict nodded reluctantly. "A hunting expedition would be most agreeable. It would be my privilege to accompany you."

"Excellent. I'm certain we will be able to find a horse for you that will suit. Buttercup, perhaps?" Richard laughed at Benedict's look of disgust.

He was sorely missing his own horse, but he hadn't intended to go traipsing across the countryside when they left him behind in London.

"Ah, here are the lovely ladies now," Granville interjected, turning to watch his wife and daughters file into the room. Dressed in their elaborate evening gowns, the young girls smiled broadly while Evie and her mother followed more serenely. White slippers peeked from beneath the gowns as the girls walked, their skirts swishing around with each step, and white gloves covered their hands.

As if of their own accord, his eyes immediately sought out Evie. Her calm manner was a distinct departure from her younger sisters'. The candlelight added a gentle, golden tint to her slightly—and unfashionably—tanned skin. The effect was surprisingly attractive. He swiftly averted his gaze. It wouldn't do to be caught as he had been in the garden earlier.

As the marquis offered compliments to the girls, Lady Granville smiled to Benedict. "Good evening, Mr. Benedict. You are looking quite rested. I trust you are enjoying your day?"

Benedict bowed before responding, "Absolutely, my lady. One cannot help but take delight in a grand house such as this."

"And the grounds? I caught a glimpse of you touring the gardens earlier." Her eyes were alight with interest, and he inwardly groaned. If she had spied him in the gardens, he could imagine with whom she spied him.

"Equally lovely." He decided to continue before she asked about his conversation with Evie. "Fortuitously, it appears I will have the opportunity to explore the estate at large. Lord Granville and Richard have just invited me on a hunt to be held at the end of the week."

A groan escaped Richard. At the same moment, Evie's features lit with pleasure. "A hunt? Oh, fantastic! I have been positively cooped up for days. A hunt would be just the thing." She rubbed her hands in anticipation.

Richard clamped a hand on Benedict's shoulder. "Oh, now you've gone and done it. I was hoping we could sneak off without her noticing so I would have half a chance at the hunt." He dropped his hand and sighed. "Now *she's* going to be there to show me up. Can't a man ever catch a break?"

Benedict blinked. Evie participated in the actual *hunts*? Apparently, a lot had changed since the last letter they exchanged. He knew very well she was an exceptional rider, but to actively participate in a foxhunt was rather beyond the pale. He didn't know whether to be massively impressed or absolutely appalled. He decided to go with the former; she was, after all, still in one piece—for now.

Evie chuckled at her brother. "Oh, don't be such a spoilsport. It will be a fair fight, I assure you." She grinned innocently at him. "I may even allow you to have a head start."

"My, aren't you just the very soul of fairness and generosity," Richard grumbled. He shook his head in Benedict's direction. "My father should have never allowed her to join us. Mother protested, but Evie is a bit, uh, strong willed, shall we say?"

He laughed when Evie smacked him, rubbing his arm before continuing. "Well, you did pester him for almost a year before he finally gave in to your demands and allowed you to accompany us on our hunts." He turned back to Benedict. "Only on Hertford's estates, mind, and so long as only family intimates, locals, and Hertford staff are involved."

Benedict's plans to avoid talking to Evie went up in a puff of smoke as he looked to her in admiration. Memories of their plans to race when she visited him that last weekend at Eton lifted a corner of his lips. The chance to see her in her glory in person was too much to pass up. "You must be quite a remarkable horsewoman, Lady Evelyn."

Pride and pleasure lit her crystalline eyes, and he felt as though he had just won a prize. "Actually, Mr. Benedict, just this once I will flatter myself and say I am indeed a skilled rider."

Richard scoffed. "Skilled, maybe. Bordering on crazy, definitely."

Evie seemed to take no offense. "Oh, pray do not listen to the protestations of losers, Mr. Benedict. Richard is merely jealous of my aptitude and flair for riding. Sadly, the Moore legacy of fine equestrianism seems to have passed over my dear brother. But what he lacks in skill, he makes up for in charm. Is that not right, Richard?" Her expression bordered on wicked as she verbally sparred her brother.

"Very funny, but you are ignoring the true issue of the matter." Richard's hands went to his hips as he turned again to Benedict. "She always manages to be at the front of the field, which is really quite annoying for us mortals. The real problem arises when she is first on the scene. If she is the first to approach the cornered fox, she clears the way for the thing to escape while heeling the dogs. She claims since she is the 'victor,' it is her prerogative to do as she wishes with the prize. It is a wonder we do not have foxes positively blanketing the countryside."

"Oh, that is just stuff and nonsense, as you well know," she countered. "First of all, I am not *always* at the front of the field; I am merely always ahead of *you*. Second, I call the dogs off only when the fox has gone to ground. It is not as if it happens often. And really, it is no fun to stand around while some poor terrier spends hours trying to dig the pitiable thing out. Call it a game of tag, if you will. Third, if *you* can look that poor, adorable creature in the eye and kill it, by all means, go right ahead." She put her finger to her lips. "Of course, you do need to get to the fox *first.* . . . Well, that *is* a problem, is it not?" She laughed merrily at Richard's comically sour expression.

"If it makes you feel any better," she said, apparently taking pity on her brother, "I suspect we will be drag hunting this time around. No foxes chased; therefore no foxes pardoned. It is the perfect opportunity to try out the hunter without involving dozens of people, and we can all be back in time for tea."

"Well, fox or no, Benedict will have the opportunity to witness the whole farce for himself, I am sure. Be nice; it is not polite to trump one's guests, after all." Richard smiled winningly to the room at large.

Lord Granville merely shook his head at his two older children's exchange. "Have no fear, Mr. Benedict. I am sure a pleasant day will be had by all."

The butler, dressed impeccably with every sparse hair on his head in place, came in at that moment and announced dinner. The group shuffled to relocate to the dining room. Each of the twins vied for the opportunity to be escorted by Benedict, then appeared crestfallen upon realizing the honor would go to Beatrice.

As he offered her his arm, she looked up to him with sly eyes. "You've made my sister very happy, *Mister* Benedict."

He clenched his jaw for a second before responding. Dipping his head closer to hers, he said in a low voice, "It is all I've ever wanted to do, Lady Beatrice."

Her eyes widened the smallest amount. She was quiet for a moment as they entered the long dining room. Then she leaned toward him slightly and whispered, "I remember how happy she used to be when the post came."

"Oh?"

"And how melancholy she was when it stopped."

As they approached her chair, he met her eyes. "Nobody regrets that as much as I do. That is why I wouldn't want to remind her of that time. My lips are sealed if yours are."

She gave him an appraising look. "They are as long as she is happy. All the paints in the world are not worth my sister's getting hurt."

Clearly she'd had time to think the issue through. He respected her willingness to stand up for her sister, even if he was the one she stood against. He held her eyes for a moment before dipping his head in a shallow nod.

"As it should be, Lady Beatrice."

He thought her a skilled horsewoman.

Evie swallowed her grin and surreptitiously stole a glance at Mr. Benedict as the footmen served the second course. Never mind that he had never actually seen her on a horse or knew anything at all about her; just seeing the admiration in his eyes had been very heady indeed.

She raised a spoonful of pea soup to her mouth, sipping dutifully but barely registering the rich, creamy flavor Cook had no doubt labored to achieve. Instead, she was focused on the delicious sound of Benedict's low, smooth voice as he conversed with her brother—discreetly, of course. Mama would undoubtedly be keen to observe any interaction between Evie and the new-comer.

It was like her own little ballet: Take a bite of soup; smile to Papa; nod at what her mother said; steal a glance at Benedict; dab her mouth with her napkin; ask one of her sisters a question; laugh at the answer; steal a glance at Benedict.

She dipped her spoon once more and was surprised when it clinked on the bottom of the empty bowl. She set the utensil down and picked up her sherry glass, continuing her spying over the rim of the crystal.

He was not what one would expect of an academic. It was hard to imagine his broad shoulders and lean, muscled limbs at home in a library or study. His physique spoke of a more rigorous lifestyle.

Evelyn put down the goblet and pressed her napkin to her lips. She nodded vaguely in agreement with whatever Papa was saying, then snuck a peek at Benedict's arms, the outlines of which were just visible through his tightly fitting jacket. Rigorous lifestyle, indeed—it was difficult not to stare. She looked up, a question about his sports of choice on her tongue. The remark, however, fled as she found herself looking directly into his slightly amused gaze.

Gads, he had caught her!

Mortified, she fought the blush she could feel rising up her neck. Clearing her throat, she rallied. "So if not communing with nature, Mr. Benedict, what activities do you enjoy?" There, that came out nicely. It was an absolutely *wonderful* recovery after being caught ogling his person.

For a moment, she would have sworn she caught a wicked gleam in his eye before it vanished behind polite interest. "There are many *activities*"—did she imagine the emphasis?—"I enjoy, Lady Evelyn. While in school,

I participated in boxing, as it was a less-structured sport that did not impair my studies. I do enjoy the occasional walk through a well-tended garden and, indeed, the odd riding excursion. And you, my lady? When not spreading goodwill to vermin across the countryside, how do you spend your time?"

She gaped at his teasing comment. Where had *that* come from? Narrowing her eyes slightly, she replied, "Aside from *rescuing* hapless animals, I enjoy reading, riding, and—"

"Arithmetic, my lady?" he cut in with a completely straight face.

"Riding, not writing, you nitwit," she replied tartly before she could catch hold of herself.

Her mother choked on her soup at the same moment her father's outraged, "Evie!" echoed across the dining table. Evie immediately clamped a hand over her mouth in horror. Merciful heavens, had she just called the man a *nitwit*?

How could she have let the insult, teasing though it was, actually leave her lips? There was no fighting the blush this time; her cheeks burned as hot as the summer sun. Cringing, she stammered, "Oh, my goodness, I—I beg your pardon, sir. I did not mean that. I have grown used to bantering with my brother, and inadvertently extended the rhetoric to you. My deepest apologies, Mr. Benedict."

She could feel Mama's eyes boring into her from across the table. Evie bit the inside of her cheek. What was *wrong* with her?

"No harm done, Lady Evelyn," Benedict responded graciously, keeping a straight face, though she felt strongly he was amused. He dipped his dark head in acceptance of her apology and said, "Please forgive my impertinence, interrupting you as I did."

She couldn't be sure, but he looked to be biting back a smile. At least the man was a good sport about it. For some reason, she wouldn't have expected that. "Oh, I do believe you may call me Evie, Mr. Benedict. I daresay you have earned the right."

A groan escaped in the direction of where her mother was seated. Evie swallowed and looked down the table—oh, yes, her mother was *not* pleased. Evie could only hope the flickering candlelight made her mother look more exasperated than she truly was.

Mama turned to Mr. Benedict. "Ours tends to be a rather informal household when we are among family." She paused to send a pointed look in Evie's direction, but Evie knew her mother would not detract the offer now that it had been made. For heaven's sake, why couldn't she have just kept her mouth shut? "I do hope this total affront to protocol does not offend you?"

"Not at all, my lady," he replied. The corners of his eyes crinkled as he turned to Evie and gave her a broad grin. "Thank you, Evie. I am honored. Nobody calls me James, but I'd be pleased if you called me Benedict. Most of my friends do." Again, the dimple creased his left cheek.

Richard made a noise not unlike a snort, but Evie ignored him. "You are too kind, Benedict." Her stomach did an odd little flip as she said his name. It didn't make any sense. She had merely dropped the mister, but for some reason, losing the formality of the title seemed surprisingly intimate.

The moment was broken as Carolyn piped up. "Carolyn—you must call me Carolyn."

Her twin was only a second behind. "Oh, *please*, call me Jocelyn!"

"Girls! Where are your manners?" her mother cried, shaking her head at her girls' impertinence. Taking a measured breath, she looked apologetically to Benedict. "It appears, Mr. Benedict, that all my children wish to toss aside convention. In for a penny, in for a pound, I suppose."

"I am pleased your children consider me a friend already."

Mama gave him a relieved smile, and when he looked away, Evie caught the warning glare she doled out to each of the girls, including her. Her mother might wish for Evie to make a match, but heaven help her if Evie pushed a toe across the line of propriety. She really needed to show more reserve—not to mention restraint.

"So, what was the third interest you were speaking of before I so rudely interjected?" Benedict's question startled her from her thoughts.

"I beg your pardon? Oh, yes, uh, that would be astronomy." She was surely making an outstanding impression. Could she please stop sounding like a scatterbrained miss? At least she had carried on a normal conversation with him in the garden. "The country affords a spectacular view of the night sky, provided one can be patient enough to wait for a cloudless night. I often enjoy sitting in the garden at night, surrounded by the sweet scents of roses, lilac, sweet pea . . . even the faint scent of evergreen in the winter. It is the perfect setting for stargazing."

The footmen began clearing away the dishes, and Benedict waited for the clinking of silverware on porcelain to die down before answering her.

"Astronomy, you say. How unusual." He furrowed his brow in thought. "Have you been to the Royal Observatory in Greenwich?" He paused, and Evie shook her head in the negative. "You can see the heavens as you have never imagined there. I was fortunate to be visiting when a meteor shower occurred several years ago. Quite the most amazing thing I have ever witnessed."

He was a student of astronomy as well? So they had

something in common after all. Most men thought the hobby tedious and pointless, save for the few naval officers she knew. As the conversation carried on around her, she found herself lost in thought, the words around her swirling meaninglessly past her ears. Perhaps while Benedict was here, he would join her in the garden if the night sky ever cleared for a night of stargazing.

A little shiver went through her at the thought—the two of them, alone in the dark, with nothing but the plants and the heavens as witness. . . . She swallowed loudly and looked down at the plate of roasted lamb a footman placed before her. The smell of rosemary and thyme barely registered in her mind as she imagined the two of them nestled among the roses and lilacs.

She could hardly wait for the clouds to clear.

As the dinner crowd thinned around him, Ned Barney shifted in his seat and shot yet another look at the door. Where the hell was his bloody employer? He'd been sitting in the godforsaken place for nearly an hour, nursing a warm ale and carefully avoiding engaging any of the other patrons in the dim, gloomy room. The pub had a dark, cavelike interior that generally suited the clientele whose purpose seemed to be to get drunk or get into trouble—or both.

The firelight barely penetrated the smoke-filled room, serving more to cast flickering shadows than actual illumination. The mutton stew before him did nothing to alleviate the pervasive smell of body odor and smoke, so Barney merely took another draft of his ale. There was a low hum of conversation and a few random angry shouts, but most of the patrons kept to themselves and their pints. The golden rule, however tarnished, was steadfastly observed: Do not nose into other people's business lest they nose into yours.

At last, the door swung open, and a tall, lean figure stepped inside. Though Barney couldn't make out the man's face, his shining, black Hessian boots and finely tailored clothes stood out among the sea of solid, working-class men surrounding him. Without glancing around, he headed immediately for Barney's table. With his hat pulled low over his brow and the collar of his greatcoat pulled up around his chin, clearly the man wished not to be seen, or more particularly, recognized.

Barney shook his head—the high-stepping fool stuck out like a sore thumb.

As he approached the table, his employer didn't hide the look of derision that clouded his features. Barney suppressed a snort; a fine guv like that would hate to be seen with the likes of him. He certainly fit in better than Lord High-and-Mighty, whose eyes raked over Barney's greasy brown hair, tied as always with an old piece of leather, and his coat, which, thanks to days of rain, was uncomfortably stiff with dried mud and shed clumps of dirt every time he moved his arms. Barney wasn't about to apologize for his appearance.

For all he cared, His Highness could look at him with all the disgust in the world. He thought he was so much better than Barney, but look who came running when Barney sent the man a missive this morning.

Sitting with his back to the wall, Barney took a moment to sweep his eyes around the room. If someone had taken notice of them, he wanted to know.

"Cease looking around so much. You are bound to only attract attention, you bloody fool," the man growled, slipping into the empty chair before tugging the collar of his coat up higher.

The peacock was dressed like that, and he had the gall to say Barney was the one who would attract attention? He wanted to tell the man where he could go, but of course that would send his money away as well. Trying to look contrite, Barney dropped his gaze and ground out, "Sorry, m'lord. Wanted to know what's what, is all."

He could tell his lower-class accent grated on the gentleman's nerves—it had since the first day they met.

"For God's sake, man, do not call me that. Have you no brain at all?"

This time Barney remained mute, staring into his ale. It was better than putting a fist through the man's skull.

"Have you managed to find him, then? Is that why you sent for me?"

"Nay, but I'm close, I know it. Just a li'l longer, 'e'll be mine." He shifted in his seat. Now, to get to the point of the meeting. "I called you because 'e went deep, 'n far at that. If I'm to chase 'im 'cross the 'ole of England, I'm going to need more funds, is all." He hazarded a glance at his employer. The anger and disdain were clear in the man's eyes, and Barney quickly looked down again. He took a bracing draft of ale to fill the silence his employer let stretch.

"I gave you what you said you needed. On what did you manage to piss it away already?" He hissed each word, and Barney shifted uncomfortably in his seat.

"There's expenses, tryin' to find a man that's gone to ground. I've been payin' servants and grooms and all sorts to track 'im."

After a few moments of consideration, the man reached into his pocket, withdrew a small leather pouch, and tossed it on the table. The heavy clink was music to Barney's ears, and he made an effort to conceal the satisfaction from his expression.

"If I do not hear of his whereabouts within five days, I will personally track you down and extract my money from your worthless hide." He stood and glared down at Barney. "Is that understood?"

Barney, still seated at the table, met his eyes and gave a curt nod. "Aye, my lor—uh, sir. I catch your meanin'."

Barney watched as the man turned on his highly polished boot heel and strode to the door. Without a backward glance, he pushed through the exit and was gone. Only then did Barney allow a smile to crack his face.

Leaning back in his chair, he tossed the bag in his hand once, feeling the weight of it, before pocketing the money. Dropping some change from his own meager supply on the table, he rose to his feet. The meeting had gone better than expected. He made his way toward the door, limping in favor of his left leg.

His employer didn't realize that at this point, the job had become personal. Having someone to pin the blame on, and getting paid to do what he already would have been doing, was just a bonus. His target was about to find out that no one made a fool of Ned Barney and got away with it. He could hardly wait for the moment when he would pay one Benedict Hastings a surprise visit.

Chapter Seven

*You may threaten all you want, Evie, but you forget I
hold the trump card. You would never betray me to my
grandmother. How do I know this? Because I would
then betray you to your parents. Of the two of us, who
do you think would suffer the greater consequences?
Were we playing chess, I believe I would have just declared checkmate. Now then, you were saying?*
— From Hastings to Evie

He had been right to sever his ties with Evie before
embarking on his career some seven years earlier.
If Benedict had met her as they had originally planned
when he graduated Eton, he would have never been
able to leave her behind to serve the Crown.

After all, a spy must have full concentration to play
his part.

Benedict closed his eyes and dropped his head back
against the curved lip of the copper tub. It was not that
he had forgotten her completely. When Lisette whisked
him off to the Continent, he had lain awake many a
night, wondering how Evie was doing and whether or
not she was happy.

Wondering whether or not she hated him.

Eventually, he had stopped thinking of her every day,
or even every week. She became a distant, fond memory
that came to him only on rare, special occasions. And

now, here he was, in the middle of the most unthinkable situation, needing nothing more than to concentrate on what the hell he would do next, and he was utterly captivated by her once more. Honestly, what was it about the girl—*lady*—that seemed to erode his willpower so effectively? She was just so damned engaging. He was quite sure it was the only time in his life a young lady had ever referred to him as a nitwit.

A small smile came to his lips. Really, it was exactly the sort of thing she might have said in one of her letters. She had never failed to put him firmly in his place back then, either. His heart tugged within his chest, and he took a slow, deep breath, filling his lungs with the hot steam rising from the water. He had made his choice seven years ago, and now he must live with that.

If he could just stay out of her way—or better yet, if she would stay out of his—then he could decide his next step and move on from this place without causing her any pain.

He slid lower into the almost painfully hot water until it lapped at his chin. He couldn't put it off much longer. He had pushed it aside earlier, but it was time to face his demons. It was time to decide which was more important to him: his loyalty to his country, or to his blood.

Damn Renault. Damn him for finding Benedict's one weakness with the precision of a master swordsman, plunging the tip of his blade into his enemy's heart. Benedict had thought himself so bloody clever when, after three years of working his way into the Renault brothers' smuggling ring, he had finally set them up for the ultimate fall.

Memories of that night almost a year ago wrapped around him like a cold blanket, pushing away the heat of the bath water: the smugness he felt at outsmarting the French bastards; the smell of the salty sea air as it whistled by in cold blasts; the crack of gunfire and the shouts of men as they tried to escape the Crown's best agents. By the end of the night, twelve had been captured, two had escaped, and one was dead.

It was to be his finest hour. He should have walked away a hero. Instead, he'd been forced to defend himself when Jean Luc Renault had aimed his pistol at Benedict's head. In that moment, Jean Luc had paid the ultimate price, Pierre Renault had escaped into the night, and Benedict had lost much of his credibility for having lost both his targets. He always knew Pierre would come after him; he just never imaged how clever the man would be when he did.

Benedict squeezed his eyes shut, wishing he could go back somehow and change what happened. The problem was how far would he have to go back? A week? A month? To the day he had eagerly accepted his first mission?

Growling, Benedict pressed his lips together and slipped beneath the water. He welcomed the scorching heat, the burning sensation on his skin, and the unpleasant prickle of hot liquid against his eyelids. It was but an echo of the betrayal that burned hotly in his gut not four days earlier, when he had arrived at the mist-shrouded manor house on the dunes of Folkestone.

When his lungs burned as achingly as his skin, he emerged from the water, gasping for air. He would make his decision, but not tonight. He simply couldn't trust himself to weigh the consequences clearly yet. And with a lifetime to live with the consequences, it little mattered if he decided now or a few days from now. In the meantime, he could have precious few days to soak up all the things he never had in life: a loving family and a few peaceful days in the country.

And a beautiful woman who stole his breath away.

"There is something you're not telling me."

Richard looked up from his deck of cards and grinned.

"Bit, there are many things I'm not telling you. It is my duty to protect you from at least some of the wicked things I do."

Evie rolled her eyes and pushed away from the door frame of the billiards room. He could be so obtuse when he put his mind to it. The faint scent of cigars still hung in the air, even though it had been hours since the men had enjoyed a friendly game after dinner. Only a few candles remained lit, most of them situated around Richard's game of solitaire.

His coat and cravat were nowhere to be seen, and his sleeves were bunched at his elbows. It was a good thing his valet, Bradford, had stayed behind in London. The man was notoriously fussy about the state of Richard's clothing.

She joined him on the sofa, tucking her bare feet up under the hem of her night rail and pulling a pillow into her lap. "I was thinking of something much more immediate than your late-night trysts. There is something odd about Mr. Benedict, and I want to know what it is."

Their guest had been much more responsive to her at dinner, but she still sensed a sort of reluctance about him. More important, she still could not recall a single mention of the man in all her correspondence and conversations with her brother. If she knew the names of even his friends' horses, shouldn't she recall hearing mention of a James Benedict?

"My, how very flattering you are. Truly, the only thing odd about Benedict is that he didn't seem to mind my sisters converging on him like a flock of seagulls on a crust of bread. Could it be that your interest in Benedict has nothing to do with how odd he may seem, and everything to do with the lovey-dovey expression in your eyes when you watched him at dinner?"

Evie gasped, hesitating only half a second before lobbing the pillow in her lap at her brother's head. "I did no such thing! Don't be absurd."

"I'm not being absurd in the least, Bit. A blind man couldn't have missed the interest in your eyes."

Heat flamed up Evie's cheeks. Surely she had not been so obvious. If anyone else had seen what Richard claimed to have seen . . . "Any interest I have in Benedict is entirely platonic, I assure you. If that. I mean, I am merely curious about his—and your—sudden appearance."

This was not going well at all. He nodded with patent disbelief, and she glared at him in return. "Now, stop trying to fluster me. Be serious, and tell me more about your friend and why he accompanied you here."

Richard sighed and flopped back onto the cushions. "Nothing much to tell. An old acquaintance from school."

"So you've said. But that doesn't tell me anything about him. You said he was from Bath, but I thought you didn't have any friends from there."

"He is from Bath, but as he stated, he rarely, if ever, returns there. Besides, Benedict is not the type to attend the parties I so enjoy frequenting."

Exactly. "Yes, I gathered that. I'm curious if you have anything in common. He is nothing like your normal group of friends."

"What is life without variety?" he asked with a flip of his hand.

She nearly growled at him. "Stop being so blasted evasive."

"As soon as you stop being so blasted nosy. You are seeing mysteries where none exist. Now, enough about Benedict. What do you care about it, anyway? You have a huge opportunity before you, and you are squandering it. Why haven't you spoken with Mama yet?"

He was right, of course. She hugged her knees to her

chest and sighed. "After calling our guest a nitwit at dinner?" She cringed just thinking about it. "I need at least another day to try to redeem myself."

"Or you might be stalling without even realizing it. Could it be because you may be giving the idea of love another chance?" He waggled his eyebrows suggestively.

"Don't say that," she replied, much more vehemently than she'd intended. He reared back in surprise, and she closed her eyes and took a breath. "Forgive me. But I'll not marry. It's just not for me." Although her brother might not have known it, she had decided many years ago never to risk her heart in a love match. She would never recover if she cared for a man, only to have him turn his back on her again. Men were fickle beasts—she knew that all too well.

She offered him a conciliatory smile. "It's late, I'm tired, and I think it is past my bedtime." She stood and stretched. "Are you coming up?"

He shook his head. "I'm still on city hours. Sleep well, Bit, and I'll see you in the morning."

She gave him a quick hug before heading for the stairs. She was halfway up when she realized someone else was coming down. She glanced up and stilled.

Benedict.

He slowed, offering a tentative smile. He somehow looked more elegant in his simple white shirt and buff breeches than he had in his evening wear earlier. She forced herself to focus on his dark eyes and not the triangle of skin exposed by his open collar.

"Good evening, Evie." In the quiet of the darkened stairway, his low voice slid over her like rough silk.

He descended the last few steps separating them until he was one step below her, bringing him nearly to eye level. Several tendrils of his damp hair had fallen across his forehead, and she had the sudden, ridiculous urge to brush them away with the tips of her fingers. Would his hair feel as silky as it looked?

"Hello, Mr. . . . Hello, Benedict." She spoke softly, not wanting to break the stillness of the moment. The spicy scent of sandalwood teased her senses, and she drew a long, slow breath through her nose. Swallowing, she asked, "Are you looking for something?"

He nodded, not breaking eye contact. "I thought Richard might still be awake. Neither one of us is accustomed to country hours yet. I'm surprised you are still up." It was the first time he had truly held her gaze, and she relished the dark, almost secretive quality of his eyes.

Though he said nothing improper, she tugged her wrapper more securely in place. There was something wicked about standing alone with a man without the benefit of unmentionables. Heat stole up her neck at the thought. Thank goodness for the dim lighting—it would not do for him to have any idea where her thoughts had meandered.

"I'm on my way up now. It's been quite an exciting day, after all."

"Yes, quite. I won't keep you then, my lady. It was . . . an experience meeting you." Though he didn't quite smile, his dimple belied his amusement.

He didn't move right away, but when she didn't say anything, he started to turn. Almost without thought, she touched a hand to his sleeve. He froze, his gaze flying up to meet hers. Heavens, what was it about him that made her heart race? Swallowing, she removed her hand. "Please, let me just say again how sorry I am for calling you a nitwit. I still can't believe I did that."

A slow smile lit his face, and he leaned forward conspiratorially. "A lady is entitled to her opinion."

Evie blinked. Their conversation in the garden came

rushing back to her, and she bit back a smile. "I guess I rather made your point, didn't I?" A wisp of delight intertwined with the embarrassment ticking her belly. He remembered her words. It was rather nice to know their conversation had resonated with him.

"The thought occurred to me. Still, no harm done. Please, don't think of it again."

"Are you certain?"

"A man can stand to be put in his place from time to time. I don't think I have nearly enough people in my life who feel comfortable insulting me."

"Just imagine the kind of insults I could give you after we've known each other more than a day."

Instead of offering the smile she expected, Benedict's expression seemed to tighten, and he took a step back. "Indeed. Well, please don't let me keep you any longer. I bid you good night, my lady."

Just like that, he turned and headed down the stairs, leaving nothing but the faint scent of his cologne and the unmistakable impression of a man escaping.

Was it something she had said? She straightened her spine and started up the stairs. Tomorrow, she was going to learn more about the enigmatic Mr. Benedict. She was going to get some answers if it killed her.

He was an idiot. And she smelled like lemons.

He hadn't expected it, but really it complemented her perfectly. None of those fussy, floral scents would have been right for her. Thank God she broke the spell of the moment by mentioning how long they had known each other. If she only knew.

He found Richard in the billiards room, staring at a stack of cards on the small sofa table. He looked up warily, but he grinned when he saw Benedict. "I thought you might be Evie, returned to pester me some more."

He motioned to the chair across from him, and Benedict took a seat. "I was right about her wanting to pin me down."

Benedict really didn't like the sound of that. "Oh?"

"Yes, and she had a few questions about you, my friend."

She wouldn't be his Evie if she didn't. "It's to be expected, I suppose."

"Yes, well, I thought perhaps you would like to get out of the house tomorrow—away from the constant scrutiny of my sisters. What do you think?"

Benedict suppressed the no that instantly came to his lips. No, he didn't want to get away from the house—or its occupants. Of course, he could never say as much to Richard. The man would *not* appreciate the thought that Benedict might be leading his sister on. It was for the best, anyhow. The less time he spent with Evie, the less likely she would discover he was Hastings; ergo less of a chance of causing her pain—or being subject to her wrath. "That sounds like a fine idea. Where shall we go?"

Richard grinned and picked up the cards, expertly shuffling them without ever looking down. "The place I have in mind the girls would never dream of accompanying us. It's perfect!"

Chapter Eight

Very well, so you have me there. I admit it. I would never betray you. Not to your grandmother, nor to anyone else, though you are a cur to call my bluff. And I confess it is not because you hold the trump card. It's because I rather like being able to say whatever I please to at least one person in this world. There really are no secrets between us, are there?

—From Evie to Hastings

Fishing.

Curled on the plush window seat near midnight the following day, Evie shook her head as she looked past the fogged glass at the darkness beyond. Whoever wanted to go fishing in the dreary weather they had endured today? As if on cue, a gust of wind rattled the window, spattering a few errant drops of rain against the glass.

Richard had whisked Benedict away shortly after breakfast, and they had not returned until dark. Drenched and exhausted, both men had chosen to have a tray in their rooms for dinner, and she was rather inexplicably out of sorts about the whole thing.

Whether it was his sudden appearance, the fact that he was something of a mystery to her, or just that when he looked at her, she felt something . . . different, she simply couldn't deny that she wanted to see him again. She had been anxiously looking forward to speaking with Benedict again ever since it had occurred to her that, thanks to the impending hunt her father was planning, she had the perfect opportunity to spend some time with him. The stables were her domain; she was exactly the right person to help Benedict pick out an appropriate mount for the hunt, and she had planned to take full advantage of her position.

It was perfect.

And now, even though she would have to wait until morning to instigate her plan, she was entirely too restless to get any sleep just yet. She sighed and got to her feet. Perhaps a chapter or two of reading would help her to relax. Shrugging into her dressing gown, she lifted the candleholder from the table next to the door and headed downstairs to the library.

The lamps were turned back and the house was nearly silent, much as it had been the previous evening when she had run into Benedict. As she entered the library, the musty smell of books seemed stronger in the darkness. She didn't bother with lighting a lamp; she knew exactly the bookshelf that she wanted.

The circle of light cast by her candle illuminated only a small fraction of the vast array of books housed on the many shelves before her. Shivering a bit—the room had not seen a fire in a while—she rubbed her arm with her free hand as she inspected her choices. Her father's old adventure novels, including *Robinson Crusoe* and *Gulliver's Travels*, were peppered among the more modern novels that she preferred. After searching for a few moments, she settled on her favorite standby—*Sense and Sensibility*.

Clasping the worn copy of the book to her chest with one hand, she lifted her candle with the other and slipped out of the library. She retraced her steps to the second floor and turned toward the west wing where her bedchamber was located.

Thump!

Letting out a little squeal at the unexpected sound, she whirled around instinctively toward the direction it had come from. The swift movement caused her candle to flicker and die, and she was immediately plunged into darkness.

For a moment, she stood stock-still, trying to listen past the thud of her own heartbeat as her eyes adjusted. *Calm down,* she chided herself. *It's probably nothing.* Still, her heart hammered as she strained to either hear or see anything.

Thump!

She started, squinting in the direction of the east wing. What *was* that? The family's chambers were located in the west wing, and the servant's quarters were upstairs. Benedict alone was currently housed in that wing.

What could he be up to? A niggling thought in the back of Evie's mind admonished her that it was none of her business what Benedict did in the privacy of his bedchamber, but it was not loud enough to make her turn away and return to her own room.

Instead, she cautiously tiptoed toward the Blue Room, only two doors down the corridor from the stairway. She struggled to make out shapes in the gloomy corridor, but mainly she was slinking along on memory.

"Oofff!"

She hopped up and down, silently cursing the blasted table that had reached out and bit her toe. Had that table always been there? Shaking off the pain, she moved on, proceeding more slowly and with exaggerated caution this time.

Thump!

The noise was definitely coming from Benedict's bedchamber. Movement caught her eye—swiftly moving shadows in the faint, flickering light spilling from beneath the door.

She paused to consider her options. She could, rather, she *should*, turn herself around and return to her bedchamber at once. She should climb into her bed and settle in with *Sense and Sensibility* for a few calming chapters before going to sleep. Tomorrow, when she saw Benedict, she should inquire if he had slept well and smile disinterestedly when he responded yes.

It was really rather unfortunate that Evie never seemed to do what she *should* do.

Squaring her shoulders, she took a few more steps, stopping several feet away from the door. At this distance, she could hear other faint noises coming from within. She leaned forward and tried to make out what was going on. It was no use—the sounds were even more mystifying now that she was closer.

Evie chewed her lip for a moment, suddenly feeling as though she were spying on the man. All right, so perhaps she *was* spying on the man, but he was the one who had drawn her attention in the first place. Yes, it was all *his* fault she was standing outside of his room in the middle of the night.

Really, she should leave. He was given the chamber to use as he pleased, with a door to close as he pleased.

But she couldn't just walk away now—her curiosity was absolutely *killing* her. Very well, she would have a quick listen at the door to make sure he wasn't injured or something; then she would be on her way. She nodded; it was a reasonable plan. Bending down, she placed the book and the useless candleholder on the floor before straightening and running her damp palms over the soft fabric of her night rail. She took a deep breath, sidled up to the door, and slowly placed her ear to the cool wood. Doing her best to ignore the thundering of her own blood in her ears, she tried to concentrate on discerning the sounds coming from within.

She could just make out odd rustling noises—and there was another thump. She wrinkled her brow. Why wasn't he sleeping? Never mind that *she* was not only awake but prowling the corridors and working on her burgeoning career in espionage.

As she listened, she looked down at her bare feet, which were illuminated by the light filtering from beneath the door. Shadows moved smoothly in the wavering light, sliding back and forth. There seemed to be a certain rhythm to motion. Was he dancing? No, the movement seemed too . . . aggressive for that.

She watched for several moments before breathing a quiet sigh. It was no use. Whatever he was up to, she wasn't going to figure it out through a two-inch-thick slab of solid wood or by attempting to interpret the vague motions of shadows. Perhaps she could figure out a way to question him.

Thoroughly frustrated, Evie turned and started to retrace her steps, then jerked to a halt. At the same time, the door rattled in its casing, the sound like a gunshot to her suddenly racing mind. Her gown had caught on the doorknob!

There was a sudden cessation of noise from the room, followed by the swift sound of footsteps toward the door. Her heart dropped to the floor. Good heavens, he was going to catch her spying on him!

Panicking, Evie wrenched the skirts of her nightgown free, hiked them knee high, and sprinted for the west wing. As she reached the staircase, she skidded around the railing, dropped to the floor, and huddled behind the massive carved banister at the very moment the door swung open.

Her heart pounding hard against her ribs, she watched as Benedict poked his head out past the frame and cautiously looked from left to right. Dim candlelight spilled into the corridor from the room behind him. She hoped desperately that she was out of his range of vision and said a small prayer of thanks for the dark night and extinguished lamps.

She fought to control her breathing, afraid any noise would alert him to her presence. Evie would never recover from the mortification if he caught her snooping outside his door. Slowly he stepped into the corridor.

As he emerged, she sucked in a startled breath, her eyes widening in shock. Good heavens, he was practically naked! He wore nothing but a loose-fitting pair of what looked to be linen pants. His bare torso glistened in the flickering light—he must have been sweating from his exertions.

Her pulse fluttered wildly as she watched him, unobserved, from her hiding place as he investigated the corridor outside his bedchamber. His chest looked as though it had been carved from marble, smooth and taut with clearly defined muscles. What would it feel like to trace a finger down the valley running the length of his belly? Fighting the sudden urge to fan her cheeks, she squeezed her eyes shut for a moment, trying in vain to maintain even an ounce of decorum—not easy to do after spying on a houseguest in the dead of night.

Seemingly of its own volition, her right eye cracked open to get another look. Evie slammed it shut again, this time laying her hand firmly across her eyes. She needed to think of something else, anything to distract her.

Kittens!

Kittens were adorable, innocent creatures. They didn't have broad, muscled chests. Their bellies weren't flat and lean, toned to perfection. . . .

Her eyes popped open again. Clearly, distraction was not working. She snuck another peek in his direction, feeling the tickle of butterflies and an unfamiliar sensation in her stomach. Good heavens, no wonder unmarried women were not permitted to look upon the male form. His lean figure must surely be as fine as any of the Greek statues of the gods she had glimpsed.

His bare feet were silent as he prowled outside the room and he squinted into the darkness, obviously trying to discern the perpetrator in the gloom. Finally, he shrugged and made to return to his room.

Evie went limp with relief. If he had—

She came up short, biting her lip when he stopped in his tracks and looked to the floor outside the room. She held her breath, her pulse roaring back to life. What did he see? Bending down, he picked up a small object, turning the item in his hands.

The blood drained from Evie's face as she realized what he had found.

Oh God.

She might never leave her bedchamber again.

Chapter Nine

There are always secrets, whether we intend there to be or not. But, if I am honest, I don't believe anyone knows quite as much about me as you do. How, I wonder, did that come to be the case?
— From Hastings to Evie

Sitting on the edge of his bed near the candle on the nightstand, Benedict flipped absently through the pages of the novel that had been abandoned outside his door. A slightly boyish grin tugged at the corners of his lips as he considered the object in his hands.

Evie. It must have been her. He simply could not imagine one of the young sisters prowling the house in the middle of the night, romantic novel in hand. Even if one of them had ventured outside his door, she would have surely tittered or giggled, or in some other way given herself away as Beatrice had when he arrived.

No, the perpetrator had been none other than the ever-curious Evie. She must have been going to or from the library. Was she just being nosy, or had she heard him? The smile quickly disappeared as he considered his carelessness.

Damn. He had best be on his guard if he was to keep his cover. He took for granted that, since he had been placed in a room in his own wing, he could practice without worrying about being discovered. He had to be more cautious—carelessness like tonight could get him killed in the real world.

He looked to the silver rapier he had tossed on the bed in haste upon hearing the noise outside his room. He had been concentrating deeply on the swift and graceful moves of fencing, charging forward and leaping back, jabbing and parrying an invisible foe. The practice was more than just keeping his body agile and his skills fresh; it was to clear his mind and spirit of all the clutter. He had always particularly enjoyed the meditative aspect of practicing fencing alone.

With the metal shaft glinting in the candlelight, he was very glad now he had the forethought to abandon the weapon before investigating the cause of the noise in the corridor. He could only imagine the trouble that would have arisen had he burst from his bedchamber brandishing a sword. Evie likely would have screamed and brought the whole household down on them.

Worse than that, it might have given her a clue as to his true identity. She knew very well Hastings was an avid fencer, his favorite of all the sports at which he was proficient.

His thoughts focused again on his golden-haired enchantress, and the smile returned unbidden. She had been so close, standing right outside his room in the middle of the night. What would he have done if she had still been there when he opened the door? He pictured her as she had looked on the stairs in her night rail the night before, her hair loosely braided and draped over her shoulder. Had she even worn anything beneath the gown? His mouth went dry at the thought.

It was a very good thing she had retreated before he pulled open the door.

Shaking his head, he returned his attention to the book in his hands. The gold-leaf lettering winked in the flickering light. *Sense and Sensibility.* Should he give it back to her? No. He rather wanted to see what she would do, first.

He rose and went to the water basin resting on the bureau by the bed. He splashed the tepid water across his face and chest and quickly toweled off. Looking up, he caught a glimpse of his own expression in the mirror above the bureau. He smiled at himself with real amusement.

Suddenly, he was quite looking forward to the morning.

After what seemed like five minutes of sleep, Evie awoke to the sound of her maid bustling into her room and swishing open the curtains to a ridiculously bright and sunny day. All at once, the memory of last night assailed her. Evie groaned and yanked the covers over her eyes.

"Ugh, Morgan, it is brighter than a dozen suns outside. Do please close the drapes."

There was a moment of silence on the other side of the counterpane. Hesitantly, Morgan said, "But my lady, it is an exceedingly fine day today. It's exactly the sort of weather you love. And Mrs. Hargrove has prepared quite a feast for breakfast this morning on account of the lovely day."

Lovely day, her foot. How on earth would she face Benedict this morning? Beneath the counterpane, she wrinkled her nose and blew out a breath. There was no help for it. She would have to say something to him. Besides the fact she couldn't stay beneath the covers forever, no matter how much she might wish to do so, it simply wasn't in her nature to let something like this fester.

With a great, gusty sigh, Evie threw off the covers. "Please tell me there is a large, steaming cup of chocolate waiting for me." If she had to eat crow, at least she could wash it down with chocolate.

Morgan gave her an odd look. "Of course, my lady. Right here on the bed table, as always."

As they bustled through their morning routine, Evie sipped her chocolate and considered what she would say. The worst-case scenario would be for him to ask at the breakfast table who left a book outside his room. One look at the title and the whole family would know she was the culprit. Her hopes of staying home for the Season would be squashed before they ever even had a chance. No, she had to talk to him—soon, before he could bring it up to her family.

Before she lost her nerve.

Twenty minutes later, Evie was holed up in the bed-chamber adjacent to Benedict's, her ear to the door. As soon as he stepped into the corridor, she wanted to be ready to pounce. Honestly, this was *not* how she envisioned beginning her day. With her stomach in knots and her heart beating like a battle drum, she wanted to get this over with—the sooner the better.

It would really help if she had any idea what, exactly, she would say to the man. *Forgive me, sir, but it appears that I dropped my reading material outside your door while spying on you last night. Do be a dear and return it.* Or better yet, *I'll give my entire stash of pin money for you not to tell my parents.* Bribery worked on most men, didn't it? Bribery always worked on Richard, but it was usually in the form of food. Perhaps if the life savings didn't tempt Benedict, a chocolate scone would.

At last, the footsteps from Benedict's chamber moved toward the door, followed by the telltale click of the latch sliding open. She counted to three, took a deep breath, and eased open the door. Stepping lightly, she padded into the corridor.

"Why, good morning, Benedict." Evie cringed as his dark head swiveled in surprise. Even to her own ears, her voice sounded overloud and entirely too forced.

He turned to face her fully, and it was all she could do not to blush. Even though he was fully and properly dressed and standing in the early-morning sunlight, all she could think about was his sweat-soaked bare chest bathed in the glow of flickering candlelight from the night before. For heaven's sake, how could she ever look him in the eye again? She forced a smile while focusing on his left ear.

"Er, good morning to you, Evie. I didn't see you there."

She smiled sweetly. "Oh? I do hope I didn't startle you. I was just—" *lying in wait for you for the better part of the last ten minutes*— "passing by."

"Ah."

She couldn't seem to think of what to say next. She had rather hoped that when she was face-to-face with him, the right words would come. Alas, she was completely without inspiration. Awkwardness settled uncomfortably between them; yet she still stood there like a proper dolt. After a moment, Benedict took a step toward the stairway. "I was just heading to breakfast, if you would like to accompany me."

A friendly stroll together might be just the thing to get her powers of speech working again. "Yes, thank you." See? She was doing better already. As they started forward, she focused on the intricate pattern of the carpet runner. Without the force of his gaze focused on her, her heartbeat settled somewhat.

"Actually, I was hoping to speak with you." There now, a whole sentence. Perhaps she was only a partial dolt.

"Indeed?" A tendril of warmth infused his voice as he spoke the single word, and she relaxed further. "Well then, you have my entire attention."

"It's about last night—"

Before she could finish her sentence, Richard stepped from his chamber down the hall. He saw them immediately and grinned. "Good morning," he called, shutting the door behind him and heading their way.

Blast it all, now she would lose the opportunity to talk to Benedict before breakfast. Something akin to panic set in. She couldn't allow him to ruin her plans, to speak of the book, and casually end her dreams. Acting on impulse, she pretended to stumble, dropping down on one knee.

As she had hoped, Benedict rushed to assist her, bending down and offering his arm. "Are you all right?"

He effectively blocked Richard's view of her, but she knew her brother was fast approaching. She grabbed hold of Benedict's forearm and squeezed, looking up to him beseechingly. "Please don't say anything to my family about what you found last night. I'll explain later, I promise."

His eyebrows rose halfway up his forehead. She could only imagine what he must be thinking. He opened his mouth to respond but closed it before saying anything. Richard was almost to them now, his boots landing heavily on the carpet runner behind Benedict, and she poured everything in her heart into her eyes. "Please," she whispered.

Benedict looked down into her eyes, his chocolate gaze unreadable. At the last second, he gave a small terse nod. "I'll be waiting," he said, then extended his free hand and wrapped it around her elbow.

Immense relief wilted her body, and she let him tug her to her feet. "Thank you, sir. I can be so clumsy sometimes."

"Good God, Evie, isn't it a bit early for swooning?" Her brother's teasing manner gave no indication he had noticed the exchange.

"Come now, Richard," Benedict countered. "It's never

too early for a woman to swoon at my feet. I generally like to have at least two such instances before noon."

Oh, bless the man. He would hold his tongue—for now at least. She rolled her eyes as she was expected to and thought fast to come up with a normal reply. "How easily you mistake stumbling for swooning. I shudder to think of all the young women of your acquaintance whose clumsiness was mistaken for regard. Worse yet if you are the one to trip them."

Richard laughed, just as she had intended, and they headed down to the breakfast room, chatting and teasing as they went. Her relief of being granted a reprieve by Benedict quickly gave way to apprehension as Evie considered what she would say to the man when they were alone. She chewed the inside of her lip, thinking of the incident. Really, she wasn't the only one who had some explaining to do. What was it he had been doing in his bedchamber last night? She would never have been drawn to spy on him if it hadn't been for the mysterious movements and thumping noises.

She watched him as he laughingly responded to something Richard said, that adorable dimple showing up again. Perhaps if she could come up with a proper excuse for the book outside his door, they could have a little time to chat. Purely for investigational reasons, of course. It would have nothing at all to do with his wide, chiseled chest or his disappearing dimple . . . or the lingering tingle where he had grasped her elbow to help her up.

"Benedict," she said, inspiration suddenly striking her.

The two men turned and looked askance at her. "It occurred to me that you will need a proper mount for the hunt this week. If you like, I can help you find just the right horse for your skill level."

"Thank you, Evie. I would appreciate your assistance very much. When are you free?"

"I have nothing planned for the whole morning. Would you like to head to the stable block after breakfast?"

Richard looked back and forth between them, his eyes narrowing slightly. "There's no need for you to worry about finding Benedict a horse, Evie. I'd be more than happy to take care of it."

Drat—Richard would ruin everything. "Oh really? And pray, when was the last time you catalogued the strengths and weaknesses of our current stock?"

She had him there, and he knew it. After a second pause, he nodded. "Yes, I suppose you're right. Well, when should we all meet, then? Half eleven, perhaps?"

Blast it all, her brother was not going to make this easy. Evie opened her mouth to tell him in no uncertain terms that he was not needed, but Benedict cut in. "Half eleven sounds perfect."

It was an effort not to growl in frustration. As they entered the sunny breakfast room, Richard nodded his agreement before heading directly for the sideboard, which was overflowing with eggs, toast and jam, ham, two kinds of scones, and baked apples and cinnamon. Though it smelled delicious, Evie had no appetite whatsoever.

She turned to Benedict and whispered, "Why did you agree to have him join us? I need to speak with you *privately*."

"And you shall—when we meet a half hour earlier."

She reared back in surprise. Well, he could be devious when he put his mind to it, couldn't he? It wasn't every day someone managed to pull the wool over Richard's eyes. She pressed her lips together to hold in a giggle. "Well. All right, then."

He didn't smile, but a hint of his dimple creased his smooth-shaven cheek. "Until then, my lady."

Chapter Ten

Happy birthday, Evie. I wish for you a day of riding, a night of stargazing, and all the chocolate scones you can eat. Perhaps someday I may offer my felicitations in person, but for now, please accept the gift I have smuggled to you with Richard's help. I saw it and thought of you.

— From Hastings to Evie

At the appointed time, Benedict waited in the garden, soaking up the bright sunshine as he lounged on a small stone bench. Evie was right; it did smell rather wonderful, though he doubted he would have noticed it if she hadn't mentioned it before. Taking a deep breath, he leaned back on his hands and glanced toward the house again. She was late.

He could hardly wait to see what she would say to him. When she had looked up at him with those pleading, blue eyes, he knew there was no way he could deny her anything she asked at that moment.

Not that Benedict planned to announce the incident at breakfast, for heaven's sake. But he rather liked being in a position where she sought out his company.

At last Evie emerged from the house and made her way toward the garden. She looked like the embodiment of sunshine with her cheery yellow gown. He watched her as she descended the terrace steps and made her way toward him. She had a way of moving that managed to seem effortless and alluring at the same time—a sort of natural grace evident in the gentle sway of her hips and in the proud line of her shoulders.

When he could simply observe her like this, the tension in his shoulders eased a bit, and the stress of his life slid away like silk gliding over satin. Of course, he knew it wouldn't last. The moment they spoke again, the unease would return in force as he tempted fate by being near her.

And it would be worth it.

The pebbles beneath her feet crunched smartly as she approached, a slightly wary smile on her beautiful lips. He rose to greet her, schooling his features to a friendly welcome to put her at ease.

"I apologize for keeping you waiting. Beatrice wanted to chat with me, and I couldn't very well tell her why I was in such a hurry."

Beatrice again. Benedict could only venture to guess what the girl wanted to talk about. He cocked his head to the side and murmured, "Oh? Anything interesting?"

Evie's cheeks bloomed with the most lovely shade of pink. "Merely sisterly conversation. I'm sure it would be of no interest to you."

The blush was at once beguiling and bedeviling. *What* had the sisters talked about that would bring about such a response? He'd bet his entire life savings that it had something to do with him, but as to what exactly, he hadn't a clue. If Beatrice had divulged his secret, he would have known it the moment he saw Evie's face.

Hiding his ravenous curiosity behind a polite smile, Benedict dipped his head. "If you say so, my lady. Shall we head to the stable block?"

He was closer than was strictly proper, and she had to tilt her head back to meet his eyes. The sun bathed her face, setting her eyes to sparkling more brilliantly than any precious gemstone could ever hope to. The long, slender column of her throat was exposed to his scrutiny, and for the briefest moment, he wondered what she would do if he pressed his lips to her pulse.

Her eyes clouded, and she gave her head a tiny shake. "In a moment. Let's take a turn about the garden. I'd like to explain what happened last night."

Ah, yes, the book. It was tucked in his jacket, pressing against his ribs; yet he had managed to completely forget about its existence. She was very, very good at making him forget himself. He pulled the leather-bound volume out and handed it to her. "I believe this belongs to you."

She blushed crimson red—something he hadn't expected of her—but continued to meet his eyes, nonetheless. Her expression was an odd mixture of embarrassment and relief. It was more than a little endearing.

She took the book from him and sighed, running a thumb over the spine. "I am sorry, Benedict. I heard noises last night on the way back from the library and went to investigate. I'm afraid that curiosity always gets this cat." She smiled sheepishly up at him.

It was all he could do not to reach out and run a fingertip across her pink cheek. He squeezed his hands into fists at his side, firmly repressing the urge. Instead, he started forward at a slow, leisurely pace, taking a moment to gather his wits. "I figured as much. I didn't mean to disturb you. It shan't happen again."

"You are free to do as you like. Whatever it was you were doing."

He nodded. "How kind of you to say."

"And do feel free to use any one of the halls or ballroom for your . . . activities. If you need more room."

He suppressed a smile. Now she was digging. "Why, thank you. I appreciate the offer."

She plucked a leaf from a perfectly manicured shrub

as they passed by and twirled it between her thumb and forefinger. "We also have various pieces of equipment."

He raised an eyebrow. "What sort of equipment?"

Her chin lifted slightly, and she regarded him with a hint of frustration. After a few seconds, she said, "If you would tell me what you need, I can tell you if we have it."

"I have everything I need."

She tossed the leaf to the ground and turned to him. "For heaven's sake, are you truly not going to tell me what the devil you were doing?" She was so impatient, his Evie. She looked to him accusingly. "Are you taking a page from Richard's book and merely torturing me?"

"Torture you? I don't know what you are talking about. Why is Richard torturing you?"

She wagged a finger in his direction. "Don't think you can distract me from the topic at hand. I know Richard said the two of you are here because of a woman, but I am becoming more and more convinced there is more to it than that. The two of you are up to something, I swear. Showing up unannounced, going off on mysterious"— she fluttered her hands in the air—"fishing trips in the rain, doing God knows what in your room last night—it is all very strange."

Benedict blinked in surprise. Well, she really was getting suspicious. He would do anything in his power to keep from lying to her any more than he already had. Perhaps it was time to go on the offensive. After all, he had quite the advantage over her. He could easily use his knowledge of her against her.

"I hadn't realized you'd feel so neglected, Evie. If you wanted to join us, you had only to say the word." Her eyes narrowed suspiciously, and he rushed on. "Let me make it up to you. I am going to need to get to know my mount before the hunt. Would you care to show me around the estate? It is a fine day for a ride."

The corners of her full lips curved upward. "If you think you can get into my good graces with a request like that—"

"You're right; never mind. I'll have Richard accompany me."

Aha—he'd hit her weakness, just as he had intended. She wrinkled her nose and said, "Good heavens, don't do that. You're liable to break your neck if you take any advice from him. No, I'll come with you. It will give me the opportunity to observe your chemistry with the mount before you take to the hunting grounds."

"As you wish, my lady." He worked to keep the satisfied smile off his face. Lord but she was easy to manipulate. "Come—let's go take a look at your horses."

Having reached a truce of sorts, they made their way down the path and through the yawning doors to the stables. Stepping into the shadowed interior, he was momentarily blinded by the contrast to the bright sunshine outside. Evie led them straight toward the stalls in the back.

As she slowed, he prudently pulled his eyes from her backside and pointed to the nearest stall, which contained a sleek, speckled gray mare that looked to be about sixteen hands. "She's a beautiful horse. Is she a good jumper?"

Evie chuckled before responding. "The very best. Unfortunately for you, Epona is mine."

So this was the fabled Epona. Many a letter had been devoted to the horse after Evie was given the foal for her fifteenth birthday. "Epona? As in 'goddess of horses'? Not very original," he scoffed good-naturedly. He had teased her about the moniker years ago when she had proudly written to him of her new horse and the grand name she had bestowed upon her.

She placed her hands on her hips in mock affront and

said, "I was practically a child when I named her. I was only fifteen when Papa gave her to me, and at the time I was just learning about the Roman gods and goddesses. I thought it was very clever and sophisticated, even after I was mocked for it by my brother and a dear friend." She grimaced, a cloud passing over her face momentarily before she shrugged. "I can't very well change the poor thing's name now. Besides, I have kind of grown to like it."

Benedict blinked. *Dear friend?* She had to have been referring to him. So she did occasionally think of him in good terms. To mention him so casually years later with a near perfect stranger—well, he couldn't deny the feeling of pleasure that coursed through him.

"I'm only teasing, of course. And I can hardly talk, as my horse is named Samson."

She grinned, looking up into his eyes. "Truly? And you thought to tease me? For shame, Mr. Benedict. For shame."

"And what have you two got your heads together about?"

Richard strode down the center of the aisle, suspicion all over his face.

Evie grinned sweetly. "Wouldn't you just like to know?"

He cut curious eyes to Benedict. Benedict merely shrugged. If Evie wanted to play her game, he wasn't about to spoil it for her.

"Well then," Richard said, looking back and forth between them. "It appears I am going to have to stay close by if I'm to keep up with the two of you."

Benedict very nearly rolled his eyes. Seeing Richard in the role of protective older brother was altogether bizarre. In all their years as friends, he was always the scoundrel of the two. Besides, Benedict's only goal was to bask a bit in Evie's presence. He had no designs on her innocence.

Evie did not seem the least bit bothered. "Only if we're traveling on foot. If we should be on horseback, you would be sadly without hope of keeping up."

"You wicked girl," Richard exclaimed in mock outrage. "Honestly, I can't imagine that we were raised by the same parents."

"I know. To think I'm related to someone with such bad form on a horse."

Richard laughed aloud and wrapped a playful arm around her shoulder. "You wound me, Evie; really you do. My form is nothing if not glorious. It's my riding that's dreadful."

Shaking her head, Evie chuckled. "Oh, I wouldn't call it dreadful. Merely passable."

He shuddered dramatically, withdrawing his arm. "God save us from passable. I think I prefer dreadful over mediocrity."

"Yes, well, some of us would settle for decent," Benedict interjected. "Which is why I wanted Evie to join us."

Richard pulled a face. "And what is that supposed to mean?" The wicked grin on his face said he knew *exactly* what it was supposed to mean.

"It means you would happily place me with a tottering old workhorse so that you may have the once-in-a-lifetime possibility of actually appearing to be the superior horseman."

"What nonsense. Buttercup is a perfectly spry mare."

Evie's tinkling laugh washed over Benedict like warm summer rain. "You are right not to trust him, Benedict. Buttercup is nearly as old as I am. Now who is wicked, dear brother?"

"Have I ever claimed to be otherwise? Now then, let's see what horse *you* think will suit our Mr. Benedict."

As they went to work on the task at hand, Benedict reveled in the opportunity to observe Evie in her element, at home in the humid, musky air as she took them from stall to stall, summarizing the virtues of each horse. He could not stop himself from studying her, seeing the pride firsthand in her eyes, watching the way she touched and stroked and spoke to each of the horses they encountered.

When they paused in front of a large black gelding, she trailed the tips of her fingers down the side of the horse's muscular neck. It was a gentle, sweet caress, and for a moment Benedict imagined the touch on his own skin. At the very thought, a shiver skittered across the skin above his collar, and he raised a hand to rub the suddenly sensitive skin.

She patted the horse and turned to Benedict. "Brutus is a little older, but he is steady and strong. He was Richard's horse of choice until Comus came along, not that Richard ever did either of them justice."

"Hey," Richard exclaimed, crossing his arms. "I'll have you know Brutus and I rubbed along perfectly well. We simply never agreed on the proper way to jump."

"Yes," she said, raising a golden eyebrow. "Poor Brutus insisted on the correct way, whereas you never had your balance right."

"So he is a good jumper?" Benedict interrupted before the siblings could get started again.

Evie smiled briefly. "One of the best. You will have to have a firm hand with him, but I don't think he will be too much for you to handle. What do you think?"

"I trust your judgment completely. If you think Brutus will suit, then it must be so." He rubbed the horse's velvet muzzle, and the beast whickered happily in response. "And thank you for taking the time to rescue me from Richard's scheming."

Richard grinned. "I don't know what you're talking

about. But I do believe I have had quite enough of mucking about in the stables. Shall we head to the house?"

Benedict shook his head. "I think I'll take a moment to get to know Brutus, if you don't mind."

Richard nodded and looked to Evie. "Bit?"

"I've work to do. But I do plan to go riding before tea. Would you like to come along?"

"Thank you, but I think not. After the ride here and our excursion yesterday, I believe I'll stay around the house today."

"Very well, I'll see you at tea."

They waited in silence as Richard took his leave, both watching his retreating form. Though he didn't look at her, Benedict could feel her presence beside him; she was a perfectly respectable distance away, yet close enough for him to smell the faintest hint of lemons.

After a moment she turned to him, looking very satisfied with herself. "Will you be ready in an hour?"

Benedict raised an eyebrow, not catching on immediately. Realization dawned on him. The crafty girl. She had just ensured that Richard couldn't complain about their leaving him behind. An entire afternoon with only the two of them and whatever servant would serve as their chaperone?

"I wouldn't miss it.

Drat the man.

Evie blew a lock of hair from her forehead in frustration. He had neatly sidestepped telling her absolutely anything about what he was doing last night. She had almost been back in her bedchamber when she realized she had completely let him off the hook. She thrust her arm into the jacket of her riding habit and grumbled.

"Did you say something, my lady?" Her maid looked at her a bit strangely.

Evie tossed a smile over her shoulder. "It was nothing, Morgan. Thank you for your help. I can manage from here."

Morgan nodded and took her leave. When the door clicked closed, Evie began to pace. Benedict might have managed to throw her off earlier, but she would have ample opportunity to pry during their ride.

Actually, she'd have ample opportunity to do just about anything during their ride. She could stare at his gorgeous profile, listen to his silky, smooth voice, smell his delicious scent. There would be no worries of her mother scrutinizing her behavior or her siblings interrupting them. A nervous flutter tickled her belly. The man was an enigma. Some of the things he said were just ridiculous. And sometimes . . . sometimes they slipped into banter as easily as old friends.

Evie shook her head and sighed. It was odd that he could prompt such a strong reaction from her. How could she feel so attracted to him one minute, and annoyed with him the next?

A light tap came from the door. Evie took a last look in the mirror and smoothed a hand over the shimmery, deep blue velvet of her habit before calling out, "Enter."

Her mother opened the door and stepped into the room, the line of her shoulders tense beneath her emerald morning gown. "Hello, my dear. I hope I'm not interrupting you."

"Not at all. Come in."

Mama closed the door quietly behind her before turning her attention back to Evie. "Do you have a moment? I thought perhaps we could talk."

"Yes, of course." Evie glanced at the gilded clock on the mantel. She was supposed to meet Benedict in less than ten minutes, but he would have to wait. Unsure of her mother's mood, Evie took a seat in one of the conversation chairs and waited while her mother did the same.

They sat in an awkward silence for a moment. Evie sat straight in her chair, her hands folded in her lap like a proper lady. Something about her mother's manner made Evie nervous, though she couldn't say what. She did her best to exude confidence and serenity, but the fluttering butterflies in her stomach really weren't helping anything. Realizing the nearby thumping noise was her own foot tapping beneath her skirts, she curled her toes within her boot and willed herself to stay still.

"You seemed rather distracted at breakfast this morning. I could tell something was bothering you, though I had no idea what."

"It was nothing, Mama. I'm afraid I didn't sleep well last night."

"Then I realized you had been acting out of character for almost a week, even before all the excitement of Richard's arrival." She paused as if waiting for Evie to contradict her. Evie said nothing.

"After your father's meeting with the estate manager this morning, I mentioned my concern to him. He told me there was something that you'd been meaning to speak to me about."

"He did?" Evie squeaked, then cleared her throat. She wasn't prepared to do this just yet, but it would appear she hadn't a choice.

"Yes, he did. I questioned what it was about." She looked down to her hands for a brief moment, then leveled her gaze at Evie. "Evie, he told me about your proposal."

Blast, blast, blast! Evie reined in her immediate reaction, swallowing the protest that sat on her tongue. "And?"

"I cannot possibly allow it."

The air in Evie's lungs whooshed out as if she had

been kicked in the gut. It couldn't be—it could simply not be the end of her dream. No, she had convinced Papa and, by Jove, she could convince her mother. It was just too important. Evie clenched her jaw and shook her head. "Mama, you must hear me out first. It is what I want more than anything."

"It is what you *think* you want." Mama leaned forward earnestly in her chair, pressing her hands together in an almost prayerlike gesture. "Evie, you must know a decision such as this will affect the rest of your life. I know how much you dislike London, but it is only a means to an end. Find yourself a nice, country gentleman with his own stables and you can have the best of both worlds."

Evie refused to let her roiling emotions get the better of her. Sucking in a steadying breath, she met her mother's gaze straight on. "Our stables are hardly interchangeable with any other setup out there. And besides, I already have the best of both worlds, Mama. I have family and my work right here at the Hall."

"*Having* a family and *starting* a family of your own are two very different things. Why are you so resistant to the idea?" Frustration colored her voice like purple dye in a glass of water.

Mama wasn't the only one feeling frustrated. Evie's clasped hands squeezed together into a tight ball in her lap. "Why are you so resistant to the thought of me following my own dreams rather than the dreams laid out for me by others?"

Pressing her lips into a thin line, Mama drew a slow breath and exhaled. "Sweetheart, you simply have not fallen in love yet. Once you find the right gentleman, your dreams will change. You can't give up and hide out here. What if he shows up and you miss him because you couldn't be bothered to come out of your shell for a few months?"

"Then I suppose it was not meant to be." Evie scooted forward on her chair, looking her mother directly in the eye. "Really, Mama, if I haven't met him in five Seasons, then I doubt he will make some sort of heroic entry during my sixth."

"How can you just give up? Society will view you as something to be pitied. Is that what you want?"

At this, Evie stood. She had endured just about enough of society's dictates. "Hang society. What has it ever done for me? Given me endless rules and restrictions to live by, that's what. I keep my work hidden away to please society, I endure dreadful posturing and gossip at the hands of society, and I have given the last five springs for absolutely nothing."

Mama's face paled, and Evie felt a pang of regret. She hadn't meant to be so blunt. "I'm sorry, Mama. It's just that it has been building within me for some time now, and I feel rather passionate about it."

"Clearly." After a few beats of silence, her mother rose to her feet. She placed a cool hand on Evie's overheated cheek, and Evie could see the sincerity in her eyes. "It's not that I am not on your side; I *am*, which is why I don't think stepping away from the marriage mart is the right thing.

"Can't you at least think about it? Consider my wishes? I am nearly three-and-twenty, Mama. Old enough to know my mind. Old enough to know what I want for my life."

Mama's eyes searched Evie's face. Evie willed her to see all the things she was feeling; to understand that she didn't want to live her life at the mercy of a man, one who might love her one day and turn his back on her the next; to acknowledge that Evie's work, and the horses, were safe, predictable, and meaningful in their own way.

At last her mother pursed her lips and gave a short

nod. "I will consider it. For *this* Season only, mind. For reasons I don't understand, your father is in support of you, so I am willing to concede that there is much to think about."

Of course Mama didn't understand Papa's reasoning. She didn't know what Papa knew—*no one* did. He had promised to keep her secret all those years ago when she had very nearly disgraced herself, and he had never waivered. Mama had never known why Papa had taken Evie under his wing at the tender age of sixteen, allowing her to work at his side. But she had accepted it. And Evie could only hope she would accept this, too.

"Thank you, Mama. I hope you'll see that this is the right thing for me. This is what I want above all else."

Smoothing a hand down her skirts, Mama sighed. "You may want to save your thanks. While I am trying to understand your father's point of view, I will also do everything I can to make him see mine."

That did *not* make Evie feel good about her prospects. But what could she do?

Mama offered her a small smile with steel in her eyes before striding to the door. She paused before opening the door, and half turned to look Evie in the eye. "I think there is someone out there for you, Evie. I think you need only open your eyes and your heart, and you will find him."

Chapter Eleven

Who knew you could be so very thoughtful? Thank
you a dozen times over for my gift. Does my handwrit-
ing look very fine now? The swan feather was the per-
fect fit for my hand, and our butler had the tip precisely
cut. Now my words are not only wiser with age, but
more attractive with my newest implement.
— From Evie to Hastings

E vie was fifteen minutes late to meet Benedict, thanks
to the conversation with her mother. The unsettled
feeling in her stomach had yet to go away, and a long
ride sounded like the perfect thing to get her mind off
the whole thing.

The horses were already saddled and waiting, and
Benedict leaned against the tack wall, his head bowed.
He looked . . . sad, somehow, as if he were balancing the
world itself on his broad shoulders. Well, with the way
she was feeling, they would be a fine pair, indeed.

"I seem to be in the habit of making you wait," she
said quietly.

He looked up, his dark eyes as fathomless as a still
lake at midnight. "You are well worth the wait, my lady."

She smiled at his sweet words, a ribbon of pleasure
fluttering through her. "Nonetheless, do please accept
my apologies. Are you ready for our ride?"

"Lead the way."

Within minutes they were mounted on their respective horses and heading across the lane toward the rolling fields surrounding the estate. Several yards behind them, a groom followed discreetly. With things as they were with Mama, appearances must be maintained now more than ever.

They lapsed into a companionable silence, and she relaxed as she took in the comforting sounds of the horses' breathing, the creak of the leather saddles, and the clomping of hooves on damp earth. She struggled to push her conversation with Mama to the back of her mind. It was out of her hands now. Fretting about it during a perfectly lovely ride with a perfectly lovely companion was not going to make things any better.

Beside her, Benedict moved easily with his mount, as if they had been on dozens of rides together, and she had to remind herself not to stare. His back was straight but loose, absorbing Brutus's steps effortlessly. They were quite the handsome pair, the dark horse and his dark rider.

Offering Benedict a warm smile, she said, "You look quite comfortable in the saddle. Where did you learn to ride?"

Benedict shrugged. "I rather taught myself." The sadness she had glimpsed earlier still colored his tone. Why would that be? One would think he would be proud of the accomplishment.

Evie glanced to his face but couldn't read his expression. "That's actually very impressive. I may brag about my skills, but I would be worthless on a horse without all of my father's instruction. To learn without a mentor must have been very challenging."

"Yes. Sometimes we have little choice in the matter."

"Did your father dislike riding?"

"No, he merely disliked me."

Goodness. Evie cringed, not sure what to say to something like that. It was hard to imagine a father who would turn his back on such a fine man. Her own father was so important to her, it was impossible to imagine her life without his support. A fleeting memory of Papa galloping toward her on a moonlit night so many years ago flashed in her mind. He had been so gentle with her, despite his fury, and had helped her move on from her heartbreak. Not many men would have been so understanding of their wayward sixteen-year-old daughters.

She pressed her eyes closed briefly and put the memory from her mind. They needed a change of subject—better yet, a change of speed. Pointing toward a pond nestled in the rolling hills halfway between where they were and the distant tree line, she said, "That is where the hunt will begin. Would you like a closer look?"

At his nod, they set off toward the pond, picking up their pace to a brisk trot. The warmth of the sun and the lovely breeze were invigorating. Riding over the ridge of the hillside, she could just make out the church's bell tower several miles away in town. The grass covering the gently sloping ground was finally turning green again, and trees proudly displayed their tiny buds and newborn leaves. In a word, it was glorious.

Their trot was about half the speed Evie wanted to go. She glanced at the silent man beside her and grinned. It was time for a little fun. Without a word to Benedict, she sent Epona into a gallop. She gripped the reins tightly and leaned forward as the mare increased her speed. The wind whistled noisily by her ears and brought tears to her eyes as they tore across the countryside. Epona's legs pounded the ground, her nostrils flared, and her muscles bunched in rhythm with her graceful gallop.

Evie laughed with abandon at the extraordinary feeling of racing over the ground. It never diminished, no matter how often she rode. She had always imagined this was how a bird must feel, gliding over the earth's surface with the crisp, clean air rushing past.

When at last she reached the pond, she slowed her horse to a gentle trot, patting her neck approvingly. "Well done, love. Didn't that feel wonderful?"

In response, Epona, damp with sweat and breathing hard, shook her head and snorted. Given her head, the mare would likely run all day.

She craned around and searched out Benedict, who was a good distance back. He held Brutus at a brisk trot with the groom still several paces behind him. It was the perfect opportunity to watch him without worry of censure. He truly was a handsome man. His hat mostly covered his dark hair, but she could still see the ends curling above his ears. The slim cut of his clothes accentuated his broad shoulders and narrow hips.

As he approached, she was pleased to see a genuine grin on his face. His white teeth flashed in the sunshine as he pulled up on Brutus's reins and brought the gelding to a stop beside her. "You and your mare are something to behold. Did you enjoy your run?"

Evie smiled easily. Galloping away had been the right thing to do. For once his facial features were completely relaxed. She set their pace to a gentle walk and said, "Yes, very much. Didn't you want to give a go of it yourself?"

"No. I was more than content to watch you in your glory." Benedict patted his mount's neck soundly. "Besides, Brutus and I were getting to know each other. You, however, are clearly accustomed to Epona. When you're galloping like that, it is hard to tell where one leaves off and the other begins. I can see why you're so proud of her."

Pleasure at his praise lifted her heart. She brushed a hand over Epona's mane. "There is no better feeling in the world to me than riding at top speed. It does give my mother fits, however."

"I can't imagine why. Perched atop an insignificant little saddle on an enormous animal, flying across uneven ground at a gallop—I can't think of what might upset her about that." His musing made her grin.

"It is a mystery," she said, lifting a shoulder in mock confusion.

Shaking his head, Benedict chuckled. The sadness from before had completely lifted, and he seemed lighter, happier, sitting beside her as they bantered. Something about them at that moment just fit. She *should* feel reserved, even aloof with this near stranger, but instead she relaxed beside him, soaking in his smiles and reveling in his praise.

Evie gave the reins a little flick and set the pace to a gentle walk. Before them, the lake shimmered in the afternoon sun, reflecting the cheery blue skies. She sighed with pleasure and looked to Benedict. "Tell me something about yourself."

He lifted an eyebrow. "What would you like to know?"

"Anything, really. I feel as though you know much about me, while I know almost nothing about you. How about . . ." She pursed her lips and searched for a topic, careful to avoid any more mentions of his father. She should probably avoid his family altogether, just to be safe. "I know, tell me about how you and Richard met."

"Let's see," he said, rubbing a hand over his chin. "Richard and I met as first years at Eton. Like many of our classmates, we became friends when we were both compelled to participate in the school's production of *King Lear*."

Heavens, they did have a long friendship. Richard had written about the play in his second or third letter after arriving at Eton. "Oh, I remember when Richard was in that play. My parents were so excited to see him in his first performance. I was crushed when I was not allowed to attend, but I begged every last detail from them when they returned. I cannot believe you were in it as well! I must know what part you played."

"Alas, my dramatic skills were not on par with your dear brother's. I was one of the unfortunate boys stuffed into black clothes and forced to tend to the *real* actors. I believe Richard and I bonded over the excellent tea I brought for him, errand boy that I was."

She tried to picture him as an eager young boy and failed miserably. It was impossible to imagine him as anything less than the tall, powerfully built man beside her, especially after having seen for herself exactly how well-built he was. She realized he was watching her, waiting for her to respond. "Well, er, I suppose that makes sense. I have a very hard time picturing you on stage waxing poetic, skull in hand." She put her own arm out dramatically, as if holding the skull in question.

"Right, well, since it was *King Lear* and not *Hamlet*, I don't think we would have had to worry about such a scene."

Drat—she knew that. That would teach her to think of his half-naked form while trying to hold a normal conversation. She dropped her arm and grinned impishly at him. "I was just testing you. Of course I know the famous grave-digging scene is from *Hamlet*."

He snorted in disbelief. "I don't believe for a moment you were testing me. Shame on your governess for not teaching an impressionable, young English rose such as yourself proper English literature," he said with mock gravity. Solemnly, he made a tsking sound, shaking his head.

"This above all else: To thine own self be true!" she replied. "See, I knew exactly what I was doing. I merely wished to see if you were as clever as fellows are rumored to be."

"The lady doth protest too much, methinks."

"I will speak daggers to him, but use none," Evie grumbled in retort. She narrowed her eyes at him in mock anger but could not keep the smile from her lips. She was having fun, and judging by his wide grin, Benedict was as well.

As a matter of fact, she could not recall a single time she had shared such a lighthearted exchange with a gentleman. It was nice—more than nice—bantering with him as if they were close friends and not newly introduced acquaintances. With all the tension with her family about the Season, she needed that right about now.

She glanced behind them to where Jasper followed on Sirius, dutifully avoiding watching them. It was rather annoying having a chaperone tagging along, even if she was the one who had insisted on it. She turned back to Benedict and winked. "Shall we take a little stroll? I should very much like the opportunity to show you around a bit."

"What a lovely idea," Benedict replied, pulling back on the reins and dismounting. He patted Brutus's neck before coming to her side.

Evie looked back at the groom once more. "Jasper, please tend to the horses while Mr. Benedict and I do a bit of exploring."

He nodded and hopped to the ground, coming forward to take the leads. Evie turned to Benedict so he could help her dismount. "I am sorry to tell you that there is not a block or tree stump in sight. Let us hope I do not knock the both of us to the ground," she said as she placed her hand on Benedict's shoulder.

The feel of his taut shoulder, even through the cloth of his jacket and the leather of her glove, was enough to steal the breath right from her lungs. The image of him wearing nothing but those loose-fitting pants came rushing back to her once more. His broad chest, sculpted muscles, lean stomach . . . She sucked in her breath and only just managed to keep from closing her eyes. She knew *exactly* what lay beneath the few layers of clothes he now wore. If only her hand were touching his skin . . .

He abruptly looked up into her eyes. *Oh no!* She averted her gaze as her cheeks flooded with heat. Of course it was ridiculous, but she felt as transparent as a pane of glass. Heavens above, what would he think of her if he knew her thoughts?

A moment later, Benedict reached up and clasped his hands firmly around her waist. His fingers wrapped around her almost possessively, and her eyes flew back to his face, wide with surprise.

What was he doing? A few moments earlier she would have said he was little more than polite to her, but now his expression was so intense, so familiar somehow, she didn't know what to think. He held her gaze, unblinking and without a polite smile to deflect the intimacy of the moment, and Evie was completely unable to look away. He almost seemed to be challenging her to say something.

She couldn't have said anything if her life depended on it.

He lifted her then, smoothly and seemingly with ease as if she weighed no more than a child. She reveled in his touch, in the intoxicating sensation of being in his arms. Slowly, gently, he lowered her to the ground, like a feather floating on a breeze. When her feet touched solid earth, she was so close to him that her boots almost touched his. He smelled of sandalwood again, and she was reminded of the feel of his solid chest when they collided that first day. Without conscious thought, she leaned toward him, her eyes settling on his lips. His hands tightened possessively on her waist.

And then Epona shifted beside them.

It was as startling as if someone had discharged a gun. In a rush, Evie became aware of where they were and the groom who stood only a few feet away on the other side of Epona. Benedict blinked and straightened, dropping his hands and stepping back. Her skin felt cold without the heat of his hands, and she had to stop herself from protesting.

He glanced at the groom and took a few more steps away, casually surveying their surroundings. She took the opportunity to make a show of putting herself to rights, all the while concentrating on slowing her racing heart and calming the lingering roar of a thousand butterflies traipsing through her stomach.

So this is what getting swept off your feet feels like.

Good heavens, a simple touch and she had been completely lost. For the first time in her life, she could imagine how her parents felt when their eyes met all those years ago in a ballroom in Brussels, and the rest of the world had fallen away. Perhaps this was what her friends giggled and blushed about after a single dance with a gentleman they admired. She never could understand their silly reactions, seemingly brought about with little or no encouragement. Evie nearly laughed at herself— apparently all her fevered emotions required was a hand down from her horse! She had known the man for only two days, for heaven's sake.

Two days. How could she possibly be so drawn to someone within two days? She drew in a slow, steadying breath. Benedict wasn't for her. He was merely passing through her life, both of them on their way to fulfilling their dreams. And very soon, he would be gone.

When she looked up, her eyes immediately met

Benedict's, and once again awareness rippled through her. Yes, he would be gone soon, but for now it was just the two of them. She glanced to the left, where the path followed the manicured shore and ended at the gazebo. In the opposite direction, it snaked along the waterfront before disappearing into the trees.

The temptation to be alone was just too much. With nervous energy shimmering deep within her, Evie turned to the right. "Shall we?"

Benedict dipped his head, though his chocolate gaze never left hers. "As you wish, my lady."

Chapter Twelve

More attractive penmanship, yes. Wisdom, we shall see. Speaking of your birthday, did you get everything you hoped for? One wonders what the daughter of a marquis wishes for when she looks to the heavens at night.
—From Hastings to Evie

Damn it, he had known better. He was well aware that he should have kept his hands off her. He should have been more careful to hold her at a safe distance, but no, at the very first opportunity, he had seized the chance to touch her once more. Now, as they strolled along the sandy path, he had never felt more aware of another person in his entire life. The trees around them could have been props in a play for all the attention he paid them.

Somehow, when she touched him, all of his worries, his circumstances, even his thoughts, had slipped away, and, for a moment in time, he was just a man filling his senses with a woman he cared for. He honestly couldn't say what would have happened if the horse hadn't brought him back to his right mind.

Although, in truth, he wasn't really back to his right mind.

If he were, he wouldn't be aching to reach out and caress her hand with his. He wouldn't be wondering at the softness of her lips or imagining the feel of her pressed against him as he kissed her senseless. What would she do if he did? He gave his head a quick shake, trying to shake loose the ridiculous thought. For good measure, he laced his fingers behind his back. Beside him, Evie fiddled with the frog fastenings of her jacket. Was it nervousness, or was she feeling restless as well?

Ahead, the path disappeared into a copse of trees that lined one side of the lake. His body hummed with the knowledge they would soon be out of sight—alone for the first time, out of view of the house, the groom, even the horses. He should be running in the opposite direction, but he couldn't make himself leave her yet. Just a little more time with her, a few more minutes with the weight lifted from his shoulders as he allowed himself just to be a man, walking alone together with an old friend in the woods—was that so terrible?

Now that they were finally alone together, he couldn't quite think of what to say to her. With the heightened state of his nerves, though, he had to break the tension or he would go out of his mind. "The lake is nice." He cringed at the uninspired comment.

She bit her lip and nodded. "Indeed." The word sounded stilted. After a pause, she added, "It is well stocked, too."

"How nice." Good Lord, did he sound like a twitter-brained idiot to her as well or was it just him? The sudden charged awareness between them seemed to rob him of the ability to hold a normal conversation.

"Did you not fish here yesterday with Richard?"

He shook his head. "We went to the stream to fish for trout."

"Ah."

This was absurd. Five years of history between them, and this was the conversation they had? He searched for a more stimulating subject, and almost immediately he thought of her favorite topic. He cleared his throat and dove in. "Tell me how you came to be such an important part of your family's business."

The question didn't relax her as much as he had expected, but at least it got her talking. "Riding was always natural to me. My father said he had never seen anything like it, that it was a natural talent that would be a crime not to encourage. It started innocently enough, a few rides with him through the estate, the occasional race with Richard, even the odd chance to accompany Papa to inspect potential purchases. It built slowly enough that Mama was never unduly alarmed."

"So your father was your champion?"

She nodded, brushing aside a branch as they passed the first of the trees. The air was noticeably cooler in the shade. "Yes. I started working at Papa's side in earnest when I was sixteen. Over the years, I think he finally came to the realization that Richard would always be merely an average horseman. And I was, well, not."

"No, I don't imagine you were." He grinned, keeping his eyes on the trail as he stepped over a protruding root. She had never been average at anything a day in her life, as far as he knew. "So, really, you have Richard to thank for your father's support."

"No, I—" She paused midsentence, an odd look on her face. "Actually, I suppose you are right. Good heavens, I never thought of it that way before." She wrinkled her nose. "You mustn't tell him that. His ego is already big enough for the both of us."

He gave her a conspiratorial wink. "My lips are sealed, my lady."

She sighed and shook her head. "It seems you are doing a lot of that for me of late. I should thank you again for holding your peace about finding the book."

"Of course. I'm a gentleman, after all." She didn't

look as assured as he hoped. What troubling thoughts had crossed her mind to cause the small vee of tension between her brows? He allowed the distance between them to close slightly. "You've nothing to fear, Evie. As far as I know, the book could have been left behind by a specter."

She offered a halfhearted smile and paused before a fallen tree. "I know it seems a silly thing to you, but it is very important to me. I must be absolutely above reproach before my family leaves for London."

What an odd thing to say. "Come now, I'm sure you have nothing to worry about. And anyway, wouldn't they be more concerned about your behavior *after* you arrived?" he asked, offering a small, teasing smile.

She ran a gloved finger over the tree's bark, chipping away a small piece. "It is my intention not to go to London this Season."

"Not to go to London?" Was her family planning to bypass the Season this year? No, that couldn't be—he'd heard them mention the trip several times since their arrival. "I'm afraid I don't follow. What exactly is your intention, then?"

She didn't say anything at first but just looked up at him with those huge blue eyes. He had the distinct impression she was appraising him and his trustworthiness. He found himself standing a little straighter beneath her scrutiny. Finally, she took a deep breath. "I have convinced my father to allow me to stay at the Hall this Season, so I may avoid the tedious posturing of the marriage mart altogether. Now I've only to convince my mother to agree to my plans, and I will be free to do the work I love. In the meantime, I cannot give her any reason to become upset with me."

Benedict stood there slack-jawed as the implications of her statement sank in. Shock did not begin to describe the way he felt. She was giving up on finding a husband? Did she plan to bury herself in the stables, never to love and be loved? "Your father agreed to this? Accolades to you and your exceptional powers of persuasion, my lady. You must be very pleased."

He clenched his teeth at the sarcastic tone of his voice. He should have kept his damned mouth shut—it was none of his business, after all.

Some of the joy faded from her eyes, replaced by something akin to wariness. "Exceedingly. It is not every day, sir, that one rises above the expectations of others and accomplishes that which has previously seemed impossible."

She was speaking nonsense. She was the most passionate, entertaining, intelligent woman he knew, and she wanted to cut herself off from the world like some dried-up old spinster? She wasn't giving herself a chance. "I agree. Of course, one must ask oneself, did one rise above, or fall below?"

She gasped and backed up a step. "What a ridiculous thing to say, Mr. Benedict! You don't know anything about me, and you presume to make such a statement? What does it even matter to you?"

Oh, how wrong she was. He *did* know her. He knew her well enough to know that she deserved to find happiness in love. She was voluntarily shortchanging her future by closing herself off from the possibility. *He* no longer had the luxury of such a choice. His prospects had been destroyed, no matter what happened when he left this place. Through no fault of his own, he would either spend the rest of his life as a shamed outcast, or burdened by the knowledge that he had betrayed his own moral code for the good of others. Either way, he would never subject a woman to his fate, and therefore marriage would never be in the cards. And here she was, the world at her feet, and she was turning her back on it.

The little fool.

He ground his teeth together to keep from saying what he really felt. Taking a long breath, Benedict inclined his head in deference to her. "It doesn't. I just hope you have thought this all through."

She crossed her arms, her azure eyes cooling considerably. "You know, I was just beginning to like you. Clearly my ability to judge one's character is slipping. Thank you for letting me see your true nature in a timely manner."

"If showing my true nature means that I present the voice of reason, then you are more than welcome, my lady."

She screwed up her face as if she smelled something rotten. "Voice of reason? You must be delusional."

"Delusional, correct," he said, pantomiming the up-and-down motion of a scale. "It's all a matter of interpretation, I suppose."

"What is there to interpret? You are presumptuous enough to assume I don't know my own mind. Why? Is it because I am a mere woman?"

"I never said—"

"You might as well have," she exclaimed, color staining her cheeks. "You don't know me well enough to have come about your conclusions any other way. Therefore, you must think that because I'm a female, I—"

"It's because you have so much to offer!"

They both froze.

Benedict looked even more surprised than Evie felt. With a muttered curse, he dragged his hat from his head and raked a hand through his hair. "Forget I ever said anything. You may do as you please, and I shall keep my delusional opinions to myself."

Evie stood there blinking, utterly mute. How could

she *ever* forget he had said such a thing? Pleasure at his praise raced through her body, warming her more effectively than even the brightest sun. "You think I have a lot to offer?"

He blushed—actually blushed—and rubbed a hand over his mouth in agitation. He gave a quick, jerky nod. "Yes, of course. Richard has always spoken so highly of you. And with all of the ingrates procreating within the *ton*, they could use as much fresh blood as they can get."

She gave a quick snort of laughter before slapping a hand to her mouth. "I cannot believe you just said that."

"You don't agree?"

"Of course I do. I simply can't believe you verbalized it."

They grinned at each other, the tension from before melting away. For a moment, neither one of them spoke; then Benedict cleared his throat and gestured for them to carry on. "Shall we continue, or would you like to head back?"

"Let's keep going. The day is young yet." Her heart felt oddly buoyed, like a cork bobbing in a lake. It was nice, walking quietly beside him. With nothing but the sound of their boots on the dirt path and the occasional chirping bird, it was very peaceful. It felt normal, as if they had been together like this before, enjoying simply being with each other. "Thank you for saying that," she said quietly, keeping her eyes on the path in front of them.

"What?"

"That I have a lot to offer. I do realize I am not the ideal example of femininity."

"Thank God for that. Do you really want to be the *ton*'s ideal anything?"

Evie grinned. Now he was catching on. "Not in the least. I may be in the minority, but I am perfectly happy just the way I am. However," she said wryly, glancing up to meet his gaze, "my unconventional nature does have a way of getting me in trouble. For example, when I un-intentionally call a perfect stranger a nitwit."

Benedict chuckled, his brown eyes alight with mirth. "I'll admit—that was a new experience for me."

With her attention wholly on him, she didn't see the rock in front of her until she stumbled over it. His hand shot out to steady her, and she gasped at the sudden contact. Their eyes met briefly, and she smiled before looking down to watch the path.

Benedict didn't drop his hand. Instead, he readjusted his grip so that he supported her elbow in the palm of his hand. She swallowed the urge to giggle. They were both adults. If he wanted to offer her a guiding hand, it was perfectly acceptable to do so. It was no one's busi-ness but her own if her whole body was positively hum-ming with awareness of the man at her side.

"So you truly are happy?" His voice was low and smooth as he spoke. "I mean, there is nothing more you want from life?"

Her muddled brain struggled to think past the tingle of his hand at her elbow. "At the moment, I enjoy my life exactly as it is." It was absolutely true. She could be with him like this all day and be perfectly content.

The path narrowed, and they were forced to move a little closer to each other. His spicy cologne blended beautifully with the mossy, earthy scents wrapping around them.

He dipped his head, lifting a single brow. "Exactly as it is?"

She slowed to a stop, and he followed suit, turning so they were face-to-face. She knew at once they were closer than was proper, but neither of them moved. She licked her lips and nodded once. "Yes. Mostly." Why was it so hard to think with his hand pressing against her, warm and sure?

The trees above them rattled in a light gust of wind, and sunny spots of light danced over the broad expanse of his chest and shoulders. "Mostly?" he said, the deep timbre of his voice nearly a caress. He tilted his head slightly, holding her gaze the whole time. "What is it that is missing from your life?"

Only yesterday, she would have said nothing. Nothing was missing from her life. So why did her long-dormant heart suddenly protest that answer? Longing, unlike anything she had felt in years, snaked within her. She opened her mouth to respond to him, but no words came to her lips. Finally, she simply shook her head. She couldn't think about it now; she couldn't answer him when she didn't know the answer herself.

A few wisps of hair that had worked free of her pins during her ride lifted in the wind and fluttered across her cheeks. As naturally as if he'd done it a thousand times before, he reached out and touched the errant strands. His fingertips whispered along her cheek as he brushed the lock behind her ear. She held perfectly still as gooseflesh tightened the skin on the back of her neck and swept down her arms. It was all she could do not to turn her cheek into his palm.

"Nothing you would wish for?" He persisted, his words barely above a whisper.

Evie's heart hammered within her chest as she breathed in his enticing scent. The new, delicious sensations coursing through her warmed her from the inside out. She looked up into his dark penetrating stare, losing herself in the velvet depths. Without even intending to, she swayed toward him, lifting her chin as she did. His nostrils flared slightly; he was not unaffected by her nearness. The knowledge weakened her knees even as it emboldened her. Instead of answering his question, she slowly shook her head, her eyes never leaving his.

He lowered his head just enough for her to feel the heat of his breath upon her cheek. The rapid rise and fall of her chest betrayed her own emotions, but she didn't pull away—not when only inches separated their lips. Was this to be her first true kiss?

"Nothing at all?" he murmured, moving his hand from her elbow and skimming up the back of her arm.

She swallowed, her gaze dropping to his lips. "Nothing is perfect, Mr. Benedict."

Chapter Thirteen

If I told you what I wished for, then surely it won't come true. I will say, however, that my dreams have nothing to do with possessions, though I am certain you already knew that. Can you truly not guess what this daughter of a marquis wants?

— From Evie to Hastings

It took a moment before her words penetrated the haze of desire clouding Benedict's mind. "Mister?"

"Benedict," she said softly. "Nothing is perfect, Benedict."

But it was too late. All at once, the truth of his situation came rushing back. He wasn't Benedict, and she wasn't his Evie. He was *Mr.* Benedict, and she Lady Evelyn. For a moment in time, he had forgotten who he was supposed to be; forgotten the role he played. As much as he might wish things had ended differently between them, he could no more change the past now than he could escape the drama he'd found himself entangled in. Damn it all to hell, how could he have forgotten himself? How could he have let himself get so caught up in the moment?

He took a small step backward, only a few inches physically, but emotionally the distance was much greater. "You are absolutely correct about that, my lady."

Evie blinked several times, confusion clouding her eyes. A tiny crease appeared between her brows, and he cursed himself for ever having gotten so close to her in the first place.

He offered her a small smile, trying to soften the sting of his disengagement. "Jasper will be wondering what's become of us. I think perhaps we should head back."

"Yes, of course," she said, visibly rallying. He could have happily flogged himself for causing the hurt coloring her voice. He had been a fool to ever think he could be alone with her and not risk losing himself. More than that, he had been reckless.

When they returned to the house, Benedict was, to be quite blunt, anxious to get out of Evie's company. Entering the paddock, he hopped down from Brutus and handed the reins to the waiting groom. Evie dismounted using the three-step mounting block, thank God. Contact between the two of them should be kept to a strict minimum.

"I must admit I am weary from all of our exercise today. I believe I shall go rest. May I escort you to the house?" He kept his expression bland and his tone impersonal as he made the offer, hoping she would refuse.

She studied him with solemn eyes, concern and a little hurt reflected in their depths. He willed her not to press him, not to make things harder for him than they already were. After a moment she shook her head. "Um, no. Thank you. I think I shall stay for a while longer and see to some business matters. Rest up, and I shall see you at dinner."

He nodded in reply and made good his escape to the house, careful not to look back at the rightly bewildered young lady behind him. If he stopped now, well, he didn't think he'd ever be able to walk away from her.

Standing in the courtyard of a weatherworn inn at twilight, Ned Barney knew he had found the right person. He was getting closer and closer to tracking down his quarry, and he felt in his bones that this was the man who would lead him to Hastings. Before him, the innkeeper eyed the tantalizing pouch of coins Barney held in his hand.

Leaning toward the man conspiratorially, Barney said, "As I said, all I need is a direction." He jostled his hand, letting the innkeeper hear the clink of the coins.

Muffled laughter filtered through the thin ivy-covered walls of the first-floor tavern. The man glanced around the courtyard again, making sure they were still alone. The lamps had not yet been lit, and heavy shadows surrounded them as effectively as a cloak. He licked his lips, settling his eyes on the coin purse in Barney's outstretched hand. Finally, the man reached forward to take the prize. Barney quickly withdrew the bait. "Uh, uh, uh. You tell me wha' I need to know, and I give you the money."

The innkeeper scowled at him and crossed his arms. "How am I to know you'll do as you say?"

Barney grinned. "I suppose you are just going to have to trust me."

"Not bloody likely. I wouldn't trust you as far as I could throw you," the man retorted.

Barney shrugged and turned away.

"Wait!"

He stopped, allowing himself a quick smile before clearing his expression and swiveling to face the greedy bastard. "Yes?"

The man lifted a finger and pointed eastward. "They went on to Hertford Hall in Alyesbury. That yellow-haired gent be the marquis's son."

Triumph! Barney executed a shallow bow. "Much obliged, sir," he said, before punching the man square in the face. The innkeeper fell like a stone, landing in a heap at Barney's feet.

Shaking his hand once, he turned and limped toward his horse, pocketing the money purse. Finally, he had a firm destination. He whistled as he mounted his horse and turned in the direction the innkeeper had pointed. Now that he had an address, it was only a matter of time.

"How was your ride?"

Evie grimaced and looked up from the letter she had been trying to compose for the better part of half an hour to absolutely no avail. Beatrice stood framed in the doorway of Evie's small study, her eyes alight with curiosity. Or was it mischief? With Bea, one could never be sure.

"Fine," Evie said, tossing her quill on the desk. The ink was dry by now anyhow. Every time she looked at the vellum, all she could see was Benedict's shadowed face in the forest, looking down at her as if she were the only person in the world.

Or so she had thought at the time. Apparently she had misread him—dreadfully so. What she thought was interest was only some sort of polite attention. Or was it even that? He could have been loathing her for all she knew. She *really* wished she knew what she had done to change his mood so drastically.

Beatrice's head cocked to the side as she looked Evie up and down as if she were a horse at auction. Evie stifled the urge to roll her eyes. Oh, superb—now she was garnering looks of concern from a sixteen-year-old. Coming fully into the room, Beatrice settled on one of the blue-and-green-patterned chairs in front of Evie's desk. "You don't look fine. Did something happen with Mr. Benedict?"

Evie gave a half snort, half laugh. She did not even know the answer to that question. *No, something didn't happen, and that is the problem.* Somehow she didn't think Bea would understand. "How did you know I was with him?"

"Well, let's see," she said, raising her hand and pointing to her pinky. "First I saw you arguing with him in the garden." She moved on to the ring finger. "Then I saw you making cow eyes at him. Next you spent ages in the barn with him and Richard. Then the two of you rode to heaven knows where with Jasper trailing behind you. Last of all," she said, wiggling her thumb, "the two of you were hardly speaking when you returned two hours later."

Evie just stared at her, almost as impressed as she was annoyed—almost. "I'm certain you can find work as a spy if the whole 'finding a husband' endeavor doesn't work out. That is uncanny. And ridiculous."

Bea's face fell. Apparently she'd expected accolades for her trouble. "It's not ridiculous! I'm concerned about you. You seem . . . unsettled. Is Benedict bothering you?"

Actually, unsettled seemed exactly the word to describe the way Evie was feeling. Drat her sister for reading her so effectively. But honestly, she hated not knowing where she stood with the man. It was all the more galling since she had been so awakened to him. From the moment he had lifted her from her horse, her entire world had tilted. She felt like nothing so much as a newborn colt, wobbly and unsure in its new surroundings. Out of nowhere, the memory of his scent assaulted her, bringing with it the unfamiliar passion that had heated her blood when his lips had been so achingly close to hers. She rubbed her arms as gooseflesh tickled her skin once more. She *really* shouldn't be thinking of such things with her sister's keen eyes watching her.

Leaning back in her chair, Evie waved a dismissive hand. "Mr. Benedict is not bothering me in the least. We shared a nice ride through the country and returned when we grew weary. Nothing more, nothing less."

Except for the shockingly intimate feel of his hands on her waist. Or the exhilarating weightlessness of being held in his arms. Or the enlightening discussion behind the sheltering limbs of the massive oak trees lining the trail. Or that heart-stopping moment when she thought he was going to kiss her—and the abrupt departure shortly after.

Beatrice looked completely unconvinced. "Has he done anything . . . untoward?"

Untoward? "Good heavens, Beatrice, what kind of thing is that to say? Of course not." Evie fought valiantly against the blush rising up her neck, but still her cheeks burned—not because Benedict had been untoward in the least, but because of how badly she had *wanted* him to be.

Her sister's eyes widened slightly—the blasted girl didn't miss a thing. "Evie, something happened that you aren't telling me."

Evie ground her teeth together in annoyance. She was feeling raw enough about what had happened—or *hadn't* happened—with Benedict without discussing the matter with her meddling sister. "I don't know what you are talking about, Bea. And truly, if he had done anything improper, you'd probably know before I did, the way you're snooping."

Her sister didn't leap to her defense as Evie had expected. Instead, Beatrice scooted to the end of her chair and whispered, "Actually, I do know something about him you should know."

Of course she did. She probably knew the man's life story by now. Evie crossed her arms over her chest and fixed her sister with a glare. "Was this knowledge gained by polite, acceptable means?"

"No, but—"

"Then I don't want to hear it. Now, you must stop this spying. I won't have my every move being watched by my little sister."

"But Benedict—"

"Is our guest, and he deserves privacy," Evie interrupted firmly, completely ignoring the fact that she herself had spied on the man not twenty-four hours earlier. "As do I."

"Yes, I know, but he—"

"I mean it, Bea. Not another word."

"Evie," Beatrice exclaimed, slapping a hand on the desk. "*Listen* to me. It's for your own good."

Oh, so now her sister thought she knew what was best for Evie? That was really too much, especially since Evie was so unsure of where things stood between Benedict and her. Abruptly she stood. "That is enough. You're behaving like a nosy child, and it has to stop."

Pressing her lips into a thin line, Beatrice glared at her. "A nosy child? Fine, if you don't wish for me to tell you what I know, then I won't. But don't blame me when you discover all is not as it seems."

Evie rolled her eyes at her sister's dramatics. "Duly noted. Now leave me be, please. I have work to do before supper."

Her sister rose to her feet and started for the door. She paused by the window, the pink light of evening slanting across the right side of her body. "Just be careful, Evie. I don't want to see you get hurt."

Without waiting for a response, she slipped through the door and was gone. Evie shook her head slowly. What had *that* been about? Whatever Beatrice's intention, she had only served to make Evie think on Benedict that much more.

By the time Evie settled into bed that night, she was precariously close to obsessing about the man. He failed to show up for either dinner or the duet pianoforte recital the twins performed, sending a note begging off in his place. In the latter she was not alone in her disappointment—the girls had balked at giving a concert without the guest of honor, but their mother had insisted the show must go on. Beatrice was the only one who seemed relieved at his absence.

Evie pulled the heavy counterpane up to her chin and rolled to her side on the soft mattress. She had to see him again. Alone. If he wouldn't talk to her, she didn't know what she was going to do. She was so on edge, her skin felt too tight for her body. Oh, who was she fooling? She didn't just need to talk to him again; she needed to feel his touch on her skin. For the first time in her life, she *wanted* a man to touch her.

She still could hardly believe the strange pull between them. A near perfect stranger, and every fiber of her being seemed attuned to him, drawn to him as a honeybee to nectar. She hardly knew herself, the way she was feeling.

In a few days he would be on to his new life, and she would immerse herself in hers. There was no future between them, and she had no desire for one. She knew better than to put her trust in a man expecting loyalty in the long run. But in between now and when he departed . . .

Alone in her darkened chamber, with naught but the silvery threads of moonlight slipping through her drapes as witness, she considered the possibilities.

She had never kissed a man before. Benedict presented the perfect opportunity. He wouldn't expect anything from her, and he wouldn't endanger her dreams. They had come so close to it, so unbearably close that she almost protested aloud when he stepped away from her.

His voice murmured in the back of her mind, and she pressed her eyes closed. *Nothing you would wish for?* A few days ago she would have said no. Now, there was something she desired. She wanted him to kiss her more than anything in her whole life.

She had to talk to him; to somehow get him alone again. She didn't think she could actually tell him what she wanted, but if she could catch him in the right mood—and that was really key, given his swings of mood—then maybe . . .

Maybe she could entice him to share one, perfect, unforgettable kiss with her. She shivered and pressed her eyes closed. She only hoped it would be enough.

Chapter Fourteen

I have a few ideas as to what might make you happy. More time in the stables with your father, to be sure, as well as less time sitting at the pianoforte pounding out mangled versions of the great classics. Richard has described these in great detail, you should know. Perhaps more opportunities to meet new people? I can think of at least one who would like to meet you.

—From Hastings to Evie

As the carriage bumped along the rutted road leading to the village, Benedict resolutely kept his eyes trained out the window on the passing countryside and off the beautiful—and devious—little minx across from him. He could feel Evie watching him, her gaze flitting back to him every third pass: first to Richard, then to the window, then to Benedict. Each time she landed on him, it was as if the sun licked across his skin, burning a hot, delicious path wherever it touched.

This was *exactly* why he had tried to avoid her this morning.

At breakfast it had been clear that she wished to see him today. After yesterday, he knew his willpower couldn't hold up to resist her should they find themselves alone again. When Richard had asked their plans for the gloomy, rainy day, Benedict held silent until she reluctantly admitted she had a new book she wished to read. He suggested a trip to town for the two men, and she had triumphantly announced that the book she wished to read was a newly arrived order she needed to pick up from the village bookseller.

One look at her face and he *knew* she knew she had him.

"It is really quite lovely here in the spring, when the trees are all in bloom." Evie's statement was softy spoken and sounded conciliatory.

Benedict stubbornly continued to stare out the window, though he barely saw the soggy, verdant scenery rolling by. The damned trees had nothing on her. "I can see that."

"I'll never understand how Richard can spend so much time in the city. All of the congestion, and bad air, and noise—I just don't see the lure. To me, this is paradise."

Richard let out a small laugh. "And I will never understand how you can prefer so much isolation, emptiness, and lack of socialization. It's downright unreasonable to expect a man to thrive. Don't you agree, Benedict?"

Benedict shrugged and said, "I prefer to think of myself as balanced. Time among each extreme will prevent one from becoming too narrow-minded."

Richard snorted. "Right. You are the most broad-minded chap I know. Why do I keep forgetting that?"

"I can't imagine. You should follow my example, Richard. We wouldn't want you turning into a congested, foul-smelling, sooty city-dweller, now would we?"

"Too late, I'm afraid," Evie quipped with a smile.

Benedict briefly met her eyes and found himself reluctantly smiling as well. He quickly broke their eye contact and returned his gaze to the passing scenery.

Out the window he saw the approaching town. Grass gave way to pavement, trees to buildings. It was not unlike any other that dotted the English countryside—an inn, a pub, a bakery, and a few clothing and accessory shops. They rumbled through the main street, the well-sprung carriage absorbing most of the jostling from the cobblestones, before turning down a smaller street and slowing to a stop.

They filed out, Richard first, with him assisting Evie before Benedict climbed down last. The rain at least had stopped, but the streets were still dotted with puddles and water dripped from nearly every surface. Only a handful of people milled about, though each seemed to have taken interest in the grand carriage's arrival. Before them was a quaint, wooden building with small shuttered windows and a weathered green sign hanging over the door proclaiming DARCY'S BOOKSELLERS.

He was *not* about to get stuck spending the entire day at Evie's side like some lapdog. Benedict turned to Richard and offered a carefree smile. "Shall we wander about town a bit? I'm sure we'll only be in your sister's way."

He started to veer in the opposite direction, when he felt a small tug on his sleeve.

"Won't you accompany me? Being the academic you are, I am sure you must appreciate a well-stocked bookshop."

He looked down to see her smiling up at him. She was clearly trying to manipulate him; he was surprised she was not batting those ridiculously long eyelashes at him.

"I am set for literature, my lady. Pray, enjoy your shopping."

She did bat her eyelashes then. "Well, perhaps you can put your schooling to work and help me to select something new."

Richard grinned and nodded toward the shop. "By all means, Benedict, go. I would love to see what you would suggest for my dear sister's reading."

Staring meaningfully at Richard, Benedict answered Evie. "If it is your wish. After you." He swept his arm with an exaggerated gesture while continuing to glare at his friend.

Richard's grin grew even more. "Why don't you two go ahead? I'll pop into Tuttle's shop and see what they have in the way of new gloves."

"Be sure to tell them I said hello," Evie said with a syrupy sweet waggle of her fingers.

Benedict swallowed a curse. Once again, she knew she had him. Of course, she wasn't the only one testing his patience. Richard was an amazing friend, but he was far and away too flippant. If pressed, Benedict could probably come up with something Richard took seriously, but at the moment he couldn't think of a thing. The man could not seem to help but have a bit of fun at Benedict's expense.

Scowling, Benedict trailed after Evie into the shop, careful to keep his eyes on the building and off the tempting sway of her hips. As soon as they opened the door, the proprietor immediately rushed forward to greet them. The thin, willowy man was obviously well acquainted with Evie. As they chatted about some new arrivals, Benedict wasted no time in escaping.

The place was a labyrinth of narrow aisles winding around the cramped shop. Books of every subject, age, and condition overflowed from the dusty shelves. He had to step around the stacks of books that extended almost to the ceiling in several places. He wrinkled his nose at the slightly musty scent that seemed to get stronger the farther he ventured into the poorly lit shop.

"Please don't be cross with me, Benedict."

Evie's softly spoken plea cut straight through his anger and right to his heart. He pressed his eyes closed for a second before turning to face her. She stood at the end of the aisle, a stack of books cradled in the crook of her arm and a hesitant smile on her lips. He knew right then and there he would never be able to resist her.

"I could never be cross with you, Evie."

She smiled slowly and took a few tentative steps forward. "I'm not sure I believe that, but I do hope that, at the very least, you have forgiven me for dragging you here with me."

"Who am I to deny a lady anything? You wished me to accompany you, and here I am. No dragging necessary."

"I thought that, as an academic, you might enjoy the shop. It is quite well stocked."

The reminders of his deception always surfaced when he least expected them. He wouldn't correct her, but he wouldn't lie, either. "I have indeed always been a lover of books. As for the shop, it is . . . unusual."

She chuckled, looking around at the chaos surrounding them. "Mr. Darcy is much too involved in the contents of the books to bother with the organization of them."

"I can see that. It is a wonder he can sell anything at all—or find anything, for that matter."

"Interestingly enough, he can find any book in the store in mere moments. I have long since given up trying to find what I need and instead simply ask for it. It does make browsing very interesting, however."

She tilted her head and read two adjacent titles on the shelf nearest where she stood. "*The Count of Monte Cristo* and *The Decline and Fall of the Roman Empire*. I cannot begin to guess why the two of these are grouped together." She looked up and snapped her fingers. "I have it! Both books involve the comeuppance of a once-strong oppressor. How could I have not seen such an obvious correlation?"

He raised his shoulders briefly in an "I don't know" gesture and looked to the shelf to his right. "Ah, I have *A Dictionary of the English Language* and *The Forest of Montalbano*. Clearly, these two have much in common."

"Oh?" she prompted, placing her free hand on her hip.

"I daresay every word in *The Forest of Montalbano* can be found in here," he said, thumping the spine of the dictionary. She laughed lightly, and he felt the corners of his own mouth lift. Hearing her joy illuminated a tiny corner of the darkness within him.

"Clearly. How could I have missed it?"

"There now, it is not your fault, my lady. One cannot expect the fairer sex to understand these sorts of things."

Without missing a beat, she arched her left eyebrow and said airily, "If that is what makes the male population feel superior, then by all means, I will leave it to you. We females prefer to use our talents on more worthwhile endeavors, such as rearing the next generation."

"Indeed? I was not aware that you were dedicating your time to the upbringing of the future generation. I bow to your superior pursuits, my lady." He sketched a shallow, mocking bow, and she made a face at him.

"Very well, you have me there. Though, I will say, being the eldest female sibling, I certainly have had a hand in my sisters' upbringing. But really, I have naught but the reins of the family business in my repertoire of pursuits."

"A very unique pursuit, if I may say so. I don't believe I have ever met a lady who was interested in working for a living."

"That is not fair. I am convinced there are many ladies who would enjoy outside pursuits but would never do so thanks to the restrictions society places on us. Somehow I doubt you have read Mary Wollstonecraft's *A Vindication of the Rights of Women*."

Benedict was momentarily taken aback. Leaning his shoulder against the shelf nearest him, he said, "Actually, I have, but I would not think the same of you. She is rather vitriolic in her assessment of the aristocracy, of which, I might point out, you are a member."

Evie shook her head. "She is disdainful of the *uselessness* of the aristocracy. In case it is not obvious enough, I am working toward being a useful member of society. I am more industrious than most men of my class."

"Of that I will brook no argument. You, Evie, are unlike any member of the *ton* I have ever encountered."

She paused for a moment, adjusting the position of the books in her arms. "I am going to take that as a compliment. Although I would never say that I work for a living, I do gain immense satisfaction from my involvement in the business. Nobody seems to care or understand that I enjoy the challenge and purpose that the position poses."

"Ah, but would not 'rearing the future generation' also pose challenges and purpose?" He knew her well enough to anticipate her reaction and was rewarded with just the response he expected: an exaggerated roll of her eyes.

"Of course it does, you— " She paused in time to save whatever insult was poised on the tip of her tongue. "I was merely pointing out there is more than one way to contribute to society."

He chuckled quietly. "All right, I call a truce. So, what books have you found already?"

He watched in fascination as her cheeks flushed and she flattened the books to her chest.

"Just a few silly novels. For the girls, of course," she said, beginning to back up. "Have you found anything to pique your interest?"

He was not about to let her get away with her attempt

at evasion. His hand shot out and snatched one of the books from her grasp. She cried out in dismay, but he ignored her as he read the title.

"Byron?" He couldn't help but screw up his face in disgust. "You read treaties on the rights of women, which, by the way, expound on the ridiculousness of false sensibilities, and then you go and purchase a book of silly, romantic poems?"

Her flush deepened, and she snatched the book back, dropping the other two books she was holding. He bent to help her, but she yelped, "Don't!" He stepped back in surprise, and she quickly snatched them off the floor.

She pushed her drooping hair off her forehead with as much dignity as she could manage and drew a deep breath. "As I said, they are not for me. Let me just leave them with Mr. Darcy while you look for something you think I might benefit from."

He pursed his lips in an effort not to laugh at her; he did not think she would respond well to it after her defensive embarrassment. He should have known after the Austen book she had left outside his door that she harbored a romantic side. Nodding his head, he agreed. "Leave it to me. I shall find something right up your alley."

She dipped her head and scurried off toward the counter, leaving him to peruse the random assortment of books in peace. He found he was smiling to himself as he browsed. He tried to straighten his features—he needed to discourage Evie from spending more time with him, not encourage her. Perhaps a bit of teasing was in order—something to break the building tension between them without actually hurting her. In a sudden moment of inspiration, he decided on just the book.

He followed Evie to the counter. "I wish for the book to be a surprise. Wait outside, if you will, and I will make my purchase and join you shortly."

She gave him an odd look but shrugged her shoulders and complied.

As the shopkeeper retrieved his selection, Benedict congratulated himself for the cleverness of his choice. Anything he could do to discourage her from being in his company was a step in the right direction . . . especially since he seemed to be more drawn to her with every passing moment.

Chapter Fifteen

*Perhaps, if someday the stars align, there is someone I
might wish to be introduced to. If this person would
also like to be introduced to me, that is a question I
cannot yet answer. Perhaps the spring will bring the
answer to that?*

—From Evie to Hastings

As she prepared for dinner, Evie was still fuming
about the joke Benedict had played on her. Handing over the package with an innocent smile earlier in
the carriage, she had eagerly torn the brown paper away.
After reading the neatly printed title, she skewered him
with a glare. "What is this supposed to be?"

Richard pulled the book from her hands as Benedict
affected a wounded expression and replied, "Don't you
like it? Only yesterday we were quoting Shakespeare to
each other, so I thought you might enjoy my favorite of
the Bard's works."

About this time Richard erupted into laughter, passing the book back to her. "He's right, Bit. I have it on the
best authority that you do love Shakespeare. Well chosen, my friend, well chosen."

She dropped the offending play on the seat next to
her in disgust. Oh yes, Benedict was *so* clever. She
crossed her arms and narrowed her eyes. "*The Taming
of the Shrew*. Ha. Ha. How exceedingly clever."

"What? I thought you would love a play you could relate to." Benedict was all innocence.

Richard laughed even harder at this, bending forward before rocking back in his seat. A grin broke out on Benedict's face; it was so smug, she longed to slap it off.

Men. And others wondered why she remained unmarried.

Now, hours later, she watched in silence as Morgan worked to create a more elaborate evening hairstyle, weaving in a string of pearls among her upswept tresses. Evie liked the way the pearls caught the candlelight, highlighting the artful curls her maid had spent an age to perfect.

Tonight, Evie wanted to look so good that Benedict would eat his *and* the Bard's words. So far everything was going to plan—her maid was doing a superb job, and the simple, elegant white gown Evie wore fit her to perfection. She debated adding a piece of lace over the low décolleté and decided against it. For the first time in her life, she wanted to attract a man specifically so she could make him as crazy as he was making her. It might be petty, but it was the only retribution she had. She couldn't *wait* to see his face when he saw her.

When at last she was alone, Evie glanced at the clock—almost a full hour until dinner. She sighed and wandered over to her window. Pushing aside the curtains, she stared out into the evening sky, which was still tinged with a faint orange at the distant horizon. As her eyes adjusted, she felt a genuine flash of pleasure—the stars were out! Well, of course, if she had not been so preoccupied with the two idiots in the carriage with her on the way home, she would have realized the emerging blue sky would give way to a starry night.

It was too good to pass up. On a whim, she slipped on her shoes and grabbed a warm shawl. Blowing out her lamp, she made a break for the comfort of the outdoors.

By some miracle, she made it all the way to the back terrace without being stopped by a single person. In a family the size of hers, that was quite a feat. The chilly air swirled around her ankles when she lifted her skirts a few inches before descending the stone steps into the garden. It was considerably cooler than it had been on their outing, and she was glad for the shawl tucked around her arms.

Once on the pebbled path, Evie dropped her skirts and grasped the ends of the shawl, crossing her arms for further warmth as she walked toward the back gardens so the lights from the windows would not diminish the view. She knew where she was going; there were many times when she escaped from the house to gaze at the familiar patterns of stars in the heavens.

She found her favorite bench, the only one with an unobstructed view of the sky in the garden. Though the flowers were not yet in bloom, the smell of fresh life, newly tilled earth, and grass clippings filled her senses. Sitting down on the cool and thankfully dry stone, she looked down at her feet and closed her eyes. Just as she had done when she was a child, she played her own little game by throwing her head back and opening her eyes to focus on the first star that caught her attention.

This night, not one but two came into focus, and she smiled happily at the coincidence. The twin pins of light were none other than Cor Coaroli, the Heart of Charles, which meant her gaze was appropriately aimed at the Canes Venatici, the Hunting Dogs. A wide grin spread across her face. Clearly, such a coincidence had to mean good luck for the impending hunt.

From the Hunting Dogs, she traced her way through several of her favorite springtime constellations, taking comfort as she always did in the fact that the stars were completely reliable and dependable. Even if the clouds rolled in and her view was obscured, she knew the stars were still maintaining their exact locations in the heavens, patiently waiting until they could shine again.

She was feeling relaxed now, no longer obsessing about Benedict or anything else. She let all those things fall away and simply observed. It was nice to revel in the quiet, without her family, the servants, or even horses causing some sort of background noise or another.

"You're shivering."

She nearly jumped out of her skin at the softly spoken statement, letting out an odd sort of half yelp, half squeal in the process. Hand to her galloping heart, she whipped around to peer in the direction of the unexpected voice. On a small bench under a tree not twenty feet away sat Benedict, innocent as could be.

"Merciful heavens, is it your intent to stop my heart?" Evie asked breathlessly. "You scared the daylights out of me!"

She could see him now, sprawled inelegantly across the wooden bench, no hat or gloves in sight. He stood and stretched before walking toward her.

"I apologize for that. I suppose I didn't think. I didn't want to intrude on your quiet time, but when your teeth began chattering loud enough to wake the dead, I felt it was my duty to speak up."

"My teeth were doing no such thing, and if you had a duty to do anything, it was to alert me to your presence," she replied peevishly, all the while trying to recall if she had done anything embarrassing when she thought herself unobserved. Thankfully, nothing came to mind.

Benedict chuckled. "Touché, my lady. I suppose I was enjoying some of my own alone time as well. May I join you?"

Evie looked down beside her to the spot on the bench he had gestured to. Why did he have to bring it to her attention that she was shivering? Now the coldness of the stone bench seeped through her gown with a vengeance, and she became aware of how cold her own ungloved hands had become. How very irritating the man was proving to be.

Feeling contrary, she said, "No."

The answer had the perverse effect of making him smile. "Come now; don't be that way. I am sorry for the fun Richard and I had at your expense today. I promise I won't do anything like that again. Please may I join you?"

Did he just say please? Evie's eyebrows hitched up in surprise. She made a mental note to thank Morgan for the extra work the maid had done on Evie's hair tonight. As she considered his request, Evie realized there was something in his manner that seemed somewhat resigned. She couldn't really put her finger on what exactly made her think so; it was just a mood she sensed.

Benedict and his moods—changeable did not even begin to describe the man. In the short amount of time she had known him, it seemed as though she had already seen a dozen different sides of him. She looked up at him and wished she had not—for all of his less desirable traits, Benedict was absurdly handsome. Really, it almost made one feel inadequate.

Evie sighed. It'd be petty to send him away. Besides, he didn't look as though he planned to leave any time soon, and she did not want to go to the house just yet. She shrugged and scooted over a bit. "Oh, very well—suit yourself. We shall have to go to supper in a minute in any event."

Benedict flipped out the tails of his jacket and sat beside her. "Time is not passing as quickly as that. We still have more than half an hour before we must return."

The bench was on the small side, and Benedict was seated only inches away. In a matter of moments she could actually feel his warmth—how completely remarkable. She made a conscious effort to keep her body from leaning into the heat, even just an inch or two. Instead, she gripped the edge on the bench on either side of her skirts and looked up to the heavens again. The faint scent of sandalwood drifted toward her. She discreetly inhaled the spicy aroma—delicious.

"Do you have a favorite?" Benedict's breath hung visibly in the chilly air as he asked the question.

She blinked. Scent? No, of course not. "A favorite what?"

He tipped his head back and pointed to the skies.

"Constellation?" she asked. He nodded, and she thought about it a minute. "I suppose it depends. Tonight I was particularly happy to see Canes Venatici."

Out of the corner of her eye, she caught his raised eyebrows. "You really do know your constellations. Impressive, I must say. So why has Canes Venatici caught your fancy this evening?"

"Why, good luck for the coming hunt, of course. What else would the Hunting Dogs symbolize?" She looked at him ruefully. "It is quite the least distinct constellation in the sky, but tonight it seems appropriate. Normally I suppose I might say Leo, or perhaps Canis Major."

"I am fond of Leo myself. Not only is the mighty lion something to behold, but it is possibly the easiest thing to see in the whole jumble, which is helpful to a layman such as myself."

Evie laughed at his observation. "That jumble, as you call it, is very neatly laid out, if you but pay a bit of attention. How else have sailors guided their ships to safety all these years?"

"Men don't need guidance. Every male is born with an innate sense of direction. A pity you women must depend on outside cues such as the stars." His tone was perfectly sober.

She rolled her eyes. "Very funny. I thought at dinner the other evening you mentioned you were a student of astronomy. Surely you must respect the field."

"No, I said I had been visiting the observatory, and you *assumed* I was a student. You never asked, and therefore I never confirmed or denied. Alas, I am not." Adopting an air of self-importance, he said, "I do, however, have *great* respect for the field."

"Well, I am certain astronomers will be much assured to learn you have given their work your seal of approval."

He grinned and shook his head. "Anyone who can stare at those tiny bits of light, string together three of them, and somehow have an entire bear or scorpion must, at the very least, have a very active imagination."

She chuckled, thoroughly enjoying their banter. When he was like this, he felt so . . . familiar somehow. There was a certain ease between them that seemed so natural. His other moods seemed more like an ill-fitting piece of clothing.

"Yes, you know all those fanciful astronomers out there, what with their telescopes and quadrants and other silly little instruments." She cut her eyes toward him. "I'll bet you don't see shapes in clouds, either."

"That is not true. I regularly see cloud-shaped clouds. Some of them even look like clotted cream."

At this she laughed out loud, her breath crystallizing between them before vanishing into the night. She placed her hands on either side of her cheeks and shook her head. If only he could be like this all the time. He was deuced annoying when he clammed up, but when she saw the other side of him, well, she thoroughly enjoyed *that* Benedict. Her laughter trailed off, and she dropped her hands back down on the bench.

Only her right hand didn't touch the bench.

It settled on Benedict's bare hand by mistake, and she

gasped at the contact. His skin was deliciously warm against her cold fingers, and she hesitated for the barest of moments before jerking her hand away. The butterflies came flooding back, wreaking havoc in her stomach again. She suddenly wished she had not let him sit so close to her. She opened her mouth to apologize, but the words fell right out of her head when he reached out and grasped her hand in his.

"Your fingers are like ice." He said the statement simply, with complete nonchalance. He pulled her hand into both of his, chafing her skin between his palms.

It felt like absolute *heaven*.

Her eyes had gone round as saucers, her gaze riveted on their joined hands. Belatedly, she realized her mouth was still hanging open, and she snapped her jaw shut with an audible click. She didn't know what to do, what to say, so she simply was still. The intimacy of his deliberate touch was overwhelming, unlike anything she had ever experienced before.

With her heart thumping in her chest, she couldn't seem to draw a proper breath. What was more, the cold night air hid nothing, each shallow puff of air a visible testament to her reaction to him.

She watched, mesmerized as he raised her hand, still enveloped in both of his, with excruciating slowness toward his lips. When she realized what he intended, her eyes flashed to his, and she saw that he was watching her face intently. Their eyes locked, and her mouth went dry. He brought her fingers achingly close to his mouth, pausing only a fraction of an inch away. She held her breath, suspended in time while her whole being waited to see what would happen next.

Good heavens, was he really going to kiss her this time?

Through parted lips he slowly drew in a deep breath;

she could see his chest rising with the action. He paused for the space of a second, though her anticipation was so great that it felt like minutes. Unconsciously she leaned forward, her own lips parting slightly.

And then he exhaled.

His breath, deliciously hot, flowed over her fingertips, down her palm, and across her wrist. Somehow, the warmth seemed to race through her entire body before settling low in her belly. She had never felt a more delectable sensation in her life, so pleasurable her toes curled within her thin slippers. If only time would stand still so she could really savor the feeling. Gooseflesh immediately peppered her arms, and she shivered involuntarily.

His lips curled into the slightest of smiles. Into the silence, he murmured mere inches from her skin, "I intended to warm you, not chill you further."

She swallowed thickly, trying to find her voice. Taking a deep breath, she said hoarsely, "I rather think you succeeded. I—I feel much warmer now."

His smile grew, and he lowered her hand. Disappointment instantly coursed through her body. *No!* She wasn't ready for it to end.

Benedict took one look at the pleading expression on her face and was lost. He couldn't think—didn't want to think. His heart hammered against his ribs, drowning out whatever protests his brain tried to make.

He had to have more.

Without conscious thought, he pressed her palm to his knee with one hand and reached out to cup her neck with the other. It was like holding the forbidden fruit, grasping that which he was never meant to have. He caressed the smooth, supple skin of the hollow of her cheek with his thumb, giving her time to protest. Instead, she turned slightly into his touch.

It was all the encouragement he needed.

Tugging her toward him, he slowly tilted his head and leaned forward until their lips were so close, he could smell her sweet breath. It was the most intoxicating scent he had ever known. He knew he should stop, should leave her now and escape before things progressed any more. But he couldn't. Damn it all, he couldn't. He wanted her, needed her, and nothing could make him walk away now.

With a groan, he closed the distance between them and pressed his lips to hers as gently as he could. The kiss was soft, and sweet, and utterly perfect. If everything went to hell tomorrow — and it probably would — he could be content in having experienced one perfect moment in time. Only . . . it wasn't enough. Her kiss was perfect, but it only made him want her that much more.

She made a soft sound in the back of her throat, and he tightened his hold, pressing his lips more firmly to hers. He turned her head with a slight pressure of his thumb and lightly kissed the corner of her mouth. She smelled delicious, but she tasted even better. He dipped his head and trailed kisses along her exquisitely formed jawline, sliding his hand farther back so he could press his lips to the sensitive skin directly below her ear where his thumb had just been.

She shivered at the contact, her hand flexing under his palm, lightly squeezing his knee. It was almost more than he could take. He returned to her mouth, and this time her lips were eager as she pressed against him. He deepened the kiss, parting his lips and experiencing a flash of satisfaction when she did the same. When he slipped his tongue into her mouth, she responded tentatively at first, but in moments their tongues danced together.

They fit as if they were made for each other. His Evie,

his most treasured friend, tasted of hope and trust—too much trust.

At last he broke the kiss. Panting for breath, he leaned his forehead against hers and closed his eyes. Why couldn't this moment last forever? To stay here, holding the woman he had known so well but still hardly at all, surrounded by gentle darkness and thousands of pinpricks of light above.

Evie blinked, her eyes unfocused as he gently pulled his hands from her and came to his feet. The moment he stepped away, reality washed over him like a rogue wave, swamping his senses. Good Lord, what had he done? How had he managed to lose himself so completely with her? He clenched his jaw against the self-recrimination that flayed him from the inside out. He had lost his mind.

All the upheaval that had happened in his life recently—which was continuing to happen—and he went and did something like this? There could never be anything between them, no matter how much he wished otherwise. And after that kiss, Benedict was *really* wishing otherwise.

As things stood now, only one thing in his life was certain: No matter which decision he made regarding the life-changing moment near the cliffs of Folkestone, the result would be a life without her. If he followed his heart, then he would never be allowed in polite society again. But if he did not stand up for what was right, then he could never live with himself.

Benedict gave his head a little shake. In all his life, he had never dreamed Evie would be the one to captivate not only his mind and his soul, but somehow even his heart. Why couldn't he have found her earlier? Perhaps things could have been different then.

She looked up to him, confusion written all over her face. It broke his heart to see her looking so uncertain.

He took a deep, bracing breath and said, "Evie, I am so sorry for kissing you. I don't know what came over me, but I promise it will never happen again. Please say you will forgive me."

Her forehead wrinkled as he spoke, and he felt his stomach drop. She wasn't going to forgive him. How could she? The liberties he had taken with her were appalling, to say the least.

He braced himself for her anger as she narrowed her eyes. "You swain."

"I know," he said miserably.

"I can't believe you are apologizing for kissing me. How completely ridiculous."

Ridiculous? That wasn't at all the reaction he had expected from her. "Whatever do you mean?"

"For heaven's sake, Benedict, didn't anyone ever tell you if you kiss a lady, it is customary to compliment her, or at the very least smile afterward? I do believe you have just insulted me." She stood and brushed her dress out.

"Insulted—how on earth did I *insult* you?"

"By apologizing, you just indicated you regretted your actions. You might as well have told me I am a poor kisser."

"Evie, now *you* are being ridiculous. I implied no such thing," he exclaimed. What was he supposed to say to a statement such as that? "I promise you, you are not a poor kisser."

"Well, that is high praise indeed. Thank you for clearing that up."

How had he managed to botch things so thoroughly? He was *trying* to make things right, and all he accomplished was angering her further. Grasping her shoulders, he looked her straight in the eye. "Listen to me, Evie. You are a wonderful kisser. I am merely trying to apologize for taking such liberties with you in the first place. As much as I enjoyed your kiss, it was not very gentlemanly of me."

She looked up at him, nibbling on her perfect little bottom lip. He could see the hurt in her eyes, despite her matter-of-fact tone. Lord, he wanted to kick himself.

He pressed his eyes closed, taking a deep breath. Before everything went to hell and there was no turning back, was it really so horrible to have wanted a moment of true happiness? He exhaled and pressed his forehead to hers. She stiffened but didn't pull away. "Evie," he said softly, "I will be leaving very soon. I'll be starting a new life, and you have all of your plans. Knowing that, it was wrong of me to kiss you. Can't we just be friends?"

She was quiet for a moment, and he wished he could know what she was thinking. Had he hurt her? Finally, she said, "Actually, I think it was a good idea for us to kiss for exactly those reasons."

What? He released his hold on her shoulders and stepped back. "What on earth are you talking about?"

She looked to her hands a moment, her brazenness of moments ago seeming to ebb away. "I don't plan on marrying, Benedict. But that doesn't mean . . . That is to say . . ." She paused and took a deep breath. "That was my first kiss. When else will I have the opportunity to . . . enjoy someone's attentions? I have made a commitment to my path in life, and with you leaving in a few days, well, I think you are exactly the right person for me to kiss."

He knew he looked like a simpleton, standing there with his mouth hanging open, but he couldn't seem to do anything about it. She wanted him to kiss her? To be together specifically for the reason he thought to keep his distance? Gathering his wits, he snapped his mouth shut and swallowed. It was tempting—absurdly tempting.

"Evie, I would like very much to agree with you"—

she had no idea just how much—"but I could never take advantage of you like that. What kind of gentleman would I be?"

She appeared almost fragile in the moonlight as she looked up to him, the white light bathing her face in a way that made her skin pale yet luminescent. "I am trying to be honest with you, Benedict. I enjoy your company, despite the rather spirited nature of some of our conversations. Set aside what you think others expect from you for a moment, and tell me if you enjoy being with me as well."

There were so many lies between them, he couldn't bring himself to lie about this. "Yes."

She took a small step toward him. "Tell me if you want to spend *more* time in my company."

She held his gaze, unblinking and earnest, and he answered her honestly. "Yes."

"Tell me you want to kiss me again."

He drank in the sight of her, memorizing the curve of her cheek, the bow of her lips, the starlight in her eyes. He knew he shouldn't say it; he knew he should turn and leave her, leave this house, and never look back. And even as he knew these things, the truth tumbled from his lips.

"Yes."

Relief spread over her face, and she took the last step to close the distance between them. His arms snaked around her waist and pulled her against him, hard and decisive. His lips crashed onto hers, and he poured everything he felt into the kiss. She groaned and dug her hands into his collar, pulling them even more tightly together, if that was possible.

She was his, if only for the moment, just as she had always been. He knew everything about her spirit, her irrepressible personality, and now he wanted to know everything about her body—her beautiful lips, which fit against his exactly right; her tiny waist, nearly spanned by his hands; and the sweet swell of her hips. He wished there were nothing between them—no secrets, no lies, no clothing, no impossible realities. Her hands slid up and settled around his neck, and he groaned with the pleasure of her touch.

In the distance, a scraping sound caught his trained ears. He tensed and pulled away—someone had opened the terrace door. Evie gave a small mewl of protest and leaned toward him once more.

"Shh," he breathed, putting a finger to his lips. "Someone is coming."

Evie's eyes widened, and she looked toward the house. The last thing either one of them needed was to be discovered alone together in the garden. "It's Richard," she whispered, nodding toward her brother's form outlined against the glow of the glass door behind him.

Richard strode across the terrace and paused at the top of the stairs. "Hastings, are you out here?"

Chapter Sixteen

Richard and I were discussing the end of term yesterday. I can hardly believe these five years have gone by so quickly. Neither my parents nor my brother are planning to attend the ceremony, not that I am surprised. I do hope, however, there will be someone in the audience who shall smile for me when it's my turn.

—From Hastings to Evie

Evie turned to stone in Benedict's arms as her brother's words fell over them like a blanket of ice. Her eyes snapped to Benedict's, utter confusion pushing out all rational thoughts. "Hastings?" she repeated numbly.

He didn't say anything at first. He didn't have to. The look of complete horror in his eyes spoke louder than any words he could have said. "Evie, wait—"

She shook her head, holding her hand up to stop him. No. It simply couldn't be. Dread wrapped cold fingers around her heart, stealing her breath. "Are you or aren't you Hastings?"

She wanted him to deny it. To laugh and tell her what an absurd notion it was. Instead, he released her and blew out an aggravated breath. "I am."

They had lied to her? They had both lied to her? The sound of boots hitting the pebbled path punctuated her rising panic, and she looked back toward the house. She couldn't be caught with Bened—this *man*, alone in the darkness.

She stumbled backward, suddenly desperate to get away. Gravel crunched angrily beneath her feet as she struggled to keep her footing.

"Benedict?" Richard called louder. He must have heard her.

"Answer him," she hissed, anger and hurt bubbling up like acid in her throat. "He knows you're here."

Benedict balled his hands at his side and muttered a black curse. "Coming, Richard. Just getting some air." His voice sounded remarkably steady. If it weren't for the tautness of his shoulders and his clenched jaw, Evie would have never known anything was amiss. She shouldn't be surprised—he was a damned good actor, it would seem.

He looked back at her, a myriad of emotions playing over his moon-kissed features. "Please, let me explain—"

"No," she snapped, cutting off his whispered plea. God, he must have thought her such a fool, blithely accepting his every word as truth. She wanted to shout at him, slap him for the deceit. But there was nothing she could do now. Now, more than ever, she couldn't be discovered with him. "Go, now, before he comes and finds me."

He hesitated, staring at her with stricken eyes. Her own eyes pricked with tears, but she'd die before she let a single tear fall. Crossing her arms tightly across her chest, she glanced to Richard. Panic swooped through her—he was walking toward them! She turned pleading eyes to the liar before her. "Please, *hurry.*"

"This isn't over," he threatened, his voice hushed but vehement. "We *will* have a proper talk." With a growl of frustration, he spun on his heel and stalked away. The panic from the fear of being discovered eased within her, but that only made room for the other, equally unwelcoming emotions roiling within her to come to the surface. Betrayal seemed to fill her lungs, suffocating her.

She collapsed onto the stone bench and dropped her forehead to her palm. *Hastings.* Her Hastings, the one she had considered to be one of her closest, dearest friends, a boy she had even imagined herself in love with, only to have the rug so cruelly pulled from beneath her. Her confidant of all those years; a person who knew her backward and forward—*this* was the man who had been staying with them these past few days? The man who had changed everything about how she viewed the world when he had blithely sent her that last letter, pulling the wool from her eyes on the true nature of men. The ground suddenly seemed to spin, and she squeezed her eyes closed, fighting for breath.

He had lied to her—lied to her *face*.

Disbelief nearly paralyzed her. He had been here all this time. He knew who she was. He knew her through dozens, perhaps hundreds of letters. Yet he had not revealed himself to her. After he had kissed her right here in the garden, looked into her eyes, and spent days conversing with her—all of it was a lie?

Up on the terrace, Benedict greeted Richard with a slap on the shoulder before herding him inside. She narrowed her eyes. She'd deal with Richard's part in this later. It was more than enough to attempt to handle Benedict's betrayal, especially with the taste of him still fresh on her tongue.

She couldn't face him. She couldn't face *anyone*. The thought of sitting across from him at supper and attempting to maintain small talk as if nothing had happened was enough to nauseate her. Maybe tomorrow she would be equal to the task of giving the man a proper thrashing. Not tonight. All the hurt, and anger, and betrayal she had felt seven years ago rioted within her.

She came up short. Oh no. Oh good heavens, no one could know she knew he was Hastings. If Richard and Benedict were keeping up the farce for her benefit, then they absolutely had to continue doing so, because if Papa discovered that Hastings was beneath his roof, he might very well kill the man.

A corner of her mouth curled up. Perhaps not *kill*, though he most definitely deserved it, but at the very least, Papa would be extremely displeased. Only he was privy to Evie's embarrassment after Hastings's last letter. If Papa became upset, then Mama would want to know why. If Mama ever discovered Evie's stupid actions of that day, she would have more than enough ammunition to demand Evie continue indefinitely on the marriage mart.

After all, if Evie had once been such a fool for love, there was hope for it again.

Evie's shiver had nothing to do with the chilly night air. She could not allow Benedict to reveal to the others his true name. She wouldn't let him ruin her chance when everything she wanted was nearly within reach.

Blast and damn, there was nothing for it. She had to talk to him—alone.

But first she had to get through dinner.

From his position just inside the tree line, Ned Barney watched the young woman open the glass terrace door and slip back into the house. She must be a family member. Her clothes were much too fine for a servant. Not that it mattered who she was—he wanted only to find Hastings, not some chit who sat for ages in the cold for no good reason.

Favoring his left leg, he pushed away from the tree he had been leaning against, its rough bark biting into his palms. There was no doubt this was the correct house—it was large enough for a king, let alone a marquis—but the enormous dwelling created some challenges. With dozens of servants milling about outside and in, he would have to wait for his quarry to leave the safety of the grounds. With his reduced mobility, he couldn't trust that he could get away in time if someone spotted him close to the house.

Barney pulled his travel-worn coat closer about his body, warding off the increasingly chilly night air. He had everything he needed to sleep in the woods, but without the luxury of making a fire, he did not look forward to the prospect. No, he would stay in the inn tonight and come round tomorrow morning to resume his vigil.

He could be patient. He'd waited this long, after all, to get his revenge on the bastard who had robbed him of so much. He paused to rub his aching leg, savoring the icy burn of cold fury filling his chest. When Hastings had snitched and blown the whole smuggling ring to hell, Barney had avoided capture by jumping from the ship into the inky black seawater below. Though he had escaped with his life, the broken leg resulting from the fall had failed to heal properly, and he would never be the man he was before the raid.

Just as he would never be able to make the kind of money he once did as a smuggler. He limped back to where he had left his horse, a grim smile on his lips.

Let the bastard sleep snug tonight. Sooner or later he would emerge, and when he did, his opponent would be waiting.

Weary to his very core, Benedict shut the door to his suite. Slowly, carefully, he shrugged out of his jacket and hefted its weight in his hand. It would have to do. With all the pent-up fury within him, he hurled it with all his might across the room. It spread out midflight and floated harmlessly to the floor on the other side of the bed.

He wished it were something breakable—his mother's prized Ming vase, for example—something that would crash to the floor and break into a million pieces. He rubbed a heavy hand over the back of his neck and dropped into the upholstered bench at the foot of the bed. But he didn't need to break anything. No, he had managed that bloody brilliantly in the garden.

As long as he lived, Benedict doubted if the look on her face would ever dim in his memory. And he couldn't even thrash Richard for unmasking him—Benedict certainly couldn't tell the man he had been locked in a passionate kiss with Richard's sister when he had inadvertently ruined everything.

One by one, he yanked off his boots and carelessly dropped them to the floor. Ghastly couldn't begin to describe how miserable dinner had been. Evie, her skin as white as the gown she wore, had sat like a marble statue across from him, pleading weariness from the day's exertions when her father expressed concern.

He'd had to call on his years of training in order to maintain a normal facade, even managing to laugh with Richard about some ridiculous thing or another. Regardless of whom he was looking at or talking to, his every sense had been trained on Evie, willing her to forgive him, to give him a chance to explain. To not hate him.

Somehow he got the impression that for her not to hate him was on the far side of impossible. And really, he deserved no less. That, however, did not stop him from wanting more.

He had to go to her. He yanked out his watch fob and checked the time. It was nearly eleven o'clock. He would wait another hour to ensure that the family and servants were abed, but not a minute longer.

With nervous energy still coursing through his body,

he stood and began unbuttoning his shirt. He needed to clear his mind. He was no good to anyone in the state he was in. He changed into the lightweight pants he used for practicing, lit a few more candles, and retrieved his foil.

The motions were so familiar to him, he didn't need to think, only move. He concentrated on each breath and listened to the pounding of his own heartbeat. *Advance, advance, ballestra, retreat, retreat, recovery. Lunge!* He went through all of the drills he had practiced for years, from simple to complicated. He ignored the pouring sweat, the screaming of his muscles, the pounding of his heart.

A soft tap at the door stopped him midthrust, his pulse thundering in his ears. Hope roared to life within him as he snapped upright and tossed his foil atop the bed. Before he could take three steps, the door swung open.

And then there she was.

Evie slipped inside and shut the door before turning to face him. Benedict swallowed, arrested in his place by the sight of her. She looked as though she had just risen from bed, wearing a voluminous, white night rail and wrapper, with her hair plaited in a long rope tumbling over her shoulder. She should have looked innocent; instead she looked like a warrior poised for battle.

She was beautiful—and nearly glowing with the force of her fury.

"You deceitful, spurious, villainous, loathsome, cowardly *bastard*."

Each word shoved a knife deeper into his chest. No one could quite craft an insult like Evie. He dipped his head slightly. "I agree completely."

She hesitated for the space of a breath, her fiery gaze flitting over his body. He was suddenly very aware of her presence here in his room, late at night, and of his wearing naught but a thin pair of linen pants. Judging by the way her chin hitched up an inch or so, he'd wager she realized the same thing.

She drew a sharp breath and pointed an accusatory finger at him. "Don't think you can sweet-talk me by agreeing with me. You've made a mockery of me in my own home, laughing at me as I trusted you, all the while knowing I would never stand for the likes of you at the Hall if I knew who you really were, *Hastings.*" She spit his name as if it were poison on her tongue.

"I wasn't mocking you, Evie," he said, nearly growling the words.

"Not mocking? Well, I should very much hate to see what you believe mocking to be if not this." Her hands swished through the air, vaguely encompassing the two of them and the interaction they had shared. "You took advantage of my ignorance, purposely spending time with me. Why? Was it so amusing to toy with me? A cat stalking its pathetic mouse?"

"I didn't toy with you—"

"You *kissed* me," she nearly shouted, cutting him off. "How could you do that?"

The hurt in her eyes plunged the knife the rest of the way into his heart. Damn it to hell, how had things come to this? How had he bungled his life so badly that he had hurt one of the few people on the planet who truly *meant* something to him? "I have no excuse, Evie. I tried to stay away, but I couldn't."

"No, you couldn't, could you? It was entirely too much fun to toy with the stupid girl who used to write you. How you and Richard must have laughed at how easy it was to make me the fool."

The low candlelight couldn't hide the twin spots of color high on her cheeks. Her eyes were shining, heavy with the dew of unshed tears. He took another step forward, wanting, irrationally, to comfort her somehow— to draw her into his arms and soothe her pain away. His advancement only made her ball her fists at her sides.

"Evie, it wasn't like that—it was *never* like that. I panicked when I realized you were here. I thought your family was in London for the Season, and when I ran into you at the stables, all I could think of was how stupid I had been so many years ago by ending our friendship the way I did. I didn't want to hurt you by dredging up old memories."

"So you lied?" She shook her head, setting loose a few golden wisps of hair from her braid. "What a brilliant plan. Lie about your name so as to avoid the repercussions, all the while convincing yourself it is all for my own good. Forgive me if I don't fall on my knees in gratitude for your magnanimous gesture."

He gritted his teeth. God, how he wanted to just tell her everything, starting with why he wrote that cursed letter, pouring his heart out about all of it, including the betrayal that had rocked him to his very soul. It would feel so damned good to have it out, to have one person in the world be privy to all his secrets and understand what he was facing. She might be angry, but he knew her well enough to know her heart would break for him. He knew without any doubt she would forgive him if he confided in her.

But he couldn't.

Not because he didn't trust her. Not because she wasn't worthy. No, as much as he wanted to explain why he did what he did, it would only be an excuse, an unburdening of his troubles that would serve only to cast his motives in a better light. It would be the truth, but in the end it would only cause more heartbreak for her. Why would he bring her into his confidence now? Especially when there was nothing she could do—nothing anyone could do—to make things better.

No, his secrets would leave with him, but somehow he had to figure out a way to vanquish the hurt and unhappiness from her eyes.

He took another step closer, keeping his gaze trained on hers. "You are right. I was an absolute idiot. I've never forgiven myself for that horrible letter. I was young, and stupid, and there have been many times when I have thought on that moment and wished I could undo it."

She stood there seething, her arms crossed protectively over her chest. "Yes, well, wishing will get you exactly nothing. You *crushed* me that day. I thought you were my friend, and you stomped my heart with only a handful of words."

"I know. It was bloody wretched of me." He rubbed a hand over the bunched muscles of his neck. He was desperate to make her feel better, to soothe her somehow. "I was scared of what I was feeling for you—a girl I had never met. I didn't know how to handle it, and I was terrified of meeting you in person. I was only eighteen, and I made a bad decision."

"And I was only sixteen," she exclaimed, her delicate eyebrows arching up with the passion of her words.

"Yes, only sixteen. Young enough to forget me. I was just an amusement to you, someone to banter with when it pleased you."

"Someone to ban—" She stopped and squeezed her eyes shut, shaking her head in protest. "You weren't some amusement to me, Benedict. It wasn't some sort of game to me, as it apparently was to you."

"It wasn't a game to me, either," he insisted, taking yet another step toward her. "I wasn't exaggerating. I cared for you."

"But I *loved* you!"

Chapter Seventeen

All teasing aside, I shall always smile for you, Hastings. Mama and Papa have agreed to allow me to come. These next few months shall be very long indeed.

—*From Evie to Hastings*

As soon as the words escaped, Evie gasped, her hand flying to her mouth as if to call them back.

Benedict's own shock kept him rooted to the floor. She loved him? *Loved him?* No one had ever said those words to him. He had never known the comfort of love or even affection. His father had ignored him, his mother actively disdained him, and his brother had viewed Benedict as his inferior. He couldn't name the silvery flash of emotion that simultaneously heated his blood and chilled his heart.

She had loved him, and he had tossed her aside. In the light of her revelation, the words of that damned letter went from harsh to heinous. He imagined her as she must have been, a beautiful, spirited girl, wounded by the strokes of his quill. And he saw her as she was now, trembling with the force of her emotions, devastated by his betrayal. Resolve threaded through him, hot and fast, steeling his bones and sharpening his vision.

He would leave tomorrow no matter what.

He would go to his superiors when he reached London. He would tell them everything and let the chips fall where they may. He wouldn't cover the sins of another, no matter how many good people would be hurt by the truth; no matter how much his reputation would be damaged; no matter how unjust the consequences would be.

A single tear spilled down Evie's cheek, and she dashed it away angrily. God, he couldn't bear seeing her hurting so much, knowing it was all his fault. He reached for her, wanting to comfort her. She slapped his hands away, backing up until she bumped against the wall. "Don't you dare touch me. I said *loved*, not love. I am no longer a silly girl with naive notions filling my head. You made sure of that."

"Evie, I am so sorry. I never wanted to hurt you."

She scowled at him, disdain wrapping around her like a cloak. "Save your apologies for someone who cares. I'm not here to be subjected to more of your lies."

Pushing away from the wall, she skirted around him and went to the wing chair before the fireplace. She clutched the high back, keeping the furniture between them like a shield. "You owe me, Benedict. You've come into my home like a battering ram, and you owe me."

What was she getting at? He walked to where she stood, allowing her to keep the chair between them. "What is it that you want?"

Evie squared her shoulders, tilting her head as if to look down on him. Candlelight flickered in her eyes, reflecting the fire within. "You mustn't tell anyone that I know who you really are."

His brow knitted in confusion. It wasn't at all what he had expected. "Why not?"

He studied her expression. With her lips pressed in a thin line and her posture one of icy composure, she seemed to be withdrawing from her fury, moving to cold indifference instead. Only the rapid rise and fall of her chest betrayed her agitation.

"I don't wish to complicate things with my family before they leave for London."

She was lying. It was a valid enough reason, but he didn't believe her for a minute. Something else was going on, he'd wager his life on it. He shook his head slowly. "No, there is something you're not telling me. What is it?"

"I don't know what you're talking about. You know very well how important it is that my parents not be upset. I don't want anything to interfere with my plans to stay here."

"That's part of it, to be sure. But that is certainly not your only reason. I know you better than that."

Her nostrils flared as she glared at him. "You dare presume—"

"Yes, I do. There is a reason you don't want the others to know who I am. What is it?"

"Fine," she bit out, digging her fingers into the cushioned fabric. "My father would call you out if he learned of your deceit."

"He'd be displeased, to be sure, but I doubt he'd call me out. Richard was part of the ruse, after all."

"You're wrong. It's not the ruse; it's *you.*"

"Why me? I know you never spoke of the way things ended. If you had, Richard would have been the first to know."

She shook her head. "Richard wasn't here. My father was, and he does know."

"For God's sake, Evie, it was seven years ago. I doubt he would call a man out for writing an ill-worded letter, especially since I was hardly more than a boy at the time."

"You don't know anything about what he'd do. He despises you, and I won't have you upsetting him."

"He *despises* me? That makes no sense at all. You're leaving something out; I'm sure of it. What is it?"

"It's none of your concern—"

"It *is* my concern! Something must have happened that would cause your father to despise me. Just knowing I sent a bungled letter isn't enough to warrant that reaction."

"Yes—"

"No! Tell me, Evie," he begged, stepping closer still. "What happened?"

"I went after you," she cried, her eyes flashing furiously.

Benedict reared in surprise. "What?"

"I packed a bag, I saddled my horse, and I went after you." She hung her head, refusing to meet his searching gaze. "A groom alerted my father when my horse was missing come morning, and he rode out to find me, galloping as hard as his horse would carry him. I nearly ruined myself for a foolish, childish infatuation."

She looked up then, her face tight. "He was very kind, despite his fury. He saw how dreadfully my heart was broken. He promised to keep my secret, and over the next few days he kept me by his side. That was when I started spending more time in the stables with him. It gave me something else to focus on other than Hastings the Betrayer."

Benedict sucked in a sharp breath. Hastings the Betrayer? No other words could have turned him inside out more effectively. He knew what betrayal felt like. It had been tearing him to pieces since the moment Henry's words had reached Benedict's ears as he crouched in the dark, fog-shrouded courtyard in Folkestone not a week earlier.

She straightened her spine, meeting his eyes straight on. "I don't want Papa to know you are here, because I don't want him to react protectively. I don't care if he thrashes you within an inch of your life, but I don't want him to feel the need to keep me by his side once more. And I can't bear to see pity in his eyes when he looks at me."

Benedict studied Evie, her stiff shoulders and stubborn, hurt eyes. Everything inside him was telling him that he could make things better by soothing her hurt and calming her soul if he could only wrap her in his arms to hold her, to say the things to her with his body that he couldn't say with words.

But she wouldn't let him near her, not without a compelling reason. He straightened as a thought occurred to him. It was risky, but what did he have to lose?

"I'll hold my tongue," he said quietly, watching her carefully, "for the price of a kiss."

Evie drew back as if he'd slapped her. How could he dare ask such a thing of her? What kind of heartless cur demanded such a thing of a lady? Especially of one who had been as thoroughly abused as she. With all the coldness she felt in her heart, she said, "You've already extracted your price, sir. This very night, as a matter of fact."

He didn't flinch; he didn't back down in the least. "It is the price of my silence now, my lady. A kiss will secure my promise, but anything less and I will tell your father everything."

She cast about for something to say, anything that would get through his thick, uncaring skull. "Why would you do such a thing? Haven't you hurt me enough? And I am not exaggerating; my father hates you for what you did to his little girl."

"Of that I have no doubt."

Evie cursed beneath her breath in frustration. Had he always been such a bastard and she had simply been blind to it? "You won't do it. You may be spiteful, but you must have some interest in self-preservation."

His dark gaze bored into her like a physical force. "If you refuse to meet my terms, then I swear to you, I will announce the truth at the breakfast table. I will *not* back down from this. If you test me, you and I will both pay the consequences."

His words were spoken with such unnatural calm, it sent a shiver straight up Evie's spine. He was serious. Blast him, he would do it.

She shook with impotent fury. "Fine, take your pound of flesh. I just hope to God I never have to lay eyes on you again."

His posture never changed, but his expression somehow gentled. He seemed . . . relieved? Through her anger, confusion niggled at the back of her mind. Why didn't he seem as satisfied as she expected? There wasn't a hint of smugness touching his features as he drew a breath and slowly stepped around the chair.

He moved like a trainer approaching a skittish colt — gently, deliberately. Candlelight bathed his chest in golden light, accentuating the hard planes of muscles beneath his smooth skin. Against her will, her heart began to flutter, the blasted traitor. Sandalwood reached her nose, masculine and enticing. She tried to hold still, but of their own volition, her feet carried her backward, retreating from the spell he cast on her.

His eyes were soft, his expression unexpectedly sweet as he followed her. She bumped into the wall; there was no more room for retreat. Steeling herself against the emotions suddenly rioting within her, she clenched her jaw and waited.

He stepped so close, they were almost touching. Then, placing his hands against the wall, one on either side of her head, he leaned down until his lips were only inches from hers, close enough that his breath fanned across her cheek. It was beyond intoxicating. Her heart raced, her blood roaring through her veins as she focused on his lips. She knew exactly how they felt against hers, and her whole body ached to feel them against her once more. She fought against her body's betrayal, forcing herself to think of his lies.

When his lips touched hers, it wasn't the crushing assault she expected. The kiss was featherlight, achingly tender. Warmth spread through her, and she balled her hands at her sides to keep from touching him.

He pulled away the slightest amount and looked at her, almost too close for her to focus on him. "Evie," he breathed, cupping her face in his hands. "Forgive me."

His pressed another kiss to her lips, then turned her head so he could kiss her on each cheek. "I'm not afraid of your father, because he could never hate me more than I hate myself for hurting you." Tilting her head down, he kissed the corners of her eyes and the tip of her nose.

"I regretted that letter almost as soon as I wrote it." He was whispering now, and he leaned down to feather little kisses along her jaw. "I tried to stay away from you this week and maintain a distance between us, but I couldn't. No matter how hard I tried, I simply couldn't."

His mouth found hers again, and this time, she couldn't resist. She kissed him back. How could she not? He had invaded her every thought for days. The man she had once loved and lost was here before her, begging her forgiveness.

He groaned against her lips as she gave in to him, wrapping his arms around her and pulling her to him. Somehow her hands were on his back, exploring the smooth expanse of his dampened skin. It was hard to think, hard to do anything but feel as he opened his mouth to her and deepened the kiss. Her fingertips slid down his back and skimmed along the rough fabric of his pants.

His hands descended as well, following the nip of her waist and then the curve of her hips. She moaned when he cupped her bottom and pulled her against him, sending heat licking through her body like a spreading fire.

If she lived a thousand years, she would never forget the feel of his body against her, the surge of desire as their tongues intertwined, the weightlessness that overcame her as she wondered what was next.

Whatever his sins, in that moment, he was hers.

He had to get a hold of himself.

If he didn't, Evie would be well and truly ruined by morning. His body sang at the thought, vivid images of the two of them tangled in his bed making his pulse thunder. His fingers itched to pull the fabric from her body, to unbraid her hair and set her naked atop the counterpane.

He groaned against her lips at the image, giving her bottom a little squeeze. No, he had to stop this, to leave her future intact. It was all he had left to give her. She couldn't be his—no matter how desperately he wished otherwise.

With an act of will greater than any he had ever achieved in his life, he pulled his lips from hers, hugging her to him as he panted for air. Why did the right thing have to feel so wrong?

He pulled back and looked at her, gritting his teeth to keep from kissing her again. Her eyelids were heavy with the unmistakable look of seduction, her lips swollen and rosy. "You are the most beautiful, enchanting, irresistible woman I have ever known."

She smiled slowly, uncharacteristic shyness touching her features.

"Please say that you can forgive me and my utter stupidity of the last decade or so."

"I suppose I can. If you truly mean it."

"After a kiss like that, can you doubt the way I feel about you?" He resisted the urge to gather her up in his arms and take her to bed right then and there.

"No, I suppose I can't."

He rubbed his hands up and down her arms, unable to let her go altogether. "I swear to you, not only will I breathe not a word to your family, but I will be leaving here tomorrow."

A frown marred her beautiful lips. "So soon?"

He couldn't help himself; he dropped a kiss to her lips once more. God, what he wouldn't give to have the option of sweeping her off her feet and making her his own. She could work in the stables until her heart was content, so long as she spent her nights by his side as his wife. He drew in a deep breath through his nose before pulling away from her.

But he wasn't free—at least he wouldn't be by the end of the week. "I don't want to risk endangering your plans any more than I already have. What if Richard slips up again, only this time in your father's presence?"

She sighed and nodded. "You are absolutely right." She threaded her hands in his and squeezed. "Please, stay as long as the hunt. We never did have that race we planned all those years ago."

He knew he should leave first thing. It was a long trip to London, and now that he had made his decision on what to do, he wanted it done with as soon as possible. He looked into her eyes, drinking in the smile she offered him—*him*, not James Benedict. He could not resist her. He had little to offer her, but he could grant her this. He nodded once. "Very well. I should love to ride by your side once more."

"Until tomorrow, then." She reached on her toes and pressed a kiss to his lips before turning and heading for the door. "Oh, and Benedict?" she said, pausing before the door.

"Yes?"

"No more secrets between us, all right?"

If she asked the right questions, he wouldn't lie in his answers. But he wouldn't volunteer the information. Besides, with him leaving tomorrow, it was unlikely ever to come up. He lifted one corner of his mouth and nodded. "You have my word."

Chapter Eighteen

After five years, I will finally learn the voice of the words I know by heart? A very interesting prospect, I must admit. Will I know you when I see you? Oddly, I think yes.

— From Hastings to Evie

She had well and properly been kissed last night.

Evie fought to keep the giddy expression from her face as her maid meticulously braided Evie's hair into a hunting-appropriate coiffure. It wasn't easy. She wanted to giggle like a schoolgirl and gush about the toe-curling, butterfly-inducing kisses she had shared with Benedict. Morgan would probably faint to hear of Evie's outrageous behavior.

All these years, her view of the world had been so tainted by the disastrous end to her relationship with Hastings—Benedict. But this morning, after she had awakened from a night full of blush-inducing dreams, it occurred to her that perhaps she had been wrong to want to shut herself off from men like that. Looking back, she realized how very young and silly she had been.

And now—now she was different. Benedict's apology had been sincere. She believed he had never meant to hurt her like that. Their kisses had been an epiphany. She had never thought to marry, but now, all she could think about was waking up to Benedict every morning, embracing him, and feeling his body against hers.

"My lady, are you quite all right?"

Evie blinked and looked at her maid in the mirror. "I beg your pardon?"

"You look quite flushed all of a sudden, and I'd hate to think you were getting sick."

If her face hadn't been completely red before, it certainly was now. "Yes, yes, of course I'm fine, Morgan. I'm simply eager for the hunt."

She smiled weakly, and Morgan nodded and went back to work. Eager for the hunt, indeed. She could hardly wait to see Benedict again, especially atop Brutus. Perhaps he didn't need to leave quite so soon. Another night couldn't hurt, surely. Perhaps they could meet beneath the stars once more, only this time late at night, without the threat of being discovered.

When at last her hair was done, Evie headed for the breakfast room. Unfortunately, everyone was in attendance except Benedict and Papa, who as usual was already at the stables. She tried to keep her mind on the conversations at hand, but after one too many looks of curiosity from Mama, Evie decided to give up. "I believe I will head to the stable block to check on the horses."

Carolyn waved, a piece of half-eaten toast in hand. "Evie, say hello to the cute little fox for us when you let him go."

Richard rolled his eyes at this. "They are not *cute,* Carolyn, they are vermin!"

"They are so cute," Jocelyn said, mischief glinting in her cornflower blue eyes. "And I wish I could pet one."

Richard dragged a hand over his face and glared at Evie. "See what you have done? I won't be surprised if there are foxes on leashes roaming the house the next time I am home."

Carolyn grinned impishly. "Really? Can I have a pet fox? They are such adorable little creatures."

Evie laughed out loud at the aghast expression on Richard's face. "They aren't vermin, but they are wild, Carolyn. Perhaps we should get you a ferret instead."

Richard threw up his hands. "Ugh, I give up. Why don't you have a wolf den in here while you are at it?"

Evie took pity on her brother. "Have no fear—we shan't be bringing any foxes, alive or dead, back from this hunt. Remember, this is to be a drag hunt. The hunt master laid the trail this morning, and we asked for him to keep the course fairly small." She patted his arm. "It will be great fun, you'll see. And really, it's not as though you would have ever seen the fox in the first place."

Richard's jaw dropped at the teasing insult. His head swiveled between Evie and their mother before he exclaimed in mock outrage, "Mother! Are you going to allow her to speak to me that way?"

Mama chuckled at Richard's outrage. "Now, now, children. We mustn't quarrel at the breakfast table."

As Evie rose, Beatrice set her silverware down. "Actually, I'd rather like a spot of fresh air. May I join you, Evie?"

Evie raised an eyebrow. Beatrice hated the stables. Now what was the girl up to? "Yes, of course."

After pausing to get their hats and gloves in place, they headed outside. The sun peaked from behind wispy clouds—the perfect weather for a ride. As they padded down the stairs and stepped onto the gravel pathway, Beatrice linked arms with her. "I'm sorry we quarreled the other day."

So much had happened since then, Evie had forgotten completely about their tiff. "Yes, me, too. You are my sister, and I love you very much."

"And I you, which is why I had to try again, when we

both weren't so upset." She looked uneasy, fidgeting with the green buttons of her spencer jacket. "He's Hastings, Evie. That was what I was trying to tell you yesterday."

She paused, cringing a bit as if waiting for an explosion. Evie cringed, too. Beatrice knew he was Hastings as well? Of course. If her head hadn't been so filled with the events of the evening, she would have realized that was what Beatrice had tried to warn her about before. Drat—what to say? Should Evie reveal that she already knew, or pretend ignorance? Either way, she had to be sure Beatrice wouldn't breathe a word of it to anyone else.

She sighed and patted Beatrice's hand. She didn't want to lie. "Yes, I figured that out for myself yesterday."

Her sister's eyes widened at Evie's revelation. "Are you all right? I thought you would have been upset."

"I was. But then we talked, and by the end of it I could understand why he didn't want me to know he was here."

They walked a few paces in silence as Beatrice worried her lip. "You're not mad that I kept his secret in the first place? Richard made me promise not to tell and threatened to stop sending me paints."

"Then we shall have to devise the perfect punishment for our bothersome brother, won't we?"

Beatrice grinned. "Yes, I think so."

"And no, I'm not mad. I do have a very big favor to ask, however." Evie hesitated before going on. "If anyone asks, you must of course always tell the truth, but if the question of Benedict's name does not come up, could you not volunteer it?"

Beatrice stopped and looked to her in confusion. "You don't want Mama and Papa knowing that he's Hastings?"

"Not if they don't ask. If I'm perfectly honest, I rather

like spending time with him, and I should hate to ruin that by upsetting Mama and Papa."

Beatrice grinned. "He is rather handsome, is he not?"

"Indeed," Evie said, her cheeks heating at the thought of last night. "So you'll keep mum? I mean, his name is Benedict, after all."

"Very well. But only because I'd like to know more about what's making you blush. Very intriguing."

She knew she loved her sister for a reason. "Thank you, Bea. I won't forget about this. If ever you need me, I promise to be there for you." She gave her sister a quick hug. "I don't imagine you want to join me in the stables, do you?"

Beatrice wrinkled her nose. "No, I'll leave that to you. I'll see you in a bit."

Alone at last, Evie hurried toward the stable block, eager to get the morning started. The faster the hunt arrived, the faster she would see Benedict once more. If she could convince him to stay for another night, then after the hunt, when darkness fell and the stars lit the garden once more, things could get very interesting indeed.

Firmly suppressing the giddy grin on her face, she pushed aside the heavy stable door. Inside, a sort of organized chaos filled the building. Horses and stable hands were everywhere, in various stages of preparation. The sounds of voices, horses whinnying, and muffled dog barking echoed in the open space, making her smile. She loved hunt day. She nodded to Jasper, who was leading Epona from her stall. Nearby, Brutus flicked his freshly trimmed tail as a groom checked his hooves.

"There you are," her father said, looking up from his inspection of Ronan's saddle. He brushed off his hands and strode toward her. "An exceedingly fine day for a jaunt through the woods, wouldn't you say?"

"Indeed it is. How is Ronan this morning?"

Pride shone in Papa's eyes. "Magnificent. I'm not entirely certain which of the two of us is biting at the bit more, so to speak."

Evie laughed. "Well, we'd best get on with the preparation so we can get you out in the field."

Behind her, the door scraped.

Evie looked up in time to see Benedict arrive. Her breath caught when he looked up and immediately met her eyes, as if he had known exactly where she would be. Their gazes held for just a moment—barely even that— before he lifted a hand in greeting and started toward them. In that brief moment, Evie's breath froze in her lungs and the hair on her arms stood straight out.

Oh, good gracious—she was in trouble.

"Are you all right, Evie?"

Evie jerked to attention. Papa regarded her queerly, his eyebrows drawn together. No, she was not all right. She was very, very far from being all right. She blinked at her father and tried to gather herself.

"Er, yes, fine. Why ever do you ask?" Evie replied with as much nonchalance as she could muster.

"Just that you look quite peaked. Are you too warm?"

The humid air of the stables was quite a bit warmer than outside. Yes, that excuse worked just fine with her. "A little. I was outside in the sun for a few minutes with Beatrice. Oh, look—there is Mr. Benedict."

Her father turned to greet Benedict, and she blew out a slow breath. She most certainly did *not* want her father to suspect the direction of her thoughts just then.

Chapter *Nineteen*

*I may not know you by your countenance, but I should
like to think that I should know you by a single phrase,
as such has been the nature of our correspondence. I
feel as if I know you best among all.*
— *From Evie to Hastings*

A sucker punch to the gut.

That was the feeling that assaulted Benedict
when he stepped inside and looked up to see Evie's un-
guarded expression. She was watching him as if . . . as if
he were something to *devour*. In that half-second space
of time before he broke eye contact, her expression had
instantly heated his blood to near boiling.

Bloody hell.

With so many witnesses around, he sincerely hoped
his expression wouldn't give something away. Something, for example, such as how mere eye contact with
Evie had him imagining all sorts of inappropriate
things—none of which involved clothing. Good Lord, if
anyone had known of the rush of desire he felt just then,
he would have been thrown out on his ear—and that
was the *best*-case scenario.

Pulling himself together, he greeted the marquis.
"Good day to you, my lord. Are you looking forward to
the day ahead?"

Lord Granville smiled warmly and replied, "There is

nothing in the world I would rather be doing today. And you, sir?"

"I'm very much looking forward to it."

And finally, he turned to Evie. "Are you eager to begin, Evie?"

Their secret burned between them, hot and delicious. The smile she gave him was slow and deliberate, as if she were imagining right then what she wanted to do with him. God knew he was imagining it. She licked those perfect lips and said, "Oh, indeed I am thrilled, Benedict. And you?"

He nodded in return, not trusting his voice to speak.

"Excellent. I do hope you won't fall behind." Her words were completely proper, but the hint of lust in her eyes was enough to make him regret his decision to stop things before they went too far last evening.

"For your sake, I shall try to keep up," he said, smiling blandly.

She nodded to him, and the marquis turned the conversation to the preparations at hand. It took an act of will to keep his eyes off Evie as he nodded and pretended interest in what her father was saying.

Within the hour, the whole family and a handful of the servants were gathered in the courtyard and ready to go. Benedict studiously avoided staring at Evie, no matter how appealing she looked sitting tall on Epona. When at last everyone was mounted—or "stuffed into carriages," depending on who was asked—Granville nodded, and they were off.

They proceeded slowly toward the lake where Lady Granville and the girls would spend the day. Ahead, the sound of giggles, laughs, and the occasional shriek could be heard from the elegant carriage as it ambled toward their destination.

With Richard chatting with his father at the head of

the pack, Benedict let his mount fall back until he was even with Evie. If not for the small, knowing smile touching her lips, no one would ever guess that they had shared such passion between them last night.

He smiled at her, taking in her brilliant eyes that mirrored the sky so perfectly, and her slightly flushed cheeks, and those lips—he knew very well how soft her lips were. "You're beautiful."

Pleasure lit her features, and the smile she gave back was enough to make him shift his position in his saddle. "Beautiful enough to keep you here for another day?"

He blinked in surprise. Last night, she had brooked no argument to his plans to leave today. Why the change? It didn't matter. He couldn't risk it. The more he was in her company, the more he wanted to *be* in her company. It was best to end things now, on a positive note. He wanted to look back on this day for years and smile at the one perfect day they shared before his life went to hell.

"*Too* beautiful to keep me near you. I find I am sorely lacking in willpower when it comes to you, my dear. I wouldn't want anything to happen that you'd regret. I couldn't live with myself if I hurt you more."

She bit her lip, adjusting her hold on the reins. It was clear she wished to say something. Benedict kept his peace until at last she took a breath and said, "I didn't really want to go last night."

He breathed in the words, savoring their meaning. She would be the death of him, he was sure. He sighed and looked to her. "I didn't want you to, either."

"But still you didn't stop me."

"I thought I was doing the right thing. I was trying to be a gentleman."

She nodded and looked down, smoothing a hand over Epona's neck. Pressing her lips together, Evie looked him straight in the eye. "What if I don't want you to be a gentleman? Tonight, I mean."

"Evie, I don't want you to get hurt. When I leave, I won't be returning any time soon." He couldn't do this. He had to move on, to leave her while she was still uninvolved with the tangles snagging his life.

"All the more reason for us to enjoy the time we have." She paused for a moment before saying quietly, "I have a feeling the stars will be out again tonight."

Damn it to hell, he shouldn't be here now, let alone ten hours from now. Why couldn't they have met when he was free to pursue her? He drew in a deep breath, settling into Brutus's rhythm. "I've already made plans to depart at the conclusion of the hunt. My things have been packed, and Richard knows of my intent."

"So?"

"So he'd wonder if I suddenly decided to extend my stay. He already knows I'm anxious to be done with the farce."

She eyed him with a single brow raised, her head tilted to one side so that the sunshine bathed the kissable column of her neck. The slightest smile curled her lips. "We'll see about that."

With that, she clucked her tongue and set off ahead.

Across the field, a few paces into the tree line, Ned Barney crouched in the underbrush, watching as the straggling pair pushed forward to catch up with their party. Pushing a stringy lock of hair from his face, he sat back and grinned. With that hot piece dangling in front of his target, Barney would have no problem completing his mission. Benedict was so distracted, Barney could probably walk right up to the man, arm outstretched and pistol in hand, and he still would not notice him.

When the servant had set to the woods this morning

dragging a cloth, Barney had known his chance was coming. He had waited until the man left before settling in a small clearing not far from one of the trees the man had marked. It was a good location, and he had already determined his overland escape route after the deed was done.

Chuckling, he struggled to his feet, wincing at the pain despite having favored his left leg. He retreated into the forest to retrieve his mount, which he had left tied to a tree limb. He shook his head and grinned. This was going to be like shooting hens in a pen.

Benedict tightened his grip on the reins as he watched Evie pull away. She sat tall in her saddle, a prim yet alluring silhouette. He wanted to go after the little minx, but of course he couldn't. That would only serve to call attention to them.

Instead, he held Brutus steady and contemplated the loss of his sanity even as he watched her body move in time with her horse's trot. The slightest hint of lemon flavored the sun-warmed air, and he found himself filling his lungs with her scent. Perhaps it was not his sanity that was the issue. Common sense—now that he *knew* had gone out the window.

Ahead of them, the carriage slowed to a gentle stop. The moment the wheels ceased turning, the door burst open, causing the footman to race around to provide his hand before the girls could jump out on their own. They spilled out of the carriage in quick succession, each brushing out their skirts and adjusting their bonnets before making a beeline for Benedict. Lady Granville appeared a few moments later, her exasperated expression suggesting she was already rethinking the wisdom of bringing the trio along for the day.

In the amount of time that it took Benedict to dismount, all three of the younger girls had swarmed him like a small flock of birds. He smiled a bit uncomfortably at them as he tried to gain his footing—and a bit of breathing room.

"Er, you ladies must be eager to spend the day in such a glorious location." Benedict said, surreptitiously backing up a step.

"Oh yes, Benedict, it is so lovely here." Carolyn batted her golden eyelashes at him.

"It is absolutely wonderful at the lake. As a matter of fact, it is a much better way to spend the day than hunting," Jocelyn added.

Beatrice chimed in, "I should think it would be a far more relaxing day here than mucking about on horseback."

"I imagine you are correct, ladies, but the hunt will not last long. I am confident I will have the opportunity to spend plenty of time here as well."

It was truer than he wished to admit—the hunt *wouldn't* last long. Before he knew it, he would be back on the road to London, his time here naught but a memory. He'd accepted his duty, but Benedict didn't want to dwell on the rapidly approaching future. For the moment, he simply wanted to live in the excitement of the hunt, savoring the anticipation of racing beside Evie at last.

Out of the corner of his eye he caught Richard's grin. "Of course he will, my dears. As a matter of fact, he should have just enough time for you to take him on a tour when we return."

Benedict smiled while shooting daggers at his friend. "How delightful." Why the man enjoyed torturing him so much was beyond him.

"I thought it was your plan to leave us at the conclusion of the hunt." Evie's statement was said with complete sweetness, her face serenely innocent.

She was good; he would give her that.

"No, Benedict, you can't leave before supper," Carolyn exclaimed, hooking an arm through his. "Jocelyn and I have only just perfected our pianoforte duet. You've missed it once; please say that you will stay for our performance tonight."

"I—," he started to say, but Jocelyn interrupted before he could get the word out.

"And if you stay through supper, it certainly wouldn't make sense to leave so late at night." She turned to their mother, her eyes imploring. "Please tell him he's welcome here for as long as he likes."

"Now, now," Richard said, for once intervening. "If Benedict must be on his way, we mustn't delay him."

Lady Granville smiled at Benedict even as she gently disentangled her daughters from his arms. "Richard is correct. Although you are absolutely welcome to stay with us for as long as you wish, Mr. Benedict, even if that is only until the conclusion of the hunt."

Lord Granville looked up from adjusting the girth of Ronan's saddle, apparently having just noticed the topic of their discussion. "Why on earth would you want to leave after the hunt? Half the enjoyment is found in recounting the whole event in vivid and exaggerated detail over port after supper."

"Oh, I'm certain Mr. Benedict has more important matters to attend to than our post-hunt rituals." Evie smiled at him serenely, though her eyes danced with mirth. "Isn't that right, Benedict?"

All eyes were on him, and he could practically hear Evie's trap snap closed around him. He cleared his throat. "I had hoped to reach Berkhamsted by night's end. . . ."

"Bah, the inn in Berkhamsted is dismal," Granville said, waving a dismissive hand. "It's hardly worth the effort for a mere two-hour jump on your journey. No, best to get a good night's rest and set out early."

With everyone's attention on Benedict, Evie grinned at him. He was her own personal fox, and she had him well and truly cornered. Even as he tamped down on the frustration welling within him, part of him acknowledged that her sly manipulation gained him something he couldn't allow on his own—the opportunity to spend one last night with her.

Dipping his head, he said, "I thank you for your hospitality, sir, and of course I will be honored to stay another night."

Following an overly enthusiastic send-off from the girls, the hunting party was under way. They made their way to the appointed meeting ground, where a handful of participants, including several of the grooms, were waiting with the head huntsman and the dogs. Allowing the animals to warm up, they deliberately started the hunt several hundred feet away from where the scent was laid. With a slight breeze stirring the air, it wasn't long before the dogs were headed toward the trees in pursuit of the elusive scent. The party followed close behind into the forestland to the south, and within minutes had vanished into the trees.

Benedict listened to the rustling of dead leaves underfoot, the breathing of the horses, and the restless whining of the dogs as they descended deeper into the woods. Though the trees were without leaves, the sunlight did not quite penetrate the canopy and the air was noticeably cooler. The sunshine of the past two days had not been enough to dry the forest floor, and the dampness of wet leaves permeated the air. As the group progressed, the feeling of excitement and anticipation was nearly tangible.

With his horse's hooves padding rhythmically on the damp earth, Benedict found himself watching Evie more than the ground in front of him. He felt as if he needed to memorize the way she looked now, in her element, perched proudly and confidently atop her sleek horse. With the gold braiding and tassels swaying from her shoulders, she looked as brilliant as any captain heading into battle.

The sharp sting of a tree branch scraping his cheek snapped him to attention. He winced and touched his hand to his injured cheek. Blood smeared on his two fingers when he pulled them away. *Damn it.* He sighed and wiped his cheek with his shoulder.

"Great Scott, man, have you managed to bloody yourself already?" Richard pulled back on the reins lightly to wait for Benedict to catch up. Reaching into his pocket, Richard pulled out a delicate, silvery handkerchief and handed it over.

Benedict accepted the cloth and pressed it to his cheek. "First blood. Does that mean I win?"

Richard snorted. "Not if you draw it on yourself. I know this is your first time in these woods, but do try and keep up, old man."

Richard laughed as he pulled ahead, but Benedict got the last word in as Richard took off ahead of him. Pinching the handkerchief between his thumb and forefinger and waving it in the air, Benedict called after him, "Am I to keep your favor, then? Why, thank you, gentle maiden. I shall cherish it forever!"

At that moment the first dog picked up the scent, and immediately a cacophony of howling and barking filled the air and the pack bolted farther south. The atmosphere changed at once, suddenly charged with excitement. As if by magic, all of the apprehension and inner turmoil he had been feeling seemed to vanish. A huge grin sprang unbidden to his face, and he felt an instant surge of anticipation. Spurring his horse, Benedict bent low over Brutus's neck and let the familiar feeling of exhilaration wash over him. He relished the cool air rushing past his face, carrying away his worries like feathers in the wind.

The group followed loosely behind the baying dogs. While his mind had wandered, most of the field had pulled ahead and were a fair distance away already. Granville was at the lead, his newly acquired Irish hunter sprinting powerfully through the brush as the marquis leaned forward in the saddle. To the right of Granville was Evie, her body moving in perfect accord with Epona as she stormed ahead. Benedict grinned, pride welling within him. She moved as gracefully as any dancer he had ever seen, particularly with her knee hooked on the sidesaddle in what had to be an exceptionally uncomfortable position.

Benedict watched in snatches, keeping an eye on his own route as well. He increased his speed and arched toward the right, breaking away from Richard and falling into line almost behind Evie. Ahead of him, Epona jumped effortlessly to clear a fallen tree, soaring through the air with perfect form before landing lightly without breaking stride. Benedict grinned as a feminine peal of laughter rang through the trees.

He allowed his mount to have his head as they charged toward the log, and he reveled in the incredible exhilaration as Brutus charged and leaped as if he were born to it. Of course, chances were he *was* born to it. The landing was firm but not as graceful as the spry mare, jarring Benedict's still-sore muscles. When Brutus again found his footing, Benedict leaned low and urged him faster, slowly closing the distance between him and Evie.

Evie never once looked back at him. She must have been able to hear him now. The rhythmic pounding of Brutus's hooves was mismatched with her own mount's stride, and she surely knew Benedict was gaining on her. Epona's legs stretched long and fast, steadily propelling horse and rider forward and finally past the marquis. Benedict caught more giggles from Evie as they pushed ahead. Her joy was contagious, and soon Benedict could make out the sound of her father's laughter, probably the sound of his conceding defeat. Benedict found himself grinning as he steadily pressed forward.

The howling of the dogs echoed through the woods, alerting them of an eastward turn. Separated by only a few yards, Benedict and Evie raced over the muddy terrain. At a brief clearing, Evie finally hazarded a glance backward, and Benedict was gratified to see her eyes widen momentarily at the sight of him on her heels before they narrowed again quickly and she jerked her attention forward abruptly.

He did not even try to stop the bubble of laughter that escaped his lips. She peeped backward again, and he watched as she lowered her stance even more and appeared to urge Epona to go faster.

Normally he would not have dared to go so fast through unfamiliar terrain, but he knew Evie was perfectly at home and he stayed directly behind her route.

"You're cheating," she shouted over her shoulder. "You must find your own way!"

He laughed at her cheek. "All is fair in love and fox-hunting, my lady!"

They were a good deal ahead of the others now, Evie lying across Epona with determination evident in her every movement. They had veered off course from the dogs and were merely racing each other now. Benedict hung low to his mount, easily absorbing the jarring stride, without a single care for all the mud Epona's hooves flung into his face. He glimpsed an opening in the woods ahead and knew she must be heading toward the clearing.

This would be his best chance to usurp her lead. As they broke through the last of the trees, he pushed Brutus faster. The pounding of the horses' hooves echoed through the trees like rolling thunder. She maintained her lead, but given just a little more time, he could overtake her.

Crack!

Before his mind had even processed the sound or what it meant, Benedict hauled up on the reins and catapulted himself off his mount and to the soft, grassy ground. His momentum was still too great to remain upright, but he instinctually compensated by tucking his body and rolling, smoothly coming to his feet and crouching defensively.

It was seconds before his brain caught up and he realized what had happened.

Bloody hell—a gunshot!

He desperately replayed the scene seconds earlier in his mind. *Oh God—Evie!*

While he had reined in at the crack of the gunshot, Epona, still a few yards ahead of him, had started at the sound, and Evie had been unseated. In his mind's eye he watched in slow motion as she flew through the air, disappearing from view in the tall grass of the clearing.

Please let her be all right!

Cursing sharply, he dashed toward where he had seen her fall, all the while darting glances in every direction, trying to find an unseen enemy, his pulse racing at an unbearable speed. He estimated the shot had come from at least a hundred yards away, maybe even two hundred. The shooter had likely used a Baker rifle so he would have adequate time to escape after sending off the shot.

His heart hammered in his chest, fear giving him a burst of speed and overriding the need for caution. Without thought, he had reverted to his training, acting on instinct alone. He kept low to the ground, well hidden in the overgrown weeds. From his crouched position, he caught a glimpse of Evie's navy blue habit several yards ahead of him.

Dear God—she wasn't moving.

Terror lodged in his chest, pressing the air from his lungs as he rushed to her, anxiously throwing looks over his shoulders for the hidden adversary. Had Renault somehow tracked him down? How was that even possible? This was all his fault. Evie had nothing to do with it—other than trusting him enough to ride beside him. Benedict simply had to have been the intended victim. Fear squeezed his heart; if she was dead, then he might as well have pulled the bloody trigger himself.

He dropped down onto his knees beside her still form, sinking slightly into the saturated earth. He saw immediately her arm was hanging unnaturally low from her shoulder, not at all in line with the gold braiding stitched over the shoulder seam. His stomach twisted violently—if she had dislocated her shoulder, there was no telling what other injuries she had sustained in the fall.

Holding his breath, Benedict felt for a pulse at the collar of her riding jacket. Immense relief—more profound than anything he had ever felt in his life—washed over him at the steady pounding of her heartbeat. He breathed deeply for a few seconds, trying to slow his own heart rate and regroup. He pulled his hand away and froze.

Fresh blood, red and wet, smeared his fingertips.

Chapter Twenty

*Why have you not written me, Hastings? Are your
end-of-term exams keeping you so very busy?*
                                    — From Evie to Hastings

Evie struggled to emerge from the fog of incomprehension flowing around her. She could hear a man's voice, tense and worried as he tried to rouse her, but she was completely powerless to respond. A flash of pain seared her upper arm, and she involuntarily gasped.

"Evie! Can you hear me? Where are you hurt?"

The pain drowned out his voice, softening the words as if they were spoken underwater. The burn spread from her shoulder, running down her arm and out across her chest. She wished the fog would come back to her now, the insulating layer of haze that had mercifully protected her from the rising wave of pain.

What was wrong with her? The last thing she could remember was soaring through the air on Epona and then . . . nothing. Dear Lord, everything hurt. And why did she feel so blasted wet and cold? She groaned and tried to open her eyes. It seemed an impossible feat—nothing seemed to be working correctly. After a herculean effort, her left eyelid cracked open, followed by her right, and she worked to focus on the blurred face above her.

"Evie, are you all right?" She could hear relief in Benedict's voice this time. "Tell me what hurts."

"My arm, my ribs, my head . . . everything," she moaned, closing her eyes and trying to curl her body up into a protective ball. The pain from the movement was so overwhelming, dizziness and nausea simultaneously assaulted her, as if someone had spun her like a top. She swallowed thickly before asking, "What happened?"

Benedict was silent for a moment before answering her. "Somebody fired a gun. You were either thrown or fell from Epona."

Evie's eyes popped open again. "Fired a gun? Oh no, Epona—is she all right?" As the fog in her brain ebbed further, panic surged within her.

She tried to sit up to look around, but Benedict held her firmly in place. She gasped at the pain her struggling caused and stilled.

"Calm yourself, Evie, for God's sake. Your shoulder is dislocated, and God knows what else may be injured. Epona is well, I assure you." He looked so pale and worried, panic lodged in her throat. His clothes were covered in mud and leaves, and his disheveled hair was pushed haphazardly off his forehead. He looked years older than he had when they were riding.

"I'm so sorry, Evie. I never imagined something like this would happen. As soon as the others come, I'll hunt the bastard down. He will pay for this; I swear it on my life."

She gritted her teeth against a wave of pain. When it passed, she suddenly realized what he wasn't saying. "You mean someone did this on purpose? Someone actually shot *at* us?"

"They weren't aiming for you, Evie."

Her eyebrows knitted together in confusion. Either it was an accident or it wasn't. What did he mean they were not aiming for her? Then her fuzzy mind caught his meaning. "You? They were shooting at you? Why?"

The pain was dizzying, and she fought against the darkness creeping into the perimeter of her vision.

Anguish flickered across Benedict's dirty face, and he dropped his forehead to his wrist before dragging the back of his hand across his eyes. Finally, he lifted his haunted eyes to hers. "Yes, I think so. I would never in a thousand years have dreamed they would have come after me. I didn't even know anyone saw me."

He wasn't making sense. What was going on? Her mind was too addled to process the ramifications of what he was saying. She stared, uncomprehending, at him before a nearby sound caught her attention.

The ground rumbled, and the sound of hooves beating the debris-littered earth assaulted her ears. Benedict glanced toward the sound and then back at her. "I have to go find him, Evie. I'll explain everything when I get back, but I can't let the blackguard get away."

He dropped a kiss on her brow, then stood to greet the rider. Evie tried to focus. "Benedict, wait. I don't understand. . . ."

The last was said on a thin thread of air as Evie slipped back into the waiting mist.

Benedict waved his hands to catch Richard's notice as he crashed through the underbrush.

"Evie's been injured. I believe her left shoulder is dislocated," he shouted tersely. "She's unconscious, so I don't know much else about her condition. See to her—I am going after whoever fired the shot."

The horror on Richard's face was almost too much for Benedict to handle. He suddenly felt as if he had been turned inside out. His friend's normally jovial face had gone white; his eyes flashed with panic.

"What the bloody hell happened?" Richard demanded as he jerked his horse to a stop. He scrambled off his mount, his movements clumsy as his eyes never left his sister. Falling to his knees besides her, his gaze flitted from the spreading bloodstain on the collar of her habit to the sickening position of her arm. He squeezed his eyes closed, covered his mouth briefly with his hand, and swallowed. After a second, he opened his eyes and went to work feeling the remainder of her limbs through her clothes in an effort to uncover unseen injuries. His voice choked, he asked, "Who did this? Why?"

Benedict's own stomach clenched at the scene. "I'm—I'm sorry, Richard. I think whoever shot at us was aiming for me. I never dreamed they would come after me—"

"Who? What are you talking about?" Richard looked completely bewildered.

"A man I know from France who has a grudge . . ." He shoved both hands roughly through his hair. How could this be happening? "I don't know what happened, but I'm about to find out," he said grimly.

Mounting Brutus, he wheeled the horse around and took off at a run, lying low over the horse's neck as the tree limbs rushed by. He pushed the animal hard, desperately afraid it was already too late.

How could he have been so stupid? To think he had never considered that Renault would try to find him. He would have bet his life that no one had seen him that night in Folkestone. What he had done instead was bet Evie's life.

God, he was the vilest of idiots. His blood ran cold as he envisioned the scene again in his head: Evie falling, her crumpled body, Richard's eyes upon seeing his injured sister.

So bloody stupid—possibly even deadly.

Right then and there, while racing through the woods in despair, Benedict promised himself only two things. First, he would leave Richard's family immediately, never to bring chaos or strife to their sweet country life again. And second, he would find whoever had perpetrated this attack.

And when he did, they would pay.

As he crested the hill, he caught sight of a horse and rider disappearing into the next copse of trees. The distance was too great to discern distinguishing features; he caught only a fleeting glance of a dark figure atop a dark-colored horse.

Anger surged inside of him; at that moment he knew there was nothing he would not do to exact revenge on the sniper. He had few weapons on his person—just a dagger and a hidden pistol, neither of which was much good unless at close range. With the fury flowing through his veins, if he was to get as close as that, it would be a hand-to-hand combat situation. He wanted to feel each blow with his fists and relish the flesh-to-flesh contact that would bring his opponent down.

And the man *would* go down.

He rode flat-out across the clearing but had to slow the pace when he plunged into the trees. The vegetation was thicker than it had been on the hunting grounds, and he was forced to slow further when he encountered a hearty thicket. He bent to dodge a low-hanging branch.

Crack!

Damn it!

He could almost feel the wind from the bullet as it whistled harmlessly through the leaves of the branch he had just ducked beneath. Brutus started at the sound and danced nervously beneath him. This time the shot had been fired from a much closer distance, and he was certain it had come from ahead of him and to the right. Cursing, he jumped to the ground and quickly lashed the reins to a nearby sapling. He patted Brutus's neck, dismayed that he needed the horse too much to let him escape the danger.

Crouching, he half ran, half crawled in the direction of the shot, glad for the mud now covering his clothes.

Bang!

Benedict ducked his head as the second shot sent up a spray of dirt and leaves only a few feet ahead of him. The shot, which sounded as if it came from a pistol this time, was fired from nearby. He was close now. Despite the danger, he did not slow his progress. The bushes ahead of him rustled, and he focused his attention toward the sound.

Through the brush, he caught intermittent glances of the man, disjointed images of the coward attempting to mount his horse and the rifle secured to the saddle. Finally he got a clear side view of the man, and he instantly recognized his adversary.

Ned Barney—*damn it all!*

Come hell or high water, he *would* bring the bastard down—this time. If Barney succeeded in escaping again before Benedict reached him, Benedict would lose precious minutes sprinting back to his own horse. The head start could be enough for Barney to have a chance to elude him, and Benedict would be damned if he was going to let that happen. The blackguard didn't know it yet, but he was going to tell Benedict exactly what he wanted to know.

And the bastard was going to suffer in the process.

Abandoning his attempt to keep low, Benedict sprang from the underbrush just as Barney wheeled his mount around and whipped the horse's flank. Benedict caught hold of Barney's boot, a tenuous grasp at best as he kicked and struggled to break the grip, yelling at the horse to go. As the horse jerked into motion, Benedict swung his other hand up, getting a firm two-handed grip on the filthy leather boot. His body dragging on the ground, he struggled to remain to the side of the beast so not to get trampled, all the while twisting and tugging on his enemy's leg.

Benedict's feet scrambled for purchase on the leafy, slick ground to no avail, and he was dragged alongside like a rag doll. While he struggled, his hip was almost immediately smashed against a tree stump. The impact ripped his already ruined pant leg and inflicted painful cuts down his right leg, but he hardly registered the trauma. The whole of his being was concentrated on the leg in his grasp and his quest to unseat Barney.

Barney screamed out in pain as Benedict grasped even tighter and tried to twist his whole body around in a bid to torque the knee again. Leaning over the saddle, Barney clung to the horse's neck with one arm. With his free hand, he struck out at Benedict, pummeling his head and shoulders from the awkward position. Benedict absorbed each blow, ignoring the onslaught as he continued his quest to bring Barney down with absolute, single-minded purpose.

"Let go, ye bloody bastard!" Barney's desperation was clear in his hoarsely shouted command.

The plea, wrenched from a place of weakness, only served to strengthen Benedict's resolve. It was like a last bellow from an antelope being brought down by a hungry predator.

At last, Benedict gave a mighty twist, and Barney shouted out in agony. In reaction to the pain, Barney's torso rocked back, his spine arching as he threw his head back with a roar and grasped his leg with his hand. All the while Benedict held tight as the horse continued to storm through the woods at an alarming pace, dragging him through the mud and leaves blanketing the forest floor. Abruptly, a branch connected with Barney's exposed neck with a sickening thud, and both Barney and Benedict were jerked violently from the horse and thrown to the ground.

Momentarily stunned, the wind knocked out of him,

Benedict lay gasping vainly for breath while stars
crowded his vision. The sudden cessation of noise as the
horse galloped away made his ears ring. Of its own volition his body writhed on the ground, his jaw locked open
as his lungs tried to overcome the temporary paralysis.
When finally his breath returned, he struggled to position himself defensively. He couldn't let Barney get the
upper hand. He couldn't fail when the stakes were so
high.

Benedict rose to his knees, maintaining a wide stance
and protecting his head with his upraised fists. His gaze
locked on Barney, who was lying facedown on the
ground nearby, and he realized at once that Barney was
not moving at all.

"Get up, you coward," Benedict shouted, spitting the
words with all the loathing that boiled within him.

Barney remained motionless. Benedict sat back on
his heels for a moment, panting for breath. He watched
warily, assuring himself that Barney was not lying in
wait for him, ready to ambush Benedict when he let his
guard down. Finally, he allowed his hands to fall to his
side. He could detect very shallow breathing, but Barney's right arm was bent at an impossible angle. If the
man had been conscious, it would have been impossible
for him not to show some signs of distress.

Panting for breath, Benedict struggled to his feet and
stumbled closer. Cautiously, he grasped Barney's shoulder and rolled him over. One look at the purpled skin of
his enemy's neck and he couldn't help but cringe. The
injury caused by the impact was sure to be painful and
debilitating for at least some amount of time, but with
the continued sound of his breathing, Benedict felt reasonably confident serious damage had been avoided. At
the very least, Barney's windpipe was still intact, which
was something.

Of course, any injury he sustained served the bastard right.

Hands on hips, Benedict debated what to do with his prisoner. He could tie the man up, but it wasn't bloody likely he would escape. No, it would be better to just leave him where he lay while Benedict collected the horses. With a wrenched knee, broken arm, and injured windpipe, Barney was unlikely to get very far if he awoke.

As it happened, Barney had not yet come around when Benedict returned with both horses a short time later. Though it was the last thing he wanted to do in the world, he had decided to tie Barney to his saddle and take the man back to Hertford Hall. There he would be able to get medical attention, but whether he would do so before or after Benedict interrogated the bastard, he had not decided.

Richard and his family would need to know the perpetrator had been caught. In addition to the fact that they would want to know for their peace of mind, Benedict had no doubt that the marquis was also the local magistrate. It was not a conversation he was looking forward to.

He hoisted Barney's deadweight ungracefully into the saddle and strapped him on as best he could. He mounted his own horse and set off for the house. Looking to the lifeless man beside him, Benedict shook his head in disgust.

"So how did you find me, Barney?"

It didn't matter, really. The responsibility for bringing the vile man to Hertford Hall was his and his alone. Ahead, two men on horseback galloped toward him, and Benedict recognized one of them as the groom who had escorted him and Evie on their first ride. He clenched his jaw and straightened his posture. It was time to face the music.

Chapter Twenty-one

Please forgive me, Evie. I wish I could explain why I must cease our correspondence, but I cannot. Can you simply trust me?

*— From Hastings to Evie; written
but burned before posted*

When Evie came to the second time, her environment had changed considerably. Gone were the stiff riding habit, the squishy mud, and crisp spring air. Now she reclined against her own bed in a soft cotton nightdress. The popping and cracking of a fire blazing unnecessarily in the hearth was the only noise in the otherwise quiet room.

Heavens, she was hot.

Why on earth was a fire burning? Sweat dampened her skin, and she moved uncomfortably in an effort to find a cooler spot on the sheets. Instantly, pain ripped through her shoulder, and she gasped and immediately froze.

"Evie! Be still, darling. How do you feel, sweetheart?" Her mother's voice was tense, fearful, and unusually strained. Her cool hands grazed Evie's cheek, and Evie turned her face into her mother's palm and opened her eyes.

"Good heavens, I feel hot." Evie's voice cracked a bit. Her mouth felt as dry as dust. As if her mother read her mind, a cool glass of water appeared at Evie's lips, and she drank deeply. She had never tasted water so good in her life. Licking her lips, she took stock of her nerve endings before adding, "And rotten. Utterly rotten."

Her mother smiled a bit at this, though it didn't reach her strained eyes. "Yes, I suspect you do feel rather rotten. I do not imagine being thrown from one's horse feels at all pleasant."

Evie groaned. "Is it as bad as all that, then?"

Mama patted her hand and sighed. "You were fairly lucky, if one can call it that. Your arm was dislocated, but the doctor was able to set it right, and he does not believe any lasting damage will result. There is a rather nasty bruise on your ribs as well, but he was fairly certain it was superficial, and thankfully no bones were broken. There is a lump on your head that must have resulted from your fall. There is a very unpleasant-looking cut on your neck, and several smaller scratches crisscrossing your face. You also have quite a few bruises, but those will fade soon enough."

Well, was that all?

Her mother paused, shaking her head as her eyes flitted over Evie's various wounds. "This is exactly why I never wanted you to go hunting. I know, I know," she said, putting her hands up when Evie opened her mouth to speak. "But I had to say it."

"This wasn't exactly normal circumstances—it could have happened on a leisurely walk." Really, how often did one get shot at? Foxhunting could hardly be blamed for her injuries. At a sudden thought Evie struggled to sit upright, ignoring the pain that burned like a hot coal. "Benedict! Is he safe?" Pain and confusion swirled within her like mists in a coming storm. Her stomach churned with dread as she remembered his ashen face and serious, regretful eyes.

What had he done?

Her mother fluttered her hands in admonishment. "Lie down, Evie. For heaven's sake, you will surely ruin the doctor's hard work."

Evie eased herself back down, but persisted. "Benedict, Mama? What happened after I, um, fainted again?"

Her mother pursed her lips. "I believe I will fetch Richard for you. He will want to know you are up, and he will best know how to answer any questions you might have." She leaned forward and kissed Evie on the forehead. Squeezing Evie's good hand she said, "My goodness, but you gave us all a scare. Mind you do not overtax yourself."

She rose gracefully from the bed and left the room.

As soon as the door clicked shut, Evie began to fret. Had Benedict returned? Had he found the person who had shot at them? What had he gotten them into? What could he have possibly done to warrant such an extreme response? She could not seem to comprehend any of it.

Someone actually shot at them.

Evie shook her head with lingering incredulity. Of all the endings to the hunt one could imagine, that possibility had certainly never entered her mind. With a sigh she decided to assess the extent of her injuries and pushed the covers back with her right hand. The air, though warm, was considerably cooler against her skin than the heavy counterpane. She never could understand why a fire must be laid whenever someone became sick or injured. Honestly, it was not as if one could sweat away a dislocated shoulder.

Looking down, she took stock of the already vivid bruises staining her arm. She cringed—it was a rather awful sight. What was more, by the feel of it, the rest of her body was just as bad off, if not worse. She craned her neck as best she could to try to get a good view of her injured shoulder, but there was nothing to see. Someone had dressed her in her night rail, and a sling was fashioned to hold her arm up.

Well, that ought to be a lovely accessory for her next ball gown.

A knock interrupted her inspection. Her brother opened the door before she could bid him to enter and rushed straight to her side.

"Oh my God, Evie. How are you feeling?" He gingerly sat on the side of the bed. He lightly touched the back of her hand as though terrified of hurting her.

"I am all right, Richard. Truly I am." *So long as I don't move,* she amended silently. "Please tell me what has happened? Did Benedict catch the culprit? And speaking of Benedict," she said, narrowing her eyes at him before continuing in a fierce whisper, "or should I say *Hastings,* would you tell me what in God's name is going on?"

Richard flinched at her uncharacteristic vulgarity. "How did you know? Never mind—it doesn't matter. Evie—," he started, then paused and blew out his breath. He covered his eyes with his hand briefly before meeting her eyes again.

"I am not entirely certain what is going on. Benedict has not returned." He held up his hand at her alarm. "I am certain he can take care of himself, so don't waste a minute of thought on him. If he comes back, I have asked to be alerted the moment his horse is within sight. We have quite a lot to . . . discuss."

Evie felt as though she had been punched in the stomach. *If* he came back? He had told her he would be back. Surely he wouldn't just abandon her. . . .

Surely, nothing. What did she even know about the man? He could be a bloody pirate for all she knew.

As the silence stretched between them, Richard looked more and more agitated. "As God is my witness,

I never imagined helping an old friend could bring harm to my family—to anyone! I don't even know what is going on. He only said a man he knows from France has a grudge, whatever that means."

"France!" Evie's voice sounded shrill to her own ears. "When has he ever been to France?" A sick, sinking feeling began to tug at her. She had trusted Benedict. She had shared intimacies with the man. Had she misread his character?

Richard's face went a dull red. "He's lived on the Continent for years and apparently just returned. He told me he wanted to get away from the city for some peace and quiet. I shall never forgive myself for allowing him to come to Hertford Hall."

She drew in a pained breath, trying to comprehend the new information. He had lived on the Continent. He had *enemies*, for heaven's sake. What else didn't she know about him?

Richard leaned toward her, grasping her good hand. "I don't know what happened. I don't know how they found him, or why they bothered. Hell, I don't even know who 'they' are! I have been doing nothing but turning it over in my head since the shooting, and nothing seems to make sense!"

Restlessly he jumped to his feet and began to pace. Evie heartily wished she could throw back the bedclothes and stalk the length of the room along with him.

After their years of correspondence, she had thought she knew him so well. She had accepted his reasons for lying about his name and had believed him when he said it was to protect her. But what if it was to protect himself? What if he had been hiding out from some nefarious person the whole time?

She'd thought she was falling in love with the man of her dreams, but that man had been in her imagination all along.

She pressed her uninjured hand over her eyes. She had fallen, all right. She had fallen for his lies. Nearly every word out of the fraud's mouth had been utter balderdash.

Why? After all they had shared, why did he do this to her?

The tears that sprang unbidden to her eyes surprised her—Evie was certainly not the watering pot type. She dashed them away angrily. She struggled to draw a decent breath. What a silly little fool she had been. How foolish to think he might have had some sort of interest in her, when all along he had been lying through his teeth. She winced inwardly at how stupid she must have seemed.

"Just go away, Richard. I would like to be alone, if you do not mind." She flicked a few more tears away with her fingertips.

"Evie—," Richard began.

"No! Richard, I don't want to see your face right now." He looked so stricken, she added, "Perhaps later, but right now I want you to leave." After all, she had never told him of Hastings's betrayal, so Richard couldn't have known how deeply he wounded her by bringing the man to her home.

"If that is what you want . . ." He trailed off, giving her a moment to contradict that it was indeed what she wanted. When she said nothing more, continuing to stare at him with all the hurt and anger she felt, he rose slowly and shuffled toward the door.

Looking back at her dejectedly, he sighed and said, "There is one more thing. Father assumed it was a poacher who fired on you. Please don't disabuse him of this notion. It will be much easier on them if it is as simple a matter as that. And really, I—I can't bear for them to know."

Evie stared at him mutinously for a moment before allowing a curt nod. Richard dipped his head in acknowledgment and retreated, closing the door behind him.

She exhaled loudly and dropped her suddenly heavy head back on the pillow.

She wished now she had told her father about Hastings the moment she learned the truth. If only she had stormed into the dining room, pointed a finger, and declared him an imposter—at least then she could have seen him properly thrashed.

She pressed her hands to her eyes. She wouldn't cry about him again. He wasn't worth it. And what was the point? The damage to her family was done. She never wanted to see him again. She never even wanted to hear his name again, or any other alias he decided to go by.

As far as she was concerned, he could ride away and never come back.

Now if only she could convince her blasted heart of it.

Benedict, his prisoner, and one of Granville's grooms rode in silence toward the estate. The other man had gone ahead to update the others of the capture. As they approached the stables, Dunley, the head groom, rushed to meet them, his face serious and drawn.

Benedict dismounted quickly and handed the reins over. "Please send for Lord Raleigh at once. I need to speak with him as soon as possible."

Dunley nodded curtly as he accepted the reins. "I sent word of your return the moment Brutus came into view." He looked uncertainly at the man draped over the unfamiliar horse.

"I will take care of our guest, Dunley. Thank you for seeing to Brutus."

Benedict waited until Dunley bobbed his head and left before untying Barney from the saddle and hauling the still-unconscious man down. Barney groaned and shifted restlessly as Benedict shouldered him none too gently.

A short distance away, the door to the house slammed

shut. He looked up to see a furious Richard storming toward him, still wearing the mud-stained clothes from the hunt. Gone was the red jacket, and the collar of the now-ruined shirt was open at the neck while the sleeves had been shoved up. Judging by his thoroughly mussed hair, he must have spent the last few hours shoving his hands through it as he generally did when he was stressed or worried.

Though the anger was expected and completely deserved, Benedict's nerves still reacted; he not only stopped walking, but he also unconsciously took a tiny step back.

"Richard, please tell me how Evie is do—" His plea was cut off midsentence as Richard, who had not slowed as he approached, landed a solid punch on Benedict's jaw, sending him flying backward. He landed hard on the gravel, the combined weight of himself and Barney driving him into the ground and the breath right out of his lungs. Barney groaned again, the impact undoubtedly jolting his injuries.

Richard stood over Benedict, his chest heaving while he clenched and unclenched his fists. "How dare you come back to this house? How dare you ask after my sister as if *you* are not the reason she was injured! Leave that degenerate bastard and get out of my sight."

Benedict sat in stunned silence for a beat, shocked by his friend's outburst of violence, even considering the circumstances. In all their years together, Benedict had never once seen Richard hit another man except for in a boxing parlor.

He kept his eyes on Richard warily as he hefted Barney off his lap and got to his feet. "Richard, I—"

But Richard was having none of it. "I don't want to hear any of your excuses. As a matter of fact, I don't want to ever see your face again—do you understand me?" The veins in his neck stood out at the violence of his reaction, while his hands remained balled into fists by his sides.

The condemnation in Richard's eyes made Benedict flinch, and he tried to breathe past the crushing shame. He had to make Richard understand why he had come here, why he was forced to withdraw while he figured out his next step. He weighed his options, considering simply turning and leaving as his friend plainly wanted. But the truth was that Richard deserved more than that.

It was time to tell Richard everything—no matter how damning it would be.

Widening his stance and preparing himself for another attack, Benedict stated calmly, "I am not leaving until you hear the truth."

"The truth? Well, that is rich, coming from you. You will leave when I damned well tell you to. You have no say in this. None!" Richard's hand sliced angrily through the air in punctuation.

Benedict raised his hands, palms out, in a conciliatory manner. "I deserve your every hateful thought. I admit that, but you deserve to know the truth of why I came here. *She* deserves to know."

Richard's nostrils flared at the reference to Evie. "As if you have any right to talk about what she deserves. Let's talk about what *you* deserve, Benedict. Let's talk about the lies you fed me, the betrayal of friendship, or, I don't know—" He gestured with disgust toward the man lying unconscious on the ground. "How about the homicidal maniac you led to my home."

"I don't deny any of your accusations, Richard. If it is your wish, we can talk about everything I deserve and then some. But not," he said, emphasizing the word clearly, "until I tell you what has transpired to lead us to this moment. Just five minutes, Richard, and you can do anything you want with me, including banishing me from ever seeing you or your family again."

Richard crossed his arms and stared mutely at him.

Taking that as acquiescence, Benedict took a calming breath and said evenly, "Let us take him"—he nodded in Barney's direction, smart enough not to admit just yet he knew the man's name—"somewhere where he can be detained, and I will explain everything. What happens next is up to you."

Clenching his jaw, Richard nodded curtly and strode off into the stables, leaving Benedict to collect Barney and follow him. Sighing deeply as he felt his integrity and honor crumble like so much dust, he bent to recover Barney, slung him over his shoulder, and followed Richard into the cool interior of the barn.

He had only one chance to get this right.

Chapter Twenty-two

I am not amused by your failure to write to me. If I said something to offend you, you must chastise me properly. I cannot bear to be subjected to the silent treatment.

—From Evie to Hastings

It was the raised voices that had attracted her attention. While Evie was accustomed to the occasional feminine shriek of excitement or even argument, hearing male voices raised in anger was altogether unusual.

Benedict—he must be back.

She tried to ignore the rush of emotion that assaulted her; she refused to even name the feelings. Instead, she forced them away and sucked in a deep, filling breath. She knew very well she was to stay put in bed at the very least for several days. It would be the very pinnacle of foolishness for her to get up now, particularly with no one around to assist her. Her mother would have a fullblown fit if she even thought Evie was contemplating leaving her sickbed any time soon.

But, as the yelling continued, she was positively *dying* to know what the devil was going on out there.

Deciding that getting out of bed was certainly preferable to death by curiosity, and deeply hoping her mother was clear on the other side of the house, she took a moment to prepare herself for the journey across the room to the window. A couple of deep breaths and a fervent prayer for safety and stealth later, she was ready to go.

She carefully pushed aside the counterpane, mindful not to jolt her injured arm or make any sudden movements, and slowly rose to a sitting position. Dizziness accosted her at the change in position, and she sat still until the room stopped spinning. She would probably be smart to take the doctor's advice and remain resting in bed for a day or two. She blew out a resigned breath. Her curiosity often got the better of her, however, and she was honest enough with herself to admit that this was one of those times, especially when she could think of only one person likely to trigger a shouting match.

After a minute of holding still to ensure the light-headedness had passed, she rose to her bare feet, gripping the bedpost for balance with her right hand. Again the dizziness washed over her, and she clung to the cool wood, pressing her cheek against it while her body fought to regain equilibrium. *Perhaps* it was not the *best* idea she had ever had to pull herself out of bed, drag herself across the room to the window, and eavesdrop on whatever was going on out there. However, she was committed now.

And furious.

And curious, always curious.

Finally, she felt steady enough to pull away from the bedpost and shuffle along the bed toward the window. When at last she reached her destination, she gratefully lowered herself onto the wonderfully thick cushions of the window seat. The area was much cooler than her bed, and she relished the refreshing air against her skin. As she struggled to relax, it took her a moment to realize she no longer heard the shouting outside.

She quickly pulled aside the curtains and scanned the grounds below her window. Her eyes promptly settled on a threesome of men: one lay on the ground, and two, obviously Richard and Benedict, were facing each other. Their postures appeared to be very tense, almost poised to fight.

So he had indeed returned.

She could not separate the anger and relief simultaneously coursing through her body. As much as she despised him, she didn't want him dead. Injured would be fine, but certainly not dead.

She might have been developing . . . feelings for the man, unwelcome feelings at that, but those feelings had been mortally wounded with one shot. And they never would have developed in the first place if she had known who he really was. She glanced down to her sling and bandages and shivered. She could not bear to think how much worse the damage could have been if the shooter had had a better aim.

Actually, what scared her most, besides the obvious fact there was a shooter at all, was that her whole family had been completely vulnerable. It could have just as easily been her brother or father. She could imagine her mother and sisters waiting peacefully by the pond, her sister Beatrice painting away while the twins made clover necklaces with the early blooms. She could picture her mother reading in the gazebo, waiting innocently for the triumphant return of her husband and two eldest children. They all had just been so . . . vulnerable! No other word really quite described their state.

Would her easygoing family be forever changed by the ordeal? Her father had been furious and worried out of his mind. He had sent every available man out on the chase, but none of them had the head start Benedict did. Her father's face had been drawn and pale when he'd come by to see her for a few moments before returning to the stables to await word. Her mother had also been anxious, and Evie had never seen her brother in such a state. She wondered how the girls were doing, as her mother did not want them overtaxing her with a visit just yet.

She squinted at the figures through the window, trying to get a clear view of their expressions. She was frustrated by the distortion of the glass, but she dared not open the windows and alert them to their audience. As she watched, Richard turned suddenly and stalked into the stables. Benedict scooped up the body of the third man before following Richard. She watched as the three of them disappeared through the open door of the structure, wishing desperately to be privy to whatever they were talking about.

Exhausted, she lay back on the pillows of the bench. The pain from her injuries no longer felt distinct, and her whole body now ached dreadfully.

Did she really care what was going on among the three men? Did any of it really matter? The damage had been done, and nothing was going to change that. Her eyelids became unbearably heavy, and with a feeling of discord still in her heart, she drifted off.

Benedict was relieved, for more than one reason, to hear the doctor had not yet left the premises. He was starting to worry since Barney had not yet come to consciousness, and Benedict really needed to question him. But more important, he felt much better knowing the doctor had already treated Evie. Thank God the man had been fetched so quickly.

He closed the door to the storage room serving as both an examination room and a prison cell. Richard, who had been silent since entering the building, strode toward the gardens. Benedict followed several steps behind, not wanting to push his friend by getting too close.

Tension settled in Benedict's stomach like a hot stone. What the hell was he going to say? How was he going to put into words the experience that changed his whole life in the space of a breath? He didn't even know where to start.

It was the cruelest of ironies that Richard chose the very same bench Benedict and Evie had shared the night before. Instead of moonlight, it was illuminated in harsh sunlight, which glared off the white stone. Last night it had seemed like a hidden escape, whereas now he saw how exposed it really was.

He had to consciously push the images from their time together out of his head so he could focus on the conversation to come. Flashes of her laughing at his silliness, of her indrawn breath at his touch, of her huge and expressive blue eyes when he warmed her hand nonetheless flitted through his brain. He could almost feel her lips beneath his, and he closed his eyes against the painful pleasure of it.

He forced himself to picture her as he last saw her: broken on the forest floor, pale, injured, and lifeless. The terrible images did the trick. Benedict was ready to relive the nightmare he had stumbled across that night in Folkestone. Facing Richard, Benedict squared his shoulders and wet his lips. His friend leveled a hostile glare at him and mutely waited for him to begin.

"The night I came to you followed the worst experience of my entire life." Closing his eyes, he began with the day he left school, and held nothing back.

"You're a bloody secret agent?!"

Benedict was startled by Richard's outburst. Lost in his story, he had nearly forgotten anyone else was listening. He blinked and focused on his old friend, whose cheeks were ruddy and eyes slightly bloodshot. Benedict winced, the guilt for the long-standing deception assaulting him. "I'm sorry I never told you. If it makes you feel any better, I never told *anyone*. Not my family, not my friends, not my staff."

"I don't even know who you are!" Richard sprang up from the bench and began pacing, running his hands through his hair roughly. "God, Evie was right all along. She knew something was wrong about our showing up unannounced as we did. She knew, and she warned me, and idiot that was, I brushed her off. I even laughed at her theories. And now she is lying in bed, wounded, damaged, hurting." His voice cracked. Benedict knew he must be tormented by the thought of his injured sister. It was nothing compared to the torment he felt. Nobody could possibly feel as horrible as he did.

Benedict took an unthinking step forward to comfort him, and Richard thrust his arm out to stop him. "Don't! Don't come near me. You play spy for the government, making fools of those who love you in the process. You lied to me; you've been lying to me for God knows how many years."

"Richard—," Benedict started, but Richard cut him off.

"No! I get where you are going. Your damned profession caused you to get into some trouble along the way. Because of your own mistakes, you dragged your family, and now my family, into the mess. I don't—"

"That's just it, Richard," Benedict cut in loudly. He was relieved that Richard stopped talking and waited, albeit with a deadly glare in Benedict's direction. He took a deep breath and continued. "It wasn't my profession that caused the trouble. That was what I was trying to tell you. Please, let me finish. As soon as I do, I will leave and never darken your doorway again, if that is what you want." He pleaded with his eyes for Richard to hear him out.

Richard crossed his arms and raised his left eyebrow, presumably his cue for Benedict to continue.

Benedict closed his eyes briefly in relief and forced himself to dredge up exactly what had happened that night. Within moments, he could feel the cold, damp air on his skin, smell the salty air, hear the distant wash of the waves. He could also feel the sickly dread in his stomach that he had experienced listening to the voices in the cottage. He took a deep breath and continued.

"Several years ago, I was charged with infiltrating a smuggling ring operating between Folkestone and Wimereux. I succeeded and within a few months was able to pinpoint the leaders of the operation, brothers by the names of Pierre and Jean Luc Renault. One night almost a year ago, I set them up, convincing them I had a high-ranking official who wished to sell sensitive—and valuable—information, but he would divulge the information only to the head of the operation.

"The Renault brothers were twins, and I knew that where one went, the other would follow. When they arrived in Folkestone on board their fastest, best ship, our agents were ready and waiting. Most of their men were captured, but in the fight, Jean Luc turned on me, and I was forced to shoot him. Pierre managed to escape, much to my superiors' dismay."

Benedict hazarded a glance at Richard, but his stony facade revealed nothing. Benedict raked his fingers through his tangled hair. "For months, I heard nothing from him, and I assumed he burrowed into some rat hole in France. Then, last week, I received information from one of my contacts that Renault had returned to England and was training a new team.

"After what happened in the raid, I couldn't risk going to my superiors unless I was certain the information was correct. So, early the next morning under the cover of darkness, I rode out to the place he was supposedly staying and investigated. My contact was correct. I heard Renault talking with another man about an upcoming shipment."

He paused, reliving the emotions he had experienced in the quiet dawn. After a moment, Richard interrupted his wandering thoughts. "What is the point? So you ran into this Renault, turned tail, and led him here?"

Benedict held his gaze and shook his head. "I was just about to leave to report my findings, when I heard the voice that stopped me cold." He swallowed past the lump that lodged in his throat. He could remember the exact words he had heard spoken in response to Renault's query on the upcoming shipment: *I assure you, I intend to see this done with all possible haste.*

"Richard, it was Henry."

Richard blinked. "Henry. As in your *brother*, Henry? The bloody Earl of Dennington?"

Benedict nodded. "I left town with a heavy heart, not sure what I was going to do, and decided I needed time to come to grips with the decision before me. My main concern was that I did not want to be found by the War Office, or anyone really, until I knew what I would do. I believed until today there was no way for my brother or Renault to know I was there. But, as it is now so completely obvious, I was wrong."

His story finished at last, Benedict bowed his head, allowing the full magnitude of the truth to settle around them like a layer of winter frost. Richard did not say a word; he did not even make a sound. Benedict silently sent up a brief, fervent prayer that the truth would at the very least help Richard to understand why Benedict had done what he had.

When at last Benedict looked up, apprehensive, almost fearful at what he would see on Richard's face, it was with a rather grim sense of validation that he saw the shock on Richard's pale features. Not wanting to push him in any way, Benedict waited patiently until Richard spoke first.

"Bloody hell." Richard shook his head slowly, then looked Benedict in the eye when he said again, "I didn't know. Of course, how could I have? You should have told me. We could have come up with some other plan, one that didn't involve endangering my family."

Richard turned away from him, stalking several paces away and running his hand through his hair in agitation again. "Damn it, Benedict! We could have gone somewhere else, somewhere that would not have dragged everyone I hold dear down with us."

He turned abruptly, slicing his hand in the air. "No, it doesn't excuse your actions. I am sorry for the bloody awful situation you got into, truly I am. But it simply does not make up for the injuries my sister now bears, or the tears my mother cried, or the violation my father feels at having his child assaulted on his own property. Speaking of which, my father believes the attacker was a poacher. It is my intention that he continue to believe it—it is simply easier and less traumatic. I have let him know I will handle the matter entirely."

Benedict was more than happy to have Richard's family believe that particular scenario. Though he doubted it, it was also his hope Evie would not know the full extent of his deceit. His head ached at the thought of her hating him. He dipped his head slightly in an abbreviated nod, not quite ready to be let off the proverbial hook. "I know that what happened in no way justifies being dishonest to you and your family, but I just wanted you to know what has been going on in my life, and what would cause me to turn to you for help while not being honest with you."

Benedict lifted his shoulders and said simply, "It was my brother. I wasn't thinking straight."

Richard walked slowly back toward him. Benedict wished he could know what the man was thinking. He just looked so . . . defeated.

God, Benedict felt like hell. He wished there were some way to undo everything that had happened. "I deeply, deeply regret my actions. I wish I had never come up with the ridiculous plan, concocted on a moment's notice. And I thought your family was away until we arrived, not that it makes things any better. I hope you believe me when I say if I had had any indication I would be followed, that any danger would be presented to you, I would have never, ever come here."

Evie's crumpled figure materialized in his mind's eye again, exactly as he had last seen her—lying prone on the forest floor. It was a physical pain to him; he pressed his palm first to his chest and then to his head in a vain attempt to alleviate it. He wished he could go to her, to see her awake and *whole*. All he really wanted in the world was for her to be vibrant and healthy again, the way she had been last night as they had sat on the bench in the moonlight.

A million years ago.

"What are you going to do now?" Richard dropped wearily onto the bench, placing his elbow on his knee and resting his chin in his hand.

"I need to finish this. I don't see that I have any other choice. I have come to terms with the fact my brother is a treasonous bastard." He scrubbed a hand over his face. Shrugging his shoulders, he continued. "I need to find my brother and apprehend him. I am still an officer of the Crown, and it is my duty to turn in any traitors I discover."

Richard sat up straight. "Turn him in? For *treason*? Benedict, your family will be ruined! The title will be lost, and you and your kin will *never* be able to set foot in polite society again."

And there it was—the real reason it had taken him so long to come to terms with what he had to do.

He could see the dawning realization on Richard's face. Benedict had already thought all of this through. Turning Henry in would be a death knell to his family. The title, the lands, the income, and any respect he or his family once demanded would dissolve like sugar in boiling water.

But he was no hypocrite. If his brother was involved in illegal activities, he could not treat him any differently than he would any other criminal he had brought down over the years.

He only wished he had left *before* the bloody hunt.

The anger surged once again inside him, and it took all of his willpower not to punch the nearest inanimate object. He particularly wanted to thrash the unconscious lowlife who had brought the fight to Hertford Hall. Of course, it was his own brother he really wanted to have a go at.

The betrayal burned deep in his gut. After dedicating years to protecting British citizens and national security, his own brother was throwing all he held dear to the wind. Henry had put monetary gain ahead of all else, and for what? He already had a title, extensive lands, several houses, and servants aplenty. Even if he was operating at a loss, it was nothing a good estate manager and some belt-tightening could not fix. Or, if all else failed, there was a veritable plethora of heiresses who would be happy to plump his coffers in exchange for the title of countess.

Benedict pictured his older brother, dripping with jewels and fine clothing, purchasing the finest horseflesh and conveyances, stocking his wine cellars and liquor cabinets with the oldest and rarest varieties. With derision he realized Henry would never personally sacrifice for the good of others, particularly the lowly tenants of his lands. He would never give up any of his own creature comforts, regardless of necessity or obligation.

With a grave face and a heart that felt as if it were carved from crumbling marble, Benedict looked his friend square in the eye. "I don't have a choice, Richard. My brother must pay for his transgressions."

Richard held his gaze for a moment, then sighed deeply. "You must do as you feel is right. Wait until that bastard has come to so that you may question him. Tell Dunley what supplies you need. And take Brutus—he will serve you well until you can retrieve Samson."

Richard stood and closed the distance between them. He stopped a few feet from Benedict, hesitation and uncertainty written on his face. At last he cleared his throat. "However I may feel about you right now, I hope you don't get yourself killed."

Benedict smiled humorlessly. "That makes two of us."

Chapter Twenty-three

My greatest regret is that I cannot meet you at last, but the timing of my departure is not my choice. Can you ever forgive me?
  —From Hastings to Evie, tossed in the fireplace before even addressed

Evie stared at the solid, infuriatingly immobile door for perhaps the hundredth time in the past hour. Why had her brother not come to her? It felt like ages since she had seen Richard and Benedict disappear into the stables, and she was anxious to discover what had transpired between them.

She stretched her neck from side to side; it was stiff and sore from her having slept on the window seat. She would probably still be there if her maid hadn't woken her, clucking like a mother hen as she helped Evie back to bed. Evie extracted Morgan's promise not to tell Mama about the incident, thank goodness, and to fetch Richard.

It was difficult to quell the desire to go find her brother herself, as he had not seen fit to respond to her summons. She blew out an impatient breath and tried to focus on the book in her hands—again. She had been staring at the same page for half an hour and still had no idea what was written on it.

Finally, there was a light tap at the door. Throwing the book aside, she called out, "Come in!"

Pushing the door open a few inches, Richard poked his hand in and waved his white handkerchief back and forth. "I come in peace."

Despite the somberness in his voice, his antics earned a snort from Evie. Shaking her head, she called out, "Oh, get in here."

He pushed the door open the rest of the way and made his way to her bedside. He looked tired and strained, but he managed to stretch his lips into a semblance of a smile as he approached her. Pulling up her desk chair and sitting with his knees almost touching the mattress, he asked, "That sling really is quite the fashion statement. I do believe it could be the start of a trend."

She smiled at his halfhearted attempt at humor. "Oh yes, it does rather frame the face, don't you agree?"

"Absolutely." He leaned forward slightly. "How are you feeling?"

"Dreadful. Sore, to be sure."

"I suppose that's to be expected. At least it's not so dreadfully hot in here anymore."

"Yes, I'm much more comfortable now."

An awkward moment of silence hung between them. She was not exactly sure how to ask him what he and Benedict had discussed. *So, I was spying on you and noticed you and Benedict were engaged in an argument. What is that all about?* Especially when she had been so angry with him the last time they had spoken. She still was angry, but at the moment, she was more curious. Curiosity always trumped any other emotion in her book. She offered him a small smile and reached for his hand.

"I am feeling a bit confined in here, cooped up like a lame chicken. What is going on in the outside world? Any word from Benedict?" Try as she might, the words did not sound as casual as she had hoped. In fact, they seemed to fall flat to the floor with an audible thump.

The muscles around Richard's eyes tightened, and he squeezed her hand. All traces of joviality were gone when he answered. "He is gone from here. There is no need to worry about him further. I doubt he will ever cross your path again."

Excellent. Perfect. Exactly what she was hoping to hear.

She nodded briskly in acknowledgment and mentally washed her hands of the man. At least she tried to. Oh, who was she kidding? If those were the words she wanted to hear, why did her stomach drop to her knees in reaction to the news? If she really had no desire to see him again, the mere mention of his name wouldn't send an enticing shiver down the back of her neck.

If what Richard said was true, he was not coming back. Ever.

Well, of course not—why should he? They hardly knew each other—other than on paper—and just look at all the trouble his visit had caused her family. She thought of their ride together across the estate . . . of his hands clasping her around the waist and lifting her down to him, then lingering a moment longer than they should have. Her fingers tingled at the thought of his breath caressing her bare skin yesterday as they sat beneath the stars. And then there were his sweet—and increasingly passionate—kisses.

Balling her hand into a fist, she could not stop herself from asking, "Where is he going?"

Richard was quiet for a few beats, glancing out the window to the gathering dusk. "He is off to find his brother."

Her eyebrows drew together. "The earl? What has he to do with anything?" Was the drivel about the Frenchman a lie as well?

"Quite a lot, actually." He blew out a pent-up breath and dropped his chin in his palm, his elbow resting gracelessly on his knee. "It's all rather complicated. Yes, Benedict lied to us, but he was going through a rather difficult ordeal and just wished to have some peace to work it out. He never imagined he would bring trouble to our doorstep."

She felt a little hysterical bubble of laughter rise up. "Trouble? No trouble! Just a bit of an accident, that's all. Really, naught but a flesh wound." And to make the day even better, tears were pricking her eyes once more. Brilliant.

Really, she prided herself on her ability to keep a stiff upper lip, and here she was tearing up over a very stupid man who had done nothing more than turn her life upside down—twice. She swallowed past the lump lodged in her throat.

"Oh, Bit, don't cry. He won't come back here. He will never cause you pain ever again."

Richard meant the words as reassurance, but for some inexplicable reason, they only caused more sadness within her. He awkwardly patted her hand to comfort her and said, "I am so sorry you had to go through this. Why don't you get some rest now?"

She nodded, giving a little sniffle. She didn't want to rest, but she really didn't want Richard to sit there and watch her cry like a ninny. She swallowed again and said, "Rest would be good. Thank you for coming to see me. And please, keep me updated on . . . anything."

Richard rose and kissed her forehead before leaving. He retrieved his handkerchief from his pocket and offered it to her with a half smile. She gratefully accepted his proffered gift and quickly set about mopping up the tears. As she watched his retreating back, she crushed the fine-linen square in her fist and willed herself to stop her foolish crying.

It was easier said than done.

*   *   *

As dusk gave way to night and the air grew cool, Benedict remained motionless among the tangle of trees that had concealed him for the better part of an hour. His eyes were trained on the flickering light spilling from one of the second-story windows. When he had left the estate hours earlier, he had made it as far as the village before suddenly wheeling Brutus around and sprinting back. He hadn't been able to do it.

He simply could not leave without seeing her first.

After the long and eventful day, the family appeared to be retiring early. One by one, the lights in the windows were snuffed, until only one remained—Evie's. It was now or never.

With Brutus tied securely nearby, Benedict set off on foot toward the house. He kept a low profile as he ran across the lawn and skirted the stables.

As far as he knew, Barney remained securely within the storage room where he had left him hours earlier. It took almost an hour, and some less-than-gentle prodding, but Benedict had finally extracted the information he needed from a groggy and pained assailant-turned-informant.

What he learned was worse than he originally expected: His own brother had hired Barney to come after him. Benedict had been spotted in the village by one of Renault's men, fleeing in the early-morning gloom as if the hounds of hell were on his heels. Fearing Benedict would ruin things for him, he had sent Barney to see to it that Benedict was taken care of.

Was there any humanity left in the man who had played by his side as a child?

According to Barney, his brother was actually fairly close by. The man had spoken of a meeting at a pub that had taken place several days ago. Henry was apparently staying at a little-used manor house that served as a hunt-

ing lodge on one of his estates roughly halfway between
Hertford Hall and London. Benedict could vaguely recall
visiting the place when he was around eight or nine years
old before the new lodge had been built on the richer
hunting grounds of one of their other estates.

When he had emerged from the interrogation room,
he had been surprised to find Richard waiting in the stables. With a grim face, he gave a curt nod. Richard offered
a simple, "Good luck," before returning to the house,
leaving Benedict to make whatever plans he needed to
get under way. Benedict appreciated both the sentiment
as well as Richard's lack of interference. Not that he could
imagine Richard rushing out to help him after the turmoil
he had caused, but still he was glad to be left to his own
devices—this was something he had to do alone.

And now here he was, going behind the man's back
again. Damn if he wasn't starting to really hate himself.
But it couldn't be helped; he simply had to see her with
his own eyes, to make sure she was recovering and taken
care of, before he could go on.

As he approached the house, he decided to try for the
doors to the library. He carefully, quietly tried the
knob—amazingly, it was unlocked. Who would have
thought luck would actually be with him for once? Silently, he eased the door open and slipped inside. He
stole through the house, creeping up the stairs and down
the corridor to the door across from Richard's room.

He paused, his heart beating in his ears as he drew in
a calming breath, raised his hand to the brass knob, and
twisted.

Evie should be asleep.

She shifted on the bed in a vain attempt to get comfortable. It was late, and she had endured a rather awful
and exhausting day. Her shoulder, though marginally

better, still ached like the devil, and the dull throbbing of her ribs made any position uncomfortable. Sleep would offer relief, but she simply could not calm her mind enough to rest.

The book she had tried to read proved worthless as a distraction and now lay discarded on the bed next to her. Really, she didn't know why she had even bothered. Her mind was so preoccupied, the thought of concentrating on something as trivial as a novel was really quite laughable.

With a sigh, she leaned over to blow the candle out, when a noise at the door brought her up short.

What was that?

She had thought her whole family was in bed already. She wiggled into a more upright position and watched in momentary confusion as the door was pushed open.

Oh good heavens, had the attacker escaped? Fear coursed through her as a dark figure slipped into the room. She gasped, and the sound caused the intruder to whip around to face her.

Benedict!

She instinctively sat up, then cried out at the pain of jostling her shoulder. Benedict rushed across the room to her.

"Evie," he whispered fiercely, looking distressed, "are you all right?"

He was at her side in moments, cupping her face in his palms as if it were completely normal for him to do so. The heat of his hands against her skin stunned her, and for a few seconds her mind went completely blank. In that moment, his touch felt soothing, wonderful . . . right.

The twinge in the shoulder as she started to reach her hand up to cover his was like a bucket of ice-cold water. As her shock gave way to anger, she tugged her chin away. He immediately dropped his hands to the bed and straightened.

"What are you doing here?" she hissed. Who did he think he was, walking into her room as if he owned the place? "You shouldn't have come."

The nerve of the man!

She grabbed the covers with her right hand and tugged them up to her chest. Thank goodness he had no way of knowing her stomach was doing somersaults at having him in her bedchamber. It was almost painful for her to look at his wounded expression.

"I'm sorry. I know I shouldn't be here," he said, sinking onto the mattress. "I had to see you, to make sure you are in one piece."

She scowled. "Just barely, no thanks to you." She struggled to put some space between them; it was too hard to concentrate with him sitting so close, looking at her the way he was—as if he actually cared about her.

"I know—it is all my fault." He rubbed a hand over his eyes wearily. "*Everything* is my fault. I wouldn't have come, but I made a promise that I would explain everything, and I mean to make good on that promise. And I wanted to say good-bye."

Her temper flared. He came to say good-bye, did he? To salve his conscience before walking away? Well, he was out of luck. "You should have—left, that is. I can't believe I ever trusted you, Benedict—or Hastings—or whatever the bloody hell you are calling yourself today."

"I know I lied to you, Evie—"

"Yes, so do I. I just didn't realize how much you were lying about."

He settled his dark gaze directly on her, unwavering in the candlelight, and she tried to ignore the sincerity she saw in his eyes. "I can't tell you how sorry I am for having been untruthful with you and your family. It is not possible for me to express the magnitude of my regret. All I can say is that I am truly sorry, Evie."

She was softening toward him, and it suddenly made her furious. "Sorry cannot help my shoulder, Benedict. Sorry cannot undo the fear and anxiety my mother and father went through today. You stirred up trouble somewhere, and then you came running to us to hide like a child behind his mother's skirts. If you had any honor, you would have faced your problems head-on, not brought them to our doorstep. You are a coward, a liar, and a complete fraud."

Benedict's face paled considerably, and through her anger she felt as though she had just plunged a dagger into his heart. She tucked her trembling hands beneath the counterpane.

"It's not as simple as that. I've come to explain why I came here," he murmured with a hooded expression.

"Oh, no need. My brother explained everything."

"Everything?" He seemed incredulous. He must not have thought Richard would tell his secrets. "You know about my brother?"

"Yes, yes," she said, waving a dismissive hand. "Your brother, France, the man with a grudge. I assure you, he explained it all."

Something in his expression changed, like a candle being extinguished. His features became harder, more haggard almost before her eyes. She looked down, focusing on the blasted sling. She shouldn't feel bad—she was the one who had been wronged.

"I see." He stood and looked down at her. "If I had to do it over again, I would have done exactly as you said. But I made my choices. I have to live with the consequences."

"And apparently, so do I," she said. The pain she saw on his face was heartbreaking, but she simply could not let go of her overwhelming sense of betrayal. "God, Benedict, you already broke my heart once. Why did you have to do it again?"

"It was *never* my intention to hurt you." His voice

was fierce and low. "When I was young, I handled things dreadfully wrong. Now . . . well, now I'm just a bastard."

She wasn't going to disagree with him. "Why don't you just go?"

"I will. I am. Obviously it is of no use to you, but I needed to offer my apology. Even though it is too late to undo the pain to you and your family, I will do what I can to make this right." Almost to himself, he added, "No matter the consequences."

He stood and locked eyes with her. She felt his gaze all the way to her toes, which curled involuntarily at his nearness. After a moment, he dipped his head and said quietly, "I shan't bother you again. I have only one suggestion. If you still have that last letter I sent you, take another look. My regret was there for you all along; you just had to read between the lines."

The mere thought of reading that heartbreaking letter again turned her stomach. She averted her face from him, closing her eyes against the sight of him leaving. Slow footsteps carried him away. When the door clicked shut, she opened her eyes and, staring at the place on her bed where he had sat, suddenly felt empty and adrift.

Why did he have to say such a strange statement in farewell? It didn't matter. He was gone now, and she didn't want to think on him again. Leaning over, she blew out the candle. As she lay back in the darkness, she tried to block out the image of his stricken expression when she had called him a coward. It was not fair that she had been the one wronged; yet, somehow, sympathy kept creeping up behind her anger. It was for the best that he was gone now. She would never have to worry about the man again.

Settling down on the stiff, slightly mildew-smelling bed in a posting inn about an hour away from Hertford Hall, Benedict fingered a scrap of fabric in his hands thoughtfully. The elaborately embroidered, silver-threaded monogram was much worse for the wear since Richard had handed it to Benedict earlier that day when he had scratched his cheek. The smear of blood caused by the branch was now indistinguishable from the multitude of stains the handkerchief had sustained since then. Pristine only hours before, it now lay limply in tatters.

How very fitting.

Benedict welcomed the slow burn of anger that seeped through his blood like poison. The handkerchief's condition was about as good as that of his personal life, and, with the exception of himself, there was really only one person to blame.

Henry.

He still was having difficulty coming to grips with the depth of his brother's betrayal. It was bad enough when his brother had been involved only in smuggling. It was nearly beyond Benedict's ability to comprehend that Henry would send an assassin after his own flesh and blood in order to keep his despicable activities secret.

How could Henry have sunk so low?

Benedict would have never dreamed his brother would go to such lengths. When Benedict had fled, he never once considered that Henry would have his own brother tracked like an animal.

God, he had been so blind.

With a deep sigh, he stuffed the fabric into his jacket pocket and stretched out on the mattress, trying to get comfortable enough to catch a few hours of sleep. Usually, it took a while for him to get to sleep, but with the exhaustion weighing on his entire body, he was more worried about waking than falling asleep.

His brother was mere hours away. If Benedict had pushed himself, he could have been there by daybreak. It wouldn't do, though. Unhappily, he had conceded that, by resting, he would be better prepared for the encounter. It chafed mightily to stop for the night, but he needed to sleep.

Desperately.

His body was screaming for a break after the intensity of the day. And after the confrontation with Evie, his emotions needed a break as well. His body longed for a hot bath to soak his aching muscles, but he settled for the dubious comforts of the hard bed.

As he relaxed each of his muscles in turn, encouraging his body to give in to slumber, he couldn't help but wonder if Evie was thinking of him. She must be cursing the day she laid eyes on him.

He had thought if she knew about the betrayal of his brother, she might, in some small way, understand how Benedict could hold the truth to his chest. Instead, she was just so . . . flippant. Some small part of him, someplace deep inside, had died a little. Any hope that she might understand him, that she might, at the very least, not hate him, had sputtered and died.

All that was left was darkness.

He wished there were some way to have everything—justice, love, happiness, honor. If that were possible, he would throw himself at her feet and beg for mercy and forgiveness. He stiffened, as a strange weight settled in his chest. *Love.* Dear God, he was in love with her. He took a slow breath, letting the realization wash over him like rainwater.

He would do everything he could to do things right by her from afar. He didn't deserve her, and God knew she probably hated him, but that didn't mean he would stop fighting for her.

Chapter Twenty-four

How can you be so cruel? I have half a mind not to come to see you at all. At the very least, I shall deny you my smile during the ceremony. No one shall be smiling for you, but at least one shall certainly be frowning.

— From Evie to Hastings

The next morning, the day dawned as dark and glum as Evie's mood. The wind had kicked up and the clouds had closed in, eradicating any traces of the beautiful days they had enjoyed that week — before the chaos, of course. Evie itched to pace her room as she usually did when she was at odds, but of course she was still stuck in her blasted bed, as effective a prison as Newgate.

The only glimmer of good news was that the pain in her shoulder and ribs had slackened more than expected. It still ached when she moved, but for the most part the absence of constant physical pain left her mind free to explore all the emotional hurt enfolding her like London fog. Her thoughts were centered squarely on the despicable liar who had left them yesterday. How could he have so carelessly brought danger to their doorstep? How could he have thought it at all acceptable to lie to the family? To her?

She squeezed her eyes shut. That was the crux of the

issue. She had somehow allowed him to weasel his way
into her affections. One eye popped open. She supposed
that was not exactly a *completely* accurate statement. If
she were honest with herself, she knew he had tried to
avoid her attentions, at least at first, and she had been
the persistent one.

Like a little fool, she had thought there was some sort
of exciting mystery behind the handsome stranger's cool
facade—a grand romance gone tragically wrong, perhaps.
She covered her face with her hand and rubbed her eyes.

What a silly, silly little idiot.

Sighing, she dropped her hand and drummed her fingers on the mattress, brooding. Though she tried not to,
she wondered what the traitor was doing now. He was
surely off to confront his enemy and try to bring the man
to justice. A flutter of fear rippled through her as she
imagined the encounter. How did his brother fit into the
situation? What if there were more people after him,
more people willing to shoot him where he stood? What
if he was already *dead*?

She broke off from that particular line of thinking
and took a few calming breaths. For heaven's sake, she
had seen him only last night. And really, for someone
she was so angry with, she was awfully worried for him.
She could not get over the queasy feeling that something dreadful was about to happen, or had already happened, to Benedict. Did he not go off in pursuit of an
attempted murderer?

She gave her head a little shake. It was not for her to
fret over—he had made his bed; now he could lie in it.
She had other things to think about.

There was a light scratch on the door, and she called
out, "Enter," expecting to see Morgan this early in the
morning.

Instead, her mother eased open the door and offered

a tentative smile. "Oh good, you are awake. I didn't wish to disturb you, but I wanted to see how you were feeling this morning." She turned to close the door before walking to Evie's bedside. Her champagne-colored gown whispered prettily as she approached and gracefully lowered herself to the bed.

"Good morning, Mama," Evie offered with a half-hearted smile. "Not *completely* dreadful. When I move it, my shoulder hurts quite a bit, but the rest of the pain feels much more dull this morning, thank goodness." The sling holding her arm in place was already driving her mad, but at least the knot on her head had diminished. The bruises along her arms, however, were blooming into all sorts of impressive colors. She grimaced—it was not an attractive look.

"Well, I am relieved to hear you are feeling a little improved." Mama smoothed a hand over Evie's forehead. "No matter how . . . colorful you are looking this morning."

Evie made a face. She was not looking forward to the sickly yellow stage that would follow the vivid purples and blues.

Her mother hesitated a moment, then cleared her throat. "Your father and I have been talking, and we decided it was for the best to stay at Hertford until you are healed." Mama paused and leveled unyielding gray eyes on Evie. "Once you are better, we shall all head to London for the Season. As a family."

And just like that, her dreams were snatched away from her. Evie blinked rapidly, struggling to maintain composure. Another hole opened up in her heart, right next to the place Benedict had once occupied. Was she to lose everything at once? "But, Mama—"

Her mother held up a firm hand. Her eyes glinted like steel in the dim light of the overcast morning. "No buts.

It is time to move past this foolishness. A life in the stables and atop a horse is not the life for a lady. And I saw you this week. I saw the way you looked at Mr. Benedict. You are not so disinterested in the prospect of marriage as you would have us believe."

Alarm welled within her, and she struggled to sit up straight. "You can't—"

"Yes, I can," Mama interrupted. "And I have. Your father and I agree, Evie. We want the very best for you, and you will not find that hidden away here at the Hall."

Her tone brooked no argument, and Evie was in no condition to fight. Her mother stood and pressed cool lips to Evie's forehead. "You may be angry with us now, but someday you will thank us."

As her mother straightened, the door swung open.

"Oh, begging your pardon, my lady, I didn't know you were here," Morgan exclaimed, dipping a quick curtsy. She balanced a tray between her hip and left hand, her right hand still resting on the doorknob. Her eyes flitting back and forth between Evie and her mother, she clearly sensed the tension.

"It is quite all right; I was just leaving," Mama replied. She turned back to Evie. "Rest up, darling. I'll be back to check on you later, after I have tended to a few things."

As Evie's mother retreated, Morgan went about setting up her tray and opening the curtains. Evie watched her in silence. As battered as her emotions felt, she couldn't imagine putting on a cheery front.

It was all for naught. All of her hard work, all of her careful arguments and well-laid plans—it was all snatched away in one fell swoop. Fury built within her, and she knew there was only one person to blame: Benedict Hastings.

Benedict awoke in a rush. One moment he was unconscious; the next he was sitting up in bed, panting with sweat dripping off his brow. He slowly became aware of where he was—an unfamiliar, nondescript room at an inn on the way to confronting his brother. He lay back down, taking slow, deep breaths, and wiped the moisture from his forehead with the back of his hand.

He reached for his watch fob on the tiny table beside the bed and squinted at the dial in the dimness. It was seven o'clock. If he saddled up and left in the next quarter hour, he could be on the Dennington estate by noon. Despite his exhaustion, he wanted to arrive as soon as he could manage.

Bloody hell, how had it come to this? A heavy, leaden weight settled on his shoulders. There was nothing about the coming day—hell, the foreseeable future—he looked forward to. He pushed the covers aside and sat up, bringing his bare feet to the cold wood floor. He sat there for a moment, running his hands through his damp hair before kneading the tight muscles in his neck.

This was it.

He still had not decided what he would actually do once he was face-to-face with Henry. He supposed it would depend on Henry's reaction to him. Best-case scenario? He shook his head. There was no best-case scenario. That option had gone out the window when Henry decided to attack him. So, what was the most palatable alternative? That was the new question.

He stood, lit a candle, and splashed some of the cold water in the basin on the bureau onto his face. The drops trickled down his bare chest in rivulets. He braced his arms on the bureau, dropping his chin to his chest, staring at the trails of water but not really seeing them. There was really only one choice.

One way or another, he would bring his brother to justice. And that justice would avenge the hurt Evie had suffered.

He pushed away from the bureau and dragged on his shirt before retrieving his saddlebag from the lone chair in the room. He sat back on the bed and opened the outside compartment, which held the items he kept with him at all times, just in case. He carefully withdrew his dagger. As always, the weapon was meticulously clean and well polished. It glinted menacingly in the candle-light as he examined the blade. Satisfied, he pushed it into the specially fitted holder in his right boot.

Next, he extracted his pistol. He very much preferred swords to pistols, but he was prudent enough to be pre-pared for both forms of combat. The weapon was loaded and ready when he was. He tucked it into his waistband at his back and pulled on his coat to conceal it.

He set aside his bag and lifted his sheathed rapier from its resting place beside the bed. This was his forte. The sword was where he felt most confident, where he knew his op-ponent would face defeat without fail. If he was forced to fight his brother, the sword would be his choice. All those years he had imagined he was fighting his brother or father, he had never actually faced either one of them. If it came to it today, this would be the weapon he would reach for.

And he would win.

After attaching the sword to his waist, he efficiently gathered his belongings, blew out the candle, and set out to the stables.

The ride was a blur—Benedict could not have said what a single feature along the journey looked like. With every step taken in his brother's direction, his resolve strengthened. He relived almost every minute he had spent alone with Evie. He heard her laughter clearly, felt her soft skin, experienced every emotion. He couldn't let her down now. He might never be able to see her, touch her, feel her, taste her again, to tell her he loved her, but by God he would do right by her.

As he drew closer to the estate, he resolutely pushed her from his thoughts to focus on the task ahead. In his mind, he played out the possible scenarios and never found a satisfactory ending. Betrayal, belligerence, boorishness—all were what he expected to find when confronted with his brother.

And blood—there was always the chance for blood.

At last, he reached the ill-used turnoff that would lead him to the old hunting lodge. His pace slowed, and he cautiously urged Brutus forward, careful to watch his back, front, and everything in between. Brutus seemed to sense his mood and tossed his head a few times restlessly. Benedict patted the horse's neck but kept his attention on his surroundings.

The tree branches, overgrown from years of neglect, reached down to sweep at his shoulders and neck, and effectively kept his view of the lodge obscured. The rocky drive angled up, following the curve along the hill, and he remembered then that the lodge had a spectacular view of the countryside behind it. If memory served, the front of the structure was fairly obscured by the vegetation around it.

He was close now—the acrid scent of wood smoke invaded his nostrils. He slowed to a halt, while the lodge was still out of view, and dismounted. He took his time double-checking each of his weapons. Satisfied, he secured Brutus to a nearby tree branch with enough rope for the horse to graze comfortably while he waited. The rope itself was tied in an easy slipknot that could be quickly undone in case he needed to make a rapid retreat.

He decided to duck into the woods and approach the house from the side where he was reasonably sure he would not be observed. He cringed at the sound his footsteps made on the dead leaves and fallen twigs, but continued to creep along as quietly as possible. After a few minutes, he was able to catch fleeting glimpses of the brick walls, but they were hard to distinguish thanks to a thick carpet of ivy obscuring most of the building, with the exception of the small windows and a few areas close to the roof.

When the property had been in use some twenty years earlier, the grounds near the lodge had been beautifully maintained. As he stepped toward the tree line that delineated the yard, he paused and surveyed his surroundings. Thank goodness for the neglect of the property. The overgrown brambles and shrubs offered adequate cover in order for him to safely approach the lodge.

He focused on the windows of the house, scanning each portal for some sign of movement. The chimney adjoining the kitchen was spewing a steady stream of white smoke into the dim, overcast skies. Shadows moved occasionally past the glass, and he had no way of knowing how many servants were housed within. Benedict shook his head in disgust; his brother might be hiding out, but he apparently had brought an entourage along with him to see to his every need.

He slipped around to the front of the house, crouching beneath each window he came across. When he was farthest from the bustle of the kitchen, he cautiously lifted his head and peered into the small library he vaguely remembered from his youth. The room appeared to be unused, with white sheets still covering the smattering of furniture left behind.

He eyed the weatherworn window, the once-white paint peeling away from the gray wood. Grasping the mullions, he gave it a good tug in case, by some miracle, the window was unlatched; it was not.

So much for luck.

He quickly shed his jacket and wrapped it around his left hand, twisting the fabric as he wound it up his arm. He took aim, averted his face, and smashed his fist through the glass. The tinkling crash of the glass shattering and raining down to the floor below seemed as loud as an explosion in the still morning.

He froze, his stomach churning as he crouched with his hand on the handle of the pistol and listened for any sound of alarm. Nothing.

After a beat, he reached his jacket-shrouded hand through the hole in the windowpane and lifted the latch. Extracting his arm, he swung the casing outward. The opening was smaller than he had hoped, but he hopped up and worked his way through anyhow, only just refraining from uttering the curse words that sprang to his lips in the struggle. At last he was in, and he paused once more with an ear cocked toward the closed door that led to the house at large. The sounds of movement deep within the lodge filtered into the room—it was probably the servant he had spied in the kitchen.

Before opening the door, he reached around and retrieved his pistol from his waistband. He had no intention of using it, but there were few things that put the fear of God into a man quite like staring down the barrel of a cocked gun. Holding the weapon in his right hand, he slowly turned the doorknob, which was resistant to the movement thanks to two decades' ill use. He held his breath and, with infinite care and by millimeters at a time, began to pull the door open.

Suddenly, the door crashed in on him, throwing him to the floor. His body, already injured from the ride through the woods with Barney yesterday, screamed in pain as his right hip hit first, followed by his shoulders before his head crashed to the floor with a bone-jarring thump.

As a tall figure stepped over him, Benedict kicked out hard, catching the man in the back of the knees and throwing him off balance. Benedict rolled swiftly onto his belly and jumped to his feet. His attacker, whom Benedict recognized as his brother's footman, Nigel, regained his footing and came at him, swinging with a wide left hook.

Benedict blocked the punch, sending it glancing off his shoulder while he struck out with a solid jab to his opponent's belly. Nigel gasped as the wind was knocked out of him, and he automatically doubled over. Benedict took advantage of the position and threw his arms around Nigel's neck, effectively securing him in a headlock. He squeezed the footman's throat with all of his strength.

Click.

At the sound of a gun cocking behind him, Benedict froze, his blood turning cold within his veins.

Bloody hell.

Evie listened to the chiming of the clock in the hall. One, two, three, four, five . . . What was she still doing up at this hour? The sudden absence of sound made the quiet even more pronounced. Was it possible for the quiet to be loud? In the complete darkness, her attention strayed to the sound of her own breathing.

In and out, in and out.

She put her hand to her forehead, squeezing her temple with her thumb and middle finger. She was going mad.

It was the middle of the night, and here she sat, staring into the blackness and latching onto the sounds of the grandfather clock. As the day had worn on, she had become more and more anxious—anxious about her future, anxious about her healing body, but also anxious about the man responsible for injuring both.

She had tried—oh, had she tried—to simply push Benedict from her mind and wash her hands of him. She had certainly refused to read the blasted letter as he suggested. But almost immediately, his solemn face and smooth chocolate eyes would materialize in her mind, and she found herself contemplating what he was doing, as he faced his demons all alone. The haunted look in his eyes when he left stayed with her, along with the pricking sense of foreboding that she could not seem to shake.

People were trying to harm him, and he had gone off in search of them alone.

A sound from the corridor caught her attention. The faint shuffling noise, whisper quiet, seemed to originate just on the other side of her door. She sat up swiftly, ignoring the twinge of pain in her shoulder and side as her nerves kicked in, and threw aside the covers. She paused, her feet hovering above the floor, and listened for the sound again.

There it was!

What if Benedict had returned? She hopped to the ground and rushed to the door, but she just managed to stop herself from throwing the door open when the thought entered her head that it could be an intruder. What if someone else had come looking for Benedict?

She shivered and stepped back from the door, her gaze flickering around the room more on memory than actual sight. What could she use as a weapon? Her eyes fell to the hearth beside the fireplace—the poker! She darted over to retrieve the iron rod, tested its solidness in her hand, then with a nod of satisfaction returned to the door. Her heartbeat had picked up pace, and she could hear the thrumming of her blood in her ears when she hesitated again with her hand on the doorknob.

The noises were still there, and what was more, she was sure now they were coming from just on the other side of the door. She steeled herself, took a few bracing breaths, and pulled open the door, simultaneously brandishing the poker in front of her while demanding, "Who goes there?"

She heard a gasp, saw a large shadow, and struck out with the poker. The weapon connected solidly with the target, eliciting a pained grunt that matched her own as the maneuver jarred her body.

"Evie! What in God's name are you doing? You could have killed me!"

"Richard?" She dropped the poker and reached out to him in the darkness. "Oh my goodness, are you quite all right? I'm so sorry! Wait a second, no I'm not! What do you mean what am *I* doing? What are *you* doing skulking around this time of night? Even you must agree I have the right to be a little skittish after the recent events." Her chest heaved as her lungs tried to remember how to breathe.

"For heaven's sake, let us get out of the corridor—we are bound to wake someone up with all this racket." He grabbed the fallen poker before guiding her back into her room.

Evie retrieved her wrapper and draped it over her shoulders while Richard went to the fireplace and lit a candle by the dying embers. With it, he brought to life several more tapers in the candelabra before sitting in one of the chairs in front of the fireplace. He rubbed at his shoulder with a grimace and motioned for her to take the other chair, which she did without argument.

"So, what have you to say for yourself? Why were you shuffling around outside my door, scaring the daylights out of me?" Evie tucked her cold feet beneath her and waited for his answer. Frightening her as he had, he had best have a good one.

Richard was fully dressed, even wearing his boots and gloves. Releasing his shoulder, he leaned forward and traced his finger over the sling on her left arm. His eyes lingered there as he took a deep breath and said softly, "I was leaving. I was trying to decide whether I should tell you or not."

"Leaving? Where would you go—back to London? Richard, we don't blame you, not really. You have no need to leave this house."

He raised his eyes to her, the firelight hiding how red and bloodshot she knew them to be. "Please don't be angry with me, Bit. You, and the rest of the family of course, you all mean everything to me. I feel terrible about what has happened, and I will do what I can to make it up to you. But the truth is . . ." Richard's voice trailed off, and his gaze flickered back to his hands, which were now resting in his lap.

"Yes?"

"The truth is, Benedict is in a horrible situation. Really unimaginable. I know I should hate him, and I even told him he would never be welcome here again, but in all honesty, I cannot hate him. He is one of my oldest friends, and I can't even fathom the stress of the situation he found himself in.

"He made a bad choice in hiding the extent of it from me when he asked for my help. He made an enormous mistake by dragging us, the whole family, into it with him. But I also know it was never his intention. He is a good man, and I find I simply cannot abandon him when he needs help the most." Richard pressed his lips together and continued to stare at his lap.

"Oh, thank God," Evie muttered.

Richard's eyes jerked up to hers in surprise, and she shrugged a little helplessly. "Well, he has wreaked total and utter havoc in my life, but I don't want to see him dead. The blackguard has been on my mind all day it seems, and if I'm to shake him out of it, I'm going to need to know that he is all right."

Richard's eyes were sharp, but he held his tongue. She took a deep breath and continued. "I really hate him right now, but . . ." She raised her right shoulder in a half shrug and let it drop limply. "I doubt I will get a good night's sleep until I at least know the man is alive. A little beaten up would be good, if you can manage it," she couldn't help but add.

"So you are not outraged that I want to help him?" Richard asked incredulously. His brow was furrowed, and he didn't seem at all moved by her dry attempt at levity. He had never seemed more serious in his life.

Evie reached out with her right hand and squeezed his forearm. "I suppose I should be, but truthfully, I'm more than a little relieved. As I recall, you may ride like a beef-wit, but you shoot like a cavalryman."

He smiled briefly and leaned back in the chair. He stared into the flickering candlelight a moment, looking heavyhearted. Turning his head to look her in the eye, he said, "His brother sent that madman after him."

What? "I beg your pardon?" Evie sat up straight at the unexpected statement.

"Benedict discovered his brother was working with a band of smugglers." The words poured forth in a rush, and she struggled to keep up. "Afterward, he needed some time to come to grips with having to turn his own brother in as a traitor. Unfortunately, Dennington decided to take matters into his own hands, and he hired that assassin to hunt Benedict down like some sort of wild game." Richard was shaking his head, a look of lingering disbelief on his face.

Shocked did not even begin to describe how Evie felt. With her brows pinched together and her mouth agape, she sat there, trying to digest what Richard was saying. Slowly she shook her head. No wonder Benedict had looked so hurt when she had dismissed his mention of his brother's involvement in the whole thing. What must he think of her?

She met Richard's eyes, sadness tugging down the corners of her mouth. "His own brother, his own flesh and blood. How, how could that be? How could anyone ever try to harm his own sibling? Iron pokers to the shoulder notwithstanding, of course. But really, I would die for any one of you." Her heart squeezed painfully with empathy for how Benedict must have felt at the realization that danger lay within his own family.

The love she had for her family was strong and unbreakable. Trying to imagine one of them betraying her to that magnitude was like trying to imagine the feel of the falling snow after having only ever lived in the desert. One knew the phenomenon existed, but it was simply beyond one's ability to envision.

Suddenly, her brain made a disturbing connection. "Wait a moment. Did you not tell me he was going to find his brother? And now you are telling me this is the very man who tried to have him *killed*?"

Richard nodded jerkily.

Good Lord!

If it came down to a fight between the brothers, Dennington would apparently have no qualms about aiming a gun at Benedict, but Evie just couldn't imagine that Benedict could do the same. She didn't doubt Benedict could take care of himself with anyone else, but . . . when it came down to it, what if Benedict couldn't defend himself against his flesh and blood?

"You must stop him! He should go straight to the authorities. Richard, you have to stop him!" She could not push back the feeling of rising panic. She restlessly rose to her feet.

Richard stood as well. "It is too late to stop him, Bit. He left over a day and a half ago, and according to the man who was interrogated, Dennington is holed up at an old hunting lodge on his estate about halfway from here to London, a few miles south of Amersham. I know I am too late to be much use to him, but I simply must try. I let him walk out of here, knowing he was going into a dangerous situation, and I will never forgive myself if I do not at least attempt to help him."

Evie stared at her brother's haggard expression. Looking at him now, she found it hard to recall his jovial countenance of just two days ago. The candlelight played across his features, highlighting his drawn mouth and adding depth to the shadows beneath his eyes. She couldn't recall another time when he had looked so troubled.

"I think it is the right thing to do, Richard." She reached out with her hand and placed it on his sleeve. "I—I hope you know I don't blame you. I was angry earlier, and I spoke rashly. You couldn't have known; after all, he was your friend, and you trusted him."

He dipped his head in acknowledgment.

"And there is one more thing." Heat flooded her cheeks at what she was about to admit, but she needed him to know. "Benedict doesn't have as big a head start as you think. He . . . came to see me last night. He said he couldn't leave without ensuring that I was all right. So he's little more than a day ahead of you."

Richard's brows rose halfway up his forehead, but there was no condemnation in his eyes. "Thank you, Bit. I'm glad you told me."

As he turned to head for the door, she asked, "When will I hear from you?"

He swiveled back around and gave a little shrug. "After whatever happens, happens, I will head on to London. I will send a note when I know something."

She tried to ignore the knot of anxiety that had formed like a brick in her stomach. "It's going to kill me to sit here and wait." She glared impotently at the sling cradling her wounded arm.

"I know," he said, patting her right shoulder. "I promise to send word as soon as I can."

Blast it all. She would do just about anything to go with Richard, to try to help in any way she could, but riding a horse in her condition would be foolish. She stood and gave him a tight, one-armed hug, ignoring the twinge of protest from her shoulder when he squeezed her back.

"Be careful," she whispered fiercely. As she watched him leave, she tried not to think of what might happen if her brother didn't arrive in time to help.

Hurry, Richard!

Chapter Twenty-five

I am glad that I will not be there to see the frown upon your lips, especially knowing I was the cause of your unhappiness. I'd rather be tossed in gaol than hurt you.
—From Hastings to Evie, torn into tiny pieces before tossed in the bin

*D*rip. Drip. Drip.

The incessant dripping was the first thing that worked its way into Benedict's subconscious. The repetitive splashing was exceedingly annoying, but he couldn't quite place where it was coming from. His mind worked sluggishly, trying to make sense of the noise that seemed out of place in his bedroom.

And why was he so bloody cold? Everywhere, he could feel cold. The damp air on his skin was cold, but not as much as the unforgiving stone he lay on. Benedict's fuzzy mind slowly identified the situation as unusual. Why was he lying on stone?

He came awake in a rush as he realized he was in the wine cellar.

Dizziness coursed through him—he had sat up too quickly. He paused for a moment until the feeling passed, then looked around at his surroundings. Dimness. There was very little light in the space, but the fact there was light at all meant it was morning. He could make out the dim outline of the flagstones that paved the floor, as well as the barrel-shaped arch of the low stone ceiling. Water was dripping in a slow rhythm somewhere at the far end of the room. Stifling a groan, he swung his legs around and leaned back against the rough stone wall.

Yesterday had not been a good day.

Hell, his head hurt just *thinking* about it. When Nigel and his cohort, a burly man by the name of William, had captured him, they had promptly tossed him in the wine cellar the old earl had commissioned some thirty years earlier. It was built into the side of the sloping earth not twenty paces from the back of the house.

Nigel, apparently still peeved from the small matter of Benedict's attempt to choke him, had grinned pleasantly before walloping him with a sickening punch to his jaw. The impact had thrown Benedict to the back wall, where his head had bounced painfully off the stone moments before he dropped to the floor. Fortunately, he didn't actually *remember* hitting the floor; he just knew it to be the case when sometime later—he had no way of knowing how much time had passed—he had awoken in a heap on the ground.

With no light to illuminate his surroundings, he had gingerly explored the space inch by inch, hoping to find a way out. When the pounding of his head had exceeded even the pounding of his heart, he knew he had to stop. The darkness would have been disorientating even without his light-headedness; but with the added obstacle of exhaustion pulling at him like a physical force, he had finally decided to give in to his body's screaming demand to rest.

Somehow "rest" must have turned into full-fledged sleep. Stretching, he blinked and focused on the sliver of light coming from the small gap between the door and the stone threshold. The door was fashioned from rough-hewn timbers secured with iron hinges and a large brass lock. At almost thirty years old, the wooden door might have rotted enough for him to bust through. It was doubtful but still possible.

Gingerly, he had pushed himself up into a sitting position, his palms pressing against the cold, damp rock. Mercifully, though it still ached mightily, his headache did feel as though it was beginning to retreat. With utmost care, he lifted his body so he was on his hands and knees, and prepared to stand up. As a wave of pain ambushed him, he sat back on his heels and pressed his palm to his forehead.

If he ever got out of this situation, he was going to live his life with the sole priority of never getting knocked in the skull again.

Gritting his teeth, he lifted his right knee so the ball of his foot was planted firmly on the ground. He braced his hand on his knee and, after taking a deep breath, rose to a standing position. For a moment he rejoiced at the lack of pain, but after a beat, it came crashing down within his skull again. He staggered to the wall and leaned against it, breathing shallowly until the feeling subsided.

Well, that had gone well.

Into the silent darkness he said, "Right. Now what?"

Not surprisingly, there was no reply. He shuffled over to the door, supporting himself against the wall with one hand as he moved. Cautiously he pressed against it; it felt as solid as the day it was made.

"Damn it," he muttered under his breath. He hadn't expected it to give, but it would have been a nice break. The next step was to kick the thing, but even thinking it made his head ache. *It's only temporary,* he reminded himself. Pain was a fleeting sensation in the scheme of things. Easy to say in the aftermath, but it was indeed difficult to convince oneself of this truth when faced with the prospect of deliberately inflicting it on oneself.

"On the count of three," he murmured. He swallowed audibly, took a deep breath, and started counting. "One, two, three!"

Bang! His heel crashed down on the door with all the strength he could muster. The wood shuddered mightily, but, to his immense dissatisfaction, it held its ground. *Bollocks.* He growled angrily, glaring at the steadfast door and doing his best to ignore the furious pounding in his head.

"I wouldn't do that if I were you," a muffled voice warned from the other side of the door.

Benedict froze in surprise. A guard? His brother had posted a guard outside the cellar? Well, of course it made sense, but somehow he had in no way anticipated it. *Bloody hell,* he thought darkly. Walking backward until his back touched the wall, he then allowed himself to slide down the rough stone onto his backside.

What the hell was Henry waiting for, anyway? Surely the man had no reason to delay further, unless he was hoping to starve Benedict to death. His stomach growled loudly; perhaps that *was* the tactic Henry planned to employ. His brother never had liked getting his hands dirty.

At least he hadn't used to. Benedict clenched his jaw. Henry's words came back to him, as clearly as if Benedict were standing outside the window in Folkestone again, breathing in the salty sea air. *I assure you, I intend to see this done with all possible haste.*

At the sound of his brother's clipped, nasal intonations, its perfectly proper King's English in stark contrast to Renault's heavy French accent, Benedict's world had suddenly tilted, and he had clung desperately to the window ledge for balance. He had stood there reeling, fighting for breath as his vision narrowed and his insides twisted like a ruined ship's mast in gale-force winds.

Benedict clenched both fists at his side, renewing his promise to Evie and to himself to make his brother pay for the chaos his actions had wreaked on so many lives.

A scraping noise at the door caught his attention. The sound of metal on metal followed—a key in the lock!

Turning to face the door, Benedict braced himself. He was about to find out what his brother had in mind for him.

Sitting in bed just past seven in the morning, Evie mentally paced her room, trying to loosen the knot of apprehension that had taken up residence inside her chest. It had been two hours since Richard had departed, and the gloomy light of another cloudy day filtered through the window. Although exhausted, she had managed to sleep only in quick snatches since her brother had departed.

Evie looked up at the sound of a knock at the door. "Enter."

Mama opened the door, looking somewhat reserved. "How are you this morning?"

It was hard not to scowl at her mother. She wanted to be furious with Mama for standing in the way of her hopes for the future, but with the threat of the challenges Richard and Benedict faced, she pushed those feelings to the back of her mind. There would be time for that later. Besides, she knew Mama thought she was doing right by her. "I am feeling reasonably better."

Her mother paused at the foot of her bed. "Richard departed for London this morning. He left a note, and I thought you might like to see it." She handed the folded paper to Evie and crossed her arms. "You look exhausted, sweetheart. Why don't you get some more rest? I'll be back in a few hours to check on you."

Evie nodded, and her mother left, shutting the door behind her. Evie unfolded the letter and scanned the contents. The letter simply stated that Richard had returned to London on an urgent matter and had indicated he would see them when they came to town. There was no mention of Benedict, the hunting lodge, or Lord Dennington.

Benedict, Richard, herself—they were liars, all of them. This whole mess was turning them into what she hated most. It physically pained her to deceive her parents about where Richard was and why the incident had happened. Was this how Benedict had felt when he had been forced to lie to her?

Evie wondered what her father felt about the mess. As far as she knew, he thought the man who shot at them was simply a poacher who had fired on them in error, thinking them a herd of deer. He had not visited her since the day she was injured, and she dared not ask her mother how he was doing. Though there had been ample activity in the yard that morning, with several men coming and going on horseback, Evie was sure her father was still in residence.

She had never felt so helpless in her entire life. She glared down at the sling on her arm, silently and creatively cursing the injury it covered. If she had not been injured, Benedict would not be chasing across the countryside trying to hunt down his brother. Her own brother would not have gone tearing off after him, racing into a dangerous and unknown situation. She knew she was irrational. It was Dennington's actions that had incurred Benedict's wrath, and Benedict would have eventually decided to turn the traitor in, whether she was involved or not.

But it did not matter. The injury represented both the catalyst that had set Benedict off, and the roadblock that prevented her from doing anything to help. Worst of all, it served as the physical manifestation of Benedict's dishonesty to her and her family.

And she hated it.

Restless beyond measure, Evie threw aside the sheets, slid from the bed, and went straight for the box that held Benedict's letters. She suddenly felt the need to see his writing, to read his words—honest words—and discover how she would feel about them almost a decade removed from their last correspondence. It was time to face that last letter, as he had requested.

But first, she wanted to read the others—the ones that had made her laugh and feel so connected to him. After his betrayal, she had intended to destroy the lot of them, but when she stood in front of the flickering flames of her fireplace, she found she couldn't do it. She told herself she should keep them as a reminder of how sweet words could turn to terrible hurt, but deep down, she knew it was because she couldn't lose him completely. Instead, she'd let the letters serve as a cautionary tale so that she would never be fooled by a man again.

Locating the bundle, she hustled back to her bed and drew the covers up. She untied the blue ribbon around them and stared at the familiar writing that spelled out her address on the top letter. She smoothed her fingers over her own name, feeling a wholly unexpected rush of emotion.

Hastings . . . her Hastings. Her Benedict.

She opened the letter and began reading.

Dear Evie,

In the absence of an accompanying parcel to the letter I received from you today, allow me to remind you that I am still waiting for the

*embroidery sample you promised me in your
letter last month. "Home of a practically illiterate,
chauvinistic dimwit" would be the perfect piece to
enliven my dormitory room, wouldn't you agree?*

One by one she read through them, and by the time
Evie emerged from the letters, it was almost nine.
Warmth tickled her cheek and she swiped a hand at an
errant tear.

She loved him.

She probably always had, and she probably always
would. It mattered not what he called himself, or what
secrets he had held to his chest. He was hers, and she
loved him.

She thought of the circumstances surrounding the
whole debacle. If what Richard said was true, Benedict
was going to try to turn his brother in. She knew what
that meant, no matter how much her mind tried to shy
away from the possibility.

His family would be ruined.

If the Earl of Dennington was found to be a traitor,
the family would be stripped of the title and all that
went with it. Benedict would not be allowed to set foot
in polite society ever again.

She swallowed thickly. So what did that mean for
her? Before she could answer that question, she pulled
the infamous last letter from the bottom and slowly unfolded it. It was distinct, easily recognizable by the odd
way he had folded it.

Evie,

*For years, I have endured the constant bother
of your barbed tongue. You are, to be quite frank,
really just an annoying little pest of a girl with all the*

grace and decorum of a common horsefly. I have had it with your constant, unrepentant browbeating, your venomous pen, and your infantile reasoning. I thought, even despite your being female, that I might improve your mind over the course of our correspondence. I was wrong. Ergo, I'm washing my hands of you at last.

Hastings

She tossed the thing aside, not wanting to look at it a moment longer. Why would he ever wish her to read that again? Did he want to rub salt into her wounds? His last correspondence had broken her heart, and it had taught her that no man could be trusted. Yet he had seemed so blasted sincere when he left her, as if the letter would reveal something wonderful.

Clenching her jaw in an effort to stave off more ridiculous tears, she glared at the slightly yellowed sheet of paper. His parting words flitted through her mind. *Read between the lines.* She pursed her lips and considered the request, then finally picked up the page once more. This was pointless. There was not a single line drawn on the paper. She saw nothing that would delineate something important or special.

She was about to toss it to the floor, when a thought occurred to her. Smoothing the paper out, she squinted at the unusual folds. A double fold ran down the left side of the page, capturing the first letter of each line along the way. *Oh my goodness.*

F-o-r-g-i-v-e-M-e.

She gasped, raising a hand to her mouth. There it was, plain as day. An odd sensation washed through her, as if somebody let a shaft of sunlight into the darkest part of her heart. He had been telling the truth about the letter. He must have had a reason for writing it in the first place. Clearly he didn't mean what he wrote.

Evie shook her head in wonder, adjusting the way she looked at so many things.

She loved him. She would give up everything she knew to be with him, were she the only person impacted by the decision. But she wasn't. She had to think of her sisters. She could never do something that would harm their chances for marriage, and tying the family name to that of a traitor could have devastating repercussions.

Her heart squeezed painfully. How could this be happening? How could she find the man she wanted to be with, only to have him taken from her before they ever even had a chance? She closed her eyes, pressing a fist to her mouth.

She couldn't have him. The truth of it settled around her and chilled her like a blanket of snow.

But, even if she couldn't be with him, Evie had to try to help him. She might not be able to fight his enemies, but she could free his mind and clear his conscience by telling him that she forgave him. Their last conversation, when she had been filled with anger and resentment, could not be the last one they shared. It pained her deeply now to know that she had hurt him with her callousness. And Evie couldn't stand for him not to know that she forgave him. She had lived too many years hurt by a betrayal that she hadn't understood; she couldn't sentence him to the same fate.

When she opened her eyes, it was with new resolve. Her mind made up, she threw aside the covers and swung her legs around. The lingering discomfort in her shoulder hardly registered, she was so focused on her determination. She strode to the wardrobe, opened the doors, and pulled out a small traveling bag.

Chapter Twenty-six

France is very lonely without your letters to keep me company. Do you ever think of me? Never a day goes by that I don't think of you.
 — From Hastings to Evie, never even put to paper

After the suffocating silence of the empty cellar, the sound of the door scraping against the stone as it opened was jarring, to say the least. Benedict squinted against the blinding daylight that flooded the void and, to his eyes, lit the room like frozen lightning. He struggled to see as a dark figure filled the doorway. Damn, he hated being at such a disadvantage.

"Hello, Benedict. How nice of you to join us." Henry's nasal voice was tinged with even more arrogance than Benedict remembered. "I trust you are enjoying your accommodations?"

Standing with his back against the wall several paces from the door, Benedict refused to rise to the bait. "Henry." He nodded in greeting. Just beneath the surface, his blood rolled furiously through his veins. This was the man who had brought about Evie's pain. This was the man who brought shame to the family. Everything that was wrong in his life at that exact moment could be traced directly back to Henry.

"Follow me, if you please. I am very interested in hearing why you attempted to break into my home, and

I would prefer to converse in the comfort of my study. Nigel here will escort you." Henry stepped out of the doorway, and the hulking footman took his place, motioning for Benedict to join them. William was waiting a few paces farther back.

Benedict ground his teeth at the mandate but followed obediently. With such a distinct disadvantage, he had to keep his head about him until the opportunity to strike presented itself. As he emerged from the cellar, Nigel fell into step immediately behind him, and William remained at a distance with what Benedict could now see was a pistol in hand.

Together, they walked up the hill to the house and entered through the double glass doors in the back. The doors led directly into the small study. Once inside, Benedict took in his surroundings. The shelves lining the majority of the wall space in the room were mostly empty with the exception of several layers of undisturbed dust. The luxurious rug that had once lined the wood floor was absent, as were any of the normal accoutrements one might expect to see in a study.

Henry walked around the small desk and seated himself, flipping out the tails of his coat with flair as if he were in the finest drawing room in London instead of a dreary, ill-used hunting lodge. Once seated, he gestured to Benedict to sit in the remaining chair, which was positioned opposite the desk.

"Thank you, I would rather stand," Benedict responded tersely. Really, the whole situation seemed rather absurd. What was his brother playing at?

Henry pressed his lips together in displeasure, then looked past Benedict and gave a flick of his wrist. Immediately a large hand came down on Benedict's shoulder and relentlessly maneuvered him into the chair.

"On second thought, I think I'll sit," he said drolly. If

their formative years had taught him anything, it was that nothing got under his brother's skin like being flippant in the face of his "superiority." Undoubtedly it was ill-advised for Benedict to taunt the man who held almost all of the cards at the moment, but Benedict simply could not help himself.

Henry gave him a patently insincere smile and leaned back in his chair, pressing the tips of his fingers in a steeple. "I am on tenterhooks waiting to learn why you broke into my house."

Henry raised his eyebrows with mock politeness, looking to him expectantly. Benedict eyed him a moment. Was he serious? What was the man playing at? Benedict was not in the mood for games.

He crossed his arms and said bluntly, "After Barney failed in his *murder* attempt, he kindly provided me with his employer's address. Imagine my surprise when the house turned out to be the very hunting lodge that has been in the family for years."

Henry's right eye squinted slightly, and his nostrils flared perceptively. "Murder attempt? Don't be absurd. Barney had his orders to bring you to me—and he was paid very well for the service. There is no need to be so dramatic."

"He shot at our hunting party without any provocation. A young lady—and I do mean lady, as her father is a marquis—had the extreme misfortune of being thrown from her startled mount, thus suffering serious injury." His stomach clenched when he said the words. He would never forgive Henry for causing her pain. "I assure you my *imagination* played no part in the lady's wounds."

Benedict watched in surprise as Henry's face paled noticeably at the disclosure of Evie's injury. Interesting. Though he betrayed nothing in his expression, Benedict's mind raced to reevaluate possibilities he hadn't considered before. Perhaps Barney had gone rogue. It could have been retaliation for Benedict's role in the downfall of the smuggling empire from which Barney profited so handsomely.

Henry leaned forward, looking Benedict in the eye. "On my word as a gentleman, it was never my intention for anyone to get hurt. I hired Barney to find you once you disappeared and to bring you to me, nothing more, nothing less."

Henry stood and began to pace slowly behind the desk, his hands clasped behind his back. "Well, that is unfortunate. Truly, I do hope the lady recovers. Barney will have to be . . . rewarded for both his loyalty and his ability to carry out my instructions. And it also appears things have come to a head between us." He paused and placed his hands on the top of the chair back. Eyeing Benedict, he said, "You were seen in Folkestone by one of Renault's men."

Benedict nodded, not trusting himself to speak just yet. His teeth ground together at the gall of his brother to mention Renault's affiliation so casually.

Henry pursed his lips. He was probably surprised that Benedict was not denying he was there. "You have made quite the nuisance of yourself. Renault wishes to speak with you, but I thought things might go more smoothly if I could find you first." He began to pace once more.

"Your sense of familial loyalty knows no bounds."

Henry snapped around to face him. "Yes, you'd best not forget it. Without me, this family would be in ruins by now."

The nerve of the bastard. "Thanks to you, this family *is* in ruins!" Benedict made to stand but was slapped back down by one of Henry's men behind him. Benedict growled in frustration. In his fury, he had forgotten their presence.

"Without me, Renault would have hunted you down like a dog."

"Why didn't you let him?" Benedict cried, resentment coursing through his veins like black tar. "It would have been easier than this."

Henry paused and looked at him in astonishment. "You ungrateful bastard."

"Ungrateful, yes. Bastard, unfortunately not. I'm still your full-blooded brother, no matter how much it grieves me to admit it. You have brought shame down on all of our heads."

Henry drew back as if slapped, his slim shoulders going rigid. "So this is the thanks I get. I try to help you, and you spit in my face."

Benedict snorted in derision. "Help me? By climbing into bed with a cold-hearted criminal? And not just any criminal, but the very man who would like nothing so much as to have the pleasure of personally watching me die. Forgive me if I am unable to properly express my gratitude."

"You have only yourself to blame. When you decided to double-cross that low-life scum, what did you think would happen? Because I agreed to his terms, he won't leak your name to the authorities. He wants the goods you stole from him, but he is not going to bloody kill you."

Benedict went rigid in his seat. Wait a second—what did he mean? Did Henry think Benedict was the one working with Renault? He cautiously considered the possibility. Is this what his years of lying to his family about his profession had earned him? If his brother believed he had to bow to Renault to protect not only the family, but Benedict . . .

"Call off your men so we can talk man-to-man."

Henry threw him an incredulous look. "Do I look like an idiot to you? I—"

"For God's sake, have them tie me to the chair if you must, but we need to speak privately." He leveled a stubborn glare at Henry and sat in silence, all the while mentally beseeching his brother to do as he asked.

Henry eyed him critically for a moment, lips pursed in thought. More than anything, his dark eyes reflected confusion, as if uncertain about what to do next. It was not an expression Benedict would have expected from his brother, the earl. Finally, Henry gave a stiff nod and instructed his men to tie Benedict tightly to the chair. Once the bindings were secure, he waved them out of the room, admonishing them to stand outside the door. When the door clicked closed, he motioned for Benedict to continue with exaggerated deference.

Benedict decided at that moment he was done with secrets. He was done with deceit, with living a double life, and with lying to his family and friends. It appeared that all the deception in his life was what led him to this exact spot—being tied to a chair in his brother's study, missing the trust of one of his oldest friends, and having caused irrevocable pain to the most important woman in his life.

He pictured Evie as she had looked sitting on the stone bench in the garden by the light of the moonlight. Innocent. Undeserving of lies, especially when they culminated in depraved men showing up with murderous intents. Undeserving of a man like himself in her life.

He lifted his eyes to his brother with new focus. "I swear to you on our father's grave that what I am about to say is the utter and complete truth. I was recruited by the War Office right out of school. My competition wins in fencing caught their eye, and my athletic skills combined with my social status and fluent French made me a perfect candidate for becoming an agent for the Crown."

Henry's eyebrows shot up his forehead in surprise. Benedict rushed on, not wanting to give him the opportunity to interrupt. "I met Renault almost a year ago, when I was charged with infiltrating his operation. My work resulted in the capture and arrest of many of his top men. He escaped arrest, but during the chaos, his brother turned on me, and I had no choice but to kill him.

"I knew Renault would want revenge, but I thought my true identity was safe. When I heard word he had set up camp again, I went to investigate. That was when I heard you speaking with him."

Henry stood mute for a moment, staring at Benedict as if trying to read his mind. "You're lying."

Benedict shook his head slowly. "I knew the estate was struggling, and I thought you wanted an easy out. I have spent the last week in agony, coming to terms with the fact I would have to turn you over to my superiors and destroy our family in the process."

There—all of his secrets were now laid bare. God, he wished he had been as honest with Evie. He shook his head. He had to focus on the present.

Henry simply stared at him for a moment before dropping back heavily into the desk chair. Benedict was well aware that by admitting he was in the service of the Crown, he had effectively just ended his espionage career. Of course, as he had been compromised by Renault, truly it was already over. Curiously, he had no feelings of regret about putting that part of his life behind him. He only wished he had made the decision before he had caused harm to the people he cared about.

Henry lifted his eyes to Benedict. "I thought you were a traitor. He had proof in the form of letters you had written to him."

Benedict thought for a moment before understanding dawned. He meant the letters sent before the raid. They would look very damning indeed. "What was it he proposed? What exactly is the nature of your relationship?"

"It was not so much what he proposed but rather what he required," Henry answered somewhat cryptically.

What the hell was that supposed to mean? "In case you have forgotten, you are the bloody Earl of Dennington. As was drilled into me repeatedly while growing up, there are *very* few people who can require anything of you. I am fairly certain Renault would not be one of them."

Henry fingered the elegant inkwell that rested on the desk, avoiding Benedict's gaze. When at last he spoke, his words were carefully chosen and quietly uttered. "He threatened to not only reveal you as a traitor, but to destroy my name as well. He had done his homework. He knew about the debt the estate is in. He had me by the bollocks."

Benedict breathed a long breath. He felt slightly sick with himself, a feeling that was regrettably becoming more and more common as recent events had unfolded. "What did he want?"

"Oversee the distribution of a few shipments of smuggled goods, basically finishing the work he said you agreed to do."

At last, he felt cautious relief spread through his body like cool water; relief born from simply knowing that his brother had not willingly joined a smuggling ring, that he wouldn't have to drag his family's name through the mud. Just as strong was the relief that he could hope to someday be able to see Evie again.

"I fear I have made a grave mistake," Henry murmured.

"You did what you thought you had to do."

"No, you do not understand." Henry swallowed thickly. "I am not talking about the past. I am speaking of the immediate future. I—I sent for Renault. That is why I was holding you here. I sent for Renault, just as he instructed me, and he will undoubtedly be here very soon."

Oh dear God. Benedict sat in mute shock for a moment, trying to grasp the full ramifications of the claim. "He is coming here? Now?" He let loose a string of curses, struggling against the bindings holding him to the chair. "Henry, for God's sake man, how much time do we have? He will murder me where I stand—probably the both of us!"

Henry stood and rushed to the door. "Release him, Nigel, quickly!"

The startled footman looked uncertainly from Henry

to Benedict. The climate in the room was very different from when they had shut the door, and his brain seemed to be having trouble processing the change.

Henry looked at him in exasperation. "Now, Nigel."

As Henry glanced uneasily at his watch fob, Benedict's heart sank even lower. He had the awful feeling they were dealing not in hours, but rather minutes until his enemy arrived.

Heaven help them now.

Dear Papa,

We've been here before, but so much has changed since then. I must tell you that Mr. Benedict is in fact Mr. Benedict Hastings. It is a very long story, all of which I promise to share, but right now I need you to know only that I have gone to see him. Fear not, for Richard is with him now, and I will have Richard escort me home when my task is complete. I love him with all my heart, Papa. I must tell him that I forgive him. There has been so much miscommunication between us; I need for him to hear the words from my own lips.

Eight years ago when I set off to find him, it was out of my own hurt and betrayal. This time it is to set his mind at ease—to prevent that same pain for him. Please do not worry for me, and I beseech you not to try to come after me. When I return, I promise to live my life with the joy of having known love, however briefly. That is not to say I will not be heartbroken, but that I will at least no longer be living in fear and doubt.

In love and with hope for understanding,

Evie

*   *   *

"I don't know, my lady. Perhaps I should send for Lord Granville."

Evie tried not to show the alarm she felt at Dunley's words. Under no circumstances could her parents know what she was up to until *after* she was gone. Having banished her maid from her room so Evie could "rest," she was counting on having at least two hours before anyone discovered her absence and the letter upon her pillow. She peered at her longtime employee with her most authoritative air. "Dunley, you know full well that I act in my father's stead. He is very busy at the moment, and I wish to take a walk about the grounds."

She was very glad she had thought to drape a shawl over the sling on her left arm. She didn't want the groom to see that she was still suffering from the effects of the fall. Though the discomfort had lessened significantly, she thought it best to keep her arm from jostling too much on the ride.

"Yes, my lady, it is just that—"

"*Mr.* Dunley," she interjected sharply. The man closed his mouth and swallowed. "The stables have been my domain for years. It is not in your job description to question my wishes. I would like for Epona to be saddled and brought to me *immediately.* Is that understood?"

Dunley's eyes were as wide as dinner plates. She had never in her life spoken to any of the servants that way. She tamped down on the tiny hitch of guilt she felt; her mission was too important to worry about offending someone.

"Still, my lady—"

"Ah, there you are."

Beatrice. She stood in the doorway, the soft gray light of the overcast day outlining her small form. She strode forward purposefully, her slippers silent on the dirt floor. Evie didn't know what to think of her sister's arrival. She had caused trouble for Evie in the past, but Evie rather thought they had turned a corner at their last talk.

"Were you looking for me?" Evie kept her expression neutral, despite the unease scraping along her already frayed nerves.

"Yes. Papa sent me to ask you what time you thought you might be back. He wanted you to be present for the meeting with the estate manager." Her eyes were perfectly innocent, her words precisely delivered.

When Dunley looked from Beatrice to Evie for her answer, Beatrice winked and offered an impertinent grin. Love for her blessed, meddling sister swelled within Evie's chest, and she offered her a grateful smile.

"Thank you, Beatrice. I plan on taking a nice long walk with Epona, so don't expect me for hours yet. Tell Papa to schedule the meeting for late afternoon, if he doesn't mind."

"As you wish."

Evie turned impassive eyes to the head groom. "That saddle, Mr. Dunley?"

He nodded and disappeared into the tack room. Evie hurried to her sister's side and swallowed her in a big hug, grateful that she finally felt well enough to do so. "You are wonderful; do you know that?"

Beatrice squeezed her back before pulling away. "I don't know why you are leaving, but I am certain it has to do with Benedict."

Evie nodded, blinking back tears. "Yes. I love him. I must go to him."

"Well, then, you'd best get a move on. I will cover for you as long as I am able—that should buy you a few hours at the least. And I saw where you stashed your bag in the garden. I added some bread and biscuits that I filched from the kitchen in case you get hungry."

When had she become such a sweet girl? Evie offered her a heartfelt smile. "I won't ever forget this, Bea. Thank you."

She nodded once, kissed Evie's cheek, then retreated from the stables back toward the house.

The groom reemerged, toting the saddle in his arms and heading for Epona's stall. She offered him a small, conciliatory smile. "Thank you, Dunley. I have had just about enough coddling over the past few days, so forgive me if I am overly sensitive. You needn't worry; I know my limits, and I merely wish to get back in the saddle, quite literally."

He nodded again and set off to do her bidding.

Thank God.

Chapter Twenty-seven

If only I knew why you wrote that hideous letter. I tried to come after you, but Papa intervened. Now I'll never know why you betrayed me.
— From Evie to Hastings, mentally composed as her father escorted her home

The pounding of horse hooves outside was unmistakable. Benedict and Henry both froze in place, their eyes riveted on each other. They had moved from the office to the front room, both frantically trying to prepare for the upcoming confrontation. It was too soon. They hadn't had time to come up with a proper plan—or any plan at all, really.

"*Shit!*" Henry hissed, a look of panic coming over him.

Benedict's mind raced. "All right, this is what we are going to do. Have your man open the door and take him to your study. Tell him I am being kept in the cellar, and ask him to accompany you there. When you unlock the door, shove him in and lock the door." The plan was haphazard at best, but what were his options?

Henry was pulling the curtain back, trying to get a glimpse of Renault. "That doesn't make any sense. There is only one man out there. Renault always travels with at least two of his cohorts. What is he planning?"

Benedict rushed to the window and eased the fabric

aside to get a view. The rider reined in, dismounted, and walked briskly toward the front gate.

Gratitude unlike anything he'd ever experienced washed over him like a tidal wave. "Richard!" Benedict exclaimed, recognizing his friend's height and gait as he approached the house. He dropped the curtain and strode to the door. Relief coursed through him like a drug. "Richard!" he exclaimed again as he flung open the door, ignoring the bang as it crashed into the wall.

Richard stopped at once, startled. Benedict couldn't recall ever feeling so relieved, and thankful, and loved, and appreciative in his entire life. He watched as the look of shock transitioned to confusion in his friend's eyes. Richard half ran to the door, and Benedict grabbed his hand in a sincere handshake before pulling him in for a hug and a sound slap on his back.

He swallowed, trying to get his emotions under control. Of all the questions swirling in his head, the only sentence he managed was, "What are you doing here?"

Richard looked more than a little baffled. "I *thought* I was coming to help you, but it appears my assistance is not needed. Is your brother even here?"

"Indeed I am, sir." Henry appeared in the foyer and bowed smartly to Richard, who in turn looked as if he had bitten into a lemon.

Benedict held his hands up. "A lot has transpired since I arrived here. Henry had no idea Renault wanted me dead. Renault convinced him I was the traitor, and he threatened to ruin the family if Henry didn't carry out his instructions." He looked back and forth between the two men. Henry's affronted expression spoke clearly of betrayal while Richard's dropped jaw conveyed incredulity.

"I'm sorry, Henry, but I no longer have any secrets from Richard. And Richard, I wish I had more time to explain, but Renault will be here soon, and I have no doubt he will happily execute me where I stand if we don't come up with a plan. While I appreciate your presence here more than you can imagine, you must leave quickly if you are to be gone before he arrives."

Richard raised an eyebrow. "After waking at the ungodly hour of four in the morning, riding halfway to London at speeds that I really don't recommend, and only just reuniting with your illustrious self, you can't possibly think I am going to turn tail and run *now*, for God's sake." He strode past them into the lodge. "Offer me a drink, and let's get down to business."

Despite everything, Benedict cracked a smile. He'd be indebted to his friend for the rest of his life. Still, he couldn't just let the man walk blindly into the face of danger. "Richard, these men are not your average rum bibbers. They have killed men for far less than the things I have done to them. They will not hesitate to slit your throat."

"Even better—I won't have to worry about my pesky conscience when things get uncivilized." Richard's words were glib, but the determination in his eyes was unmistakable.

Benedict nodded once and knew his gratitude showed in his gaze. "Well then, let's adjourn to the study. Hopefully inspiration will strike and we'll actually come up with a viable plan." He headed down the corridor without waiting for the other men's agreement. The whole way, his mind was spinning, furiously trying to come up with a strategy. Renault was coming here to collect him. The Frenchman would have two to four men, armed and fully capable of combat. Benedict had no intention of killing or even wounding anyone if he could avoid it. He wanted them captured so he could deliver them to the home office himself, if possible.

The three men entered the room and fanned out,

Richard and Henry taking the two chairs in front of the desk while Benedict took a seat behind it. The room was cool and silent as he looked both men in the eye.

"I first want to say that my choices in life, and the deceptions thereafter, have led to this moment. Henry, I should have trusted you as my brother, my only sibling, with the truth about my career. Those choices resulted in a rather evil man showing up on your doorstep and pulling both you and the entire Dennington estate into the whole debacle. Your choices in the matter aside, it was ultimately his desire to retaliate against me that brought us to this moment."

At Henry's solemn nod, Benedict turned his attention to Richard. His friend had been part of his life for so many years; almost every school memory involved him. "Richard." He paused, struggling to find the right words. "Richard, I cannot express my sorrow for bringing this fight to your doorstep. I shall never forgive myself for Evie's pain. And there is simply no way for me to express my gratitude for your presence here. Your support, both physically and emotionally, is—well, just let me say thank you. From the absolute soul of my person, thank you."

He took a deep breath and moved on to the business at hand. "Now, I have dealt with Renault in the past. He is ruthless and dangerous, and we must be very careful how we handle him." Benedict turned to face Richard.

"Henry has sent for Renault, and he will be expecting to see me under Henry's control. Henry originally was holding me in the cellar, located a few paces down the hill behind the lodge. Here is what I have in mind." Benedict filled them in on the plan forming in his head. If they were exceedingly lucky, no one would be hurt and, by nightfall, they would have the Frenchmen en route to London. All they could do at this point was stick to the plan and pray that everything worked out.

*   *   *

Three hours later, everyone was in place when the thunder of horses' hooves announced Renault's arrival. Richard, who would be acting as one of Dennington's servants alongside Nigel, eyed Benedict's brother from his station by the front door.

It really was a pity this was deadly real and not an encounter at Gentleman Jackson's. After the chaos Dennington had put his family through, however unintentionally, Richard would dearly love the opportunity to thrash the man. But this *was* real, and they were allies with their common enemy fast approaching.

Dennington wiped a shaky hand across his forehead, smearing the sweat that dampened his brow. He looked like a frightened rabbit, ready to flee at the first sign of danger. Damn it, if Dennington didn't get over his blasted nervousness, he would blow the whole thing. Their plan was thin at best, but they were committed now, and Richard, for one, was going to do everything in his power to see it through.

"Deep breath, man," Richard said in a low voice. "Trust the plan."

Dennington looked up and met Richard's eyes. He drew in a sharp breath and nodded jerkily.

Richard suppressed the urge to give the man a quick throttle. Nothing serious—just enough to loosen him up a bit. "Dennington, trust your brother. He knows what he's doing."

A wry smile cracked Dennington's stiff facade. "I suppose it's about time I started trusting him. If I'd done so in the first place, none of this would be happening."

"Exactly," Richard said, nodding approvingly. A bit of the fear eased from the earl's face. Now he merely looked constipated. It was a slight improvement, at least. "And he's lying in wait in the cellar, ready to strike when the moment is right. Renault and his men won't stand a chance."

William was standing guard outside the cellar, keeping up the appearance that Benedict was a prisoner. In order for the plan to work, Renault had to believe all was in order. If he was put on the offensive, things would turn bad in a heartbeat.

Footsteps approached the front door, and Richard took one last, calming breath. This was it. Nigel nodded once to him before pulling the door open before Renault could knock, and he ushered the Frenchman and his three men into the room where Richard and Dennington waited. The man in front was undoubtedly Renault. His great, slightly crooked nose was exactly as Benedict had described. His black hair was slicked back from his face, and his dark gaze settled unerringly on Dennington, ignoring Richard completely.

The tall, stick-thin man behind him looked to be the man Dennington had described as Armand, and the white-haired crony had to be Charles. The third man, whose thick, muscular build and sandy blond hair didn't match any of Benedict's or Dennington's descriptions, hung nearest the doorway.

Without prelude, Renault asked, "He is here?"

Dennington paled visibly under Renault's scrutiny. "Y-yes," he said, his voice cracking slightly. "He is in the cellar down the hill."

Richard bit the inside of his cheek, narrowing his eyes at the earl. *Get it together, Dennington.*

"I wish to see him." Renault's French accent seemed exceptionally pronounced within the confines of the English hunting lodge.

Dennington nodded and gestured to the doorway. "Of course. We've been keeping him in the old cellar behind the house. If you will follow me, I will take you to him."

Renault's face contorted at the suggestion. "I have no wish to slosh through the mud to your cellar. Bring him here, if you please. It is much more civilized."

Dennington's face betrayed a hint of panic, and Richard ground his teeth to keep from intervening. Already things were veering from their plan—and they had no real contingency plan.

"Is there a problem, Dennington?" The calm in Renault's gravelly voice was chilling. Was he beginning to suspect things were not as they should be? The weight of the gun tucked in Richard's waistband was little comfort if the four Frenchmen turned on them now.

"No! Of course not. Nigel," Dennington barked, and his servant immediately appeared in the doorway. "Please escort my brother from the cellar. Take care that he is . . . properly restrained. Please."

"Yes, m'lord." Nigel turned and strode from the room.

Renault nodded to one of his men. "Lawrence, perhaps you would accompany Monsieur Nigel. Another set of hands may prove useful." The man named Lawrence nodded and trotted out of the room.

As the minutes ticked by, Richard could do nothing but watch the sweat beading on Dennington's forehead. Each tick of the grandfather clock was like the clapping of hands, and the earl grew more and more agitated with each swing of the pendulum.

Richard willed the earl to stay calm, to sit it out and wait for his brother to adapt to the new plan. His heart dropped when Dennington took a step for the door.

"I will just see what is keeping them."

"Sit!"

At Renault's command, Dennington promptly dropped back into the chair like a trained dog.

Renault put a heavy hand on the earl's shoulder. "We are in no hurry. Please, do not trouble yourself."

A shuffling noise in the corridor caught Richard's attention, and he turned in time to see William appear in the doorway, his eyes trained on Dennington. One look at his master, and William sprang forward, lashing out at the nearest of Renault's men, Charles. Richard barely took a single step before William landed a punch square on the man's temple.

No!

"*Sacré bleu!*" The curse rang over the ensuing chaos as Renault swung around, dropping his hand from Dennington's shoulder. The earl bolted from his seat, stumbling backward. In front of him, Charles shook his head like a dog and turned on William. Bloody hell, there was no going back now. Richard rushed into the melee, headed for Armand.

"Armand, *en garde*!" Renault shouted, brandishing a pistol that seemed to have materialized out of thin air. Immediately Armand responded, knocking over his chair in his rush to stand and draw his pistol.

Richard came to a dead stop, thrusting his hands in the air. Damn it, he should have drawn his own bloody pistol, but his first instinct had been to fight. William backed up as well, panting as he raised his palms face out. Charles, looking furious when he wiped his cheek and came away with blood, quickly drew his own weapon. Moving so rapidly the motion almost seemed like a blur, he lashed out at William with the butt of the pistol, connecting with the footman's forehead. Blood flowed down William's face before he even dropped to his knees.

Dennington uttered a strangled sound, horror plain in his widened eyes as he gaped at his servant's injuries. Richard started to react, but Armand immediately waved his gun at him.

"Go ahead, monsieur. I will be only too pleased to kill you."

Richard stilled, grinding his teeth with impotent fury. The smile on the Frenchman's face showed how happy the man would be to put a bullet in Richard's chest. William groaned, pressing a hand to his bleeding head.

"Here, allow me help you with that." Charles's polite tone, with its melodic French accent, was chilling. When William turned to look at him dazedly, Charles swung at him again, this time nailing him directly in the right temple. Like a felled tree, William pitched forward, hitting the dusty wood floor face-first.

Richard would feel worse for the man if the fool hadn't started the whole thing. A soft sound drew his attention to the earl, who had gone as white as a sheet. He sat heavily on the sofa, visibly swallowing. When his eyes met Richard's, Richard could almost hear his thoughts. *First William—who was next?*

"What is the meaning of this? Do you dare to try to deceive me, you stupid, stupid man?" Renault spat furiously, his knuckles white as he gripped the pistol.

Dennington raised his hands, his eyes snapping back and forth between the barrels of Renault's and Charles's pistols. He opened his mouth to speak, but nothing came out but a moan.

Richard took advantage of the Frenchmen's attention being on the earl and reached slowly behind his back. The warm metal was digging into his back, taunting him with its nearness.

"Let's go," Renault snapped, motioning to the door. "Both of you, outside. Hands up!"

Richard froze at the command as Renault's black gaze landed on him. If he moved now, Richard had no doubt he'd be joining William on the floor. Angrily, he thrust his hands back into the air and moved toward the foyer and out the front door. As he passed Armand, the Frenchman lifted Richard's jacket and snatched the pistol from where it was tucked at his back. Richard's whole body tensed, but Armand just laughed as he thrust the gun into his own waistband and pushed him forward.

Bloody. Bloody. Bloody. Hell.

Once outside, they fanned out and faced one another once more. Dennington swayed on his feet, staring fixedly at the end of Renault's pistol. As his gaze flicked back and forth between the three enemies, Richard's mind whirled with possible scenarios of attack. Unfortunately, each avenue led to a dead end, possibly literally.

"On your knees—both of you," Renault said, fairly spitting the words.

Henry and Richard exchanged glances before doing as they were told. Things were far outside any possibility of this going to plan.

Renault stalked over to Dennington. "Where is your brother?"

"I don't know," the earl exclaimed, his voice much higher than usual.

Viciously, Renault slapped his face with the shiny metal barrel of the pistol, sending him flying sideways into the gravel. Blood poured to the ground in a red river, shockingly stark against the white gravel of the drive. Richard's hands fisted at his side. If he moved now, one of the blasted idiots holding a gun on him would surely pull the trigger.

"Do not lie to me! Where is he?"

Dennington, lying prone in the sharp gravel, remained silent and covered his face with his hands. Richard couldn't fault the man for his reaction. However angry Renault was, the truth would only make things worse. Blood stained the once-white cuffs of his shirt, and Richard had the sudden image of an injured bull emboldening its bloodthirsty matador.

After a few seconds of silence, Renault lashed out with his foot, clipping the earl soundly in his right kidney. Dennington cried out in pain and curled into a protective ball.

"Where is your brother? You sent for me so that I could collect him, so where is he?"

"Right here, Renault."

Standing in the doorway to the house, Benedict felt hot fury slide like molten lava through his veins as he surveyed the scene in front of him. His brother lay crumpled on the ground at Renault's feet; Richard was on his knees a few feet away with his hands frozen at his sides.

At the sound of Benedict's voice, Richard immediately took advantage of the distraction and launched himself at the closer of the two enemies, Armand. His head caught the unsuspecting man in the belly and knocked him to the ground.

Upon impact, Armand's pistol discharged. The rogue bullet thudded harmlessly into the trees. As the two scuffled on the ground, Renault and Charles swung their pistols wildly between Richard, Henry, and now Benedict. Two pistols were at least better than three.

Henry tried to scuttle backward on his hands and feet but succeeded only in snagging Renault's attention. The Frenchman lunged for Henry's collar and dragged him to his feet in front of him, using him as a human shield. Though Benedict's aim never wavered, his trigger finger immediately relaxed.

Bloody hell.

Renault smiled. "It appears, Monsieur Hastings, that we are at an impasse. I hold your brother's life in my hands. How appropriate—an eye for an eye, a brother for a brother." There was no mistaking the cold malice in the Frenchman's eyes. Benedict's heart slammed in his chest, but he did not move even a fraction of an inch.

"However," Renault continued, his voice deceptively calm, "if I kill him, you will surely kill me. What is it that you suggest, I wonder?"

Benedict regarded his enemy through squinted eyes. The answer sprang easily to his lips. "A duel."

"A duel?" Renault laughed derisively. "You expect me to fight you to the death? But of course, monsieur. What will it be, pistols or swords? I assure you, I am much more accomplished than my brother was. You are no match for me at either one, so you may choose."

"Swords," Benedict replied tersely.

"How do I know your friends will not simply try to kill me if I succeed?" Renault's eyes were narrowed to slits.

"The same way I know your men will leave if I am the victor. We are all gentlemen here, and we have standards. In an honorable duel, the winner must be respected. Now, I assume your man here will be your second?" Benedict nodded to Armand, who was currently being sat on by Richard.

"But of course. And I assume your brother will be yours?" Renault asked with amused condescension.

"You assume wrong. Richard, if you will do me the honor, please?"

Richard's eyes went momentarily wide, and he nodded quickly.

"Excellent. Gentlemen, please lay down your weapons and let us take our places. I believe the drive will suffice." Benedict lowered his weapon first, and Richard got to his feet.

Renault pushed Henry away, causing him to stumble in order to keep on his feet. Slowly, Renault lowered his own weapon and stepped back. "Where is Lawrence?" Though his weapon remained pointed at the ground, Benedict had no doubt he was poised to attack at the slightest provocation.

"Not to worry, he is alive. He is being tended to by Nigel."

Renault nodded and finally released the cock on his weapon.

Warily, everyone got into place. With Henry standing in front of the door and the seconds behind their primaries, Henry called out, "Ready!"

Both Benedict and Renault brandished their swords. Henry lifted Benedict's pistol skyward and let off a single shot.

The duel had begun.

Chapter Twenty-eight

*Will you ever stop haunting my dreams? I sincerely
hope not.*
  *—From Hastings to Evie, spoken into the hush of
      dawn a year after his last letter to her.*

Eyeing the freshly trampled ground leading to an ill-
used driveway several miles outside of Amersham,
Evie breathed a heartfelt sight of relief. This had to be it.
The turnoff looked exactly as the old farmer just south
of the small village had described it.

She slowed Epona to a walk as she turned the horse's
nose up the drive. She had long since abandoned the re-
strictive sling, and she took advantage of the slower
pace to rub her shoulder. She ached in places she had
never felt before, in ways she had never experienced before. Nothing, however, ached as much as her heart. She
could only hope she wasn't too late.

During the ride, she freed her mind from the discomfort and relived his breath on her skin, his silken voice in
her ear, his heat against her lips. She recaptured the love
she had fostered for him all those years ago. She hadn't
even known that was what it was until now. No wonder
she had been so crushed, so utterly distraught at his final
letter. He was her first—and her only—love, and she
would fight for him now.

She rubbed a weary hand over her eyes and squinted

up the drive ahead of them. The curving path made it impossible to see what lay ahead. Who knew what she was walking into? She had little in her favor as far as protection or weapons, so maintaining stealth was probably the best tactic. Urging Epona off the drive, she steered them into the forest, keeping the drive in sight.

What was that? She yanked back on the reins, stopping Epona in her tracks. Indistinct, odd sounds rang through the woods from the direction of the house. A flash of movement caught her eye. She pressed her heels into her mount's flanks, and they surged forward toward the edge of the clearing. Something was happening, and she had to know what. At last she could see a clearing and then the house, and she hauled up on the reins before breaking from the cover the forest provided.

The clashing of steel rang clearly through the air. She quickly drew aside the leaves blocking her view and gasped when she saw two combatants locked in swordplay. Benedict! She urged Epona closer still, until she was almost at the tree line. Ahead of her, the men wielded their weapons, their movements graceful and deadly all at once. The blades flashed with blinding speed as they attacked and counterattacked, parried and thrust.

As if joined, their feet moved forward and back as one, knees bent and stances wide for optimum balance. Both men's shirts were beginning to darken with sweat.

She dragged her eyes away from the fight long enough to take stock of the others watching the duel. She recognized Richard, and the man standing beside her brother bore a rather striking resemblance to Benedict. It had to be the earl. Two other men stood alert nearby.

Unable to keep her eyes from Benedict for long, she returned her attention to the escalating fight. She felt no physical pain in that moment, nothing at all. Every fiber of her being focused on the movements of the two men locked in battle.

Benedict's movements were as graceful as a waltz, each move gliding smoothly into the next. His opponent was shorter, more compact, and he executed his maneuvers as a blacksmith wielded his hammer. The contrast was striking, and her heart pounded unbearably within her chest.

What if the other man wore Benedict down? What if Benedict slipped, or fell, or his aim was off? Everything within her longed to scream out, to make them stop. But she didn't move or make a sound. She would not be responsible for distracting Benedict, not when distraction could lead to injury.

Or worse—much worse. Evie pressed her hand to her mouth and waited.

Renault was better than Benedict had expected, easily countering his every move, putting him on the defense several times. He concentrated hard on learning his opponent's technique and was gratified when he quickly began to see a pattern in the way the other man fought.

At last Benedict had the upper hand, and his movements became more forceful and dynamic. Renault was retreating more than advancing now, and the diabolical grin was diminishing. The Frenchman's confidence began to waver, and his technique suffered. He began to lash out in frustration, clumsy jabs that Benedict easily parried.

Suddenly, Benedict saw his chance, and he attacked with a second intention. Exactly as he wanted, Renault responded with a riposte, in which he was open to Benedict's powerful counter-riposte. He knew victory was his as his blade sank into the flesh of Renault's side, drawing an agonized growl of pain.

Benedict quickly drew back his sword and stepped away, panting. Renault's left hand went immediately to his injured side where blood was quickly blooming.

Benedict bowed his head slightly, "First blood, sir. Victory is mine. I ask that you please remove yourself and your men from this property at once."

"First blood," Renault spat. "What has this to do with anything? This is a duel to the death."

Benedict looked down at the injured man, silently considering him. "I have no desire to kill you, Renault, just as I had no desire to kill your brother. I am satisfied that the battle is won, and I should think you would appreciate my benevolence. Now I ask you again: Be gone from this place, sir."

Renault straightened, grunting with the effort, and regarded him silently for several seconds. Finally, he bowed his head. "Merci, Monsieur Hastings."

Thank God. Benedict nodded and turned to walk away. He had not taken two steps when he heard Renault's hoarse roar and swiveled to see him lunge forward with his sword. Benedict swung up his own sword even as he knew it was too late to stop the onslaught.

Crack!

"No!"

Evie shot from the brush and into the clearing, screaming as Benedict and his opponent hit the ground together. Benedict's brother held a smoking pistol in his hands while Richard and one of the unknown men wrestled for another pistol.

Dear God, had the earl shot his own brother? It couldn't be; it simply could not be. Her last words could not be words of anger, their last encounter full of animosity. She had to reach him. *He has to be alive!* She urged Epona faster, stopping only when they reached the low rock-wall border lining one side of the drive. Heedless of her soreness, she scrambled down onto the wall before jumping to the ground and running for Benedict.

The second unknown man had already reached the prone pair and pulled Benedict's groaning opponent off him, dragging him several feet away.

She was too late. She could see the blood soaking his shirt, the thin fabric clinging to his heaving torso. Her stomach clenched violently at the sickly, metallic smell clinging to him like an aura. She wanted to smell his sandalwood scent; she wanted to cleanse away the horrible smell of blood. She collapsed on the ground at his feet, desperately glad he was still breathing.

"Benedict! Benedict, say something. Anything." She grasped his shoulder in her right hand, shaking him roughly. Tears pricked her eyes as her gaze took in his beautiful, haggard face.

He blinked and looked at her as if she were a ghost. "Evie?"

She nodded jerkily. "Benedict, you've been shot."

"Evie, what are you doing here?" His hand went to the back of his head, and he winced.

Was he delusional? Disoriented? She placed her hands on either side of his face and said earnestly, "Didn't you hear me? You've been shot."

He gave her a small smile and shook his head, wincing again. "No, Renault was shot. I just hit my head when he knocked us to the ground."

Evie's hammering heart froze completely before roaring back to life. Could it be true? She eyed the blood on his shirt uncertainly. "But the blood . . ."

Benedict pushed to a sitting position and patted a hand across his chest. "Is his, not mine." He reached a hand up to cup her cheek, and she pressed into his hot, dirty palm. "I'm all right, Evie; I promise."

Relief surged through her so strongly it made her light-headed, and she sagged against him. Footsteps approached, intruding on their moment. Evie looked up to see the earl standing over them. He looked to Benedict, his expression dazed. "He was going to kill you. He was going to stab you in the back."

"I know. I know. Henry, you saved my life." Benedict looked to her again and pressed a kiss to her cheek. "I'll be right back, sweetheart. Don't move."

He stood and crushed his brother to his chest, hugging him tightly as Dennington's legs seemed to give out. She didn't understand what was happening, but she knew they had shared a strained relationship. It looked as though they had just found each other again. Evie stood and turned away, giving them a bit of privacy.

She looked to Richard, who was watching her with drawn features. He didn't look at all pleased to see her. A man emerged from the house, and her brother handed over the pistol he had trained on the enemy and trotted over to her.

"What in God's name are you doing here? Papa may very well kill you when he discovers what you have done." Despite his harsh words, he wrapped an arm around her and gave her a quick, tight hug.

She ignored the lingering burn of her shoulder, having become accustomed to it hours ago. "I couldn't stay away. I had to come, to tell him I forgive him."

He shook his head, clearly disapproving. "And this couldn't have waited a few days? You could have gotten yourself killed."

"Leave her be, Richard." Benedict left his brother's side and came to stand beside Evie. "I'd like to have a word with your sister, if you don't mind."

He and Richard stared each other down, engaging in a silent battle. At last, Richard stepped back and nodded. "Go get yourself cleaned up. We'll take care of everything out here."

Benedict nodded and pressed a firm hand to the small of Evie's back, guiding her inside. He directed her up the stairs and to a stale-smelling bedroom. "I need to clean up. Can you give me a minute?"

She nodded, not trusting her voice after the violent swing of emotions she had experienced in such a short time. He disappeared through the door, and she collapsed on the stiff chair positioned in the corner.

She thought she had lost him. When she saw the blood covering him, her world shattered, falling down around her shoulders like broken glass. Without a shadow of a doubt, she knew she couldn't live without him. What was she going to do? She couldn't ruin her sisters' marriage prospects because of her own choices. Was it enough to know that he was alive and safe, even if she couldn't be with him? Her heart constricted at the thought. She squeezed her eyes closed. She would do what she had to do for the good of her family.

Perhaps they would pick up their quills once more and share their lives through ink and paper. It had served her well for years, and it might be the only way to make life bearable when she lost him.

"May I come in?" She looked up to see him framed in the doorway. Wearing a fresh white shirt that seemed a little too small for him, he looked like a new man, his hair wet, his skin scrubbed clean, the stubble scraped away. Holding her gaze, his eyes were at once playful and searching.

It took a few seconds for Evie to realize she had stopped breathing completely. Thank goodness she was already sitting down. Quickly she drew in a desperate breath of air, trying all the while to convince herself that the man before her was not an apparition. Her mouth abruptly parched, she swallowed and said softly, "Yes, please do."

His eyes never left hers as he walked across the room to the settee where she sat and lowered himself down beside her.

"Evie," he said, so much warmth infusing his voice, she actually blushed. He licked his lips and started again. "Please allow me to introduce myself. My name is Benedict Hastings, and I am an old friend of your brother's. I hope you will forgive the lack of proper introduction."

His lips curved upward slightly, and he reached out to take her hand. The touch was featherlight and so pleasurable that she closed her eyes and shivered. It was so perfect a moment that she was reluctant to open her eyes. What if it was a dream?

He touched a finger to her chin, and her eyelids fluttered open. It was definitely not a dream.

"Benedict—," she started to say, but he placed a gentle finger over her lips.

"Please, let me say something first." She closed her mouth and nodded, and he lowered his finger and claimed her free hand. "Evie, I have no right to ask for your forgiveness for the deception I brought into your life. It was not fair to you that I presented myself as someone I was not, thereby forcing your whole family to take part in a ruse without the benefit of knowledge or choice. If I had it to do over again, I would have run in the opposite direction. But I cannot undo what is done, however I may wish to. And I do wish that I could, please make no mistake."

He paused and looked away from her, his gaze flitting around the room. Her own eyes dropped, and she studied their joined hands. She had already forgiven him in her heart, but it was still somehow gratifying to hear the remorse in his voice. She knew he could have never wished for things to unfold the way they had, but it was reassuring to hear him say so nonetheless.

There was a tiny part of her, one that she was reluctant to acknowledge, that wished he had not regretted meeting *her*. She stared intently at their coupled hands and fervently hoped it was more than just a comforting touch from an old friend. She wanted him to crave her as she did him. She wanted him to feel the same intensity of feelings toward her that now swirled within her own heart.

"Evie, look at me," he said gently, lifting her hand to his lips and pressing a firm kiss upon the inside of her wrist.

Her eyes flew up to meet his the moment his lips touched her sensitive skin, for the intimacy of the gesture could not be denied.

She sucked in her breath and did not even try to slow her fluttering heart. He placed her open palm against his cheek and covered her hand with his own. His cheek was warm, the skin smooth and soft. The sensation of touching his face could only be described as delicious. Slowly he lowered their joined hands and took a deep breath.

When he spoke again, his tone was noticeably lighter. "But I would be a liar if I said I regretted *everything* about that ill-fated plan. I was stunned when you ran into me that first day." He smiled briefly before looking at her questioningly. "Did you ever wonder why I always responded to your letters?"

Cautiously Evie nodded. How could she not question why a schoolboy two years her elder had taken an interest in the faceless little girl tucked away in the country?

"You were the only person who had ever written me. My family could not have cared less about my well-being. I had no letters from home as the other boys did, regaling them with anecdotes and the latest gossip. When I arrived at Eton, I was an isolated, lonely young boy who was grateful to have found a real friend for the first time in his life.

"And then came a surly letter from my new friend's little sister. Evie, you must have known how comical it was to me. But at the same time, I was in awe of a person who could love her sibling so ferociously, and greedily." He offered her an amused smile, which she returned self-consciously.

"And so I wrote you back." He shrugged. "I purposely goaded you, hoping to get another letter from you. It certainly worked."

"What happened, Benedict? I saw the message between the lines, but what prompted you to send it in the first place?" She pressed a hand to her chest. "You broke my *heart* that day." And every day after that, really. The pain of his betrayal softened over time, but had never truly left her.

He shook his head slowly, pressing his lips together. "I was a stupid arse of an eighteen-year-old buffoon, and I handled everything abysmally. The government recruited me to be an agent for the Crown, and I had to break ties with my old life before moving on to my new one."

An agent for the *Crown*? Her expression must have given away her incredulity, because he shook his head. "I will tell you absolutely everything about that time in my life later. Suffice it to say, I handled it all wrong, and there really aren't words to express how much I regret hurting you.

"When things blew up in my face last week, I foolishly turned to my oldest friend to help me. I was devastated when I thought my brother had purposely affiliated himself with a man who was not only a known smuggler, but a man who wanted me dead. I had a choice to make: I could turn Henry in to the authorities and effectively destroy my family and the Dennington earldom, or I could hold my silence and destroy my honor, my integrity, and my self-respect."

Evie squeezed his hands. How could one possibly choose between such horrible options? He had been through so much. She was ravenously curious about his being an agent of the Crown, but she didn't want to interrupt him—not yet, not when he seemed so close to . . . something. She nodded, encouraging him to continue.

"I needed time to come to grips with the situation. I could not bring myself to tell anyone, even Richard, everything that had transpired. When I came face-to-face with you, I was shaken. First was the shock of seeing you at all when I believed your family was in London. After that, I was in awe of you. I would have expected this brusque bluestocking, and here was this beautiful, captivating woman."

He thought her captivating?

He gave a little half smile. "The breath was taken right out of my lungs. With all that was going on in my life, nonetheless I became completely preoccupied with my old correspondent." The smile on his face quickly faded to a grimace. "I lost my focus, and in the process you were hurt. I am so very sorry for that. I'm sorry for a lot of things."

She found herself suppressing an unexpected grin. He was here with her now, and she did not want to dwell on the ills of the past anymore. She raised an eyebrow and said with mock haughtiness, "As you should. In case you did not know, getting shot at and thrown from one's horse is not *at all* a pleasant experience. I really don't recommend it."

There was no mistaking the instant flash of relief in his warm chocolate eyes. He grinned impishly at her. "Consider me educated, my lady."

"And I must tell you," she said, wanting to set things straight, "I didn't really know what I was talking about when I said I knew about your brother. I didn't—not until later. I'm sorry if I wounded you with my lack of concern."

He closed his eyes for the space of a breath before meeting her gaze once more and nodding. "Thank you for that."

She looked him in the eye, letting him see into her soul. "I forgive you. It's why I came. I needed you to know that I forgive you." *And that I love you.* She wasn't ready to voice those words yet.

She relished the joy that spread over his face. "I think those are the sweetest words I have ever heard. Even better than when I learned my brother was an unwilling accomplice to Renault. Henry thought he was protecting me, believe it or not."

She gasped. "Truly? Then you don't have to turn him in?" Hope swelled like a cresting wave within her. Did that mean she could have him? Would he want her? Her mind raced with the possibility.

Benedict shook his head. "We will have to go to the War Office and explain the whole mess to them, but I am confident things will work out fine, and no one will be the wiser."

"So you are free? There is nothing left to worry about?"

"Nothing that can't be dealt with. At the moment, my biggest worry is that both our brothers are downstairs, keeping me from doing all the things with you that I couldn't when secrets were between us. As a matter of fact," he said, spreading his arms wide while holding her hands so to draw her close against him, "I'd like nothing more than to explore exactly how little there could be between us."

Evie *really* liked the sound of that. Pressed against his chest as she was, she found it hard to care that their family waited so close by.

Stepping back, he raised her hands and kissed them one at a time. "I will admit, I am a little miffed about something myself."

She blinked, trying to see past the image of the two of them intertwined on the bed. "And what, pray tell, is that?" She was glad that the misery and seriousness were lifting from his expression. A thrill raced through her as he idly rubbed his thumbs over the tops of her hands.

"You promised years ago that should we ever meet, you would know me by a single phrase. I gave you many a phrase, my love, and still you did not know me. How could that be?"

Her heart sang at the endearment—he had called her *my love*! "Oh, Benedict, I knew you—I just did not *realize* I knew you. My heart was sure of its feelings; my soul felt that you were my match. Inexplicably, I fell in love with a stranger in the space of a few days, only to find that the stranger was my soul mate whom I have known half my life."

A smile spread slowly across his full lips, a smile so heated and full of promise, warmth flooded her entire body. Without another word, he withdrew his hands from hers and clasped them behind her neck. Slowly, he drew her to him until their lips were less than an inch apart.

Pressing his forehead to hers, he whispered, "Forgive me?"

Without a moment's hesitation, she breathed, "With all my heart."

His lips spread into a delicious grin before he pressed his mouth hard against hers, kissing her with all the bottled-up passion that had been building be-tween them since the day James Benedict had walked into her life.

And she kissed him back, with all the love she pos-sessed for her dear Mr. Benedict Hastings.

Epilogue

One year later

Evie greeted the butler as she entered the front door, handing over her overcoat. "Thank you, Grayson. Is Hastings in his study? Oh wait. Don't tell me. What a silly question—of course he is."

"Indeed, my lady." He smiled briefly before clearing his expression to one of dignified indifference. He wasn't quite as splendid as her parents' butler, but he was close. In a few years, he might just surpass Finnington.

"Thank you, Grayson," she said over her shoulder as she headed for the study. She paused to collect herself before pushing open the door and letting herself in. As she crossed the carpet, Benedict looked up from his work. A grin quickly lit his face.

"Hello, my lovely wife. How are you today?"

She returned his smile as she walked around the desk and said offhandedly, "Oh, I am well. Are you very busy today?"

"I am very busy *every day*," he replied with a little shake of his head. "Henry asked me to look over some numbers for him regarding the upcoming harvest. He believes that, barring disaster, he may just have enough left over to do some repairs for some of the tenants this year. Things are turning around much quicker than we had hoped."

Pride swelled within her—what a clever man she had married. "Well, of course they are. With you overseeing the management of the estates, it is bound to thrive," she said loyally.

He chuckled and pushed his chair back from the desk. "My, what faith you have in my abilities." He held a hand to her, and when she grasped it, he tugged her into his lap.

"Well, I have learned that there are very many things that you . . . excel in," she said, wagging her eyebrows suggestively. She groaned with pleasure when he rewarded her by pressing his lips to hers and kissing her rather thoroughly. His kisses still stirred butterflies within her, and she reveled in the delectable feeling. Perhaps they could finish their conversation upstairs. . . .

"To what do I owe the pleasure of your company? How are things at the stables?" He nuzzled her neck, making her giggle when he flicked his tongue across her earlobe.

"I don't know, actually. I never made it to the stables."

He pulled back, surprised. "You didn't? Why not?"

Shortly after their marriage in June, Benedict had surprised her with the lease of a lovely little manor house not six miles from Hertford Hall. He had wanted her to have the option of helping her father in the stables whenever she chose to. She had been ecstatic at the gesture—as were her parents, who until then had been less than thrilled with the chaos Benedict had brought to their lives—and ever since they moved in, she spent two days a week at the Hall.

"Well, I started the day with a conversation with my mother. It is very helpful for a woman to have her mother so close by, you know," she informed him before planting a kiss on the tip of his nose.

Benedict smiled and gave her waist a little squeeze. "And what was it your mother helped you with today?"

"Well, let's just say I wanted to confirm something with her. And she did."

"She did what, my love?" he asked distractedly, pre-occupied with tugging at the lace tucked above her bod-ice.

"Confirm what I suspected."

She felt the moment Benedict's muscles tightened, and he pulled back to look her in the eyes.

"Evie, are you . . . ?" His voice trailed off as he failed to ask the question on the tip of his tongue.

She smiled broadly now and nodded her head. "I am in the family way, it would seem."

Benedict let out a whoop and, cradling Evie gently in his arms, sprang from the chair and did a quick spin. They laughed together, and he set her down and kissed her again.

When at last he pulled away, he had a very smug expression on his face. "Well, then, the gift I ordered for you could not have arrived at a more advantageous time."

"A gift? For me? Oh please, you must tell me what it is." She spun around in a circle, but she didn't see any-thing out of the ordinary in his tidy study.

He chuckled and took her hand. "It is not in here. Fol-low me, if you please."

He led her out of the glass door that led to the gener-ous terrace out back. And there it was—she could not have missed it. A telescope! And not just any telescope. "Oh my word, it's a Newtonian sweeper!" she exclaimed.

He nodded proudly. "The very one. I wrote to a cer-tain astronomer—perhaps you have heard of him—a Mr. John Herschel?"

She squealed in unladylike delight. "John Herschel?

Only the most famous astronomer of our time. Why, how positively extraordinary!"

He squeezed her hand, laughing as he continued. "I thought you might know of him. I will have you know that this is the exact model he had built for his own sister. I wanted the perfect gift to commemorate the anniversary of our meeting. No matter how convoluted the circumstances, it is what brought us together. That night in your parents' garden was when I knew I wanted you forever."

She felt so full of happiness and goodwill, she could not believe it. She placed her hands on either side of Benedict's face and looked into his eyes. "Thank you, my dear husband. You have given me everything I have ever hoped for in life, and then some. I will never stop being grateful for the day you came into my life again. It was worth every bump, bruise, and tear shed along the way. No matter the name, no matter the station in life, it is *you* I love."

"And I love you," he said as she drew him down for another kiss. "Just don't be surprised if while you are looking to the heavens, I am looking to you. You, my dear Mrs. Hastings, are all the beauty, guidance, and light I will ever need."

Please read on for a preview of the next
delightful romance,

A Taste for Scandal

by Erin Knightley.

Coming in December 2012 from Signet Eclipse.

"Buy an apple, guv? Best in London, they is."

Richard paused as a plump middle-aged woman wearing a kerchief over her dark hair stepped in his way. Offering his most charming smile, he said, "The best in London, you say? Well, I have no doubt they are, madam. However, I am quite set for apples. If only you had said scones. I do so adore a great scone." He winked at her, and was pleased to see a blush rise up her tanned cheeks. "I will, however, buy one for your next customer."

He flipped her a coin, and she giggled as she caught it. "That's right decent of you, guv. Sure I can't offer you nothin' else?" She gave her ample bosom a shake, and he chuckled and shook his head.

"Tempting, madam, but alas, I fear you are just too young for me." She laughed out loud at this, and he sketched a shallow bow. "I bid you good day."

"Cor, 'tis sure to be, now!"

He grinned and walked on, dodging a gangly young man as he darted past. Everyone seemed to move with great purpose, shouting to be heard above the clanking wagons and clomping of horse hooves. It had a rather—he searched for the right word—bustlely charm to it.

What was that?

Richard came up short, glancing around. He would have sworn he'd heard a woman scream. Around him, harried vendors continued to call out their wares as vehicles rumbled noisily up and down the cobblestone street. No one showed any sign that they had heard a cry of distress, too.

Still, he was certain he had heard it. He squinted past the glaring sunlight reflecting off the surrounding shop windows to peer at the interiors. Nothing amiss in the spice store or the candlemaker's shop. Striding forward, Richard looked into the small bakery past the spice shop just in time to see a large man in dark clothing advance on a young woman who stood behind the waist-high counter. Her eyes were wide with shock as she pressed her hands over her mouth.

Damn it all—the bounder was going to attack her!

Without a second thought, Richard pushed through the door and leapt at the man, slamming against a back that was every bit as solid as a stable door. Richard had the advantage of a running start, and his momentum knocked them both over the counter in a cloud of powdered sugar and curses. Together they crashed to the wood floor with a bone-rattling thud, pastries raining down on them as glass and pottery shattered nearby. Good God, the man was an ox—easily twice the size of the dainty young woman who yelped and scrambled out of the way as they flailed about on the floor.

Jamming his elbow between the man's shoulder blades, Richard landed a solid punch to the attacker's lower back. Pain erupted in his knuckles and Richard cursed and shook his hand. Bloody hell, perhaps the man was made of wood after all. Barn Door grunted and squirmed, calling out hoarsely for him to get off.

As if Richard would have mercy on the moralless man—and if that wasn't a word, it bloody well should be. Attacking a defenseless woman in broad daylight was utterly unconscionable. For good measure, Richard ground his elbow harder into his opponent's spine. It wasn't every day one had the opportunity to rescue a lady and thrash the scurrilous villain.

"I'm going for help!" the woman shouted, and he looked over his shoulder in time to see her dash for the door and disappear. Barn Door took the opportunity to twist around and land a meaty fist against Richard's temple, slamming him into the purple cabinets lining the wall. The screech of more breaking dishes clashed with the ringing in Richard's ears as he fought back, grappling with the larger man to maintain his position.

Richard finally got his arms hooked around the bounder's elbows and locked them into place behind the criminal's back. Panting, his hair hanging limply in his eyes, Richard secured his hold on the struggling man beneath him. He wasn't going anywhere.

"What the bloody 'ell do you think you're doing? Get your filthy hands off me, you betwattled fool."

Instead of responding, Richard simply tightened his hold, drawing his opponent's arms back even farther behind him. He adjusted his position so he was more or less sitting on the man. Barn Door tensed and sputtered beneath him, grunting with pain as Richard tugged sharply upward. Served the blackguard right; Richard's left eye hurt like the devil. He tsked and said, "I wouldn't struggle, were I you. It will only make me pull harder, in case you haven't noticed."

Richard chuckled as the rotter growled in frustration. He hadn't had this much fun since university. Things were always so damned civilized at Gentleman Jackson's, it had been ages since he had been able to really let loose. He was no bruiser, but he could certainly hold his own. As he had just proved. He grinned to himself, tossing his head in an attempt to get the hair from his eyes.

The front door burst open, causing the bell situated

above it to jangle violently at the intrusion as the woman and two men stumbled into the room. She was smaller than he'd realized, dwarfed by the two brutes beside her. She was damn lucky he had shown up when he did.

"That's him, right there!" she panted, pointing to where Richard and his prisoner lay on the floor. Rather obvious, in his opinion. Who else, exactly, would they think was the perpetrator? The mouse in the corner?

Now that assistance had arrived, Richard eased his grip and jumped to his feet. The cavalry rushed forward, each one grabbing one of the intruder's arms and yanking him none too gently to his feet. It was no less than he deserved. One couldn't go around terrorizing innocent women, for God's sake.

"Not him," the shop girl yelped. She thrust her arm in Richard's direction, her finger extended accusingly. "Him!"

Him? *Me?*

Jane watched with satisfaction as Mr. Black and the watchman released Emerson and tackled the crazed man to the floor. He grunted sharply as one of the men jabbed a knee in his back. Good. She hoped it hurt. How dare he burst into her store and attack her cousin like that. She'd never been so happy to see someone in her life, and she hadn't even been able to properly greet him.

With her heart still pounding painfully in her chest, she turned her attention to poor Emerson, who was shaking out his arms and moving his neck from side to side. He was covered from the top of his short sun-kissed hair to the bottom of his massive brown leather work boots with the precious sugar that had moments earlier topped her beautiful treats. "Heavens above, Emerson, are you quite all right?" She wasn't willing to move closer to him, since he was still standing next to the luna-tic attacker.

He threw a disgusted look to where the men scuffled with the protesting intruder before skirting around them, glass and porcelain crunching beneath his boots as he walked. The sight of her mother's china shattered on the floor was nearly enough to bring her to tears, but Jane willed herself not to cry. She would not give the criminal the satisfaction of seeing her upset like that. The delicate periwinkle pattern winked up at her from the broken shards littering the wood planks, and she clenched her jaw against the memory of Mama offering her a sample of fresh-baked ginger biscuits from the now destroyed platter. She noted with approval that the crazed man, who was still sprawled on the floor with his cheek pressed into a cream-filled pastry, had yet to recover his breath. She hoped he would be *very* sore in the morning when he woke up in Newgate.

Looking away from the source of all the upheaval in her shop, she glanced to the damaged cabinet and breathed a sigh of relief. At least *some* of the cherished pieces survived, including her favorite piece, the large vase in the place of honor at the top shelf of the cabinet. Thank the Lord for small favors.

Emerson wrapped her into a warm embrace, his surprisingly solid chest a comfort to her jangled nerves. Pulling away he offered her a reassuring grin. "I'll live, to be sure. Are *you* all right? That must have given you quite a scare. I'm just glad I was here, so you didn't have to face him alone."

He looked so different, with his lean frame now padded with muscles and his deeply tanned skin. He had certainly grown into himself since shipping out so many years ago. But his easy grin and clear green eyes were exactly as she remembered them. She could have cried with relief at having him home.

"I am not so much scared as angry. I haven't seen you

in ages and you are ambushed before I even get to say hello. I'm so sorry."

"You *know* him?"

The strangled, rasping question came from the man on the floor, and Jane and Emerson turned in unison to look at him. He looked a fright, his blond hair—and the pastry crumbs—plastered to his red face. Powdered sugar coated his surprisingly well-fitting clothes. Apparently, a life of crime paid rather nicely.

"I *thought* he was attacking you," he ground out, then craned his head to look up at his captors. "I thought he was attacking her. I was trying to *help*, for the love of God."

Ignoring his blasphemy, Jane couldn't stop the inelegant snort of disbelief. "Right, my dear cousin, fresh from years at sea, came all the way here to London to assault me."

"I didn't know you bloody well knew him!"

She scowled at his vile language as Mr. Black thumped his side with the toe of his boot in warning. Who did he think he was, saying something like that in her own shop? Besides, what did it matter if it was her cousin or a customer—attacking an innocent person was inexcusable. "So you chose to attack first and ask questions later?" She was not about to let the man snake his way out of the punishment he was due. In her experience, that happened all too often. She clenched her teeth, pushing away the powerful emotions that the injustices of her past evoked. Lifting her chin, she addressed her two rescuers. "Sirs, this man is a nuisance and a lunatic. Please take him away."

None too gently, the two men dragged the horrible man to his feet. He was quite a bit taller than she had realized, and she took a few involuntary steps backward. Despite his fancy clothes, he looked strong and powerful, and she wanted nothing to do with the man. Especially with the look of fury darkening his bloodshot eyes. He looked as though he would gladly throw her into the Thames if given even an inch of leeway.

"I am *not* a lunatic," he growled, jerking his arms against the hands that held him. "I'm the bloody Earl of Raleigh!"

New York Times bestselling author

Jillian Hunter

A BRIDE
UNVEILED
The Bridal Pleasures Series

Violet Knowlton is betrothed to the sensible, if
tedious, Sir Godfrey Maitland. When Godfrey escorts
her to a fencing demonstration, she looks forward to
the adventurous diversion, but everything changes
when she realizes the swordsman displaying his skill—
and dashing good looks—is none other than her
childhood friend Kit.

Soon the flames of their forbidden past ignite into a
passion neither can refuse. Although Violet has been
promised to another, Kit remains her first and only
love. He vows he will possess her, no matter what
stands in his way...

**Available wherever books are sold or at
penguin.com**

JAN 0 3 2014

S0325